SUMMER HOUSE WITH SWIMMING POOL

SUMMER HOUSE WITH SWIMMING POOL

HERMAN KOCH

TRANSLATED FROM THE DUTCH BY
SAM GARRETT

Atlantic Books
London

First published in the Netherlands in 2011 as *Zomerhuis Met Zwembad*
by Ambo Anthos, Amsterdam.

First published in Great Britain in 2014 by Atlantic Books,
an imprint of Atlantic Books Ltd.

10 9 8 7 6 5 4 3

A CIP catalogue record for this book is available from the British Library.

Trade Paperback ISBN: 978 1 78239 071 8
OME Paperback ISBN: 978 1 78239 099 2
E-book ISBN: 978 1 78239 073 2

Printed in Great Britain by CPI Group (UK) Ltd, Croydon, CR0 4YY

Atlantic Books
An Imprint of Atlantic Books Ltd
Ormond House
26–27 Boswell Street
London
WC1N 3JZ
www.atlantic-books.co.uk

1

I am a doctor. My office hours are from eight-thirty in the morning to one in the afternoon. I take my time. Twenty minutes for each patient. Those twenty minutes are my unique selling point. Where else these days, people say, can you find a GP who gives you twenty minutes? – and they pass the information along. He doesn't take on too many patients, they say. He makes time for each individual case. I have a waiting list. When a patient dies or moves away, all I have to do is pick up the phone and I have five new ones to take their place.

Patients can't tell the difference between time and attention. They think I give them more attention than other doctors. But all I give them is more time. By the end of the first sixty seconds I've seen all I need to know. The remaining nineteen minutes I fill with attention. Or, I should say, with the illusion of attention. I ask all the usual questions. How is your son/daughter getting along? Are you sleeping better these days? Are you sure you're not getting too much/too little to eat? I hold the stethoscope to their chests, then to their backs. Take a deep breath, I say. Now breathe out nice and slow. I don't really listen. Or at least I try not to. On the inside, all human bodies sound the same. First of all, of course, there's the heartbeat. The heart is blind. The heart pumps. The heart is the engine room. The engine room only keeps the ship going; it doesn't keep it on course. And then there are the sounds of the intestines. Of the vital organs. An overburdened liver sounds different from a healthy one. An overburdened liver groans. It groans and begs. It begs for a day off. A day to deal with the worst of the rubbish. The way things are now, it's always in a hurry, trying to catch up with itself. The overburdened liver is like the kitchen in a restaurant that's open around the clock. The dishes pile up. The dishwashers are working full tilt. But the dirty dishes and caked-on pans only pile up higher and higher. The overburdened liver hopes for that one day off that never comes. Every afternoon at four-thirty, five o'clock (sometimes earlier), the hope of that one day off is dashed again. If the liver's lucky, at first it's only beer. Beer passes most of the work along to the kidneys. But you always have those for whom beer alone isn't enough. They order something on the side: a shot of gin, vodka or whisky. Something they can knock back. The overburdened liver braces itself, then finally ruptures. First it grows rigid, like an overinflated tyre. All it takes then is one little bump in the road for it to blow wide open.

I listen with my stethoscope. I press against the hard spot, just beneath the skin. Does this hurt? If I press any harder, it will burst open right there in my office. Can't have that. It makes an incredible mess. Blood gushes out in a huge wave. No general practitioner is keen to have someone die in his office. At home, that's a different story. In the privacy of their own homes, in the middle of the night, in their own beds. With a ruptured liver, they usually don't even make it to the phone. The ambulance would get there too late anyway.

My patients file into my practice at twenty-minute intervals. The office is on the ground floor. They come in on crutches and in wheelchairs. Some of them are too fat, others are short of breath. They are, in any case, no longer able to climb stairs. One flight of stairs would kill them for sure. Others only imagine it would: that their final hour would begin on the first step. Most of the patients are like that. Most of them have nothing wrong with them. They moan and groan, make noises that would make you think they see death staring them in the face every moment of the day, they sink into the chair across from my desk with a sigh – but there's nothing wrong with them. I let them reel off their complaints. It hurts here, and here, sometimes it spasms down to here… I do my best to act interested. Meanwhile, I doodle on a scrap of paper. I ask them to get up, to follow me to the examination room. Occasionally I'll ask someone to undress behind the screen, but most of the time I don't. Bodies are horrible enough as it is, even with their clothes on. I don't want to see them, those parts where the sun never shines. Not the folds of fat in which it is always too warm and the bacteria have free rein, not the fungal growths and infections between the toes, beneath the nails, not the fingers that scratch here, the fingers that rub there until it starts to bleed… Here, Doctor, here's where it itches really badly… No, I don't want to see. I pretend to look, but I'm thinking about something else. About a roller-coaster in an amusement park, the car at the front has a green dragon's head mounted on it; the people throw their hands in the air and scream their lungs out. From the corner of my eye I see moist tufts of pubic hair, or red, infected bald spots where no hair will ever grow again, and I think about a plane exploding in the air, the passengers still belted to their seats as they begin a mile-long tumble into eternity: it's cold, the air is thin, far below the ocean awaits. It burns when I pee, Doctor. Like there are needles coming out… A train explodes just before it enters the station, the space shuttle *Columbia* shatters into millions of little pieces, the second jet slams into the South Tower. It burns, here, doctor. Here…

You can get dressed now, I say. I've seen enough. I'll write you a prescription. Some of the patients can barely conceal their disappointment: a prescription? They stand there for a few seconds, staring blankly, their underwear down around their knees. They took a morning off from work, now they want value for money, even if that money has come out of the pockets of healthy taxpayers. They want the doctor to poke at them at least, they want him to pull on his rubber gloves and take something – some body part – between his knowing fingers. For him to stick at least *one* finger into something. They want to be *examined*; they aren't content only with his years of experience, his clinical gaze that registers at a single glance what's wrong with a person. Because he's seen it all a hundred thousand times before. Because experience tells him that there's no sudden need on occasion one hundred thousand-and-one to pull the rubber gloves on.

Sometimes, though, there's no getting around it. Sometimes you have to get in there. Usually with one or two fingers, sometimes with your whole hand. I pull on my rubber gloves. If you would just roll onto your side… for the patient, this is the point of no return. Finally, he is being taken seriously, he is about to receive an internal examination, but his gaze is no longer fixed on my face. All he can look at now are my hands. My hands as they pull on the rubber gloves. He wonders why he ever let things get this far. Whether this is really what he wants. Before putting on the gloves, I wash my hands. The sink is across from the examining table, so I stand with my back to him as I soap up. I take my time. I roll up my sleeves. I can feel the patient's eyes at my back. I let the tap water flow over my wrists. First I wash my hands thoroughly, then my lower arms: all the way up to the elbows. The sound of running water blocks out all other sounds, but I know that once I've reached the elbows the patient's breathing has quickened. It quickens for a few seconds, or stops altogether. An internal examination is about to take place, the patient – consciously or unconsciously – has insisted on this. He had no intention of letting himself be fobbed off with a prescription, not this time. Meanwhile, though, the doubts arise. Why is the doctor washing and disinfecting his hands and arms *all the way up to the elbows*? Something in the patient's body contracts. Even though what he should be doing is relaxing as much as possible. Relaxation is the key to a smooth internal examination.

Meanwhile I have turned around and am drying my hands, my forearms, *my elbows*. Still without looking at the patient, I take a pair of plastic-packed gloves from a drawer. I tear open the bag, press the pedal of the rubbish bin with my foot and throw the bag away. Only now, as I pull on the gloves, do I look at the patient. The look in his eyes is, how shall I put it, *different* from what it was before I started washing my hands. Lie down on your side, I say, before he has a chance to express his misgivings. Facing the wall. A naked body is less disgraceful than a body with trousers and underpants down around its ankles. Less helpless. Two legs with the shoes and socks still on, and bound together at the ankles by trousers and underpants. Like a prisoner in a chain gang. A person with his pants around his ankles can't run away. You can submit someone like that to an internal examination, but you could also punch him right in the side of the head. Or take a pistol and empty the clip into the ceiling. I've listened to these fucking lies long enough! I'm going to count to three... One... two... Try to relax, I say again. Turn on your side. I pull the rubber gloves tighter over my fingers and further over my wrists. The sound of snapping rubber always reminds me of party balloons. Balloons for a birthday party, you blew them up last night in order to surprise the birthday boy. This may be a little unpleasant, I say. The important thing is just to keep breathing calmly. The patient is all too aware of my presence, right behind his half-naked body, but he can't see me any more. This is the moment when I take time to submit that body, or at least the naked part of it, to a further look.

I have, until now, been assuming that the patient is a man. In the example we are dealing with, a man is lying on the table with his trousers and underpants pulled down. Women are a different story; I'll get to women later. The man in question turns his head slightly in my direction, but, as I've mentioned, he can no longer get a good look at me. Just relax your head now, I say. All you have to do is relax. Unbeknown to the patient, I now turn my gaze to the naked lower back. I've already told him that what follows may be a bit unpleasant. Between that remark and the unpleasant feeling itself, there is nothing. This is the empty moment. The emptiest moment in the entire examination. The seconds tick by silently, like a metronome with the sound turned off. A metronome on a piano in a silent film. No physical contact has yet taken place. The bare back bears the mark of the underpants. Red bands left on the skin by the elastic. Sometimes there are pimples or moles. The skin itself is often abnormally pale; it's one of those places where sunlight rarely reaches. There is, however, almost always hair. Lower down, along the back, the hair only increases. I'm left-handed. I place my right hand on the patient's shoulder. Through the rubber glove I feel the body stiffen. The entire body tenses and contracts. It would like to relax, but instinct is more powerful, it braces itself, it readies itself to resist invasion from the outside.

By then my left hand is already where it has to be. The patient's mouth falls open, his lips part, a sigh escapes as my middle finger goes in. Something between a sigh and a groan. Take it easy, I say. It will be over in a moment. I try to think about nothing, but that's always difficult. So I think about the night when I dropped the padlock key for my bicycle in the mud in the middle of a football field. It was a patch of mud no bigger than one yard square, and I knew for sure my key was there. Does this hurt at all? I ask. Now my index finger joins my middle finger, using both of them will make it easier to find the key. A little... Where? Here...? Or here? It was raining, a few lights were on around the field, but it was still a bit too dark to see well. Usually it's the prostate. Cancer, or just an enlargement. Usually there's not much you can say about it after the first examination. I could have walked home and come back the next day, once it got light. But my fingers were already in there, the mud was already up under my nails, there wasn't much sense in stopping now. Ow! There, Doctor! Fucking hell! Excuse me... Oh, fucking hell! And then there was that one fraction of a second, my fingers feeling something hard amid the goo. Careful, it could also be a piece of glass... I hold it up to the light, the dim light from a lamppost beside the field, but in fact I already know what it is. It glistens, it gleams, and I won't have to walk home after all. Without looking at my hands I pull off the gloves and toss them in the pedal bin. You can sit up now. You can get dressed. It's too early to draw conclusions, I say.

It was eighteen months ago when Ralph Meier suddenly appeared in my waiting room. I recognised him right away, of course. Could he talk to me for just a moment? It was nothing urgent, he said. Once we were in my office, he came straight to the point. Was it true, what so-and-so had told him, that I was fairly accommodating with prescriptions for...? here he looked around somewhat skittishly, as though the place might be bugged. 'So-and-so' was a regular patient of mine. In the long run they all tell each other everything, which is how Ralph Meier ended up in my practice. It sort of depends, I said. I'll have to ask you a few questions about your general health, so we don't run into any unpleasant surprises later on. But if we do that? he insisted. If everything is OK, would you be willing... I nodded. Yes, I said. That can be arranged.

Now we're eighteen months down the road, and Ralph Meier is dead. And tomorrow morning I have to appear before the Board of Medical Examiners. Not for what I helped him out with that time, but for something else, about six months later: something you might describe as a 'medical error'. I'm not so worried about the Board of Examiners; in the medical profession we all know each other. Often enough, we even went to school together. It's not like in the States, where a lawyer can ruin a doctor after a misdiagnosis. In this country you really have to have gone too far. And even then – a warning, a few months' suspension, no more than that.

All I have to do is make sure the members of the board actually see it as a medical error. I'll have to keep my wits about me. I have to keep believing in it, one hundred per cent – in the medical error.

The funeral was a couple of days ago. At that lovely, rural cemetery by the bend in the river. Big old trees, the wind blowing through the branches, rustling the leaves. Birds were twittering. I stayed as far to the back as I could, which seemed prudent enough, but nothing could have prepared me for what happened next.

'How dare you show your face here!'

A brief moment of absolute silence, as though even the wind had suddenly died down. The birds went quiet too, from one moment to the next.

'You piece of shit! How dare you! How *dare* you!'

Judith Meier had a voice like a trained opera singer, a voice that could reach the audience in the very last row of a concert hall. All eyes turned in my direction. She was standing beside the open back of the hearse, out of which the pallbearers had just shouldered the coffin containing her husband's body.

Then she was trotting towards me, elbowing her way through hundreds of mourners, who stepped aside to let her through. For the next thirty seconds, her high heels on the gravel drive were the only sound in an otherwise breathless silence.

Right in front of me, she stopped. I was actually expecting her to slap me. Or to start pounding her fists against my lapels. To make, in other words, a scene; something she had always been good at.

But she didn't.

She looked at me. The whites of her eyes were laced with red.

'Piece of shit,' she said again, much more quietly now.

Then she spat in my face.

2

A general practitioner's task is simple. He doesn't have to heal people, he only has to make sure they don't sidestep him and make it to the specialists and the hospitals. His office is an outpost. The more people who can be stopped at the outpost, the better the practitioner is at what he does. It's simple arithmetic. If we family doctors were to let through everyone with an itch, a spot or a cough to a specialist or a hospital, the system would collapse entirely. Entirely. Someone did the arithmetic on that once. The conclusion was that the collapse would come more quickly than anyone expected. If every general practitioner referred more than one third of his patients for further care from a specialist, the system would begin to creak and buckle within two days. Within a week it would collapse. The general practitioner mans the outpost. Just a common cold, he says. Take it easy for a week, and if it's not over then, well, don't hesitate to come back. Three days later, in the middle of the night, the patient suffocates on his own mucus. That can happen, you say. A rare combination of factors, we see it in no more than one out of every ten thousand patients.

Patients don't realise that there's strength in numbers. They let themselves be ushered into my office one by one. There I spend twenty minutes with them, convincing them that there's nothing wrong. My office hours are from eight-thirty to one. That adds up to three patients an hour, twelve to thirteen a day. For the system, I'm the ideal family doctor. General practitioners who think they can make do with half the time per visit see twenty-four patients in a working day. When there are twenty-four of them, there's more of a chance of a few slipping through than there is when there are only twelve. It has to do with how they feel. A patient who gets only ten minutes' attention feels shortchanged sooner than a patient who gets the same song and dance for twenty minutes. The latter patient gets the impression that his complaints are being taken seriously. A patient like that is less likely to insist on further examination.

Mistakes happen, of course. Our system couldn't exist without mistakes. In fact, a system like ours thrives on its mistakes. After all, even a misdiagnosis can lead to the desired result. But usually a misdiagnosis isn't even necessary. The most important weapon we general practitioners have at our disposal is the waiting list. The mere mention of the waiting list tends to do the job. For this examination there's a waiting list of six to eight months, I say. With that treatment your symptoms might be a little less acute, but there's a waiting list... Half the patients give up as soon as the waiting list is mentioned. I can see it on their faces: relief. One of these days is none of these days, they figure. No one wants to have a tube the size of a garden hose pushed down their throat. It's not a particularly comfortable procedure, I say. You could also decide to wait and see whether it goes away with a combination of rest and medication. Then we'll take another look in six months' time.

How can there be waiting lists, you might ask yourself, in a wealthy country like the Netherlands? For me, the association is always with the gas bubble, with our reserves of natural gas. I brought it up once during an informal gathering with colleagues. The waiting list for hip operations: how many cubic yards of gas would you have to sell in order to do away with that within a week? I asked. How, for Christ's sake, is it possible that in a civilised country like ours people die before they reach the head of the waiting list? You can't look at it that way, my colleagues said. You can't tally gas reserves against the number of postponed hip operations.

The gas bubble is huge, even worst-case scenarios predict that there will be enough natural gas for the next sixty years. Sixty years! That's bigger than the oil reserves in the Persian Gulf. This is a wealthy country. We're as rich as Saudi Arabia, as Kuwait, as Qatar – but still, people die here because they have to wait too long for a new kidney, infants die because the ambulance that's rushing them to the hospital gets stuck in traffic, mothers' lives are endangered because we, we general practitioners, convince them that home-birthing is safe. While what we should actually say is that it's only *cheaper* – here, too, it's clear that if every mother claimed the right to give birth in a hospital, the system would collapse within a week. The risk of babies dying, of babies suffering brain damage because no oxygen can be administered during a home birth is simply factored into the equation. Every once in a great while an article appears in a medical journal, and sometimes a summary of that article will actually make the Dutch papers, but even those summaries show that infant mortality in the Netherlands is the highest in all of Europe and indeed the Western world. But no one has ever acted on these figures.

In fact, the family doctor is powerless in the face of all this. He can put a patient's mind at ease. He can see to it, for the time being at least, that a patient doesn't seek specialist assistance. He can convince a woman that home-birthing poses no risks whatsoever. That it's all much more 'natural'. Whereas it's only more natural in the sense that dying is natural too. We can give them salves or sleeping pills, we can burn away moles with acid, we can remove ingrown toenails. Nasty chores, usually. Like cleaning the kitchen, using a scouring pad to remove caked-on remains from between the burners.

I lie awake at night sometimes. I think about the gas bubble. Sometimes it resembles a bubble like the ones you blow with soapsuds, only it's right under the earth's crust, all you have to do is poke a hole in it and it deflates – or blows up in your face. At other times the gas is spread out over a much greater surface. It has permeated into the loose earth. The natural-gas molecules have mixed invisibly with the soil. You can't smell it. You hold a match up to it and it explodes. The little fire becomes an inferno that spreads within seconds across hundreds of square miles. Underground. The earth's surface becomes hollowed out, there is no more support for bridges and buildings, not enough solid ground beneath the feet of humans and animals, entire cities sink into the burning depths. I lie there with my eyes open in the dark. Sometimes our country's undoing takes the form of a documentary. A documentary on the National Geographic Channel, with charts and computer animations, the kind of documentary they're so good at: documentaries about dam-bursts and tsunamis, about avalanches and mudslides that wipe whole towns and villages off the map, about the entire side of a volcano that breaks off from an island and slides into the sea, causing a tidal wave that, eight hours later and thousands of miles away, reaches a height of almost four thousand feet. *The Disappearance of a Country*, tomorrow night at nine-thirty, on this channel. Our country. Our country consumed by its own reserves of natural gas.

On rare occasions, lying awake at night like this, I think about Ralph Meier. About his role as the Emperor Augustus in the television series of the same name. The role suits him to a tee; both his fans and his detractors are in total agreement about that. First of all, of course, because of his build, the corpulence he nurtured through the years. An obesity achieved exclusively by means of systematic pig-outs in restaurants with one or more Michelin stars. By lavish barbecues in his garden: sausages from Germany, hams from Bulgaria, entire suckling lambs roasted on a spit. I remember those barbecues as though it were yesterday: his hulking frame beside the smoking fire, singlehandedly flipping the hamburgers, steaks and drumsticks. His unshaven, flushed face, the barbecue fork in one hand, a 16-ounce can of Jupiler in the other. His voice always carried right across the lawn. A voice like a foghorn. A voice that tankers and container vessels might use to find their bearings in distant estuaries and foreign ports. The last barbecue wasn't even that long ago, it occurs to me now, only about five months. He was already ill by then. It was still he who flipped the meat, but now he had pulled up a plastic lawn chair, he had to sit while he did it. It's always fascinating, how an illness – an illness like his – attacks the human body. It's a war. The bad cells turn against the good. At first they attack the body from the sides, a flanking manoeuvre. An orderly little attack is all it is, a glancing blow, designed only to divert attention from the main force. You think you've won: you have, after all, repelled this first minor assault. But the main force is still in hiding, deeper inside the body, in a dark place where the X-rays, the ultrasounds, and the MRI scans can't find it. The main force is patient. It waits until it has reached full strength. Until victory is assured.

The third episode was on TV last night. The emperor consolidates his power. He changes his name from Gaius Octavius to Augustus, and sidelines the Senate. There are ten more episodes to come. There has never been any suggestion of cancelling or postponing *Augustus* just because its star is dead. Ralph Meier is formidable in his role, the only Dutch actor in a cast of Italians, Americans and Englishmen, but he outplays them all.

Last night, I believe I must have been the only one who watched the series in a different way. Through other eyes, perhaps that's the way to put it. The eyes of a doctor.

'Can I go anyway?' he'd asked me at the time. 'It's a two-month shoot. If I have to pull out halfway through, it would be a disaster for everyone involved.'

'Of course,' I told him. 'Don't worry. It doesn't usually amount to anything. We'll just wait for the tests to come back. There will be plenty of time afterwards.'

I watched the Emperor Augustus as he spoke to the Senate. It was an American–Italian co-production, and they hadn't cut any corners. Thousands of Roman soldiers, entire legions cheering from the hillsides around Rome, tens of thousands of swords, shields and spears raised high, fleets of hundreds of ships before the port of Alexandria, chariot races, gladiatorial contests, roaring lions and mangled Christians. Ralph Meier had the illness in its most aggressive form. It was something you had to act on immediately, otherwise it was too late. Radical intervention: a first strike, a carpet-bombing to knock out the malignant cells at a single blow. I looked at his face, his body. Inside that body, in all likelihood, the main force had already begun its offensive.

'Senators!' he said. 'From this day forth I am your emperor. Emperor… Augustus!'

His voice carried, as always – at least it still did then. If there was anything wrong with him, he didn't let it show. Ralph Meier was a real trouper. If need be, he could upstage anyone and anything. Even a fatal illness.

3

Over the years, one by one, the normal people have disappeared from my practice. I mean, the people who work from nine to five. I still have a couple of lawyers, and the owner of a fitness club, but most of my patients work in what are called the 'creative professions'. For the moment, I'm not counting the widows. There are quite a few of those. One could refer to a widow surplus. The widows of writers, of actors, of painters… the women hold out longer than the men; they're cut from other, *tougher* cloth. You can reach a ripe old age standing in the shadows. A whole life spent making fresh coffee and running to the wine shop for the geniuses in their studios. Fresh Norwegian salmon for the writers in their studies, where you always have to walk on tiptoe. It looks like a real chore, but of course it's a cakewalk. The widows grow old. Old as dirt. As soon as their husbands die, they often enter a brief, second bloom. I've seen them here in my office. They're sorrowful, they dab at their eyes with a hankie, but they're relieved as well. Relief is an emotion that's hard to hide. I look with the eyes of a doctor. I have learned to see through the tears. A prolonged illness is not an easy thing to endure. Cirrhosis of the liver is a drawn-out, painful affair. The patient often gets to the bedside bucket too late; the blood is already welling up. Changing the bedclothes three times a day, sheets and blankets heavy with puke and shit, that's more demanding than fixing coffee and making sure there's enough gin in the house. How long is this going to last? the prospective widow wonders. Will I be able to hold out till the funeral?

But then the day comes at last. The weather is beautiful, blue skies with fluffy clouds, birds singing in the trees, the smell of fresh flowers. For the first time in her life, the widow herself is the centre of attention. She's wearing sunglasses, so no one can see her tears – everyone thinks. But in fact the dark lenses serve to hide her relief. His best friends carry the coffin to the grave. There are speeches. There is booze. Lots of booze. No watery coffee at an artist's funeral, just plenty of white wine, vodka, and old gin. No slices of cake or almond pastries with the tea, but oysters, smoked mackerel and croquettes. Then the whole club goes to their favourite haunt. 'Well here's to you, old boy, wherever you may be! Old bastard! You old goat!' Toasts are made, vodka is spilled. The widow has taken off her sunglasses. She smiles. She beams. The puked-on sheets are still in the dirty clothes basket, but tomorrow they'll go in the washing machine for the very last time. Life as a widow, she thinks, will always be like this. The friends will go on proposing toasts for months (for years!). To her. To their new centre of attention. What she doesn't know yet is that, after a few courtesy calls, it will all be over. The silence that will follow is the same silence that always falls after a life in the shadows.

That's usually the way it goes. But there are also exceptions. Rage makes for ugly widows. This morning there was suddenly a ruckus at the front door of my office. It was still early; I had just ushered in my first patient. 'Doctor!' I heard my assistant call out. 'Doctor!' There was a sound like a chair being knocked over, and after that I heard a second voice. 'Where are you, you piece of shit?' the voice shrieked. 'Are you scared to show your face?'

I smiled broadly at my patient. 'Excuse me for just a moment, would you?' I said and stood up. Between the front door of the practice and my office is a corridor, first you have to walk past a desk where my assistant sits, then past the waiting room. It's actually more of a waiting area than a waiting room; there's no door separating it from the hallway.

I glanced over as I went by. As I said, it was early, but there were already three patients flipping through old copies of *Marie Claire* and *National Geographic*. By that point, however, they had stopped their flipping. They had lowered their magazines to their laps and were staring at Judith Meier. Judith had not become any prettier after her husband's death, and that was putting it mildly. The skin on her face had reddened, but not everywhere, making it look blotchy. Behind Judith's back, my assistant was gesturing that there was no way she could have stopped her. Further back, behind my assistant, a chair was lying on the floor.

'Judith!' I said, opening my arms as though I were pleased to see her. 'What can I do for you?'

For a couple of seconds my greeting seemed to stun her – but for no longer than a couple of seconds.

'Murderer!' she screamed.

I glanced over at my patients in the waiting space; I knew all three of them by sight. A film director with haemorrhoids, a gallery owner with erectile dysfunction, and a no-longer-so-very-fresh-faced actress who was expecting her first child – albeit not from the blond, hulking and permanently unshaven actor she had married seven months earlier in a Tuscan castle: all paid for by the 'celebrity' programme on the commercial TV channel that had been granted exclusive broadcast rights to the entire ceremony and after-party. I shrugged and winked at them. An emergency case, that's what the shrug and wink were meant to say. A typical case of acute hysteria. Alcohol or drugs – or both. Just to be sure they'd seen, I winked again.

'Judith,' I said as calmly as possible. 'Why don't you come with me, then I'll see what I can do for you.'

Before she could reply, I turned and strode back into my office. I placed my hands on my patient's shoulders. 'Could I ask you to go to the waiting room? My assistant will write out a prescription.'

4

Judith Meier was sitting opposite my desk. I looked at her face. The red blotches were still there. It was hard to tell, in fact, whether her face was white with red blotches, or red with white.

'*You're finished*,' she said. Then she continued: 'This whole flea circus is going to shut down so fast it will make your head spin.' She nodded towards my office door, with the full waiting room behind.

I put my elbows on the desk. Then, forming a tent with my fingertips, I leaned forward slightly. 'Judith,' I said – but suddenly I didn't know how to go on. 'Judith,' I tried then, 'isn't it a bit early to draw such drastic conclusions? Maybe I did diagnose Ralph's illness incorrectly at first. I've admitted that possibility already. And that will come up tomorrow at the hearing. But I never intentionally—'

'Why don't you just save it and see how the Board of Medical Examiners reacts when I tell them the whole story myself?'

I stared at her. I tried to smile, but my mouth felt the way it had the time I broke my jaw in a cycling accident. A pothole. Men at work. A little barrier had been set up to alert oncoming cyclists to the hole in the road, but some joker had removed it. At the emergency ward they wired my upper and lower jaws together;

for six weeks I could neither talk nor consume anything but liquids, through a straw.

'Are you going to be there too?' I asked as calmly as I could. 'That's not exactly custom—'

'No, that's what they told me. But they thought the charges were serious enough to make an exception.'

This time I really did smile. Or at least I succeeded in twisting my mouth into something that could be said to resemble a smile. But it felt as though I was opening my mouth for the first time after remaining silent for a whole day.

'Wait, let me check with my assistant for a moment,' I said, rising from my chair. 'I'll get together all the test results and the files.'

Now Judith started to get to her feet too. 'Don't bother. I've said everything I have to say. I'll see you tomorrow at the hearing.'

'No, really, I'll only be a moment. I'll be right back. I have something that might interest you. Something you don't know about.'

She was already almost upright. She looked at me. I tried to breathe normally. She sat down again.

'One moment,' I said.

This time, without so much as a glance at the patients waiting outside the office, I went straight to my assistant's desk. She was on the phone.

'Is that only the ointment, or is it the cream too?' she was saying.

'Liesbeth,' I said , 'could you just...'

'Just a moment,' she said, placing her hand over the mouthpiece.

'Could you send all the patients home?' I said. 'And call the others to cancel their appointments? Come up with some excuse, it doesn't matter what. And then I need you to leave too. Take the rest of the day off. Judith and I have to… It would be better if I had a little more time…'

'Did you hear what she called you? You can't just do…'

'I'm not deaf, Liesbeth,' I interrupted her. 'Judith is extremely upset. She doesn't know what she's saying. Maybe I underestimated the seriousness of Ralph's illness. That's bad enough. First I'm going to… I'm going to do something with her, go out, grab a cup of coffee somewhere. She needs a little extra attention. That's understandable. But I don't want the patients to see me going out with her. So send them all home as quickly as possible.'

When I came back into my office, Judith Meier was still seated.

She turned her head to look at me. She looked at my empty hands and then, questioningly, at my face.

'I think that file must be in here somewhere,' I said.

5

A medical practice like mine has its drawbacks. You get invited to everything. The patients think you sort of belong – with the emphasis on 'sort of'. Gallery openings, book launches, film and stage premieres; not a day goes by without some invitation arriving in the post. Not going is not an option. When they send you a book, you can lie and say you're only halfway through it, that you don't want to express an opinion without finishing it first. But an opening night is an opening night. And when it's over, you have to say something. It's what they expect, for you to say something. But never tell them what you really thought. *Never*. What you thought is your own business. For a while, I tried to make do with being non-committal. Things like 'I thought there were some really good parts', or 'What did the rest of the cast think?' But such inanities aren't enough, not for them. You have to say that you thought it was amazing, that you're grateful for the chance to have been present at this historic occasion. Film premieres are usually on a Monday evening. But even so, you can't just rush off afterwards. You have to put in an appearance. You don't want to get home too late, you're the only civilian there; no one else has to start work at a normal time the next morning. You stand with the star or the director and you say that you thought it was amazing. An excellent alternative is to say that you found it 'compelling'. That's what you say about the end of the film. You have a glass of champagne in your hand and you look the star or the director straight in the eye. You've already forgotten how the film ended, or rather you've succeeded in suppressing any memory of how the film ended. You adopt a serious expression. 'I found the ending entirely compelling,' you say. Then you're allowed to go home.

I never know what I loathe more: the film itself, the actual stage performance, or the hanging around afterwards. I know from bitter experience that it's easier for my mind to wander during a film than it is during a play. At a play you're more aware of actually being there. Of being there and of the passing of time. Of your watch. I bought myself a watch with a luminous dial, especially for opening nights. Something happens to time during a play. Something I've never quite been able to put my finger on. It doesn't stand still, time, no: it coagulates. You observe the actors and actresses, their movements, you listen to the lines leaving their mouths, and it's as though you're stirring some substance that gets thicker and thicker all the time. At a certain point the spoon stops moving altogether. It remains standing upright in the substance. To go on stirring would be impossible. For the first time, I glance at my watch. As surreptitiously as possible, of course. During a play, no one wants to be caught looking at his watch. I draw the sleeve of my jacket up a bit, carefully. I scratch my wrist, as though it's itching. Then I steal a quick look at the glowing dial. Each time I do that, I witness living proof that real time and stage time are two very different entities. Or rather: two times that run in different, parallel dimensions. You think (you hope, you pray) that half an hour has passed, but your watch tells you that barely twelve minutes has gone by since the lights went down. During a play, you're not allowed to moan or sigh. By moaning or sighing, you unnecessarily draw attention to yourself. Those who moan or sigh too loudly might just break the actors' concentration. But not to sigh or moan at all, that's asking too much. By the same token, that's also the biggest difference from a film: you can't get up and walk out. During a film you can sneak away in the dark, unnoticed. Even during a premiere. People think: well, he must have to go to the toilet pretty badly, and then they forget about you. They don't notice that you never come back at all. You can do that. It's possible. I've done it more than once during an opening night at the cinema. The first time it happened I actually did go to the men's room, I spent the last hour of the film sitting on the toilet seat, my head in my hands, moaning, sighing and cursing. But also pleased. Pleased and relieved. Anything, anything but the film itself. In time I got better at slipping away unnoticed. I would saunter towards the exit, casually, my hands in my pockets. Just out for a breath of fresh air, I would say, if I ran into anyone in the foyer. The next thing I knew, I was already outside. The street, trams, scooters, people. People with normal faces, with normal voices. Voices that said normal things to each other. 'One more for the road? Or shall we call it a day?' Rather than: 'We have to be awfully damned careful, Martha, that Father's estate doesn't fall into the wrong hands.' How many sentences like that can a person stand in the space of an hour and a half? 'No daughter of mine goes around dressed like a trollop! And if she does, she's no longer my daughter!' Films have a soundtrack. They turn the volume up louder each year. You can sigh and moan without anyone hearing. But it's like when you're in pain. Your breathing becomes faster and deeper. When a dog's in pain, it pants with its tongue hanging out of its mouth. Oxygen. The trick is to direct as much oxygen as possible to where it hurts. Oxygen is still the best painkiller around. I'm out on the street. I see the people. I breathe in fresh air. During a stage performance, you can't do any of that. There's no escape clause. If you go out, you have to do that before the play begins. You have no choice, even though it's not without its attendant risks. Because once you're out on the street, tempting thoughts besiege you. Don't go back in, that's the most tempting thought of all. Go home, kick off your shoes, put your feet up, zap the TV on and watch some old B-movie you've seen five times already. Anything, anything but the play.

It also has to do with my profession. In my profession, true relaxation is a necessity. I see and hear things all day long. Things you need to get off your mind at night. The fungal growths. The bleeding warts. The folds of skin between which things have become much, much too warm. The three-hundred-pound woman you have to examine in a place you hoped you'd never have to go again. None of this is what you want to think about during a play. But the lights have barely dimmed when these things start taking liberties with you. It's dark, they figure. Now we've got him! The only light now is on stage. And from the luminous dial of your watch. The endless time begins. The Big Clot. During a working day, there's nothing I look forward to more than an evening of nothing at all. A meal. A beer or a glass of wine. The evening news on TV. A B-movie or a football match. A working day like that gets off on the right foot. It's a day with promise. With perspective, I should say. A countryside of hills rolling on and on, and in the distance the glimmer of the sea. But a day that ends with a play is like a hotel room with a view of a blank wall. That kind of day can't breathe. There's not enough air, but the window is stuck and won't open. The moaning begins at eight-thirty in the morning, when I think about it for the first time. Normally I only *sort of* listen to my patients, but on a working day that ends in a play I don't listen at all. I run through ten possible escape routes in my mind. Illness. Flu. Food poisoning. A relative killing himself by leaping in front of a train. I think about the scene from *Misery* in which Kathy Bates shatters James Caan's ankles with a hammer. I feel like doing something drastic to myself. During the siege of Stalingrad, soldiers on both sides shot themselves in the hand or the foot to keep from being sent to the front. Anyone who was caught faced the firing squad. My patient goes on whingeing about his lower back pain, but all I can think of are gunshot wounds. In Mexico, the drugs cartels' death squads carve a cross into their bullets to make them spin slower. A bullet that spins slowly causes more damage as it goes through the body. Or doesn't come out the other side at all. I think about taking drastic steps. No halfway measures. With a broken little finger you can always attend an opening night with your arm in a sling. A hundred-degree fever is seen as a cowardly excuse. No, I think about other things. Like an oyster knife slipping and ramming its way straight through the palm of my hand. The tip of the knife protrudes out of the back. The bleeding only really starts once you pull it out.

The worst plays are the ones that are 'based on improvisation'. There's always a lot of mumbling. Bits and pieces of narration and dialogue 'taken from daily life'. The actors and actresses wear costumes they've assembled themselves. Plays based on improvisation tend not to last as long as plays with a regular script, but that's like the wind-chill factor. Sometimes it feels a lot colder or hotter than the thermometer says. You look at the homemade costumes. According to wind-chill time, half an hour has already passed, but the dial of your watch tells no lies. You raise the watch to your ear. Maybe it's stopped. But the watch runs on a lithium battery that lasts up to eighteen months. Time passes soundlessly. You have to count to sixty and then look again.

An oyster knife brings with it the risk of blood poisoning, of course. Normal people are better off going to A&E right away. But I have everything I need right on my office shelf. Tetanus. Yellow fever. Hepatitis A. I have little vials here, one drop of which is enough to knock you out for twelve hours. Another drop and you never wake up again at all. Dogs and cats get an injection from the vet, but human beings can drink the poisoned cup themselves. A shot glass. Ninety per cent water and flavouring. The chance to bid a dignified farewell to family and loved ones.

To make one last witty remark. I've been there and seen it often enough. Only rarely do people on their deathbeds fail to take advantage of that last chance to make a witty remark. No one's ever heard them make a witty remark in their life, but still. You can tell with most of them that they've given it some thought beforehand. As though that's how they want to be remembered. Last words. Flippant last words. Death's approach demands a little flippancy, they figure. But death doesn't demand anything. Death simply comes to get you. Death wants you to come along, preferably without too much of a struggle. 'And have one on me while you're at it,' they say, and knock back the contents of the shot glass. A minute later they close their eyes, another minute later they're dead. The last drink is rarely taken with tears. I've never heard anyone say to his wife: 'You're the one I love most in the whole world. I'm going to miss you. And you'll probably miss me too.' Never. Flippancy. A laughing matter. It's like with funerals. They are, first and foremost, expected to be *fun*. There is laughter and drinking and bad language. To keep the whole thing from being too bourgeois. A bourgeois funeral is an artist's worst nightmare. 'This is exactly how Hank would have wanted it,' they say, and smash their whisky bottles against the lid of the coffin. 'A real blowout. No weeping and wailing, fuck no!' I figure they started about fifteen years ago: the fun funerals. Pink coffins, white coffins, coffins decorated with dragons and shark's teeth, coffins from IKEA, plastic coffins, or coffins wrapped in rubbish bags. I always feel sorry for the children. It's bad enough whenever there are children involved, but when an artist dies the children are also expected to keep things fun. To decorate Daddy's coffin with stickers or poems. To put his favourite coffee mug, the one with 'fuck you!' printed on it, into the coffin along with him. For later. For there. For the end of his long, long journey. So he can drink coffee from his favourite mug, the one with 'fuck you!' printed on it, on the far side too. Above all, the children are not supposed to cry. Their faces are painted and they get balloons and whistles and party hats. Because that was Daddy's dying wish, that his children should have fun at his funeral. That they should play hide-and-seek amid the gravestones. That there be punch afterwards and cake and a big bowl full of sweets and Snickers and Mars bars.

And they all want to go to the same cemetery. The cemetery at the bend in the river. There's a waiting list for that one. Normal people with a nine-to-five job don't even make the waiting list. Seeing as the cemetery is at the bend in the river, there are at least four funerals a year in which the dead person arrives by boat. With a boat you have a better chance of making the papers the next day. The boat leaves from the centre of town and makes its way over the canals and under the bridges, which makes for some nice pictures. The boat is always decked out like a party boat too: flowers and wreaths, men and women in tie-dyed gowns and pointy hats. Women with butterfly wings on their backs, men with moustaches dyed red or green. On the forward deck, dressed in clown costumes, four trumpeters from the Funtime Brass Band are playing a fun tune. By that point, everyone on the funeral boat and the boats behind it are already three sheets to the wind. The normal people stand on the quayside and watch the procession go by, but the drunken relatives don't even give the normal people a second look.

I have to hand it to Ralph Meier or maybe, in fact, to Judith: his funeral was more or less normal. No boat, just a regular old hearse. There were at least a thousand people there. There were camera crews from a couple of broadcasting companies. When the car bearing the coffin turned into the gravel drive, I only had to take a couple of steps back to be out of sight of the immediate family. Judith was wearing a pair of big sunglasses and a black headscarf with little white dots on it. It was probably the headscarf that reminded me then, more than on other days, of Jackie Kennedy, although I don't think Jackie Kennedy would have spat in the face of an unwelcome guest in front of a thousand people at a funeral.

After the incident, I didn't leave the cemetery right away. I walked back to the gate, then a bit further, to the river. A scull went past; a man on a bicycle came by clutching a megaphone and shouting directions at the oarsmen. The two swans with cygnets bobbing in their wake underscored the feeling that 'life goes on', as they say. After standing there for a few minutes, I turned and walked back to the cemetery.

The chapel couldn't hold a thousand people, so the speeches were delivered outside. The mayor spoke, and so did the Minister of Culture. Fellow actors and directors talked about Ralph and told juicy anecdotes. There was the occasional volley of laughter. I stood right at the back, half hidden between the bushes, a few yards from the gravel path. A comedian gave a speech in which the central role was reserved for himself. It didn't sound so much like a speech as a dry run for his next show. There was laughter, but it was uneasy laughter, as though people found it more embarrassing than funny. I thought of Ralph's final moments, in the hospital, a little less than a week ago. The shot glass with the lethal cocktail sat on the nightstand beside his bed, along with a half-eaten pot of fruit yogurt with the spoon still in it, the morning newspaper, and a biography of Shakespeare that he'd been reading for the last few weeks. There was a bookmark in it, no more than halfway through. He asked Judith and his two boys to leave the room for a moment.

When they were gone, he gestured to me to come over. 'Marc,' he said; he took my hand, placed it on the blanket, and put his other hand on top of it.

'I want to tell you that I'm sorry,' he said.

I looked at his face. It was a reasonably healthy face, maybe a bit on the skinny side. If you had seen how round and plump it had been just a few months before, only then would you have realised that this was because of the disease. His eyes were clear.

Every time I see it, I'm amazed. People choose a given date to die on, but on the day itself they suddenly perk up. They talk and laugh more than usual, as though they're hoping someone will stop them. That someone will actually tell them that it's nonsense to just put an end to it all like that.

'I shouldn't… I should never have…' Ralph Meier said. 'I'm sorry; I guess that's what I'm trying to say.'

I didn't say anything. With the right medication and a couple of extremely unpleasant treatments he might have been able to postpone the end for a month or so. But he had opted for the shot glass. A dignified farewell. The shot glass keeps you from having to burden your family with memories that might be hard to forget.

But still, it was strange. A self-ordained death. A self-ordained date and time. The towel in the ring. Why not tomorrow? Why not a week from now? Why not yesterday?

'How is it going these days… with her?' he asked. I saw him hesitate; I saw how he gulped back her name just in time. I don't know what I would have done if Ralph Meier had spoken her name out loud.

I shrugged. I thought about the holiday we'd taken a little over a year ago. At the summer house.

'Marc,' he said. I felt the pressure of his hand on mine. He tried to tighten his grasp, but I could feel how little strength he had left. 'Could you tell her… from me… could you tell her what I just said to you?'

I averted my eyes; effortlessly, I pulled my hand from his grasp – out of the same hands that had once possessed the strength to make other people do things they didn't want to do. Against their will.

'No,' I said.

6

Half an hour later it happened. I was in the corridor; both their boys had gone down to thc hospital cafeteria to get something to eat. Judith Meier came back from the ladies' room where she'd applied some lipstick and fixed her make-up.

'I'm glad you were there,' she said.

I nodded. 'He went with dignity,' I said. That's the kind of thing you say at such moments. Even if you know better. It's like saying you thought a play was amazing. Or that the ending of a film was compelling.

A man came walking up to us, a man in a white doctor's coat. He stopped right in front of us and held out his hand to Judith. 'Mrs Meier?'

'Yes?' She shook his hand.

'My name is Maasland. *Dr* Maasland. Do you have a moment?' He held a Manila folder clutched under one arm. In the upper right-hand corner of it was a sticker with 'Mr R. Meier' written on it in felt-tip, and beneath that, in smaller, printed letters, the name of the hospital.

'And you are?' Maasland asked. 'A relative?'

'I'm the family doctor,' I said, holding out my hand. 'Marc Schlosser.'

Maasland ignored my hand. 'Dr Schlosser,' he said. 'That's... well, that's a coincidence. There are a few things I'd like...' He opened the folder and began to leaf through it. 'Where was it? Oh, here.'

Something about Maasland's body language put me on guard. Like all specialists, he went to no trouble to disguise his profound disdain for general practitioners. Whether it was a surgeon or a gynaecologist, a urologist or a psychiatrist, they all gave you that same look. Did you get enough of studying back then? that look said. Or were you just too lazy to commit to another four years? Or maybe just too scared of the stuff that really counts? We cut into people, we delve into the organs, the circulation, the brain, the operational centre of the human body, we know that body the way a mechanic knows a car engine. All a general practitioner is allowed to do is to peek under the bonnet – and then shake his head in wonder and amazement at such a miracle of technical ingenuity.

'Yesterday we ran through Mr Meier's full case history with him,' he said. 'That's common practice in a euthanasia case. But if I'm right, it wasn't you who finally referred Mr Meier to us, was it, Dr Schlosser?'

I pretended I had to think about it. 'No, that's right,' I said.

Maasland ran his finger back and forth across the sheet of paper he'd removed from the folder. 'I ask you that because it says here... yes, here it is.' The finger came to a stop. 'Yesterday, Mr Meier stated that in October of last year he came to you for a check-up.'

'Could be. He didn't come in often. If he was in doubt about something. Or for a second opinion. I was… I am a friend of the family.'

'And why did he come to see you in October, Dr Schlosser?'

'I couldn't say. I'd have to look it up.'

Maasland glanced at Judith, then back at me. 'According to Mr Meier, you told him in October of last year that there was nothing for him to worry about. Even though by then he was already displaying the early symptoms of his illness.'

'I wouldn't know about that, not off the top of my head. It's possible that he asked me about something then. Maybe he already sensed something and just wanted to hear a comforting word.'

'During that particular consultation in October, Dr Schlosser, did you remove some tissue from Mr Meier's body? And did you then send that tissue to us for analysis?'

'If I had, I think I would remember that.'

'Yes, I would think so too. Especially since removing tissue is not entirely devoid of risk. In the worst of cases, it can even accelerate the course of the disease. I trust you're aware of that, Dr Schlosser?'

The bonnet. I was allowed to peek under the bonnet, but I should not have touched the hoses and wiring.

'The odd thing is that Mr Meier remembered all this quite clearly,' Maasland went on. 'That you were going to send the tissue away for testing. And that he was supposed to call you later for the results.'

Ralph Meier was dead. His body, probably already a good bit cooler by now, was lying only a few yards away from us, behind the green door bearing a sign that read 'Silence'. We couldn't go in and ask him whether yesterday he had perhaps made a mistake about the dates.

'I can't recall, not right now,' I said. 'I'm very sorry.'

'Whatever the case, that tissue never arrived here.'

See? I almost said. You see, on the next-to-last day of his life, Ralph Meier was already getting things mixed up pretty badly! Because of the medication. Because of his weakened state. But I didn't say anything.

Then Judith Meier spoke. 'October,' she said.

Maasland and I looked at her, but now Judith was looking only at me.

'Ralph was worried,' she said. 'He had to go on a shoot in Italy, it was supposed to last almost two months. He was going to leave in a few days. He told me you thought it wasn't anything serious, but that you were sending a tissue sample to the hospital just to be sure. For his own peace of mind.'

'We never received anything here,' Maasland said.

'Well, that really is very peculiar,' I said. 'That's not something I would easily overlook, I think.'

'Well, in fact, that's why I wanted to talk to you, Mrs Meier,' Maasland said. 'We consider this too serious just to pass over. We'd like to take a closer look at the entire case. I wanted to ask your permission for an autopsy.'

'Oh, no!' Judith said. 'An autopsy? Is that really necessary?'

'It would give all of us, and you too, Mrs Meier, in time, more certainty about exactly what happened. We can see, for example, whether a tissue sample was actually taken, and when. Methods have become very sophisticated in the last few years. If a tissue sample was taken, we can determine quite precisely when that was done for the first time. Not only whether it was in October or later, but almost down to the exact day.'

7

A little less than three weeks after Ralph Meier suddenly showed up in my office for the first time, about eighteen months ago, an invitation to the first night of *Richard II* came in the post. Opening the envelope, I noted the physical symptoms I experienced whenever an invitation arrived. Dry mouth, slackening pulse, clammy fingertips, a sensation of pressure at the back of the eyes, and a feeling like being in a bad dream: a nightmare in which you drive into the low-traffic maze of a new residential neighbourhood; you turn left, you turn right, but you can't find your way back out, you are going to have to drive around in circles for the rest of your life.

'Ralph Meier?' Caroline said. 'Really? I didn't know he was one of your patients.'

Caroline is my wife. She never comes to opening nights. Nor to book launches, gallery openings or film-festival retrospectives. She finds them even more burdensome than I do. I rarely press the point. Sometimes, though, I beg her on bended knee to come with me. When I do that, she knows it's serious, and she accompanies me without any further objections. But I don't abuse that power. I save the begging on bended knee for real emergencies.

'*Richard II*,' she said, unfolding the invitation. 'Shakespeare... Well, why not? I'll go with you.'

We were in the kitchen having breakfast. Both our daughters had already left for school. Lisa, our youngest, to the primary school around the corner, Julia by bike to her secondary school. My first patient would be arriving in ten minutes.

'Shakespeare. Are you sure? The play's going to last at least three hours.'

'Sure, but it's Ralph Meier. I've never seen him perform live.'

There was something dreamy in my wife's eyes when she spoke the actor's name.

'What are you looking at?' Caroline asked. 'I'm not trying to hide anything. For a woman, Ralph Meier is nice to look at. So three hours is no big deal.'

And so, two weeks later, we attended the opening night of *Richard II* in the big old municipal theatre. It wasn't the first time I'd been invited to a Shakespeare production. I'd already seen about ten of his plays. A version of *The Taming of the Shrew* in which all the male roles were played by women; *The Merchant of Venice* with the actors in nappies and the actresses wearing rubbish bags for dresses and shopping bags on their heads; *Hamlet* with an all-Down's-Syndrome cast, wind machines and a (dead) goose that was decapitated on stage; *King Lear* with Zimbabwean orphans and ex-junkies; *Romeo and Juliet* in the never-completed tunnel of a subway line, with concentration camp photos projected on the walls, down which sewage trickled; *Macbeth* in which all the female roles were played by naked men – the only clothing they wore was a thong between their buttocks, with handcuffs and weights hanging from their nipples – performing against a soundtrack consisting of artillery barrages, Radiohead songs and poems by Radovan Karadžić. Besides the fact that you didn't dare to look at how the handcuffs and weights were attached to (or through) the nipples, the problem once again was a matter of how slowly the time passed. I can remember delays at airports that must havc lasted half a day, easily, but which were over ten times as quickly as any of those plays.

In *Richard II*, though, the cast wore period costumes. The set consisted of a throne room in a castle, recreated with the greatest possible authenticity. When Ralph Meier came on stage, something happened; the audience, which had at first been simply quiet, was now hushed. When Richard spoke his first words, everyone held their breath. I looked over at Caroline, but she had eyes only for what was happening on stage. Her cheeks were flushed. Three hours later we were out in the foyer, each with a glass of champagne. Crowding around us were men in blue blazers and women in ankle-length gowns. Lots of jewellery: bracelets, necklaces and rings. In one corner, a string quartet was playing.

'Shall we...?' I looked at my watch. For the first time that evening, I realised.

'Come on, Isis can wait a bit,' Caroline said. 'Let's have another one.'

Isis was our babysitter back then. She was sixteen, and her parents didn't like her to come home too late. Julia was thirteen at the time, Lisa eleven. In a couple of years' time we would have no qualms about leaving our younger daughter with her big sister. But not then, not yet.

When I came back from the bar carrying two more glasses of champagne I saw, about ten yards away, Ralph Meier's head towering above the others. It nodded left and right. It *grinned*, the way a head grins when it is used to receiving congratulations.

'There he is,' I said. 'I'll introduce you.'

'Where?' My wife only comes up to my shoulder, she hadn't seen the head yet. She quickly adjusted her pinned-up hair and brushed imaginary crumbs or fluff from her blouse.

'Marc.' He shook my hand. It was a firm handshake, the handshake of someone making it clear that he's using only ten per cent of his strength.

He turned to Caroline. 'And is this your wife? Well, well, you certainly did not exaggerate.' He took her hand, bowed, and kissed it. Then he turned to one side and laid his hand on the shoulder of a woman whose presence I hadn't noticed, because she was entirely blocked from view by his huge frame. Now she moved, almost literally, out of his shadow, and held out her hand.

'Judith,' she said. She shook Caroline's hand first, then mine.

Only much later, when I saw her for the first time by herself, did I realise that Judith Meier was not really a small person. She was only small when standing beside her husband, like a village at the foot of a mountain. But that evening in the foyer of the old municipal theatre I looked from Ralph to Judith and then from Judith back to Ralph, and I thought the things I often think when seeing couples together for the first time.

'So, did the two of you enjoy it?' Judith asked, talking more to Caroline than to me.

'I thought it was fantastic,' Caroline said. 'A fantastic experience.'

'Maybe I should leave for a bit,' Ralph said. 'Then you can say what you really thought.' He laughed his thunderous laugh; a few people turned their heads and laughed along with him.

As I said earlier, in the line of duty I sometimes have to ask patients to get undressed. When all other alternatives have been exhausted. With only a few exceptions, most of my patients are husbands and wives. I observe their naked bodies. I superimpose the images. I see how the one body approaches the other. I see a mouth, lips pressed against other lips, hands, fingers that search, fingernails across a stretch of bare skin. Sometimes the room is dark, but often it isn't. Some people have no qualms about leaving the lights on. I have seen their bodies; I know that, in most cases, it would be better to turn the lights off. I look at their feet, their ankles, their knees, their thighs, and then further up, the area around the navel, the chest or breasts, the neck. The actual sex organs I usually skip over. I look, but the way you might look at a dead animal in the road. My gaze is usually only held for a moment, like a hangnail on a loose thread of clothing – no more than that. And I haven't even got to the rear views yet. The back sides of bodies are a different story altogether. Buttocks, depending on their shape or shapelessness, can summon up tenderness or blind rage. The nameless spot where the crack between them merges into the lower back. The spine. The shoulder blades. The hairline at the back of the neck. The back side of a human body contains more no-man's land than the front does. On the dark side of the moon, both capsule and lunar lander lose all radio contact with ground control. I put on my interested expression. Does it also hurt when you lie on your side? I ask, thinking the whole time about couples with the lights on or the lights off, groping at each other's backsides. All I really want, in fact, is for it to be over quickly. For them to get dressed again. For me to be able to look only at their talking heads. But I never forget the bodies. I connect one face to another. I connect the bodies. I let them become intertwined. Breathing heavily, one head approaches the other. Tongues are stuck into mouths and poke around probingly inside. In big cities there are streets lined with skyscrapers where the sun rarely shines. Between the paving stones grows moss or grass that is almost dead. It is cold and clammy there. Or sometimes even warm and clammy. Little flies everywhere. Or clouds of mosquitoes. You can get dressed. I've seen enough. How is your husband doing? Your wife?

I looked at Ralph Meier, and then at Judith. As I said, she wasn't so small in and of herself. She was too small for *him*. I thought about the things. The things people do with each other in the dark. I looked at Ralph's hand clutching a champagne glass. All things considered, it was a wonder that the glass didn't break.

And then, suddenly, there was that moment. The moment I would think back on often, later on – the moment that should have been a warning to me.

Judith had taken Caroline by the elbow and was introducing her to someone. A woman whose face seemed vaguely familiar, probably one of the actresses in *Richard II*. That was how Caroline happened to be standing half turned away from us, with her back to Ralph and me.

'In any case, I was never bored for a moment,' I told Ralph. 'It was a unique experience for me too.'

It took a couple of seconds before I realised that Ralph Meier was no longer listening to me. He was no longer even looking at me. And, without following his gaze, I knew immediately what he was looking at.

Now something was happening to the gaze itself. To the eyes. As he examined the back of Caroline's body from head to foot, a film slid down over his eyes. In nature films, you see that sometimes with birds of prey. A raptor that has located, from somewhere far up, high in the air, or from a tree branch, a mouse or some other tasty morsel. That was how Ralph Meier was regarding my wife's body: as if it were something edible, something that made his mouth water. Now there was also some movement around his mouth. The lips parted, his jaws churned, I even thought I heard the grinding of teeth – and he breathed a sigh. Ralph Meier was seeing something delicious; his mouth was already anticipating the tasty morsel that he would, if given the chance, wolf down in a few bites.

The most remarkable thing perhaps was that he did all this without the slightest embarrassment. As though I weren't even there. He might as well have unzipped his trousers and stood there pissing on me. It would have made no real difference.

Then, from one moment to the next, he was back again. As though someone had snapped their fingers: a hypnotist releasing him from his trance.

'Marc,' he said to me. He looked at me as though seeing me for the first time. Then he looked at the empty glass in his hand. 'What do you say? Shall we go for one more?'

Later that evening, in bed, I told Caroline about it. Caroline had just removed the elastic band from her hair and shaken it loose. She seemed more amused than shocked. 'Oh really?' she said. 'What kind of look was that, exactly? Tell me again…'

'Like he was looking at a tasty morsel,' I said.

'Really? So? But I *am* a tasty morsel, aren't I? Or don't you think so?'

'Caroline, please! I don't know how to put it any more clearly… I… I thought it was *dirty*.'

'Oh, sweetheart. It isn't dirty, is it, the way men look at women? Or women at men, for that matter? I mean, that Ralph Meier is a real ladies' man, everything about him. It's probably not very nice for his wife, but OK, it was her choice. A woman can tell that right away, the kind of man she's with.'

'I was standing right beside him. He didn't give a shit.'

Now Caroline turned to face me, she slid up a little until she was lying against me, and placed a hand on my chest.

'You're not jealous, are you? It sort of sounds like it, like a jealous husband.'

'I'm not jealous! I know exactly how men look at women. But this wasn't normal. This was… this was *dirty*. I don't know how else to put it.'

'My sweet, jealous little man,' Caroline said.

8

In a practice like mine, the key is not to worry too much about medical standards. About what is, strictly speaking, medically responsible. In the 'creative' professions, excess is more the rule than the exception. Collectively, my patients account for ten well-filled bottle banks a week. I could tell them the truth. The truth is somewhere around two or three glasses a day. Two glasses for women, three for men. No one really wants to hear that truth. I press my fingertips against the liver. I test it for hardening. How many glasses of alcohol do you drink in the course of a day? I ask. They can't fool me. Alcohol comes out through the skin. A beer before dinner and after that no more than half a bottle of wine, they say. Alcohol seeps out through the pores and evaporates right off the skin. I have a good nose. I can smell what they drank the night before. Painters and sculptors stink of old gin or eau de vie. Writers and actors of beer and vodka. Female writers and actresses, when they breathe, give off the sourish smell of cheap Chardonnay on ice. They might hold a hand up to cover their mouths, but the eructations can't be stopped. Of course I could say something. I could try to get to the bottom of things, as they say. A beer or half a bottle of wine: don't make me laugh! The patients would leave. The same way they left to escape their previous family doctor. A doctor who, like me, pressed his finger against their livers and felt the same thing I did – but who then went on to tell them the truth. If you go on like this, your liver will rupture within a year. The end is an extremely painful one. The liver can no longer process the waste. It spreads out through the rest of the body. It piles up in the ankles, the ventricles, the whites of the eyes. The whites of the eyes first turn yellow, then grey. Parts of the liver die off. The actual rupture is the final stage.

So the patients leave and come to me. Someone – a good friend, male or female, a colleague – told them about a GP who doesn't worry too much about how much alcohol you knock back in the course of a day. Well, listen, that maximum number of glasses a day stuff is all pretty relative, I say. You only live once. Clean living is one of the major inducers of stress. Just look around. Has it ever occurred to you how many artists live to be eighty or more, even though they've always lived a life of riot? I see my new patient starting to relax already. A smile appears on his or her face. I name names. Pablo Picasso, I say. Pablo Picasso knew how to bend an elbow. Mentioning the name serves a twin purpose. By referring to my patients in the same breath as a world-famous artist, they feel like Pablo Picasso himself, even if only for a moment. I could put it differently. You're a much bigger lush than Pablo Picasso ever was, I could say, the only thing is that you don't possess a tenth of his talent.

When you look at things clearly, it's simply a waste. A waste of alcohol, that is. But I don't say that. And the other names I don't mention. The names of the geniuses who drank themselves to death. At the end of the afternoon on the last day of his life, Dylan Thomas returned to his room at New York's Chelsea Hotel. 'I've had eighteen straight whiskies, I think that is a record,' he told his wife. Then he lost consciousness. At the autopsy it turned out that his liver was four times the normal size. I say nothing about Charles Bukowski, about Paul Gauguin, about Janis Joplin. The important thing is *how* you live, I say. People who can enjoy life last longer than the sourpusses who eat only plants and slurp organic yogurt. I tell them about the vegetarians with terminal intestinal disorders, the teetotallers who die in their late twenties after a cardiac arrest, the militant non-smokers whose lung cancer is detected too late.

Look at the Mediterranean countries, I say. People there have been drinking wine for centuries, but they tend to be healthier than people here. There are certain countries and peoples I omit on purpose. I don't talk about the average life expectancy of the vodka-swilling Russian. If you don't live, you'll never get old, I say. Do you know why the Scots never come down with the flu? You don't? Let me tell you… Having reached this point, I have a new patient almost in the bag. By heart, I reel off a list of the whisky distilleries: Glenfiddich, Glencairn, Glencadam – and here I reach the crucial moment in our first appointment: I hint at the fact that I enjoy the occasional drink myself. That I'm just like them. One of them. Not completely, of course. I know my place. I'm not an artist. I'm only a simple family doctor. But a family doctor who happens to value quality of life more than a one-hundred-per cent healthy body.

My patients include a former secretary of state who weighs over three hundred pounds. A former secretary of state for culture with whom I swap recipes. Though I shouldn't be swapping anything with her at all. Sometimes I almost can't breathe, Doctor, she says, after sinking down panting in the chair. I ask her to unbutton her blouse, just to bare her upper back, and I raise my stethoscope. The sounds from inside a body that's too fat are not like those from a body with enough room for all the vital organs. It all has to work a lot harder in there. There's a struggle for space going on. A struggle that is lost before it's even started. The fat is everywhere. The organs are hemmed in on all sides. I pick up my stethoscope and listen. I hear the lungs, which have to push the fat aside with every breath. Breathe out very slowly, I say. And I hear the way the fat moves in to resume its place. The heart doesn't beat, it pounds. The heart is working overtime. The blood has to be pumped in time to the furthest points of the body. But the arteries are surrounded by fat too. Now breathe in slowly, I say. The fat moves aside a little when the lungs try to fill with air, but it never fully surrenders its ground. It's a fight for thousandths of an inch. Invisible to the naked eye, the fat is readying for the final offensive.

I move the stethoscope around to the front of the body. Between the former secretary of state's breasts there glistens a little runnel of sweat, like a waterfall viewed from a distance, a waterfall somewhere far up a mountainside. I try to avoid looking at the breasts themselves. As always, I think the wrong kinds of thoughts. I can't help it. I think about the former secretary of state's husband, a 'dramaturge' who spends most of each year out of work. About who gets to be on top or who lies underneath. First he's on top. But he can't get a grip anywhere. He slides off her body the way you might slide off a half-filled waterbed, or a carelessly inflated bouncy castle. Or he actually sinks into it too far. His hands clutch at the flesh. What he needs, in fact, are ropes and grappling hooks. This isn't working, his wife pants, and pushes him off. Now he's on the bottom. I imagine the breasts above his face, how they descend slowly. First there is a total eclipse. The light goes out. Then there is no room to breathe. The 'dramaturge' shouts something, but all sound is muffled by the breasts. Now they're covering his entire face. They're too warm, and not completely dry any more either. A purple nipple the size of a pudding plate seals off his mouth and nostrils. Then, with a dry pop, the first rib breaks beneath the weight of his wife's three-hundred-pound body. She doesn't notice a thing. She gropes around for his dick and stuffs it inside her. Everything down there is too fat as well, so it takes a while before she's sure he's really inside her. Meanwhile, more ribs give way. It's like when a ten-storey building is being razed; the contractor didn't pay much attention to the drawings, the builders start pulling down a supporting wall on the ground floor. At first there are only a few deep fissures, then the whole construction begins to sway. Finally, the building collapses. She starts licking his ear. That's the last thing he feels. And hears. A St Bernard's tongue filling his auricle. Exhale, one more time, I say. How is your husband? Is he working again? I could tell her that things can't go on like this any longer. It's not just that the vital organs have too little space. The joints, too, are overtaxed. Everything is being destroyed. The kneecaps, the ligaments in her ankles, the hips. Like an overloaded artic. On a downhill run the brakes overheat, the truck jackknifes and then shoots through the guardrail into a ravine. But I open my desk drawer and pull out a recipe. An oven dish of pork loin, with plums and red wine. It's a recipe I cut out of a magazine. The former secretary of state likes to cook. Cooking is her only hobby, nothing else interests her. Sooner or later she'll cook herself to death. She'll die face-down in a saucepan.

Ralph Meier was too fat as well, albeit in a different way. A 'more natural' way, you might say. At first, his true girth was hard to identify. The extra weight hung all over his body like a roomy overcoat. But during his first appointment I once again heard noises one rarely hears inside healthy people. I placed my stethoscope on his bare back. First of all there was the breathing. It sounded heavy and laboured, as though the air, scarce enough already, had to be drawn to the surface from a well that was far too deep. There was an audible echo to his heartbeat. An echo like the ringing of a bell. And further down, in his intestines, in the pit of his stomach, I heard a brewing and a bubbling. He had a fondness for shellfish and game birds, as I would witness later. Small birds – quail, partridge – he pulled the skeletons apart and stuck them in his mouth. He slurped the marrow from the cervical vertebrae, ground spinal cords between his teeth to get the last juices out of them. 'I'm on stage every evening,' he said.

'And in the afternoon we're rehearsing a new play. I can't keep up the pace.' A colleague had mentioned my name, he said. A colleague who had been a patient of mine for years. He's the one who had told him about the pills. About how easy I was about prescribing those pills – Benzedrine, amphetamines, speed – whatever I, as his doctor, thought was best for him. I bent over the stethoscope. I seriously asked myself what havoc those pills would wreak on this body. Benzedrine, amphetamine, speed – all different names for the same thing, in fact. The pulse quickens, the pupils dilate, the blood vessels too. For a few hours, we are able to go back into overdrive.

You could, indeed, call me 'easy' when it comes to prescribing certain medicines. That's right, I'm easy. Why should anyone lie awake half the night when one milligram of lorazepam will knock them out till noon? Medicines are what boost the quality of life. I have colleagues who warn their patients about the dangers of habituation. They prescribe Valium, but when the patient asks for a renewal they suddenly get all fussy. I'm not like that. Some people need a kick up the arse; others just need to think less for a couple of hours. The beauty of all these medicines is their simplicity. Five milligrams of Valium really does calm you down; less than three milligrams of Benzedrine is enough to make someone bounce off the walls till five in the morning. Some men are afraid to go into shops or talk to girls. After two weeks on Seroxat, though, the patient will return home with twelve Hugo Boss shirts, an Alan Setscoe desk lamp, and five new pairs of trousers from the G-Star Raw retail store. After three weeks he's chatting up every girl at the club. Not one or two, no, all of them. He no longer lets himself be put off by silly giggles or outright refusal. He has no time for giggling or for refusals. 'The night is still young' is for losers, for the pizza faces who hang around for seven hours with beers in their hands and then go home alone. The night is not young – if there's one thing Seroxat has taught him, it's that. The night starts *now*. The sooner it gets going, the longer it lasts. He has a perfect pick-up line. Or rather, he doesn't have to think about lines any more. All lines are good. They're especially good when you've forgotten them already, thirty seconds later. They're conspicuous by reason of their simplicity. You're looking good, he says to the girl who looks good. Is there also a *Mr* Mulder? he asks the woman who introduces herself as Esther Mulder. I never used to be able to come up with lines like that, the Seroxat-user says. Your place or mine? Your eyes are prettiest when you smile. If we leave now, we've still got the whole evening ahead of us. May I touch you there, or would you hold that against me? After five minutes with you I felt like I'd known you all my life. It's – he doesn't know how else to put it – *liberating* to come up with lines like that.

Simplicity, that's what it's all about. Simplicity is telling a pretty woman that she's pretty. You never say: do you know that you're very pretty? A pretty woman already knows that. Do you know that you're very pretty? is something you only say to an unattractive woman. A woman who's never heard that before. Her gratitude will know no bounds. Later in the evening she'll put up with anything: a dirty, unwashed dick right in her face.

An unwashed prick that sprays a month's backlog of old sperm all over her. All over her navel, her lips, her eyelids. Yellow sperm. Yellow as the pages of a book that no one wanted to read, which is why it was left out in the sun beside the deckchair. Filthy, worthless sperm that smells like a half-finished bottle of fermented dairy drink stuck on a back shelf of the fridge and then forgotten. On the other hand, though, it *does* happen sometimes. No, let me put it differently: you can be dead sure that a pretty woman almost never gets to hear how pretty she is. That none of the other men at the party have the courage to say that. You often hear pretty women complaining to each other about that: that their looks are so much taken for granted. As though it were all just par for the course, like the Mona Lisa, the Acropolis, or the view of the Grand Canyon from Grandview Point. We have no words to describe pretty women. We're speechless. Tongue-tied. We talk around their beauty. Been to any nice restaurants lately? the tongue asks. Got any plans for the summer? The pretty woman replies normally. At first she's relieved to be talked to so normally. To have someone just talk to her about day-to-day things. So normal. So ordinary. As though she's not pretty at all, just a person like anyone else. But after a while something starts bothering her. Because it *is* kind of weird. The pretty woman wears her beauty like a feather headdress. So it's kind of weird when someone goes on talking without making any reference to the headdress.

'You have a very lovely wife,' Ralph Meier said, for instance, the first chance he got. He was sitting opposite my desk and at least he didn't beat around the bush. It was during his second visit to my office, a little less than a week after the opening night of *Richard II*. He had simply shown up again, unannounced, without an appointment. 'Could I just bother him for a moment?' he'd asked Liesbeth, my assistant. 'It'll only take a minute.'

I thought at first that he had come back for a new prescription, but the pills weren't even mentioned during that second visit. 'I was in the neighbourhood anyway,' he said. 'So I thought, I'll swing by and ask him in person.'

'Oh yeah?' I tried to look at him as blandly as possible, but I couldn't help it, I couldn't stop myself: all I could think about was that look on his face the week before, when he examined my wife from head to foot.

'We're throwing a party on Saturday,' he said. 'At our place. If the weather's nice it'll be in the garden. I wanted to invite you and your wife.'

I looked at him and thought my own thoughts. Would he have invited us if I had been married to a woman other than Caroline? I wondered. A less tasty woman?

'A party?' I said.

'Judith and I. Saturday, it will be twenty years ago that we met.' He shook his head. 'Unbelievable. Twenty years! Where does the time go?'

9

'He doesn't waste any time,' I said. 'He goes straight for the kill.'

We were sitting at the kitchen table. The dishwasher was bubbling. Lisa had already gone to bed; Julia was in her room doing her homework. Caroline divided the last of the wine between us.

'Marc, come on!' she said. 'He just likes you, that's all. You shouldn't always go looking for ulterior motives.'

'Likes me! He doesn't like me at all. He likes *you*. He told me so, in so many words. "You have a very lovely wife, Marc!" That's how he looked at you in the theatre. The way a man looks at a *very lovely* woman. Don't make me laugh!'

Caroline sipped her wine, then tilted her head slightly and looked at me. I could see it in her eyes: she found this entertaining, this unexpected attention from the famous actor Ralph Meier. I couldn't really blame her. If I were to be completely honest, I found it entertaining as well. It was in any case a lot more entertaining than having famous actors not even notice your wife, I told myself. But then I thought about that dirty look of his. His raptor look. No, it wasn't all pure amusement.

'You're saying he only invited us to his party because he's after me,' Caroline said. 'But that doesn't make sense. He invited us to that opening night too, didn't he? And he hadn't even seen me then.'

She had a point there, I had to admit. Still, these were two different things, an invitation to an opening night and an invitation to a party at someone's private home.

'So turn it around for a moment,' I said. 'Your birthday's next month. Would you invite Ralph Meier to your party?'

'Well…' Caroline looked at me teasingly. 'No, OK,' she said. 'I don't suppose I would, no. You're right as far as that goes. All I'm trying to say is that you shouldn't always assume the worst. Maybe he really does like us. Both of us, I mean. It could be that, couldn't it? I talked to his wife for a long time the other evening. I don't know, sometimes you have that feeling, that you click immediately. I had that with Judith. Who knows, maybe she told Ralph to invite us.'

Judith. I'd forgotten her name again. The first time I'd forgotten it was less than a second after shaking her hand in the theatre foyer. The second time was this morning, when Ralph Meier had started talking about the party.

Judith, I admonished myself inwardly. *Judith*.

I'll be honest. When she held out her hand and told me her name, I looked at her the way every man looks at a woman who enters his field of vision for the first time.

Could you do it with her? I asked myself, looking her deep in the eyes. *Yes*, was the response.

And Judith looked back. It's only ever a matter of a few fractions of a second, of making eye contact for just that little bit longer. That's how Judith and I looked at each other. Just a little longer, strictly speaking, than one might consider entirely respectable. And while I was forgetting her name, she smiled at me. It wasn't so much her mouth that smiled, it was above all her eyes.

Yes, those eyes said back to me. *I could with you too.*

Respectable is not the right word. Respectable belongs in sentences you'd rather not hear yourself say out loud. Sentences like: 'I thought we were going to at least keep things here to a minimum of respectability.' No, respectability is not something I can claim for myself. I look at women that way because I have no idea how to look at women any other way. It may be too bad for the 'likeable' women, for the 'really rather nice' women, but to be safe I never look at them for too long. I'm not rude, I'll launch into an animated conversation if I have to, but my body language leaves no room for misinterpretation. *Not with you,* my body language writes in big block letters on my forehead. *I don't even want to think about it. Not with a ten-foot pole.* Likeable women compensate for their lack of physical attractiveness with talents natural or unnatural in other areas. At meetings attended by more than a hundred people, for example, they make all the sandwiches themselves. Or they go out and hire party hats and masks for all the guests. Or they arrive on a delivery bike carrying more firewood for the braziers. 'She's so lovely, Wilma,' everyone says. 'Such a lovely person! Who else would come up with something like that? Who else would think of that?' Wilma of course is plainly too pale or too thin or just too unattractive, but at the same time she does so many lovely things out of the goodness of her heart that you'd have to be a complete bastard to say anything negative about her.

In the end, at one of those meetings of more than a hundred people, there is always some man who remains hovering around Wilma. Often literally. It's the same man who we saw hanging around at the edge of the dance floor. He was making the moves along with the dancers, but never stepped out onto the floor itself. The bottle of beer in his hand was rocking to the beat of the music. But that was the only thing about him that moved rhythmically. 'Remember that guy?' people ask each other later. 'That guy at the party? Did you know that he and Wilma...?' From that day on he's the one who buys the two hundred whole-wheat buns from the bakery and chops wood for the braziers. Wilma takes a break from years of being 'lovely'. And who can blame her? Then the children come along. Usually plain children. Highly gifted and socially handicapped. Children who actually *like* going to school. Who skip a few grades but are always the ones who get bullied. Later on, when the only jobs they can find are shovelling stalls for an organic dairy farmer, it's mostly society's fault. Meanwhile, Wilma's friends wonder what she could ever have seen in that guy with the motor skills of a wooden clothes peg. But they understand. What it is they understand exactly they never say to Wilma. But they say it to each other. 'I mean, it's really nice for her that she at least has *someone*,' they say. 'Maybe it sounds weird, but in some strange way they're actually a pretty good match.'

Could you do it with this one? During my days at medical school, we always asked each other that, during autopsy class. Whenever a fresh cadaver was laid on the dissecting table. One time it might be an emaciated old man who had donated his body to medical science, the next time a traffic fatality whose inside pocket had been found to contain a donor card. It was our way of breaking the tension. The tension that precedes cutting into a human being. 'Could you do it with this one?' we whispered to each other, out of earshot of the professor. We mentioned sums of money. 'For a hundred grand? For a million? No? What about five million?'

And even then we were already sorting the corpses into categories. 'All right' meant just plain ugly; 'attractive' was someone with a friendly or cute face, but with an undercarriage you could smash a bottle of champagne against; 'good-looking' meant that we had nothing short of a fashion model lying on the cutting table. The kind of body that made you bewail the fact that it was so cold and could no longer move.

Caroline looked at me. 'What are you laughing about? One of your private jokes, I suppose?'

I shook my head. 'No,' I said, 'I was just thinking about Judith. And about Ralph. The way he looked at you. That she probably has no idea what kind of explosives are being planted beneath their twenty-year anniversary when you walk into their house.'

'Marc! I'm not out to ruin their anniversary party.'

'No, I know you're not. But you have to promise me this: that you'll stick to my side the whole time?'

Caroline couldn't help laughing. 'Oh, Marc! It's so marvellous, having a husband like you. A husband who watches over me. Who protects me.'

Now it was my turn to tilt my head to one side and look at her teasingly. 'So what are you going to wear?' I asked.

10

Any father would rather have a son than a daughter. Any mother would too, in fact. Our classes in medical biology were taught by Professor Herzl. During our first year at medical school, he lectured us on instinct. 'Instinct can't be eliminated,' he said. 'Years of civilisation can render instinct invisible. Culture and law and order force us to keep our instincts under control. But instinct is never very far away. It's simply waiting to pounce as soon as your attention flags.'

Professor Aaron Herzl. Should that name sound slightly familiar to you: this was indeed the same Aaron Herzl who was later drummed out of the university because of his studies of the criminal brain. The conclusions Herzl drew from his research have become widely accepted today, but back then – back during my years at medical school – such opinions could only be expressed in a whisper. Those were the years when people still believed in the good in mankind. The good in every human being. The fashionable opinion of the day said that a bad person was open to improvement. All bad people.

'"An eye for an eye, a tooth for a tooth" is in fact much closer to human nature than we dare to admit publicly,' Herzl taught us. 'You kill your brother's murderer, castrate with a butcher's knife the man who raped your wife, chop off the hands of the burglar who invaded your home. The legal system often leads only to endless delays before arriving at much the same verdicts. Dead. Gone. We never want to see the murderers and rapists back on the streets again. When the father dies, the son takes over. He chases the intruders from the house and kills the barbarians who try to rape his mother and his sisters. When a child is born, not only the father but also the mother breathes a sigh of relief to see that the firstborn is a boy. Those are facts that two thousand years of civilisation cannot simply eradicate. Two thousand years? What am I saying? This was the status quo until not so long ago. Twenty, maybe thirty years ago at most. It is important that we do not forget where we came from. Sweet, gentle, *kind-hearted* men, all well and good. But that is a luxury one must first be able to afford. In a concentration camp, sweet, gentle men are no good to anyone.'

Let me be perfectly clear about this. I love my daughters. More than anything or anyone in this world. I'm only being frank. I wanted a son. I wanted it so deep down inside me that it almost hurt. A son. A boy. I thought about human instinct as I cut the umbilical cord. Julia. From the day she was born, she was the dearest thing to me in the world. My little girl. It was love at first sight. The kind of love that brings tears to your eyes. But instinct was stronger. Better luck next time, it whispered. Within a year or two you'll get another chance. When Lisa was born, it was all over. We talked about it a few times, about having a third child, but my curiosity about having yet another daughter was only theoretical. Things go the way they go. The chance of having a third daughter was a hundred times greater than that of having a son. A man with three or more daughters tends to be a laughing stock.

It was time for me to face up to the facts. To learn to live with it. I began drawing up a list of the advantages and disadvantages, checking them off as I went. The way you might do when deciding whether to move to the countryside or remain in the big city. In the country you can see more stars, it's quieter there, the air is cleaner. In the city you have everything you need within arm's reach. It's noisier, true, but you don't have to drive five miles to buy a newspaper. There are cinemas and restaurants. In the countryside there are more insects, in the city more trams and taxis. I probably don't have to explain to you that in my equation the countryside was a girl and the city was a boy. People who live in the country go to great lengths to present even the disadvantages as advantages. An hour's drive and I'm in the city, the rural resident says. I can catch a film there and go out to eat, but I'm always so relieved to get back to the peace and quiet and to nature.

An hour there and an hour back: I don't know any better metaphor for the distance between having a daughter and having a son. After Lisa was born I resigned myself to country life. I decided to accept the disadvantages and, above all, to enjoy the advantages. Girls are less reckless. Girls are sweeter. A girl's room smells better than a boy's. You have to take care of girls more, for the rest of your life. The latest they're allowed to get home after a school party is a lot earlier than it is with boys. Between school and home lies a warren of darkened cycle paths. On the other hand, all girls are in love with their fathers. The eternal battle for elbow room is one they fight out with their mothers. For Caroline, that was tough at times. 'What was this all about, can somebody please tell me?' she would shout in exasperation when Julia slammed the bedroom door in her face again. 'And what are *you* laughing at?' she asked when Lisa went on to roll her eyes and wink at me. 'You never do anything wrong. What am I doing wrong? What do you do that I don't?'

'I'm their father,' was my reply.

'But what exactly is he in, Dad?' Lisa asked as we were parking the car a few streets away from Ralph Meier's house. We had driven past first, along a hedge and then past the bushes surrounding a garden in one of our city's quieter, more exclusive neighbourhoods. Through the bushes you could see the guests on the lawn with their glasses, and plates of food. There was smoke, probably from a barbecue: through the open car windows we caught a whiff of grilled meat.

'People know him mostly as a stage actor,' I said. 'You don't see him on TV that often.'

To Lisa, a famous actor played in *films*, or at the very least in a regular soap opera. An actor was probably young too, in any case no older than Brad Pitt. Not someone Ralph Meier's age, throwing a party because he had been married to the same woman for twenty years.

'Can you also get famous from acting in plays?' she asked in astonishment.

'Lisa! Don't be such an idiot! Of course you can.' Julia had the earbuds of her iPod in, but apparently that didn't keep her from following the conversation.

'I can ask, can't I?' Lisa retorted. 'Is that possible, Dad? Can you be famous from acting in plays?'

It hadn't been our plan originally, taking both the girls along to Ralph Meier's party. But it was a Saturday afternoon, so we asked if they wanted to go. At first neither of them reacted too enthusiastically. But to our surprise, half an hour before it was time for us to leave, they announced that they wanted to go after all. 'Why? You two don't have to, you know,' I said. 'Mum and I will be back in a few hours anyway.'

'Julia says there might be famous people there,' Lisa said.

I looked at Julia.

'Well, what are you looking at?' she said. 'It's possible, isn't it?'

After we had locked the car, as we were walking past the bushes and the hedge to the front door, I tried to formulate an answer to my youngest daughter's question. Yes, I thought to myself, you can still become famous from acting in plays, but it was a different kind of famous from fifty years ago. Any number of attempts had been made to let Ralph Meier's talent loose in front of the cameras too – with highly varying degrees of success. I remembered the police series that had been cancelled after only eight episodes, and the gravity with which Ralph Meier had spoken the line 'Tell it to 'em down at the station, buddy!' – a gravity that only provoked mirth. His role as a resistance fighter in *The Bridge Across the Rhine*, the most expensive Dutch feature film ever made, hadn't been much of a hit either. What I remembered most from that film was the raid on the registrar's office in Arnhem, and the line 'We ought to take that Nazi whore and put a bullet through her fucking head!' Ralph Meier had tried to look grim as he said it, but his expression was mostly one of bewilderment. It was hard for people to accept a hero of the Resistance who weighed more than one hundred kilos, so Ralph Meier had gone on a diet. You could see that he had lost a lot of weight, but it didn't make his body any thinner, at best only emptier. Half an hour before the end of the film, as he was facing the firing squad, the look on his face had been largely one of relief. He was probably glad that it was all over and that he could finally go to the catering van and get himself a sandwich.

'A lot of people still go to the theatre,' I said. 'To them, Ralph Meier is famous.'

Lisa turned her face towards me and hit me with her sweetest smile. 'Yeah, right, Dad.'

11

There are times when you run back through your life, to see whether you can locate the point at which it could still have taken a different turn. *There it is!* You say. *Look there…* This is where I say that we're planning to head more or less in that direction during the summer holidays and that it might ('Sure. Yeah. Why not? Who knows?') be an idea to pop in on them. That was when we were saying goodbye, right at the end of the evening, when it had already been dark for a while, and Ralph and Judith had mentioned the summer house for the first time.

You hit pause, then rewind frame-by-frame. Here's Judith throwing her arms around Caroline and kissing her on both cheeks. 'We'll be there from mid-July to mid-August,' she says. 'So if the four of you are in the area…' A little further back you see Ralph Meier, laughing at some joke you can't hear – and can't recall either. 'We're renting a house this summer,' he says. 'A house with a pool, not far from the beach. If you people feel like it, just drop by. Plenty of room.' He slaps you on the back. 'And I bet Alex wouldn't mind either.' He winks and looks at my eldest daughter. At Julia. But Julia turns her back on us and pretends she hasn't heard.

Alex was their eldest boy. I was standing there when Alex and

Julia were introduced. We were still in the hallway, we had just come through the door. It's not something you see very often, and precisely because you don't, you recognise it right away when it's real. The spark. The spark that literally jumps the gap.

'Would you girls like that?' Caroline asked in the car on the way home. 'To drop by and see them during the holidays?'

There was no reply from the back seat. In my rear-view mirror I saw Julia staring dreamily out of the window. Lisa had the buds of her MP3 player in her ears.

'Julia? Lisa?' Caroline said, turning and laying her arm over the headrest. 'I asked you something.'

'Yeah,' Julia said. 'What was it?'

My wife sighed. 'I asked if you would like it if we went by to visit them during the summer holidays.'

'Whatever,' Julia said.

'Oh… I thought you sort of liked that boy of theirs. We didn't see you for most of the afternoon and evening.'

'Mum…'

'OK, I'm sorry. I just thought: maybe you'd like to see him again. During the holidays.'

'Whatever,' Julia said.

'What about you, Lisa?' my wife asked. She almost had to shout to get Lisa to remove her earbuds. 'How would you like that, to drop by and see them during the summer holidays? They're renting a house near the beach. A house with a pool.'

Lisa had gone with Alex's younger brother and a few other kids to a corner of the living room, where they had watched DVDs and played with the PlayStation on a huge plasma screen on the wall. Thomas! Extraordinary that I could remember his name right away. Thomas. Alex and Thomas. Thomas seemed to me to be about Lisa's age, but Alex was probably a year or so older than Julia. Fourteen or fifteen. He was a fairly good-looking boy, with curly blond hair and a voice that was quite deep for his age. In all his movements, both in the way he walked and the way he turned his head to look at you, there was a kind of studied languor, as though he were trying to play a more sluggish, slow-motion version of himself. Thomas was more the ADHD type: boisterous, loud. Glasses, and bowls of crisps were knocked over regularly in the corner by the plasma screen, and the other children roared with laughter at his jokes.

'Yeah, a pool!' Lisa said.

I had spent the first few minutes after our arrival wandering aimlessly around the living room and kitchen, then I strolled out into the garden. There were lots of people I vaguely recognised, without knowing why. A few of my patients were there too. Most of them were seeing me for the first time in my natural state, probably, in normal clothes and with my hair mussed up, which explained why they looked at me as though they recognised *me* vaguely too but couldn't quite put a name to the face. I made no effort to help them out. I simply nodded and walked on.

Ralph was standing at the barbecue, wearing an apron that said 'I LOVE NY'. He was poking at sausages, flipping hamburgers, and ladling chicken wings onto a platter. 'Marc!' He bent down, stuck his arm into a blue icebox and pulled out a 16-ounce can of Jupiler. 'And your wife? You did bring your ravishing wife along, I hope?'

He handed me the ice-cold can of beer. I looked at him. I couldn't help myself: I had to laugh.

'What's so funny?' he asked. 'You're not going to tell me that you had the bloody gall to come here all alone?'

I looked around the garden, as though trying to find Caroline. But I was looking for someone else. And I found her almost right away. She was standing beside the sliding glass doors I'd come through just a few minutes earlier.

She saw me too. She waved.

'I'll go and see what she's up to,' I said.

Before going on, I need to say something about my own looks. I'm no George Clooney. My face would not make me eligible for a supporting role in a hospital series. But I do have the air, or more accurately, the look. The look common to all doctors, high or low. A look, I don't know how else to put it, that *undresses*. A look that sees the human body for what it is. *That body of yours holds no secrets for us*, our look says. *You can put clothes on it, but underneath them you're naked.* That's how we look at people. Not even so much as patients, but as the temporary inhabitants of a body that, without periodic maintenance, could simply break down.

I was standing with Judith in front of the sliding glass doors. Music from the house murmured its way into the garden. Something South American: salsa. But no one was dancing. Little groups stood around talking. We weren't conspicuous, Judith and I. We were a little group too.

'Have you two been living here for long?' I asked.

We were both holding plastic plates, which we had just filled at the buffet in the living room. I had taken mostly cold cuts, French cheese, and things with mayonnaise on them, she had more tomatoes, tuna, and something greyish-green that looked like artichoke leaves but probably wasn't.

'It used to be my parents',' Judith said. 'Ralph and I lived on a houseboat for a few years. That was fun, romantic, whatever you want to call it, but when the boys came along it became too small and cramped. Plus all that water around with two little children. We were so ready for something else. We were completely tired of bobbing up and down on that houseboat.'

Strictly speaking, she hadn't said anything funny, but I laughed anyway. I knew from experience that that was how it worked: the sooner you laugh during a conversation with a woman, the better. They're not used to it, women, to making people laugh. They think they're not funny. They're right, usually.

'And your parents…?' I allowed the question to hang in the air, at the same time describing a little circle above my plate with my plastic fork. *Within the plate*: it could only mean that I was asking if her parents were still among us. Among the living.

'My father died a few years ago. My mother felt like the house was too big for her, so she moved to an apartment downtown. I have a brother who lives in Canada. He didn't mind us getting the house.'

'And does that feel strange?' I asked, gesturing with the fork more broadly. *Outside* the plate. 'Is it strange, living in the house where you grew up? I mean, it must be like going back in time. To when you were a girl.'

When I said the word 'girl' I lowered my gaze a bit. To look at her mouth. Her mouth, chewing on a lettuce leaf. I gazed unambiguously, the way a man might look at a woman's mouth. But also the way a doctor does. With the look. *Don't tell me about mouths*, the look said. *Mouths hold no secrets for us either*.

'It was, at first,' Judith said. 'At first it was kind of weird. It was like my parents still lived here. I wouldn't have been surprised to find them around somewhere: in the bathroom, in the kitchen, here in the garden. My father more than my mother, actually. I mean, my mother comes here all the time, of course, so it's different. But we had the place redone pretty quickly. Knocked down a few walls, joined a few rooms, put in a new kitchen, that kind of thing. Then that feeling disappeared. Never completely, but still.'

A mouth is a mechanism. An instrument. A mouth inhales oxygen. It chews food and swallows it. It tastes, it senses whether something is too hot or too cold. By now, I was looking Judith straight in the eye again. And I kept looking at her while I thought those things about her mouth. A look says more than words alone. That's a cliché, of course. But a cliché also says more than words alone.

'And your own room?' I said. 'I mean, your old bedroom, back when you were a girl? Did you knock down its walls too?'

When I said the words 'your own room' I squinted and raised my eyes, as though looking up at the upper floors of the house. It was an invitation. An invitation to have her show me her old bedroom. Right now, or later in the afternoon. In her old bedroom we would look at pictures together. Old pictures, stuck into a photo album. Sitting on the edge of the single bed that had been hers when she was a girl. Judith on the swings. In a swimming pool. Posing for the school photographer on the playground with her classmates. At the right moment I would take the photo album out of her hands and press her gently back onto the bed. She would resist, but only for appearance's sake. Giggling, she would place both hands against my chest and try to push me away. But the fantasy would win out. It was an old fantasy, as old as the girl's bedroom itself. The doctor pays a house call. The doctor takes your temperature. The doctor places a hand on your forehead. The doctor sends the worried parents away and remains sitting for a moment on the edge of your bed.

'No,' Judith said. 'My old room is Thomas's room now. He painted the walls himself. Red and black. And, well, if you really want to know, the walls used to be purple and pink.'

'And you had a bed with lots of pink and purple pillows and furry stuffed animals,' I said. 'And a poster of' – I was taking a gamble; a rock star or film idol was too risky, too dated – 'a baby seal,' I said. 'A cute little baby seal.'

In addition to my looks, I should now also say something about my character. I'm more charming that most men. On those lists of crucial male characteristics you see in the women's magazines, the majority of women vote for 'sense of humour'. I used to think that was a lie. A lie to cover up the fact that, when it comes right down to it, they would always go for George Clooney or Brad Pitt first. Now, though, I know better. By 'sense of humour' women don't mean that they want to be doubled over with laughter all the time at the jokes of some cretin. They mean something else. They mean that a man should be 'charming'. Not funny: charming. Deep in their hearts, all women are afraid that in the long run they will get bored with the overly handsome men of this world. That such men spend enough time in front of the mirror that they know how good they look. That they don't need to make any real effort. Women on tap. But not long after the honeymoon, they run out of things to talk about. Boredom yawns. And it *is* tiring, spending all day around a man who only admires himself in the mirror. Day in, day out. Time becomes a long, straight road through a beautiful but tedious landscape. An unchanging landscape.

'You're warm,' said Judith.

'A horse. No, a pony. You read horse books.'

'Yes, sometimes I read horse books. But there wasn't a horse on that poster. Not a pony either.'

'Daddy…' I felt a hand on my elbow and turned to look. There stood Julia with the languid boy who had shaken my hand earlier, but who I had already forgotten was called Alex. Standing slightly behind them were two other boys and two girls. 'Can we go out to get some ice cream?' she asked. 'It's really close.'

In terms of timing it was both a good and a bad moment. There was a chance that the slight sultry edge to our – superficially – innocent conversation about teenage bedrooms, baby seal posters, and horse books might be lost for good. On the other hand, here I stood with my thirteen-year-old daughter, living proof that this charming man – me – was capable of siring a child. And not just any child, but a dreamy-eyed blonde who threw fifteen-year-old boys' hormones into overdrive the moment they saw her. I won't try to deny it: I take pleasure in being with my daughters in places where everyone can see us together. At a sidewalk café, in a department store, on the beach. People look. I *see* them looking. I also see what they're thinking. *Holy Christ, didn't those children turn out well!* they all think. *What a lovely pair of girls!* The next instant they're thinking about their own children. Their children who didn't turn out quite as well. They become jealous. I feel their begrudging looks. They start searching for defects: teeth that aren't completely straight, a skin disorder, a shrill voice. But they can't find any. Then they get angry. They become angry with the father who has had better luck. Biology is a force to be reckoned with. An unattractive child is a child you love with all your heart and soul too. But it's different. You're pleased with your third-floor walk-up too, until someone invites you over to dinner at a house with a pool in the garden.

'Where?' I ask as calmly as possible. 'Where are you going to get ice cream?'

I look at the slow boy the way all fathers look at boys who want to go to buy ice cream with their daughters. If you so much as lay a finger on her, you're dead. On the other hand, there is also a voice that whispers that you need to let her go. There is a point at which the protective father needs to step back, in the interests of the propagation of the species. That, too, is biology.

'It's really close by,' Judith said. 'You only have to cross one busy street to get there, but there are lights.'

I looked at her. I fought back the urge to say: 'My daughter is thirteen, love, she already cycles to school on her own.' I pretended to think about it. To relent. A nice, worried father. But above all a fun father.

'OK,' I said, turning to the boy. 'Just be sure to bring her back in one piece.'

Then we were alone again, Judith and I. But indeed, the moment was over. It would have been a mistake to try to lead the conversation back to seal posters and horse books. To the teenage bedroom. As a man, it would give me away immediately. Apparently he's run out of things to talk about, the woman thinks, and she comes up with an excuse to walk away. 'Oh sorry, I've got a cake in the oven.'

I looked at her. I held her gaze; that's more like it. I had seen how Judith had looked at my daughter. Her look, too, was as old as the world itself. A good match, her eyes said. A good match for my son. And now we were looking at each other. I searched for the right words, but my eyes told her already. Judith had no need to be jealous or angry with me. Her son, too, had turned out well.

He too was a good match. By letting Julia go with him so easily, I had only confirmed what everyone could see with their own eyes. Ninety per cent of all women find a married man more attractive than a single man, my professor of medical biology, Aaron Herzl, had taught us back then. A man who already has someone. A man who is married, preferably with children, has already delivered proof. That he can do it. Free-ranging single men are like a house that has been empty too long. There must be something fishy about that house, the woman thinks. Up for sale for six months and it's still vacant.

That's the way Judith looked at me now. As a married man. The message was clear. Our children had turned out well. We had, independently, enhanced the species by bringing into the world well-turned-out children who represented solid market value. Our children would never remain vacant.

'Does he have a girlfriend?' I asked.

Suddenly, there was a blush on Judith's cheeks. She didn't turn a bright red, but it was unmistakably a blush.

'Alex?' she said. 'No.'

It seemed as though she was going to say something else, but she bit it back in time. We looked at each other. We were both thinking the same thing.

12

When Julia and Lisa were little we sometimes went camping. But we stopped. It had mostly been Caroline's idea; she had done a lot of camping before we met. And I didn't want to disappoint her. When your wife loves opera or ballet, you go along to the opera or ballet, it's that simple. Caroline loved to sleep in a tent. So I tried to sleep in a tent too. But what I did most of the time was lie awake. It wasn't so much the idea that you were completely outside – *unprotected* and outside, separated from the world only by a stretch of canvas – that caused me to lie staring into darkness with eyes wide open. And it wasn't the rain on the canvas, the thunder that seemed to explode inside your earlobes, or the locker-room smell when you woke up too late and the sun had been burning down on the canvas for hours. No, those weren't the things that kept me awake. It was *the others*: the humans who were just on the other side of the flimsy tent-cloth. I lay awake and I heard things. Things you don't *want* to hear coming from other people. It wasn't the tent that produced my insomnia, but the place where it was pitched: on a campsite, amid other tents.

One morning something snapped. I was sitting in my low-slung folding chair in front of the tent, my legs stretched out in front of me on the grass. Julia was pedalling her tricycle back and forth along the path to the toilet block. A few yards away, in the shade of a chestnut tree, Lisa was playing in her foldable playpen. 'Dad, Dad!' Julia shouted, and waved. And I waved back. Caroline had gone to the campsite shop to buy milk – that morning we had found two fat bluebottle flies floating in yesterday's leftover milk.

A man came walking down the path. He was wearing red shorts. Not normal shorts or Bermudas, but a design that left his white legs bare almost all the way up to his crotch. With every step he took, the orthopaedic sandals the man wore slapped with audible pleasure against the undoubtedly equally snow-white soles of his feet. In his right hand, right out in the open, for all to see, he was carrying a roll of toilet paper.

It was a feeling, nothing more. A loathing. It felt loathsome to me, the fact that this man could be walking only a few steps away from my daughter and her tricycle. I saw Julia stop pedalling for a moment and look up at him. That made it even more loathsome. The idea that my daughter's barely three-year-old eyes were taking in this far-too-white and exposed human body. It was, I don't know how else to put it, a *befoulment*. The man was befouling our view with his bare legs, his wooden-soled sandals and his loathsome white feet. My child's view.

As I rose from my folding chair, with some difficulty, and followed him towards the toilet block, I had no idea what I was going to do. 'Stay on the path, sweetheart,' I said to Julia as I walked past. I took a quick look at Lisa in her playpen, and went into the building. I soon found what I was looking for. All I had to do was follow the noise. The cubicles were the kind that have a large gap between the floor and the bottom of the door. At the top, the cubicles also shared the same public space. They had no ceilings. Anyone climbing up onto a toilet seat could look down into his neighbour's cubicle. I squatted down, then kneeled. The man's red shorts were down around his ankles. I saw the feet in their wooden-soled sandals, the pale toes large beyond proportion. The nail on one of the big toes had a yellowish tint, like a smoker's fingertips. A nicotine hue. I took a deep breath. There were treatments for such nail conditions, I knew, there was no reason to walk around like this. On the other hand, sometimes those treatments had no effect. But anyone with even a minimum of decency would spare his fellow humans the sight. Only a stupid shithead, a *loathsome*, stupid shithead with absolutely no fellow feeling would leave his sick feet uncovered. Anyone who drew further attention to them by wearing sandals that slapped when he walked had lost all right to clemency – to the mercy of anaesthesia during an emergency procedure.

I was still down on my knees in front of the cubicle. Now I was looking through the eyes of a doctor. I thought about what I had to do. Toenails like that are not very tough, I knew, they come away easily as soon as you succeed in putting something underneath them: a pair of pincers, a cotton swab, a used iced lolly stick, it makes no difference, you barely have to apply any pressure. I looked at the big toe and its doomed nail. There was no stopping now. I thought about a hammer. Not the hammer Caroline and I had used to drive the tent stakes into the ground. That was a soft hammer. A hammer with *give*. You couldn't do much damage with a rounded rubber hammer like that. No, a real hammer was what was needed. An *iron* hammer that would pulverise the brittle toenail with one well-aimed blow. That would make it break into a thousand pieces. There was softer tissue beneath, I knew. There would be a bloodbath. Loose bits of toenail would fly in all directions, against the walls and the doors of the cubicle, like plaque atomised under a dental hygienist's drill. Everything went hazy. *I saw red*, people often say, but I was seeing grey: the grey of a gust of rain, or of sudden mist. I could grab the man by his ankles and pull him out under the door. But I still didn't have a hammer.

'Goddamn it...'

Everything was still for a moment, and precisely because I was aware of the silence, I realised that I was the one who had just sworn out loud.

'Hello?' the man's voice sounded. 'Is someone there?'

A fellow countryman. A Dutchman. I should have known. But in fact, of course, I had already known it from the start: from the moment he wandered into my line of sight with the roll of toilet paper under his arm.

'Pervert!' I said. I saw the man's hands reach for his red shorts and start to pull them up. I stood up. 'Dirty pig. You should be ashamed. There are children on this campsite. They have to look at your filth too.'

From the other side of the door came only a total silence. He was probably trying to decide whether to come out or not, or whether it might be wiser just to stay put until I went away.

In the end, that was what I did. As I stepped out into full sunlight, I blinked my eyes – and saw right away that something was wrong. I saw our tent, I saw the playpen with Lisa in it beneath the tree, but Julia and her tricycle were nowhere to be seen.

'Julia?' I shouted. 'Julia?'

I knew that feeling, I had lost my eldest daughter once before. At a carnival. I had pretended to be calm, I had tried to let my voice sound normal, but inside my chest the cold thud of panic was already pounding much louder than the music from the carousel and the shrieks from people on the roller coaster.

'Julia!'

I walked down the path to where it curved and disappeared behind a high hedge. Behind the hedge was another field of tents.

'Julia?'

In front of a little blue tent, two women were squatting as they washed dishes in the bowl before them on the grass. They stopped for a moment and looked at me questioningly, but by then I had already turned away. To the left of the path, a few yards down, I could hear the burbling of the little river where we often went to swim in the afternoons.

'Julia?'

I twisted my ankle, stumbling on a big, round stone. A thorny branch tore across my cheek, just below my eye. In three, no more than four, stumbling steps I reached the riverbank.

The tricycle was standing in a sort of shallow cove, its front wheel in the water.

I started to run through the water, slipped and landed hard on my backside on the stony riverbed, in a fountain of droplets.

There stood Julia. Not in the river, but up on the shore. She was tossing pebbles, but when she saw me sitting wide-legged in the water she began laughing loudly.

'Dad!' she shouted, raising her arms above her head. 'Dad!'

Within a split second I was back on my feet. Another one, and I was standing beside her.

'Goddamn it!' I said, grabbing her roughly by the wrist. 'What did I fucking tell you? Stay on the path! Stay on the path, goddamn it!'

For what must have been a full second my daughter looked at me with eyes that still believed it was all a joke – Dad fell in the water just to be funny, now Dad is being angry just to be funny – but then something in her expression broke. Her face twisted in pain as she tugged at her wrist.

'Daddy...'

For years afterwards I would think back on that look; and every time I did, tears came to my eyes.

'Marc! Marc! What are you doing?'Caroline was standing up there, in the trees. She was holding a bottle of milk. She looked from me to Julia and back. 'Marc!' she shouted again.

'I can't take it any more,' I said half an hour later, once Julia had calmed down and was rolling up and down the path again on her trike as though nothing had happened.

Caroline looked at me. She took both my hands in hers and said: 'You know that little hotel we saw in the village? Close to the market? Shall we go there for a couple of days?'

From that day on we only stayed at hotels. Or we rented a small house somewhere. At the hotels and houses too there were sometimes swimming pools where you saw the uncovered parts of other people, but at least you could get away from them. You were able to take a couple of hours off from such sights. A couple of hours lying on the bed in your own room, with your eyes closed. The human filth was no longer forced down your throat twenty-four-seven. After a few of those holidays in houses and hotels we sometimes dawdled around the windows of estate agents. We looked at the pictures and the prices. For Caroline, a second home abroad would have been a consolation prize for having to give up camping. We could afford it. As long as you stayed away from the coast, most of those houses cost almost nothing. But even as we gazed misty-eyed at a photo of an old watermill with a pear orchard, we also started thinking out loud about the drawbacks. It might be a shame that one only visited during the holidays, we told each other. We spent a long time in front of a photo of a renovated farmhouse with a pool. You'd have to have someone for that pool, we said. Someone to take care of it. The garden too. Otherwise you'd spend your whole holiday cutting grass and weeding nettles.

We kept putting off our dream of a second home abroad, pushing it ahead of us little by little. Occasionally we would let a local estate agent show us around. We ducked under low, sagging doorways; we caught the smell of stagnant water from a pool covered in algae and filled with croaking frogs; we ducked to avoid spider webs in what had once been the pigpen; we saw a bend in the river glistening in the valley far below; we ducked down to inspect an old outdoor oven, and watched the swallows flying back and forth from their nests beneath the eaves of the main house.

Too windy, that was often Caroline's verdict during those viewings. Too hot. Too cold. Not much of a view. Too exposed. Too close to the neighbours. Too remote.

'We'll call you,' I told the estate agent. 'My wife and I need to think it over for a few days.'

I could hardly believe my eyes when I saw the tent in the boot of the car, the morning before we left for our summer holidays. It was tucked in all the way at the back, maybe so that I wouldn't spot it. But just then Caroline appeared in the doorway, carrying two rolled-up sleeping bags.

'Aha,' I said. 'And what is this supposed to mean?'

'Nothing. It's just that I thought: sometimes you find a pretty place where the only possibility is to camp out. Where there's no hotel, I mean.'

'Aha,' I said again; a light-hearted approach seemed best, to approach the matter as though my wife was really only sort of joking. 'And I suppose that means I'll have to commute from the hotel to the campsite every morning?'

Caroline put the sleeping bags in the boot, up against the tent.

'Marc,' she said. 'I know how you feel about camping. I won't try to force you into anything. But it's such a waste to stay in a hotel sometimes. I looked around on the Internet; they have campsites there with all the trimmings. With restaurants. And you're only a hundred yards from the beach.'

'Hotels have restaurants too,' I said, but I knew I was fighting a losing battle. Caroline missed camping. I could come up with arguments. I could say that the tent and sleeping bags took up half the room in the boot, but then I would be ignoring the simple fact that my wife longed to hammer stakes into the ground, to tighten guy lines and wake up in the morning in a sleeping bag covered in dew.

And there was something else I realised. After the garden party at Ralph and Judith Meier's, I had asked Caroline if she had talked to Ralph. And more specifically, whether he had made a pass at her.

'You were completely right,' she'd said.

'About what?'

'About him being a dirty old man.'

'Really?' We were lying in bed, the reading lamps on, but we weren't looking at each other. I don't know what expression I would have had to wear if we had been.

'Yeah, you were right. I don't know, I guess I started paying attention after you said that: to the way he looked at me. Something in his eyes... he licked his lips while he was looking at me. He smacked his lips. As though I were a hamburger. We were standing beside the barbecue, he was stabbing his fork into the meat to see if it was done, and flipping the hamburgers. Then he lowered his eyes. Like a bad actor in a film that's meant to be funny. He rolled his eyes a little when he looked at my breasts. Don't get me wrong: that can be nice. Sometimes a woman likes it when a man admires her body. But this… this was different. This was, what did you call it again... filthy? Yeah, that's it. A filthy look. I didn't know what to do with myself. And then he started telling a joke. I don't remember how it went, but it was dirty. Not funny-dirty, dirty-dirty. And you should have seen the look on his face as he was telling it! You know how some people, when they tell a joke, they laugh as though they just made it up themselves? Well that's the way he laughed.'

'And now I suppose you don't want to go by and visit them at their summer house,' I said a little too quickly.

'Marc! How could you even consider that? No, thank you very much, no. I'm not really into that anyway, visiting other people while I'm on holiday, but now there's no way. I wouldn't get a moment's rest there beside that pool with Ralph around.'

'But when we left you acted like you thought it was such a great idea. At the door, when we said goodbye. And in the car you even asked Julia and Lisa about it. About what they thought.'

Caroline sighed. 'So we'd all had a little bit too much to drink, all right,' she said. 'Then you don't really say that you have no intention of visiting their summer house. And in the car I was only thinking of Julia. About that boy she liked. It's a good thing she wasn't too enthusiastic either.'

'Well, we'll see,' I said. 'There's no real obligation.'

All this time we were still standing beside the open boot of our car. I sensed an opportunity, but it meant I would have to give up my resistance to taking the tent along. And the quicker the better.

'You know,' I said. 'It's been a few years. Sometimes I miss it too: a little camping. Let's give it another try. But I don't want any messing around with pans and gas burners. We're going out to dinner every night.'

Now it was my wife's turn to look at me dubiously, as though I might be joking. But the next moment she threw her arms around me.

'Marc?' she said. 'That is so, so sweet of you!'

I held her tightly. I couldn't help it though; I was thinking about the last half-hour of that garden party. I had looked everywhere, and finally found Judith in a corner of the yard, where she was picking up glasses and half-empty bowls of crisps and peanuts.

I took her by the wrist. She turned to me with a start. But when she saw that it was me an almost dreamy smile appeared on her face.

'Marc…' she said.

'I have to see you again,' I said.

13

We left on a Saturday. The first night we spent at a hotel. The second one too. As usual, we had no fixed plans. Or, to be more precise, to all appearances we had no fixed plans. To an observer we would have looked like an ordinary couple with two daughters. A family with no fixed plans, making its way south. In reality, we were edging almost imperceptibly towards the summer house where Ralph and Judith Meier were spending their holidays.

On the third morning, still lying in the hotel bed, I flipped through the camping guide we'd brought along with us at the last moment. There were three campsites in the immediate surroundings of the summer house, all within a six-mile radius.

'So what do you guys think?' I said. 'Shall we pitch the tent somewhere tomorrow?'

'Yeaaah!' Julia and Lisa cheered, in unison.

'But only if the weather's nice,' Caroline said with a wink.

That was the plan. My plan. We were going camping. We would spend a few days, a week if need be, at the same campsite. Somewhere – on the beach, at the supermarket, in a sidewalk café in the nearest town – we would run into the Meiers, entirely by accident.

A few weeks before we left I had visited a travel bookshop and bought a detailed map of the area. So detailed that it showed each individual house. I couldn't be a hundred per cent sure, but using the address and directions Judith had e-mailed us a few days after the party, I thought I could tell which house on the map was the Meiers'. I went to ViaMichelin and typed in the address. Then on Google Earth I zoomed in so close that I could see the blue of the pool, and even the diving board.

Of the three campsites, one lay along the same road to the beach as Ralph and Judith Meier's summer house. But to my horror I saw that the guidebook referred to it as a 'green' campsite. A campsite with 'farm animals', 'environmentally-friendly toilet blocks', and 'simple facilities for the true nature-lover'. I could almost smell the stench. But a collateral plus of a campsite where detergents and deodorant were presumably taboo was that it would make the contrast with the summer house all the greater. One dive and Julia and Lisa would never want to leave.

In her e-mail, Judith had sent me both her phone numbers. A week after the garden party I tried to reach her mobile phone a few times, but only got her voicemail. At first, no one answered the landline either. I thought about leaving a message, but decided against it.

Three days later – when I had, in fact, already given up and was about to hang up – a woman with a voice I didn't recognise answered the landline.

I gave her my name and asked to speak to Ralph or Judith.

'They're not in the country right now,' the voice said – not a very young voice, I registered. 'And at this point I'm afraid I can't say when they'll be coming back.'

I asked where they had gone.

'And who are you?' the voice asked.

'I'm the family doctor.'

There was a two-second silence.

'Ralph got an offer all of a sudden,' the voice resumed. 'From America. A part in a new TV series. That's where he's gone. And my daughter liked the idea of going along. So I'm taking care of the boys for the moment.'

Judith's mother. I vaguely remembered a woman in her seventies wandering around at the party, looking rather lost. The fate of all elderly parents. Your children's friends exchange a few words with you for courtesy's sake, then try to shake you off as quickly as they can.

'Can I...' Judith's mother said. 'Can I take a message?'

I fought back the urge to say 'I'm sorry, but I'm bound by professional confidentiality'. Instead I said, 'I have some test results here on my desk. Your daughter was in to see me a few weeks ago. It's nothing serious, but it would be good if she could contact me. I've been trying to reach her on her mobile, but she doesn't answer.'

'Oh yes, that too. Judith called to tell me. That she forgot her phone. I'm in the kitchen now. I can see it from where I'm standing.'

*

Early the next morning, Judith called. My first patient of the day had just settled down across from me at my desk. A man with thin grey hair and burst blood vessels in his face. He was suffering from erectile dysfunction.

'I can't talk for long,' she said. 'What is it?'

'Where are you exactly in America?' I asked, looking at my patient's face. He had a face like a piece of waste ground, a place where nothing would ever be built again.

'We're in California right now. In Santa Barbara. It's after midnight here. Ralph's in the bathroom. I talked to my mother. She thought it was kind of weird. She may be old, but she remembered that my own doctor is a woman. I had to come up with an excuse really quickly, that I'd gone to you for a second opinion. But that only upset her even more.'

I imagined Ralph Meier in the bathroom. His big body without clothes. The jets of water from the showerhead. The drops that spatter as they strike that body: his shoulders, his chest – his stomach, which hung like a lean-to over his genitals. I tried to summon up an image of Ralph's stomach, from that first time he'd come in to see me and I'd asked him to take off his shirt. I wondered whether he could see anything when he looked down, or whether everything was all hidden from sight by that belly.

'I can't talk too long now either,' I said. 'I just wanted to hear how you were doing. And when the two of you are coming back.'

As I said this, I looked directly at the man with erectile dysfunction. There are pills to combat erectile disorders. But they remain a ruse. Those pills simply make it stand upright regardless, whether it's for a sick horse or an empty bin or the window display at a shop selling stationery. If I were a woman, I at least wouldn't want to know when my partner was using medication.

'I don't know,' Judith said. 'Ralph still has to do a couple of screen tests. It would be great if it actually went ahead. It's going to be a huge series. On HBO - they did *The Sopranos*. And *The Wire*. Thirteen episodes. Set in ancient Rome in the days of Caesar Augustus. They want Ralph to play the lead. To be the emperor.'

'I got your mail,' I said, 'with the address of your summer house.'

'Marc, I really have to go now. We may be going down there in early July. That depends on how things go here. We may even fly straight from here. And then my mother can come down with the boys later on. Once the summer holiday starts.'

I wanted to say something else. An innuendo. A flirtation. Something that would make Judith remember right away what a charming man I really was. But the presence of the dead mouse on the other side of the desk kept me from anything except platitudes.

'We'll be in the neighbourhood,' I said. 'I mean, we're heading that way anyway. It would be fun if we...'

'Bye, Marc.'

For five seconds or so I sat there with the receiver pressed to my ear. The receiver that was not producing an engaged tone, but simply static. I thought about the day that lay ahead. It was as though that day was now filled with static too.

'You can go into the examination room and drop your trousers,' I said at last to my patient, putting down the phone. 'I'll be right with you.'

The green campsite was better than I could have hoped. I have to admit, it was a lovely, shady spot surrounded by pine trees. In the distance, through the trees, you could see a narrow blue strip of sea. But I smelled something strange. The smell of sick animals. Caroline breathed in deeply through her nose a few times. Julia and Lisa looked doubtful. And we were no further than the barrier gate at the entrance. We could still turn around and leave. The gate itself was fashioned from a simple, unpainted tree trunk. A trunk that wasn't entirely straight, the way things are in nature. Beside it sat a log-cabinish kind of office. We had climbed out of our car and were leaning against it a bit indecisively. Of course I knew that this campsite was nearest to the summer house, but there are limits to what one can take. The sick-animal smell was already stirring up a dull rage inside me. It was an odour I sometimes smelled in my office too. Coming from patients who were 'living at one with nature', as they themselves put it. Patients who refused to have body hair removed from places where no body hair belonged; who preferred to wash themselves with water from a well or a ditch, and who refused 'as a matter of principle' to use chemical or cosmetic products for their personal hygiene. If one could even speak of hygiene in such cases. From all their pores and orifices came the smell of stagnant water. Water mixed with dirt and dead leaves in a blocked gutter. When they undressed, the smell was worse. Like taking the lid off a pan. A pan that's been forgotten at the back of the fridge. I am a doctor. I took an oath. I treat one and all, regardless. But nothing or no one could compare with the degree of rage and disgust I felt at the ecologically sound stench of so-called nature-lovers.

'So what do you guys think?' I asked my family. 'There are other campsites around.'

'I don't know…' Caroline said.

Julia shrugged. Lisa asked whether they had a pool. I was just about to tell her no when a man stepped out of the log-cabin booth. He glanced at our licence plate, then came towards us, holding out his hand.

'*Goedemiddag!*' he said in Dutch, with no trace of an accent: he got to Caroline first, he took hold of her hand before she had time to back away.

A Dutchman! Dutch people abroad. Those Dutch people who set up shop abroad. They convert a total ruin into a hotel or *pension*, open a Dutch pancake restaurant on the loveliest beach along the entire coast, or set up a campsite in a quiet stretch of forest. I've never been able to shake the feeling that they're helping themselves to something that actually belongs to the local population. Something that could be done just as well by that same population. Most of them don't last for very long. The locals either give them the cold shoulder, or simply harass them until they leave. The roofing tiles for the *pension* arrive too late, the permit for the miniature golf course gets lost in the post, the cooker hood in the Dutch-style pancake restaurant fails to satisfy local fire and safety regulations. The Dutch entrepreneurs complain loudly about the obscure machinations of the bureaucracy in the country in question. 'What do they want, anyway?' they ask rhetorically. 'No one was doing anything with that ruin. Those woods were completely deserted. No one ever went to that beach. We're the ones who rolled up our sleeves. We Dutch know how to get things done. So why are they giving us such a hard time? People around here couldn't organise a piss-up in a brewery anyway.' After two or three years of cursing the indigenous population and lazy foreigners in general, they pack their bags and return home in a huff.

As I reached out to shake the hand offered by the campsite owner, I tried to read his expression, to establish which phase he was in. It's like a malignant illness. First you have hope. Then comes denial. And only right at the end is there resignation.

'Welcome, welcome!' the man said; his handshake was firm but contrived, he was clearly making an effort to look at me as openly and cheerfully as he could, but in his eyes I saw the symptoms of a chronic lack of sleep. Little red veins in the whites of the eyes, undoubtedly caused by nights of tossing and turning over debts, or goods that had been delivered too late or not at all. I gave him one year, tops. Before next summer he would have the farm animals put to sleep and go back to Holland.

In the little log hut he first began flipping repeatedly through a book that contained a map of the campsite. He shook his head and sighed deeply a few times as he ran his index finger over the map, but he was a bad actor.

Once he had assigned us a space, after even more sighing and chin-rubbing, he asked, 'Could I ask how you happened to find us? We've only been open for two years and we're not in all the guidebooks.'

Two years. I couldn't help smiling. I had pinpointed it pretty well. After denial comes resignation. The counting of the days. 'We've developed a nose for this kind of place,' I said. 'For campsites where the real outdoor experience is of paramount importance. Camping out under the stars, no frills like pool tables, arcade games, or swimming pools with giant slides.'

14

Sometimes things simply go too fast. Too fast to pass for coincidence. I had prepared myself for a few days of peace and quiet. Days marked by no major events. A book. A little game of badminton. A walk. First a vacuum had to be established. The emptiness of the first few days of the summer holidays. After that emptiness, you're all too pleased when something finally happens. You're open to new encounters. To change. To new people. That first evening we were going out for shrimp and calamari at a beachside restaurant. We were tired from the trip. We were going to go to bed early. I would lie awake for hours. I would listen to the regular breathing of my sleeping family. But things went differently. Things went, above all, too fast.

With Caroline's blessing ('Go on. You'd only get in the way here anyway, right?') I went for a walk around the campsite while she and the girls put up the tent. I took the first path through the trees that I came across. There weren't many other tents. Not a single trailer. I came past the little wooden building that housed the 'environmentally friendly toilets'. That, for me, is the biggest nightmare about camping: that you have to leave the tent at night in order to take a piss. I always postponed it as long as I could. So long that it hurt. Then I would squeeze my feet into my wet shoes.

Not even at gunpoint could you have forced me to go to the toilet block in the middle of the night. The toilet block where moths crashed into the outdoor lights, their wings aflutter. Where all exposed parts of your body were stung by insects that never sleep. I would unzip the door of the tent and take a few steps at most. Sometimes there were stars. Sometimes the moon was full. I have to admit that I also had happy moments at times, standing among the trees, hearing my own piss hissing in the grass, against the stalks of stinging nettles. Then I would look up. At thousands of stars. This is it, I thought at moments like this. This is what there is. The rest is bullshit. Nothing came before moments like that. And nothing came after them either. We bought the tent during our first trip to America. It was big enough for four. Back then, though, there were just the two of us. We zipped our sleeping bags together and snuggled up close. There was plenty of extra room beside us. Space left over for the future. After pissing, I always waited a while before going back into the tent. I looked at the moon overhead and the moonlight on the grass. Inside, beside my wife, my two daughters were asleep. I was standing outside. Only when the first shiver ran down my back did I crawl back into the warmth of the sleeping bag.

The environmentally-friendly toilets consisted of nothing but a few wooden planks with round holes cut in them. Down in the hole it was dark; you couldn't see the bottom, only smell it. Both inside and outside, the door was covered in fat blue flies that didn't take off when I flapped my hand at them. I closed the door and walked on. Then I came to the fenced plot where the 'farm animals' were kept. I saw a llama, a couple of chickens and a donkey. There was no grass, only mud. Droppings everywhere. The llama's dark-brown coat was clotted with faeces and mud. The donkey was too skinny. It stood closest to the fence. I could see its ribs; the animal was shivering all over and swinging its tail wildly to chase away the flies. The chickens were huddled together motionlessly in a corner.

I felt a clammy rage rise up in me. I felt like walking right back to where Caroline and the children were putting up the tent; I felt like announcing that we were leaving this very minute, when I felt a soft touch on my left hand.

'Daddy…'

'Lisa.'

My youngest daughter had wrapped her fingers around my index and middle fingers. Together, for a moment, we looked in silence at the animals on the other side of the fence.

'Daddy?'

'Yeah?'

'Is that donkey ill?'

I took a deep breath before answering. 'I don't know, sweetheart. It's just that there are a lot of flies. The flies bother him, you see that?'

I looked at the shivering donkey; at the same moment, the animal took two shaky steps forward and stuck its head over the fence. I felt my eyes grow moist.

'Can I stroke him, Dad?'

I didn't say anything. I gulped something down. A lump in my throat. That's what they say at moments like that. But it's softer than a lump. Softer and more fluid.

Lisa placed her hand on the donkey's head. A cloud of flies rose up. The donkey blinked its eyes. I looked the other way and bit down hard on my lower lip.

'Daddy?'

'Yes, sweetheart?'

'Can we buy something for him, later? Carrots or something?'

I lay both hands on my daughter's shoulders and pulled her against me. First I cleared my throat. I didn't want the sound of my voice to alarm her needlessly.

'That's a really good idea, sweetheart,' I said. 'Carrots, lettuce, tomatoes. You'll see how much he likes that.'

There was only one restaurant at the beach, and the tables and chairs were set up right in the sand. It was crowded, but we were lucky and got the last table. We ordered two beers for Caroline and me, a Fanta for Lisa, and a Diet Coke for Julia. The sun had already gone down behind the rocks, but the air was still warm and pleasant.

'Can we go down to the water?' Lisa asked.

'All right,' Caroline said. 'But look at the menu first and choose something. We'll call you when it gets here.'

They took a quick look at the menu. Lisa wanted macaroni with tomato sauce, Julia only a salad.

'Julia, you have to eat something substantial too. At least order a hamburger along with it, or some macaroni, like Lisa.'

'Don't need it,' Julia said. She stood up. 'You coming?' she asked her little sister.

'Be careful,' Caroline said. 'And don't go into the water when we're not there. Stay on the beach.'

Julia sighed deeply and rolled her eyes. Lisa had already threaded her way past the other tables and was running onto the beach. Then, holding her flip-flops in one hand, Julia walked off after her little sister. All she was wearing was a T-shirt and the red bikini bottoms she'd bought just before the holidays, and I saw two men a few tables away turn their heads and watch her go.

'She really hasn't been eating enough lately,' Caroline said. 'She has to stop that.'

'Oh, come on,' I said. 'It's not that bad. Better too little than too much. Or would you rather have a roly-poly daughter with rolls of fat hanging out everywhere?'

'No, of course not. It's just that I worry sometimes. She does the same thing at home too. She eats all the salad first, then says she's not hungry any more.'

'It's her age, I think. She's imitating the models in the magazines. Kate Moss doesn't eat much either. But better that than the other way around. And this is not the husband speaking, but the doctor.'

We both ordered another beer and a bottle of white wine. The sun had gone down completely by now. Rocks rose up sharply behind the restaurant. There were a couple of villas up there, their lights already on. I could hear the surf, but the beach ran down fairly steeply to the water, so we couldn't see the girls from our table.

'Shall I go and check on them?' Caroline said.

'Let's wait till the food gets here. What could happen?'

In fact, I was always as worried as she was. This just happened to be our established division of roles. Caroline expressed her concern first, at which I said that she shouldn't exaggerate. If I had been here alone with my daughters, I would have been down three times already to check they hadn't been washed out to sea.

Caroline took my hand. 'Marc,' she said, 'do you think you can handle it, this campsite? I mean, it is *radical* camping, right off the bat. We could have gone to one with a few more amenities.'

'I went down to see the animals this afternoon. They're malnourished. And probably diseased.'

'Do you want to go to another campsite? We could spend the night here and go somewhere else tomorrow.'

'What we should really do is set a health inspector on that bastard. They'd close the place down pronto. But then the animals would probably be put to sleep.'

A boy in a T-shirt and jeans brought the wine. He pulled the cork and put the bottle in a simple cooler on our table. He didn't ask whether we wanted to taste it first. But that proved unnecessary. The wine was ice-cold and tasted like grapes that had been left to soak in a mountain stream overnight.

'We could leave tomorrow, you know?' Caroline said. 'Would you really report that man for a couple of sick animals? It would probably put him out of business.'

'I have a few things with me. Mostly first-aid stuff. But also some antibiotics, that kind of thing. I'll take a look tomorrow, see what I can do.'

'But Marc, you're on holiday. Don't start in on a project right away, not on the first day already. Even though it is a really nice project, of course, helping sick animals.'

This was what Caroline accused me of at times. It was, in fact, the only bone of contention between us: that I always had to have something to do when we were on holiday. Caroline could spend hours reading a book beside the pool. Or lie on a lounger on the beach with her sunglasses on and just gaze into the distance. While after half an hour I needed to do something. On the beach I built dams and castles in the sand, at the summer rental I would weed the path from the front door to the road. Sometimes even my daughters got tired of me. At first they would help dig the canal that would carry off the backwash of high tide and protect our castle, but after an hour they usually gave up. 'Time for a rest, Dad,' they said. And Caroline would say: 'Marc, come and lie down. It exhausts me just looking at you.'

I was about to object that I considered it my duty as a physician to help sick animals, and that it wouldn't take much time, when we heard Julia's voice.

'Dad! Mum!'

Caroline put her glass down on the table with a thud and sprang to her feet. 'Julia!' she shouted. 'What is it?'

But it was nothing. Julia was walking towards us across the beach. In the light of the terrace lanterns we saw her waving. We also saw that she was not alone. Walking beside her was a boy. I had seen him only once before, but still, I knew right away who he was. His blond curls. And even more than that, something in the way he walked: his languid tread, as though walking through sand was simply too hard for him.

'Guess who else is here?' Julia shouted, before they had even reached our table.

15

Sometimes things just go too quickly.

'Did you know about this?' Caroline asked much later that evening, as we were drinking a final glass of wine in front of the tent. Julia and Lisa were already asleep. 'Yes, you knew,' she said without waiting for a reply. It was dark. I was glad I didn't have to look at her. 'Why, Marc? Why?'

I said nothing. I toyed with my glass, then took a quick sip. But the glass was empty. We were sitting in our low folding chairs, our legs stretched out across a bed of pine needles. Every once in a while I felt something tickling my ankles. An ant. A spider. But I didn't move.

'I thought you wanted to keep Ralph as far away from me as possible,' Caroline said. 'I even told you that myself. That I didn't want to go. And then you choose a campsite that's a stone's throw from their summer house.'

Caroline had hung a candle holder on the pole that stuck out from the front of the tent. One of those candle holders with little glass windows. But the candle had died, and we were sitting in darkness. Above our heads, thousands of stars sparkled among the treetops. Far below you could hear the soft booming of the surf.

'Yes, I knew,' I said. 'But I didn't think it was any reason not to come to this particular place. Like it was off-limits or something, just because you might run into people you don't really want to see.'

'But Marc! There are hundreds of places like this along the coast. Hundreds of other beaches where the Meiers haven't rented a summer house.'

'I talked to Ralph about it again, later on. Right after that garden party. He told me how beautiful it was here. Still fairly unspoiled. I was sort of curious.'

Caroline sighed deeply. 'So what now? What are we going to do? Now we have to go over there tomorrow. It would be really weird if we didn't.'

'It's just a dinner. They'll probably have a barbecue again. If you want, we can leave right after that. Go to some other beach. Some other campsite. But if you really don't want to go to dinner there, we won't. We'll make up an excuse. That you weren't feeling well. Or that I wasn't. And then we'll go away, the day after tomorrow.'

Neither of us said a word for a few moments. I ran the tip of my tongue over my upper lip, which felt dry and hard.

'Is that what you want?' I asked. 'Like I said, I don't mind at all. We'll come up with some excuse.'

I heard my wife sigh a few times. I heard her swat at something on her bare leg. An insect. A pine needle, fallen from a tree. Or maybe, in fact, nothing at all.

'Oh well. It doesn't really matter. It was just that I was looking forward to a couple of days or a week with just the four of us. If it had happened later in the holidays I wouldn't have minded nearly as much. Meeting up with other people. But this is so sudden. I don't feel at all like being around a bunch of people. Having long conversations on the patio with lots of wine.'

I reached out and laid my hand on her thigh. 'I don't either, really,' I said. 'I don't feel like being around other people yet either. I'm sorry. It's my fault.'

'That's right, it's your fault,' she said. 'So you can call them and say we're not coming.'

I closed my eyes. I gulped, but my throat was empty. Except for the surf in the distance, all I could hear was a faint buzzing in my ears. 'OK,' I said.

'I'm only kidding,' Caroline said. 'No, it would be ridiculous to cancel now. To be honest, I'm kind of curious. About that house of theirs. And it will be fun for the girls. The boys, I mean. And that pool.'

Earlier that evening on the beach, this is how it went: Julia brought Alex over to our table, followed closely by Lisa and the younger brother, Thomas. Then the rest of the Meier family came strolling up. Ralph and Judith, and the woman in her seventies who I had seen at the garden party: Judith's mother. And two other people. A man in his late fifties with longish grey hair, streaked with a few black locks – a face that seemed familiar, but I couldn't figure out why, not right away. And a woman.

A woman who I assumed was with the man, although she was at least twenty years younger.

'What a surprise!' Ralph said. He grabbed Caroline, who was already halfway out of her chair, by the shoulders and kissed her three times on the cheeks.

'Hi,' Judith said. We kissed each other too. Then we looked at each other. *That's right, I really showed up*, I told her with my eyes. *Yes, so I see*, she looked back.

'Why didn't you two call to say you were coming?' Ralph said. 'We could have had dinner together. We bought a whole suckling pig at the market today. That's the real thing, suckling pig on a spit!'

Caroline shrugged and looked at me.

'Really, we only just got here,' I said. 'We weren't planning to… we're staying at the campsite.'

'At the campsite!' Ralph roared, as though this was the funniest thing he'd heard in days. At that point, the grey-haired man stepped forward. 'Oh, excuse me,' Ralph said. 'I forgot to introduce you. Stanley, this is Marc. He's my doctor. And this is his delectable wife, Caroline.'

The man Ralph had introduced as 'Stanley' shook Caroline's hand first. 'Stanley Forbes,' he said. 'Stanley,' he repeated, only his first name, as he shook mine. I suddenly knew why his face looked familiar. Stanley Forbes wasn't his real name. He'd had a different one when he left Holland for America about twenty-five years ago. Jan? Hans? Hans Jansen? – one of those basic Dutch names in any case, I just couldn't remember it right away. For the first few years you heard very little about him, but then the Dutch film director, who by then called himself Stanley Forbes, suddenly made a name for himself in Hollywood.

'And this is Stanley's girlfriend,' Ralph said. 'Emmanuelle.' He rested his hand lightly on the young woman's shoulder. 'Emmanuelle, these are some friends of ours from Holland. Marc and Caroline.'

It would be an understatement to say that Emmanuelle was a real beauty. She shook Caroline's hand, then mine – it was like having someone reach out to you from the cover of *Vogue*. A small, fragile hand, almost that of a child. From close up I now saw that she couldn't be much more than five years older than Julia. Seventeen? Eighteen? Not a day older than twenty, for sure. I looked from her face to that of the grey-haired man. I had been wrong about their ages. She wasn't twenty years younger than Stanley Forbes, she was *forty* years younger. Had she secured a role in his next film by accommodating him between the sheets? I looked at the director's face, forty years older than hers. At his forty-year-older body, draped in a pair of white, almost transparent linen drawstring trousers, and a shirt of the same material. Luxuriant grey chest hair curled up from his open collar.

For a few seconds I visualised how he forced that old body on her. How he crawled up beside her and let his hand slide down over her belly. Till it reached her navel. How he would run his index finger in a circle around her navel, then go lower. The smell of old man beneath the sheets. The flaking skin. About how she had to think about other things while it happened. About the role she'd been promised, that above all. Was this what Hans (?) Jansen (?) had dreamed of when he left Holland? Of young girls who, out of admiration for his talent, or in exchange for a role in one of his films, were willing to play with his dick?

Now, last in line, Judith's mother stepped forward. As I shook her hand I took a good look at her face, but I didn't get the impression that she made a direct connection between me and the conversation I'd had with her a few weeks earlier on the phone.

'Mr Schlosser,' she repeated, after her daughter had introduced us.

'Marc,' I said.

I looked around to see whether a table had become available while we were talking, but there were only a few empty chairs. At that same moment, the boy in jeans came back with our order.

'Ah, you folks still have to have eat,' Ralph said.

'We could...' I said. 'Maybe there will be a table in a while. Or a couple of chairs.'

'Let's leave these people to eat in peace,' Judith said. 'Besides, Mama is tired. If you three want to stay,' she said to Ralph and Stanley Forbes, repeating everything in English for Emmanuelle. 'I think it's better for my mother to go home now. She's very tired.'

What followed was a brief moment of indecision. Ralph looked around now too, in search of vacant tables or chairs. Caroline glanced over at me, then lowered her eyes. Julia leaned over to Alex, who was sitting across from her in Lisa's chair, and whispered something in his ear. Thomas ran after Lisa down the beach. Stanley Forbes had his arm around Emmanuelle's waist and pulled her up against him. Judith's mother stood between the tables as though none of it had anything to do with her.

'You'll be staying a few days, won't you?' Judith asked. 'Why don't you come to dinner tomorrow?'

16

It was Professor Aaron Herzl who first explained to us why a man's biological clock works differently from a woman's. About how the hands of the clock show the same time, but that it means something different. 'It's just like with real time,' he lectured. 'Sometimes a quarter to seven can be early. And sometimes six-twenty is already rather late.'

Every week we had two hours of medical biology, which in those days was still an elective. There were usually more women in the auditorium than there were male students. Aaron Herzl was approaching sixty, but the girls always began to giggle and blush when he addressed them directly. In that respect, he was the living proof of his own theories. The same theories for which, a few years later, he would be run out of town on a rail.

'What I'm going to tell you now is probably not very pleasant for my female students,' he said, peering into the lecture hall. 'On the other hand, it's simply the way it is. Nothing can be done about it. It is perhaps unfair, but a long and happy life lies in store for those women who are able to accept this injustice rather than resist it.'

A little muffled giggling could already be heard coming from around the hall. We, the male students, had feelings of our own concerning our professor of medical biology. Mixed feelings, that above all. The fact that most of the girls found this bald old man attractive threw certain biological principles for a loop. We were young. We had young sperm. The chance of having a healthy child was eight hundred times greater when sperm was young; we had already learned that during the lectures on gynaecology. But we *recognised* it nonetheless. We recognised Professor Aaron Herzl as a serious rival. At the intellectual level, whenever the girls were around, we tried to ridicule the professor by alluding to his undoubtedly wrinkled and age-spotted genitals, but there was something about him – an aura, or better yet a charismatic vibe – that put the girls' hormone receptors on red alert. At our expense.

Professor Herzl coughed a few times and cleared his throat. He was wearing jeans and a grey polo-neck sweater. No jacket. Before moving to the lectern, he rolled up his sleeves. Then he ran his hands through the grey hair that now grew only at the sides of his head.

'First of all, we have to accept that everything is oriented towards preserving the human race. Or at least keeping it from extinction. And when I say everything, I mean *everything*. The attraction between the sexes, infatuation, horniness, whatever you choose to call it. Pleasure. The orgasm. Taken together, all this is what sees to it that we are attracted to the other. That we like to touch that other. That we want to merge with that other. Creation is much, much more perfect than some progressive thinkers these days would like us to believe. Food smells nice. Shit stinks. The stench serves as a warning to us not to eat our own faeces. Piss stinks too, but less, because in an extreme emergency – a shipwreck, a crash landing in the desert – we have to be able to drink our own piss. Nine per cent of the population is homosexual, nine per cent is left-handed. Throughout the course of fifty thousand years of evolution, those percentages have never changed. Why? Because that's what's tolerable. Higher percentages would endanger the continuation of the species. As a matter of fact, a homosexual is nothing more than a walking contraceptive. To say nothing of left-handed homosexuals, a category not included in the statistics.' Laughter in the auditorium, this time perhaps more from the boys than from the girls. 'The continuation of the species. That is what it is all about. I'm not talking now about *why* the species should continue to exist. Bacteria, too, struggle to survive. Cancer cells reproduce to their hearts' content. Survival is the single motor behind creation. But why should that be so? In other words, what value judgement should we attach to this? Humans have already landed on the moon. Nothing grows there. No life has ever been detected there. But what's wrong with a barren moon? A moon without plants and animals and traffic jams? And what would be wrong with a barren earth? Or, once again, what *value judgement* would one attach to a barren earth like that?'

Here Professor Herzl paused to take a sip of water from the glass on the lectern. 'Anyone wishing to reflect on the purpose of creation, the purpose of life if you will, should first pause to consider the dinosaur,' he went on. 'The dinosaurs inhabited our planet for one hundred and sixty million years. Then they died out quite suddenly. A few million years later, humans came on the scene. I've always wondered why. What was the purpose of those one hundred and sixty million years? What a waste of time! No direct evolutionary link has ever been shown between the dinosaur and the human species. If humanity and the continuation of the human race were really so important, what was the point of those dinosaurs? And why did they stay around so long? Not a thousand years, or a million, no, *one hundred and sixty million years*! Why not the other way around? Why not the humans first? Why didn't things start with the evolution of fish to mammals and on to bipedal humans? And then, in a few tens of thousands of years, from the cave dweller to the inventor of the wheel, of movable type, of the transistor radio and the hydrogen bomb? And then have that go on for a few thousand years, or even a few million as far as I'm concerned, until suddenly, as suddenly as he arrived, mankind dies out. Because of a meteorite, a solar eruption, or a nuclear winter, whatever. The human race dies out. Its bones are buried beneath a thick layer of dust, along with its cities, its cars, its thoughts, its memories, its hopes and desires. Everything gone. And then, after another twenty million years, the dinosaurs come along. They have all the time they need. It no longer matters, we're not around any more. They are given a hundred and sixty million years. Dinosaurs are not excavators, they're not interested in the past. They were never awarded a degree in archaeology. They don't go out to investigate that layer of dust, not the way we would. And so they find no vanished cities. No four-lane highways, television sets, typewriters.

No mint-condition, ready-to-drive Mercedes buried beneath the dust. They find, at most, by accident, a human skull. A skull they sniff at and then, because it no longer contains anything edible, toss away as far as they can. Dinosaurs are not curious about who roamed the earth before they did. They live in the present. That's something we might do well to learn from the dinosaurs. To live in the present. Those who are ignorant of history are doomed to repeat it, we're told ad nauseam. But isn't the essence of existence found precisely in repetition? Birth and death. The sun that comes up each morning and goes down each evening. Summer, autumn, winter, spring. A new spring, we say. But there's nothing new about it. We talk about the first snow, but it's the same snow that fell a year ago. The men go out hunting. The women keep the cave warm. In one day, a man can impregnate several women. But for nine whole months, a pregnant woman is no longer available to perpetuate the human race. These days we can calculate how many times a woman can give birth before she is worn out. The answer is: twenty. After that the risks become too great. The woman becomes less attractive. In this way, the man is warned not to impregnate the woman again. Soon afterwards, fertility comes to a halt. That's how intelligently the world is put together. A man's sperm remains viable for much longer. The health risks for a child born to an old father are negligible. These days we tend to laugh at a seventy-five-year-old man siring a child with a twenty-year-old woman. But in fact, there's nothing funny about it. A child is a child. One more child. A child that otherwise would not have been there. A man ages, but his attractiveness barely declines. That too is the ingenuity of nature. Fresh food smells good. Rotten food stinks. We sniff at a carton of milk to determine whether the best-before date has been exceeded. That's the way we view each other as well. Not that one, we say. That one's too old. God, not in a thousand years. A woman who is past her best-before date is no longer desirable to us, because there is no reason for her to be. She does nothing to promote the continuation of the species. I'd like to stop for a moment to consider the injustice. I sympathise with those women who feel that this is all unfair. Women are the football stars of creation. At thirty-five, they're ready for retirement. They have to make sure they're home and dry before then. A roof over their head, a husband, children. Women are quicker to bind themselves to a man. Any man at all. You see this with women who are approaching the dangerous age. Beautiful women, who could have any man they like, suddenly opt for an ill-favoured, boring prick. Instinct is stronger. The continuation of the species. An ill-favoured, boring prick with a car and an endowment mortgage. The roof over one's head. Not even so much for themselves, but for the child. The cradle must be in a dry, easily heated space. The boring prick provides a better guarantee that the mortgage will be paid each month than the handsome man who knows that he can pick and choose. The handsome, tomcatting man may suddenly pack up his bags and leave. Instinct is so powerful that the woman isn't even acting out of self-interest. She too would prefer to cuddle up to that handsome man each night. But the handsome man has different plans. To impregnate as many women as possible and so pass on his powerful and healthy genes, that is item number one on his agenda. It's the biological clock. The hands tell the same time. For the woman, it's time to settle down. The man feels that it's still too early for that. And then, by way of conclusion, there are cultures that provide for women who are left high and dry. We tend to look down on those cultures. Here, in the West, an abandoned woman pines away in loneliness. Yet we consider ourselves superior. Those same cultures I'm talking about also make sure that girls are set up while they are still very young. You might think it's unfair that a man cannot get pregnant. But you'll never hear a man complain about that. We're all too relieved not to have to walk around for nine months with a huge belly. A belly that would only get in the way of what our instinct tells us we should be doing. You people are young. Do what you want to do. And do it as much and as often as you like. Don't think about the future. Make sure you have something to look back on. And let injustice stew in its own juices. That will be all for today.'

The summer house was on a hillside amid other summer houses, a little less than three miles from the beach. Less than two from our campsite. Too far to walk, though, so we took the car.

'Huh, I was expecting something different,' Caroline said. We had the windows rolled down and were trying to read the house numbers, which wasn't easy because most were either missing or completely covered by ivy or other climbers.

'First it was fifty-three, then fifty-five, but now the numbers are going down again,' I said. I touched the brakes and stuck my head out of the window. 'Thirty-two, damn it! What do you mean, something different?'

'I don't know. Something a little more arty, perhaps?'

When we got to the top of the cul-de-sac, I turned the car around. From here you could see a blue strip of sea and the road as it zigzagged its way to the beach. I looked over at my wife. Years ago, she too had been about to marry a boring prick. The first time I saw her was at a party. Just a friend's birthday party. Caroline and the birthday boy's wife had been friends since childhood. The boring prick had no friends. The boring prick was with her. 'I don't know anyone else here,' he told me. We were standing by the hors d'oeuvres. He put down his glass of Coke and pulled out a pipe. 'I came with my girlfriend.' I looked at his fingers as he filled the pipe with tobacco. What kind of woman would want a man who smoked a pipe? I wondered. The next moment, Caroline showed up at his side. 'Shall we get going?' she asked the boring prick. 'I don't feel so great.' Sometimes the contrast between a man and a woman is so huge that you start wondering whether there might perhaps be other factors in the mix. Financial factors, for example. Or factors of status and fame. The twenty-year-old fashion model with the sixty-year-old millionaire. The devastating beauty with the ugliest football player you could imagine. Not a third-division player, not even a third-division player with the looks of David Beckham. No, an international star. An international star with thin, greasy hair and a smile that shows more gum than teeth. It's an agreement. The model looks good in the spotlights. She can shop till she drops in Milan and New York. The ugly footballer and the old millionaire can let everyone know that they have snagged the most beautiful women in the world. But sometimes the agreement isn't immediately obvious. How can this be, for Christ's sake? you think. What does she see in this boring prick?

'Oh, excuse me,' Caroline said, and held out her hand.

'Marc,' I said, taking her hand. At first I had to fight back the urge to hold that hand a little longer than might be considered respectable. After that I suppressed the urge to say something 'charming'. I glanced over at the boring prick, who had meanwhile stoked up his pipe and exhaled a couple of thick clouds of smoke. It was pure intuition. I didn't have to say anything 'charming'. I *was* charming. In any case, I was a lot more charming than this boring prick.

I've already mentioned my looks. What I should add is that, at a first glance, I don't look like a doctor. At least not at birthday parties. Is there a doctor in the house? people shout when someone has fainted or cut his hand on a broken glass. They always look right past me, or over my head. A man wearing gym shoes that are none too new, jeans that are none too clean and a T-shirt hanging over his belt. His hair carefully mussed. I have the kind of hair you can do that with. Before a birthday party, I stand in front of the mirror. I lay my fingers alongside my head and move them briefly up and down. Then it looks just the way it should.

I looked at the woman who had introduced herself as Caroline. I suddenly realised why she was with the boring prick. The biological clock. She had looked at the clock and decided time was running out. But it would be such a waste. I glanced at the boring prick again. I saw weak genes. Perhaps even fugly children. Fugly children whose pipe-smoking father would pick them up from school. She'd said she wasn't feeling 'too great', and my heart suddenly started pounding. What if I was too late? The thought was so horrendous that I skipped all the formalities and moved right to the crux of the matter.

To me, as a man, a pregnant woman would no longer be interesting. With a pregnant woman I would exchange a few pleasantries and then leave her to the boring prick. The child would grow up in a house where the stench of pipe smoke clung to clothing, furniture and curtains.

'Some women think they're not allowed to drink alcohol when they're pregnant,' I said. 'But one glass of red wine really can't hurt. In fact, it's better. For the nerves, but also for the unborn child.'

Caroline blushed. For a moment I was afraid that I had guessed right, then she looked over at the prick and back at me.

'I… we… we're trying,' she said. 'To get pregnant. But it hasn't worked out yet.'

I breathed a deep sigh. It was a sigh of relief.

'Forgive me,' I said. 'You're probably wondering why I think it's any of my business. It's sort of an occupational disability. When women say that they're nauseous, I immediately think… well, I think that.'

She peered at me through her eyelashes. Occupational disability? those eyes asked. What occupation is that?

'I'm a general physician,' I said.

Without taking my eyes off her, I ran my fingers through my hair and brushed it back nonchalantly, mussing it even more. Meanwhile, I had stopped looking at the boring prick altogether. I pretended he wasn't there. That we were alone, just the two of us. Looking back on it, I think that was true too.

'A general physician,' Caroline said. She smiled. She also did nothing to disguise the brief, assaying glance she gave the rest of my body. Apparently she liked what she saw, for her smile broadened, showing her lovely white teeth.

What were you thinking then? I asked her later. Not just once, but about twice a year. Long after our first kiss, we both still enjoyed reconstructing our first encounter.

I thought, that's the last thing I would have guessed, Caroline always replied. A general physician! What a cute GP, I thought. With his tousled hair and his shabby clothes. And you? What did you think?

I thought, what the hell is she doing with that boring prick? What a waste of a beautiful woman. A sweet young thing like that, sitting around breathing pipe smoke.

'If you really don't feel well, Caroline,' we heard the voice of the pipe-smoking prick say somewhere off-camera, 'we should probably go now.'

'I think I'll stay for a bit,' she replied. 'I think I'll have another glass of red.'

*

'Look, Daddy! There!' Lisa shouted from the back seat.

'What?' I said, hitting the brakes. 'Where?'

'There! That boy walking over there. That's Alex.'

17

'More sardines, anyone? There's plenty.'

Ralph wiped his fingers on his T-shirt and looked at us beseechingly, one by one. 'You, Caroline? Emmanuelle, you want some more? You can have it. No, wait, how do you say that in English?' He turned to Stanley with a wink. 'She can have it. We'd have to be careful. Marc, you ready for more? Come on, you're the doctor. Sardines are good for you. Good fats, am I right?'

'Yeah, absolutely,' I said. I rubbed my stomach. 'But I'm completely full, Ralph. Thanks.'

We were all sitting on the patio, at two white plastic tables set end to end. The patio was surrounded by a circular, waist-high wall of fake rock, with shells and the fossils of marine animals mortared into it. The barbecue was built into a niche in the wall, it even had a chimney decorated with red roofing tiles. Despite the chimney, however, the odour of grilled sardines hung greasily and thickly between us, like smoke from a fire. It was a smell that clung to everything: to our clothes, our hair, to the vines and palm fronds above our heads. I had been hoping for meat. For lamb or pork. Even drumsticks, if need be. I have a total aversion to sardines. Not to tinned sardines, where all the little bones are dissolved in the vinegar, but to fresh ones, where the mucking around takes longer than the eating itself. You think you've removed all the bones, but with every mouthful about twenty of them seem to slip through. Little bones that then jab cruelly into your gums or the roof of your mouth, or else find a way to stick in your throat. And then there's the smell. Or should I say, the stench. The stench that warns me, at least, that I'd be better off steering clear of this kind of food. It's on your fingers for days. Under your nails. Your clothes have to go in the laundry right away. And you have to wash your hair. But even when all that has been taken care of, it's the belches that go on reminding you all night and the next morning of what you had for dinner last night.

'Vera?' Ralph turned now to Judith's mother. 'You're not going to let me down, I hope?'

It was the first time I'd heard anyone call her by name. She had short grey hair. Practical hair. Vera, I repeated the name to myself. Her hair looked more like a Thea or a Ria. She had a sweet but vacant face, with very few wrinkles for her age. A practical, healthy woman who had, in all probability, lived a cautious life without much in the way of major excesses, and who began to nod off after the first glass of white wine. I expected her to leave the table at any moment, to excuse herself and go up to her room.

Shortly after we arrived, Judith had given us a tour of the summer house. The first and largest floor housed the living and dining rooms, the kitchen, and three bedrooms. Even without Judith's guided tour, it wouldn't have been hard to guess whose bedroom was whose. The one with the double bed and the piles of books and magazines on the bedside tables belonged to her and Ralph; the slightly smaller room with two single beds, the floor of which was littered with clothes, shoes, tennis balls and swimming goggles was for Alex and Thomas, and the smallest room with one single bed was the mother's. I don't know why, but it was in the doorway of that last room that I lingered for a while, after Judith and Caroline had already gone back to the living room. The bedroom was virtually empty, almost like a nun's cell. Hanging over the back of the only chair was a brown sweater; beneath the chair, neatly side-by-side, lay a pair of slippers. On the wall above the bed hung a charcoal drawing of a fishing boat pulled up onto a beach. There was a framed photograph – or at least I assumed it was a photograph, the frame was turned with its back to me – on the bedside table. I listened to the voices of Judith and my wife. I could have done it. I could have taken two steps to see who (or what) was in the photograph, but I refrained. Later, I told myself. Later, there's plenty of time. At the front of the house was a large picture window running across the full breadth of the living room. It looked out over the hills that marked the coastline in these parts, but you couldn't actually see the sea. The living-room furniture was mostly ugly. A green sofa and two green easy chairs, upholstered in either plastic or leatherette, it was hard to tell. A low rattan table with a smoked-glass top. The dining table was made of heavy, dark wood, the backs of the matching chairs were covered in red velveteen. 'The owners are British,' Judith said.

On the ground floor were a garage and a separate apartment with its own entrance. That was where Stanley and Emmanuelle were staying. I vaguely hoped that we would get a tour of the apartment as well, but Judith only opened the door slightly and shouted something, upon which Stanley appeared in the doorway. Around his waist was a white bath towel that reached to just below his knees. 'Emmanuelle is taking a shower,' he said. I looked at the naked part of his body. For his age, his belly was tight. Tight and tanned. But the skin itself was dull. The hair on his chest and beneath his navel was almost white. 'Are you two coming up for a drink?' Judith asked.

Finally, we got a tour of the garden. Beside the house was a roofed-in area with a ping-pong table. Above the garage door hung a basketball net. The soil in the parts of the garden that were not covered in paving stones was dry and brown, almost red. From the patio, a tiled flight of steps led down to the pool.

'Or maybe you'd like to go for a dip first?' Judith said. Caroline and I looked at each other. 'Well, maybe later,' Caroline said.

The swimming pool was in the shape of a figure of eight. In the middle was an island of stone less than a yard across; a thin jet of water sprayed up from it. Lilos, rubber rings and a green inflatable crocodile with handles on both sides of its head floated in the water. At the far end, the wider circle of the figure of eight, was a diving board.

'This is where we spend most of our time,' Judith said. 'Getting them to go to the beach is a real ordeal.'

Just then, Lisa and Thomas came running out of the house. Judith's youngest son didn't even slow down when he reached the edge of the pool. At the last moment it looked as though he couldn't quite decide between a dive or a cannonball. Half falling, half slipping over the wet tiles, he landed in the pool with a huge splash.

'Thomas!' Judith shouted.

'Come on, Lisa! Come on!' he yelled. He flailed his arms and we had to step back to avoid getting wet. 'Lisa! Lisa! Come on!'

And there was my youngest daughter. She paused for a moment at the edge, but then tipped over into the water.

'Lisa,' Caroline said. 'Lisa, where is Julia?'

Lisa had climbed up onto the crocodile, but Thomas pulled her down right away. 'What did you say, Mum?' she asked after she surfaced.

'Where's Julia?'

'I don't know. They're inside, I think.'

After the sardines came the skate. The skate was so big that it almost covered the entire grill. Smoke billowed up. On a little iron table beside the barbecue, Ralph had laid out a platter with even more marine creatures. Mostly squid, from the looks of it. All possible variations on squid: squid with round, white bodies and tentacles on the front, squid with mushroom-shaped bodies from which the legs hung down in a clump, and the more octopus-shaped squid with the familiar suction cups on long tentacles that dangled over the edge of the platter.

'We buy all our fish here from a shop in the village that gets them right off the boat,' Ralph said, fanning the smoke out of his eyes with one hand. 'From the outside you can't even see that it's a shop. It's got those rolling steel shutters, you know, that they only open when the catch comes in. You can't get it any fresher than this.'

As discreetly as I could, I was busy trying to extract a sardine bone that had drilled its way into the roof of my mouth at an impossible spot, behind my front teeth. I only growled to indicate that I had heard him. Sitting closest to the barbecue, I got most of the smoke in my face. The smoke from the skate stank less than that from the sardines, but I'd lost my appetite anyway. I filled my glass again with white wine and took a big swig. As I swilled the wine around in my mouth I tried at the same time to use the tip of my tongue to dislodge the sardine bone; as a result my tongue was skewered painfully a few times.

'Apparently there will be thirteen episodes,' Stanley was telling Caroline. 'Thirteen times fifty minutes. It's probably going to be the most expensive production in the history of television.'

Caroline and I were sitting beside each other, across from Stanley and Emmanuelle. Emmanuelle had lit a long filter cigarette and tapped the ash onto her plate with the remains of the sardines. Even though darkness had almost fallen, she was still wearing her sunglasses. Their disproportionately large lenses made it impossible to see where she was looking.

'Have you seen *The Sopranos*?' Stanley asked Caroline. 'Or *The Wire*?'

'We have almost all the seasons of *The Sopranos* on DVD,' Caroline said. 'I think it's fantastic. Great acting too. And a lot of people have told me that *The Wire* is very good. But we haven't got around to that yet. But *Desperate Housewives*? You know *Desperate Housewives*? We have a couple of DVD sets of that too.'

'*The Wire* is really the best. You have to see it, you'll be addicted right away. Most of the actors are black. That's why the ratings are so much lower than *The Sopranos*. But *Desperate Housewives*… I'm sorry, but I usually find that a little too far-fetched. A little too ha-ha funny. But maybe it's more of a series for women. Emmanuelle here, for example, thinks it's great. Don't you? Emmanuelle? You like *Desperate Housewives* a lot, right?'

He had to tap her forearm before she realised that he was talking to her. And then he had to repeat the question.

'*Desperate Housewives*… is nice,' she said at last, to no one in particular.

'OK, so we've got that straight,' Stanley said. He grinned at Caroline. 'Anyway, so this series is being produced by HBO, the ones who did *The Sopranos* and *The Wire*. The most expensive series ever. Or did I already say that?'

'Yes, you did,' Caroline said. 'But that's OK.'

'It covers the rise of the Roman Empire. The entire golden age, if you know what I mean. From Julius Caesar up to and including the Emperor Nero. That's the only thing that hasn't been decided yet. What to call it. They can't decide between *Rome* and *Augustus*. But since seven of the thirteen episodes will take place during the reign of Caesar Augustus, I think it's going to be *Augustus*.'

'And what about Ralph?' I asked.

'Ralph is going to be the emperor,' Stanley said. 'Caesar Augustus.'

'Yeah, I know that. That's not what I meant. I was wondering how you ended up with Ralph. How you hit on Ralph for the part.'

'I worked with Ralph years ago, when I was still living in Holland. I don't know, but did you ever see *Sweet Darlings*?'

I had to think about it. Then I remembered. As far as I could recall, I hadn't seen it at the cinema at the time, but much later, on TV. *Sweet Darlings*... something about kids hanging around on motor scooters, fairly explicit sex for that era, and equally explicit violence. It had one of those scenes that people keep talking about for years. The kind of scene that can immortalise even a bad film. A couple of boys string a wire across the road. At neck height. A scooter comes along, racing at high speed. And then the head, rolling across the tarmac. The head that ends up in a drain. No, in a ditch. The head barely rises above the water. You see an amazed-looking eye amid the duckweed. An eye that blinks. Then the point of view changes. We see what the eye was looking at. At a frog sitting on the bank. A shocked frog. A frog that looks at the head in as much amazement as the head does at him. Then the frog croaks and the screen goes blurry, then black. The suggestion was clear. The head severed by the wire was still *alive* when it landed in the ditch.

'My parents wouldn't let me watch that,' Caroline said.

'Oh really?' Stanley said, looking amused. 'Were you that young?'

'Was Ralph in that?' I asked. 'In *Sweet Darlings*? I don't remember that at all.'

'My neck *still* hurts from that scene!' cried Ralph, who had clearly been eavesdropping. 'Ha ha ha!'

'Was that him?' I asked Stanley. I turned to Ralph. 'Were you the one in that ditch? I never realised that.'

'Good to know that you're up on your classics, Marc,' Ralph said. 'So what do you think, Stanley? Great to hear, isn't it, that people still remember a scene like that?'

'Oh God, yuck, now I remember!' Caroline said. 'That severed head in the ditch! Oh, I was too afraid to look. I realised later on that my parents were right, not to let me go.'

Ralph's booming laugh rang out. Stanley laughed too. Emmanuelle raised her head for a moment. A dreamy smile appeared on her face, but she didn't ask what everyone was laughing at. I couldn't help thinking about the films Stanley Forbes directed later. The ones he made in Hollywood. I hadn't seen them all, but in those films too, the director had relied heavily on explicitness. They were films that *showed everything*, as people liked to say. On the one hand the severed limbs and bleeding stumps, and on the other the sex organs with blue veins standing out on the sides. You forgot what the films were about soon after they were over, but the explicit scenes had become his trademark.

'Where's Judith?' Ralph said. 'I'm dying of thirst.'

And indeed, where was Judith? A few minutes earlier she had stood up from the table to get some more white wine, and she still hadn't come back. Judith's mother, who was sitting at the far end of the table, held her hand in front of her mouth and began yawning. 'Oh my,' she said. They were the only words she'd spoken in the last half-hour.

I leaned back in my chair and looked around. First at the stone steps up to the first floor. Then to the roofed area at the side of the house, where Lisa and Thomas were playing ping-pong under the yellowish fluorescent lighting. Their first course of sardines had been enough, and they had been allowed to leave the table. As were Julia and Alex. But where those two had got to was beyond me. I looked at the pool, where the underwater lighting was now on. That evening there wasn't even a breath of wind. The green inflatable crocodile lay motionless on its side. While I was fussing around with the sardines, I hadn't dared to look at Judith. And she too seemed to do little to try to establish eye contact with me. On one occasion she had laughed too loudly at an observation of Caroline's that wasn't all that funny, and laid her hand on Caroline's forearm. I wondered whether I'd missed something. A glance. A gesture. Something that should have told me that I should wait a minute and then follow her into the house. *Shall I go and see what Judith's up to?* I rehearsed the sentence a few times in my mind, but it remained a line from a bad film.

Then suddenly, there was movement at the top of the steps. First I saw Alex, and then Julia coming down, with Judith a few steps behind. Julia's hair was mussed, I saw when she came closer, and her cheeks were flushed. I hadn't known Alex long enough to tell if his hair was mussed too.

'Daddy?' said Julia. She had come up and was now standing behind me, laying her hands on both sides of my neck and gently kneading my shoulders. That's what she always did when she wanted something from me: a bonus on her allowance for an expensive sweater she'd seen in town; the 'poor little' hamster in the pet-shop window that she wanted with all her might to bring home; the school party where 'everyone' was going to stay until midnight. 'Hmm?' I replied. I took her left hand in my right and squeezed it gently. I also looked over at Caroline. Julia never asked Caroline anything first. She knew that I was a softer touch. *Wishy-washy*, Caroline always said. *You never dare to say no.*

'Can we stay here?' Julia asked.

'Stay here?' I said. 'What do you mean, stay here?' I tried to make eye contact with Judith, but she had just put two bottles of white wine on the table and was handing the corkscrew to Stanley. I felt my face grow warm. My heart began to pound. 'Do you mean you want to stay over here? I don't think there's enough space.'

'No, I mean all of us,' Julia said, and she squeezed my shoulders a little harder. 'That all of us stay over here. And not at that stupid campsite any more.'

Judith stepped aside, away from the table, to just behind my wife. She looked at me.

'We invited you on the evening of the party,' she said. 'But then Stanley and Emmanuelle dropped in from America, and now there's really no more space in the house. But I figured, you have a tent. Why don't you pitch it here in the garden?'

I looked back. The way she stood there, her face just out of range of the candlelight, I couldn't see her eyes clearly.

'*Please?*' Julia said quietly in my ear. 'Please?'

'I don't know,' I said. 'Where would we do that? I mean, it seems like way too much bother for you. You already have guests. That would be an awful lot of people all of a sudden.'

'Nonsense!' That was Ralph. 'Many hands make the merrier...' He laughed loudly. 'Or however it goes. There's enough room here.'

'I was thinking of over there, at the side of the house,' Judith said. 'Where the ping-pong table is. There's enough room there for a tent. And you can all shower inside and everything.'

There was a loud pop. We all looked at Stanley, who had pulled the cork out of the bottle. 'Sorry,' he said. 'No, I also mean sorry that we got here before you did. We didn't know you'd been invited.'

'It doesn't seem like a good idea to me,' Caroline said. 'The ground back there is hard as a rock. You can't pitch a tent there. We'll just go back to the campsite later on.' She looked at me, then spoke to Julia. 'You two can come over here whenever you like. And we can meet up at the beach. But at the campsite we have more room. It's more relaxed for everyone.'

'I think that campsite is stupid,' Julia said.

'Listen, the ground isn't much of a problem,' Judith said. 'And you're out of the wind there. There's a pile of bricks in the garage, you wouldn't even have to use tent pegs. Not much danger of getting blown away here.'

'Can we, Daddy?' Julia said. She squeezed my shoulders so hard now that it almost hurt. 'Can we, please?'

18

It was almost midnight by the time we drove back to the campsite. Caroline didn't say a word the whole way, but after we'd said goodnight to the girls, she announced that she was going to sit outside the tent and smoke a cigarette.

I was tired. I'd had too much white wine. What I felt like doing was crawling into my own sleeping bag, beside my two daughters. But Caroline had stopped smoking two years ago. She hadn't answered me earlier in the evening, when I'd asked what she thought about moving our tent to the garden at the summer house. She had simply tapped a cigarette out of Emmanuelle's pack and lit it in silence. Later, after the skate and the squid, she had smoked a few more. I didn't count them. More than five, I reckoned. When we said goodbye, Emmanuelle had handed her the almost empty pack.

It seemed to me like a good idea, in other words, to join my wife outside the tent for a while.

'So tell me, what was I supposed to say?' she asked, only moments after I had sunk down into my folding chair. She tried to whisper, but it sounded louder than a whisper. She spat the words out. I thought I even felt saliva hit my cheek. 'If you just sit there and say that it sounds good to you, to camp out in those people's garden? And then, *only after that*, do you ask what I think about it!? With the kids standing there? What was I supposed to say? The only thing I can do is ruin it for Lisa and Julia. Which makes me the nagging mother who always ruins things again. And it makes you the fun daddy who always thinks everything is OK. Damn it, Marc, I could have curled up in a ball and died!'

I didn't say anything. I saw the tip of her cigarette flare up in the darkness. Flare up *in a rage*. When we first met we were both still smokers. In bed we lit each other's cigarettes. I had quit a couple of years before she did. After the children were born, we had only smoked in the garden anyway.

'I say to you that when I'm on holiday I don't feel like having other people around. Especially not during the first week. And you say OK, that's fine, we can leave tomorrow if you want. And we sit there for one evening eating fish and listening to all that la-di-dah about an expensive TV series and you make a complete about-face. '

'It was because of Julia,' I said. 'I know. I'm a spineless softie. I can't say no. But it's just that I saw how much fun they were having in the pool and with the ping-pong table. The boys are nice. That's something we have to take into consideration, isn't it? I find it more relaxing too, with just the four of us on holiday. But it can't hurt, every once in a while, to look at it from their perspective. How much fun is it for our girls to be off alone with their parents?'

'Marc, that's not the point! Don't start acting like you're the only one who thinks about how to make the holiday fun for the girls. I can see that they have fun with those boys. But that doesn't mean we have to turn around and give up all our privacy just like that. What really gets me is the way it went. The way you put it, there was no way I could say no.'

I sensed an opening. The proverbial light at the end of the tunnel. A curtain slipped aside: outside the window, day was dawning. During a normal argument I would have stubbornly kept insisting that she couldn't whine about her own privacy when we were on holiday with two teenage girls. That as a mother she shouldn't always try to worm her way into the role of victim. But this was no normal argument.

'I'm sorry,' I said. 'I didn't really realise that. I should have asked in a different way. Or at another moment. Sorry.'

Then neither of us said a word. For a few seconds there I thought she was crying. But it was her lips sucking on the cigarette filter.

I leaned over and found her wrist in the darkness. I wrapped my fingers around it gently. 'How many cigarettes do you have left?' I asked.

'Marc, please. Don't be ridiculous.'

'No, really. How much can it hurt, one cigarette? Tonight I feel like smoking a cigarette. Here, outside. With you.'

'You know what it is? Lately, sometimes, I've really been worried. About you. About how you view your patients.' I fished around in the dark, trying to locate the pack of cigarettes. At last I found it, amid the pine needles under my wife's chair. 'You always used to talk about them in a way that made it clear that you stood above all that. Above all those artists and wannabes. You considered yourself better than them. And rightly so. You hated those opening nights and gallery openings and book launches just as much as I did. All that hollow rubbish from people who think they're superior to the rest of mankind just because they do something with art. So-called painters who never sell a painting, directors who make films that sell maybe a hundred tickets. But who, meanwhile, look down on people who can make their own living. Even on people who can heal other people. Like you.'

'Caroline...'

'No, wait, I'm not finished yet. That's what hurts me the most. The way they look at you. I sometimes wonder whether you even notice it yourself. I do. They look down on you, Marc. Deep down in their hearts they think you're just a dead-average, dumb little doctor. A doctor who doesn't amount to anything because he can't paint some stupid fucking painting that no one wants to buy. Who refuses to beg for money to produce another disgusting play or some dismal film that no one wants to see. I see it in everything they do. Even in the way they look at me. In their eyes, of course, I'm even lower than you are. The doctor's *wife*. The scum of the earth. How much lower can you get? That's what I see them thinking. And then they look around to find more interesting company to talk to. The faster they can ditch this dumb, boring doctor's wife the better.'

'Caroline, you shouldn't...'

'Shut up. I'm not finished yet. I want you to just listen to me. After this I'll never talk about it again. Never. I promise.'

I took Caroline's cigarette from between her fingers and used it to light mine.

'I'm listening,' I said.

'I can't take it any more. Or rather, I *could* still take it, as long as you knew deep in your heart that you stand above them. But is that still true? Do you still feel like you're above all that, Marc?'

I thought about it. I thought about what I felt deep in my heart and I knew the answer. I'd fantasised about it often enough, at moments when it all became too much. What would be lost, really, if I just gave them all an injection? I fantasised from time to time. Which films 'that absolutely needed to be made', as a patient once put it, would then remain unmade? Which paintings would remain unpainted? Which books unwritten? Would it really be such a loss? Would anyone even notice?

Sometimes, in between patients, I would spend thirty seconds sitting alone at my desk. Then I would imagine how it might go. I would call them in, one by one. Left arm? Right arm? Could you roll up your sleeve? It's just a little pin-prick, done in no time. Within a week I could finish the job. The film-production schedules would be shelved. The performances cancelled. The books would remain unwritten. Would anything really be lost? Or would a sense of relief soon gain the upper hand?

'What are you laughing about?' Caroline asked.

'No, I was thinking what it would be like if they weren't around any more,' I said. 'My patients. I mean, if I were to set up my practice all over again. A sign on the door: as from today we accept only normal patients. Patients who work from nine to five.'

I drew on my cigarette and sucked in the smoke. It felt good. It felt like the first time. The first time in the schoolyard. And just like the first time, I had a coughing fit.

'Careful, Marc,' Caroline said. 'You're not used to it any more.'

'But what do you mean exactly, about me no longer standing above it? Why do you think that?'

'I don't know, but I think it started after you met this Ralph Meier. It's like... it's almost as though you *admire* him. You never did that before, admire a patient. You hated all of it. All those opening nights you had to go to. You thought it was all a waste of time, that's what you always said.'

I took a second drag on my cigarette. A bit more carefully this time, to keep from having another coughing fit.

'Well, maybe "admire" is putting it too strongly, but you have to admit, Ralph's got talent. Anyway, he's different from those so-called artists who find themselves so interesting. He really *can* act. I mean, you thought he was good too. In *Richard II*.'

'Sure, I thought he was very good, despite his loathsome personality. You have to be able to keep those things separate, as far as I'm concerned. A person's talent and what they get up to in private. But I'm talking about something else. It's not so much that you admire his talent, it's more like you think that their lives are interesting. I noticed that back at that garden party. And now there's this. All the trouble you went to to find a campsite near them. And how enthusiastic you were about the idea of setting up our tent in their garden. It's as though, consciously or not, you're overly eager to be around them. I think that's weird. You're not like that, Marc. You *weren't* like that. That's not the Marc I know. And it's not the Marc I admire… or *used to admire*. The Marc who would never, ever, consider spending his holiday at the summer house of one of his patients. Not even if that patient was a famous actor. *Especially not* if he was a famous actor.'

I heard the sound of the tent being unzipped. Then Lisa was standing there, in her pyjamas. She was rubbing the sleep from her eyes.

'Are you two fighting?'

I reached out and pulled her to me. 'No, sweetheart. We're not fighting. What makes you think that?'

'I can hear you talking all the time. I can't sleep.'

I had my arm around her waist and pressed her against me. And Lisa placed her hand on the top of my head and ran her fingers through my hair.

'Daddy!'

'What is it, sweetheart?'

'You're smoking!'

By reflex, I made a move to stub the cigarette out on the ground, but that would only have made me look even guiltier.

'You never smoke, do you?' Lisa asked.

'No,' I said.

'So why are you doing it now?'

In the dark I saw the glowing tip of Caroline's cigarette dive for the ground and then go out.

'Listen, it's just once. Only for really special—'

'But you mustn't smoke! Smoking is so bad for you. If you smoke, you die. I don't want you to smoke, Daddy. I don't want you to die.'

'I'm not going to die, sweetheart. Look, I'm already putting it out.'

I crushed the cigarette firmly into the ground.

'You two never smoke,' Lisa said. 'Mum never smokes. So why are you smoking?'

I took a deep breath. I felt my eyes stinging, but it wasn't from the smoke.

'Daddy never smokes either,' Caroline said. 'He just wanted to try it, to see how filthy it tastes.'

None of us spoke. I pulled my daughter more tightly against me and ran my hand up and down her back.

'Are we going to that pool tomorrow?' Lisa asked.

I didn't say a word. In the darkness, I counted the seconds. One, two, three… I heard Caroline sigh deeply.

'Yes, darling,' she said. 'Tomorrow we're going back to that pool.'

19

That was how our stay at the Meiers' summer house began. *Next to* the summer house, I should say. *Beside* the summer house. In the end, the earth turned out not to be too hard for the tent pegs. Once I had unrolled the groundsheet, as I started putting the poles together, I looked questioningly at Caroline.

'No, love,' she said. 'This time you get to do it all by yourself.'

Then she walked off to the pool.

We had thin, self-inflating air mattresses. The ground wasn't as hard as everyone had thought, but it was hard. Through the air mattresses you could feel every bump and every stone I'd overlooked while setting up the tent. And our site was more or less next to the ping-pong table. I went to sleep at night and woke in the morning to the tick-tock of the balls. Alex and Thomas didn't have to go to bed at a fixed time. When they weren't playing ping-pong, you would hear them bouncing off the diving board until long after midnight.

Caroline didn't say anything. She didn't say, 'So, are you happy now? This is what you wanted, isn't it?' She just looked at me. And then she smiled.

We went along with the Meiers to the local markets. Markets where Ralph haggled loudly over the price of fish, meat and fruit.

'They all know me,' he said. 'They know I'm not just your average tourist. You don't have to tell me what two pounds of prawns are supposed to cost.' We went to restaurants where he always made a point of waving away the menu. 'At places like this, you don't order from the menu. You ask them what's fresh.' Which he then did. He patted the waiters on the back and pinched their bellies chummily. 'You won't get this anywhere else,' he told us. Platters of marine animals were set before us. Always marine animals. In all shapes and sizes. Marine animals, some of which I didn't even know existed. Marine animals, some of which left you having to guess which end you were supposed to start eating first. I'm a meat-eater myself. Ralph didn't even give me time to look at the menu. A few times I succeeded in catching a waiter's eye and pointing to a dish I'd seen on a neighbouring table. A meat dish. A dish smothered in a dark-brown sauce, with bones sticking out of it. 'What have you gone and ordered now?' Ralph would cry, shaking his head. 'This is a place where you eat fish. Tomorrow we'll buy meat for the barbecue. We've got a farm where they sell fresh lamb and pork right from the yard. The meat here comes from the supermarket. This is a *fish* restaurant. So *bon appétit*!'

On days when we weren't hanging around the pool, we went to the beach. Or, more precisely, we went to little beaches. The normal beach where we'd run into each other the first time wasn't good enough. 'Everyone goes there,' Ralph said, without bothering to explain what was wrong with that. The little beaches Ralph took us to were above all hard to get to. From where we parked the cars it was usually an hour's scramble over almost impassably rocky paths, overgrown with thistles and thorns that left your bare legs scratched and bloody. Insects with abdomens striped red and yellow buzzed through the shimmering hot air and stung you in the calf or neck. Far below you could see the blue sea. 'Nobody ever comes here!' Ralph would cry. 'Just wait and see. It's a paradise!' We always went loaded down with things. Ralph and Judith took *everything*: deckchairs, parasols, a cooler with cold white wine and cans of beer, and a picnic basket full of French bread, tomatoes, olive oil, charcuterie, cheese, and tinned tuna, sardines and the inevitable array of squid. Once at the beach, Ralph would immediately take off all his clothes and plunge into the water among the rocks. 'Jesus Christ, isn't this lovely!' he would splutter. 'Alex, toss me those goggles! I think there are crabs here. And sea urchins. Ow! Damn it! Can you look for me, Judith? I think my flip-flops are in that blue bag. Marc, what are you waiting for?'

Indeed, what was I waiting for? I've already explained where I stand with regard to naked bodies. The naked bodies of my daily practice. A naked body in a doctor's office is something different from a naked body out of doors. I looked at Ralph when he emerged from the water and slid his feet into the flip-flops Judith had taken from the blue bag. I looked at the drops of water falling from his body. He shook his head like a wet dog, and even more water flew from his hair. Loudly he blew his nose on his fingers, then wiped them on his thigh. Long ago the first animals had come onto dry land. After that, most of them had gone further inland. Only something less than two hundred years ago did humans, at first only in small numbers, begin returning to the beach. I looked at Ralph's hairy groin, from which so much water dripped that you couldn't tell whether it was seawater or if he was simply pissing unashamedly where he stood. 'Marc, come on in, man. You can see all the way to the bottom here.' He rested his hands on his hips and looked around contentedly, at 'his little beach', the existence of which only he was aware. For a few seconds he blocked out the sun with his enormous bulk. Then he turned and, with a few giant steps, the flip-flops slapping loudly against his heels, went back into the sea.

I'm not prudish, it's not that. No, let me rephrase that: I *am* prudish, I'm proud of being prudish when it means that you don't go flaunting your dick and other spare body parts all over the place in the out-of-doors. I feel, in other words, that a certain circumspection should be observed when bodies are bared. Nude beaches, nudist campsites and other places where the naked-by-principle gather, are places I avoid like the plague. Anyone who has ever seen naked people playing volleyball on the beach knows that nudity creates no erotic attraction, to put it mildly. In mass graves, too, people often lie naked on top of each other. The point is to preserve a modicum of human dignity. Nudists don't understand that. Under the pretext that it is more natural to take off all your clothes, they thrust an unimpeded view of their dangling dicks, jiggling tits, pendulous labia and dank bottom cracks right in your face. They point their fingers in accusation. They say that *you* are small-minded when you claim that all of this might be better unseen.

I looked around to see what the others were doing. The two boys had slipped on many-coloured swimming shorts. Shorts that reached down over their knees. Caroline had taken off her blouse and was lying in her bikini on a towel she'd spread out on the shingle. My two girls were in bikinis. Lisa, strictly speaking, didn't yet need a top, but it was understandable that she didn't want to be one-upped by her older sister.

Finally I looked at Judith. Judith was squatting in front of the same blue bag from which she had produced Ralph's flip-flops. She took out a bottle of suntan lotion and began rubbing it on her arms. I saw it all perfectly clearly. She was wearing only her bikini bottoms. I glanced only quickly. I was afraid she would catch me staring at her breasts, and so I averted my gaze right away and turned my attention back to the sea. No sign of Ralph. I took another good look, but I couldn't see him anywhere. This particular little beach opened onto a cove. Where cove and sea met was an outcrop of rock across which the waves came crashing in. It would be a strange start to our holidays, it occurred to me, were Ralph to drown on the very first day at the beach. Or maybe not drown completely, but have to be dragged up onto the pebbles, coughing and retching and gasping for air. Yes, there was a doctor in the house. I was the obvious candidate to apply mouth-to-mouth resuscitation. To lie him on his back and massage his stomach, to make him retch up the seawater he'd swallowed. I thought about my mouth on Ralph's. It would undoubtedly taste of squid. *This is a fish restaurant!* I thought, and burst out laughing.

'Marc! Marc!'

There he stood, on the highest point of the rocks. He had slid his goggles and snorkel up onto his forehead. He waved.

I made a decision. It was a decision that would have far-reaching consequences for the rest of our holidays, I realised at the time. I took off my T-shirt, shorts and underpants. With my back to the beach, as close as possible to the line between land and sea, at the point where the waves rolled in over the shingle. That way, for about five seconds, anyone who wanted to could see my completely naked body, albeit only from behind. The least offensive side, one might hope. I took my swimsuit from my rolled-up towel and bent over to pull it on. It was a simple pair of swimming shorts; the legs came to just above my knees. No bright colours. But with a sort of floral motif. Albeit in black and white. I put them on and tied a bow in the cord that kept them from falling down. That I was putting on my swimming shorts on this first day at the beach meant that from now on I would *always* wear shorts – even by the pool.

'Here, Marc. Here, take a look at this.'

After I had clambered up onto the rocky outcrop, Ralph handed me the snorkel and goggles. 'Right down under here, man. Stuck up against the rock, a huge one.' He indicated the dimensions with his hands. 'An octopus. A bruiser. That'll be great on the barbecue tonight.'

Stanley and Emmanuelle never accompanied us to these remote coves and shingle beaches. They usually remained at the summer house; Stanley sat at a table on the patio and worked on the scripts for *Augustus*, while Emmanuelle did lazy laps in the pool. Or they went off on excursions to local towns and villages, to visit museums, churches and monasteries. Stanley had a digital camera with a large screen. When they came back he would show us the pictures he'd taken that day. Pictures of church spires, cloisters and monastic gardens. I tried to feign interest, but it was hard. There were also lots of pictures of Emmanuelle: Emmanuelle hugging her knees on a low wall beside an equestrian statue; Emmanuelle looking kittenish beside a pond with a fountain in the shape of a carp; Emmanuelle at an al fresco table covered in white linen, the neck of a bottle draped in a white napkin and emerging from a wine cooler beside her; Emmanuelle sucking on the leg of a crab or lobster. The photos of Emmanuelle vastly outnumbered the rest. Sometimes Stanley would pause a little longer when a photo of her appeared on the screen. 'Here,' he would say then, a dreamy smile spreading across his face. 'Isn't she gorgeous?' He was right. In front of the camera, something happened to Emmanuelle. She left herself behind. Left behind her physical presence, which mostly emanated lethargy and a lack of interest. I saw how Stanley seemed to forget himself when he looked at the pictures. As though he had torn her out of a magazine. The kind of magazine that an adolescent boy hides under his mattress.

There were also days when we spent every minute, from morning to evening, beside the pool. Around noon Ralph would light the barbecue and Judith would take the first beers and bottles of white wine out of the fridge. Then we would enjoy a 'light meal' on the patio. The rest of the afternoon we spent slumped in the deckchairs around the pool, where most of us soon drifted off to sleep. The boys had strung a length of rope from the second floor to the diving board. They would climb out of the window and descend hand-over-hand down the rope until they were over the pool, then drop into the water. To loud applause from our girls, whom we had forbidden to use the rope. Ralph kept his shorts on when he was manning the barbecue, but you could tell that he almost couldn't wait for lunch to be over so that he could take them off again. When he dived into the pool with a loud cry, the water rocked and splashed over the edges. I always observed this first dive with particular interest. I observed it as a physician. Twenty years ago one was always severely warned not to go into the water so soon after eating. That idea has become outmoded. The school of thought these days is that you actually shouldn't wait too long. Digestion only really gets under way after an hour. After an hour there really is a risk. The blood moves to the stomach and intestines. Neural activity decreases. Thought processes slow, and eventually come to a halt. Too little blood flows to other parts of the body as well. Too little oxygen. The legs suffer a shortage of oxygen and can no longer apply force. The arms begin to tingle and lose all feeling. Anyone who goes into the sea during digestion runs the risk of becoming a plaything of the waves. Of being pulled out to sea by treacherous currents. But just after eating, there's not much to worry about. The stomach is full, true enough. It's not entirely free of risk.

Dishes containing melted cheese may suddenly coagulate. The cheese cools too quickly and becomes a solid lump. The opening between the stomach and the duodenum shuts down. The flow to the intestines becomes blocked. Sauces can start roiling, like oil in the hold of a supertanker. The tanker runs into trouble during a storm, it hits the rocks and breaks in two. A sauce may slosh against the stomach walls and rise up through the oesophagus. The swimmer runs the risk of choking on his own vomit. Vomit flows back into the windpipe. One last time, he raises his hand above the water and cries for help. But on the beach, no one can see him. No one can hear him. He sinks beneath the waves, only to wash up days (sometimes even weeks) later on some beach miles away.

That's how I looked at Ralph when he dived into the pool. Every time, I considered the possibility that he might not surface again. Or that he would bash his drunken skull against the bottom and be paralysed from head to toe. But each time he surfaced again, coughing and sneezing and hawking, and dragged himself up the ladder. Then he would spread a towel over a deckchair and lie down in the sun to dry. He never covered himself. He lay with his legs spread, his body too large for the deckchair, his feet hanging over the end: all loose and lazy, tanning in the sun. 'Is this a holiday or is this a holiday?' he said, burping and closing his eyes. A minute later his mouth had dropped open and he was snoring loudly. I looked at his stomach and his legs. At his dick, hanging to one side and resting on his thigh. And then I looked at my two daughters. At Julia and Lisa. They didn't seem offended at all. They were playing games in the pool. They played tag with Alex and Thomas. Or else Caroline would toss coins into the water and they would dive to retrieve them. I wondered whether perhaps I was, indeed, narrow-minded. Whether it was my own fault that the sight of Ralph Meier's naked dick so close to my young daughters seemed so filthy. I couldn't quite decide – and as long as I hadn't decided, I continued to consider it filthy. I remember one afternoon when a repairman from the letting agency came by. There had been problems with the water pressure: by evening water was only dripping from the shower. Without first putting on his shorts or grabbing a towel, Ralph got up from his deckchair and shook the man's hand. I saw the way he looked. Or rather: the way he *didn't* look. He was at least two feet shorter than Ralph. He was closer to it than someone of normal height would have been, his face couldn't have been more than ten inches from Ralph's dangling dick, he would only have had to lower his eyes a fraction of an inch to have an almost full-screen view of it. Ralph stepped into his flip-flops and led the repairman up the steps. They disappeared into the house, and when they returned about fifteen minutes later, Ralph still hadn't put on trousers or wrapped himself in a towel. 'It's the reservoir on the roof,' he said. 'It's blocked. To make things even worse, it's been months since it rained.'

The next morning, no water at all came from the shower. The taps and the outdoor shower beside the pool had also gone dry. Ralph cursed and picked up his mobile phone. 'We're paying a goddamn fortune to rent this place,' he said. 'They're going to have to solve this somehow. No rain, my arse.' But at the agency, no one answered. Ralph put on his flip-flops again, and this time, for a change, he also put on trousers. 'I'm going down there,' he said. 'I'm going to let them know exactly what I think of their water reservoir.'

It was then that Caroline said that the two of us would be happy to go to the letting agency. Ralph protested, but she said: 'No, listen, Marc and I can do some shopping at the same time. Tonight *we'll* make dinner.' As she spoke these words, she looked at me. She was smiling, at least there was that, but I could tell from the look in her eye that she was deadly serious. I mumbled something, then went to the tent to look for the car keys.

20

All the way down the hill to the village, Caroline was quiet. As I was getting ready to turn left onto the main road, towards the letting agency office on the outskirts of the next town, she laid her hand on my forearm. 'No, first we're going out for breakfast,' she said. 'At the beach.'

A few minutes later we were on the terrace of the same restaurant where we'd run into the Meiers that first evening. Caroline dunked her croissant into a large cup of foamy *café au lait*.

'Alone at last,' she said with a sigh. 'I was really ready for this.'

She was right, I couldn't deny it. Without being able to do much about it, we had become caught up in the typical dynamics of a group holiday rental. That field of forces that sweeps you away unnoticed, like a riptide invisible to the naked eye. That field of forces in which you are seldom or never alone. Privacy had been put on the back burner. A few times I had tried to go to buy bread in the village on my own, but there was always someone else who wanted to come along. Usually Ralph. 'You going into the village, Marc? Great. Today's the street market. We can buy fresh fish and fruit while we're at it.' Then I would find myself standing beside the car for at least half an hour, keys in hand. 'The boys are coming along too,' Ralph would say when he finally appeared at the top of the steps. 'They can help us carry the groceries. It'll only be a minute, Alex is almost done in the shower.'

'You're right, I was ready for this too,' I told Caroline. 'This was a good idea.'

I watched a father flying a kite with his little son. It was one of those kites with two pairs of strings, the kind you can make spin and dive. Every time the father handed the strings to his son, the kite would smack down hard into the sand. Out to sea at this hour you saw only the occasional white sail. A white cruise ship was moving almost imperceptibly from left to right, along the horizon.

'How long do we have to keep this up?' Caroline asked.

'Keep what up?'

'Marc… you know what I'm talking about. It's fun for Julia and Lisa, but how long do *we* have to keep it up? How long before we can leave without feeling guilty?'

'Come on, is it that bad?' I started to say, but then I saw the expression on her face. 'No, sorry. You're right. It *is* bad. I mean, it's hard for me too sometimes. All those people. Ralph…' I looked at her questioningly. 'Is it still bothering you? Does it still bother you, the way he looks at you?'

'Thanks to our stunning fashion model, not any more, no.'

I detected something in her tone: a not entirely clear and uncomplicated undertone as she spoke the words 'stunning' and 'fashion model'. Women think that men find them mysterious, but in the main they are all pretty transparent.

'So Ralph has traded you in for a younger model,' I said, laughing. 'And when it comes right down to it, you're sorry about that. That you, as a woman getting on in years, are no longer whistled at by window cleaners and famous actors.'

Caroline flicked her spoon at me, a few drops of foamy milk hit me in the face. 'Marc! Don't get funny! I'm really glad to be off the hook for a while. Really I am. But have you noticed how he looks at Emmanuelle?'

I shrugged.

'Yesterday?' Caroline went on.

'Before that repairman came by? It's like he doesn't care who notices. Stanley was working at his little table and Emmanuelle was lying in her deckchair. You know, when Ralph was going around with the white wine? First he leaned down almost right on top of her to get her glass. And then he just stood there looking as he poured the wine. At everything except her face. He started at her feet, then moved up slowly. And then the same route back again. It was like he didn't notice what he was doing, or didn't care. He ran the tip of his tongue over his lips. As though he had some tasty fish on his plate. But then… then. Oh no, it was too terrible!'

Caroline covered her face with her hands and leaned over till her forehead almost touched the tabletop.

'What?' I said. 'What?'

'He had the bottle in one hand and the glass in the other. But after he had put the glass back down, he had one hand free.

First he rubbed it slowly over his stomach. Around his navel. But then he just moved it down. To his dick. He grabbed it, Marc. He sort of squeezed it. All very casually, as though it were the most normal thing in the world. If anyone had caught him at it, he probably would have pretended he had an itch. Well, believe me, he did! Less than a minute later he put the bottle down on the ground and dived into the pool! You could almost hear the water hiss!'

I laughed. Caroline couldn't help laughing too. But she grew serious again right away.

'Sure, it's hilarious,' she said. 'But I still find it nasty. Loathsome.'

'Oh listen, Emmanuelle kind of provokes that reaction on purpose. I don't think she really minds. The way she has old Stanley wrapped around her little finger… and she just happens to be a very pretty girl. One mustn't forget that.'

Caroline squinted as she looked at me. 'Do you think she's pretty, Marc? Do you think she's a pretty girl? Do you sometimes sneak a look at her, the way Ralph does?'

'Yes, I think she's a pretty girl. Any man would think that she is a pretty girl. And yes, sometimes I look at her. I'm a man, Caroline. It would be almost suspect if I *didn't* look at her.'

'OK, all right. But that's not what I mean when I say I find it loathsome, the way Ralph looks at her. You said so yourself. A pretty *girl*. Emmanuelle is still just a girl. How things are between her and Stanley, I don't need to know. That's their business. But there are also other girls around the pool.'

I stared at her. I'd found it loathsome as well: the proximity of Ralph's dick to Julia and Lisa playing in the pool, but I hadn't thought about it in these terms before.

'I've been paying attention,' Caroline said. 'And I have to admit that I haven't really been able to catch him at it. But still… he's no fool. Maybe he controls himself as long as we're around. I don't know how he behaves with them when we're not.'

I said nothing. I blinked my eyes in the bright sunlight reflected from the beach. I saw black spots. Black spots dancing from left to right across my field of vision.

'They're still only children, our girls,' Caroline said. 'At least, that's what we tell ourselves. But look at Julia. How much difference is there between Julia and Emmanuelle? Two years? Four years? A couple of hundred miles south of here, Julia might have been married off by now.'

I suddenly remembered something. A few days ago. Ralph playing ping-pong with Alex, Thomas, Julia and Lisa. Not a real game of ping-pong. They all had a paddle in one hand and they were running around the table. You had to knock the ball back to the other side, then it was the next person's turn, and so on. If you missed the ball, you were out. What I remembered most of all was Ralph. He was wearing shorts for a change, admittedly, but it was a weird sight, that big body running around the ping-pong table among those other little bodies, which were so much smaller and above all slimmer. A *comical* sight, if you looked at it that way. He was barefoot, and there was a puddle of water on the ground. He slipped and fell, landing with his full weight on the tiles. I had just stood up from my deckchair and was walking towards the ping-pong table with a can of beer in my hand. At the moment when Ralph crashed down onto the tiles you could feel the ground shake. As though a lorry was driving down the street outside. 'Damn it!' he roared. 'Goddamn it! Cunt! Cocksucker! Fucking cunt! Ow! Ow! Damn it...' He was sitting with his shorts in the puddle, rubbing his knee. You could see the nasty scrape on it. A graze with stripes of blood across it where the skin had been dragged across the rough tiles. 'Jesus' fucking whore!' he shouted.

The children had stopped running around the table right away. They stood a little way away from him and looked at the large body on the ground. With a certain awe, but also in amazement, the way one might look at the carcass of a stray whale that has washed up on the beach. But after that last three-word oath, I believe it was Alex who started laughing. Then Thomas yelped and began to giggle. That was the signal for Julia and Lisa to burst out laughing too. They looked at Ralph one more time, and then surrendered completely to a liberating fit of laughter. It was laughter that wailed, that shrieked the way only girls' can. Weak-kneed, hysterical laughter. The kind of laughter that sounds as though it will never end. And deadly too. A deadly laugh for us boys. They slap their hands over their mouths and explode with it: often behind your back, sometimes right in your face. Like now.

It was not only Ralph who was being laughed at, it was all men. Man as a species. Normally speaking, that man was big and strong. Stronger than a woman. But sometimes he fell. Due to a force greater than his own. The force of gravity.

'Oh, I'm going to wet myself!' Lisa shrieked, tears running down her cheeks.

I looked at Ralph, his big, clumsy body on the tiles, the graze on his knee. It was – I don't know how else to put it – a *childlike* injury. The injury incurred by a little boy who has fallen from his tricycle. A scraped knee that you run crying to show to your mother: proud on the one hand of so much blood, afraid on the other that she might put iodine on it. That was also what you heard in Julia and Lisa's laughter – if you listened closely. The laugh of all mothers. The mothers who chuckle at the eternal clumsiness of boys. Ralph inspected the cut on his knee one last time, his face contorted with pain, and shook his head. Then he did the only thing you can do in such a situation: he started laughing along with them. He laughed along with his sons. With my daughters. He laughed at himself. Or at least, it seemed as though he was laughing at himself, as though he had a capacity for self-mockery. In reality, of course, it was above all a laugh to save face. A damage-containment laugh. A grown-up man who falls down hard is laughable. A man who can laugh about it himself is that much less so.

'Goddamn,' Ralph said laughing, as he struggled to his feet. 'You rabble! Laugh at an old man, would you!?'

And then it happened. It was a detail, no more than that. A detail to which you pay no attention at first. That takes on meaning only later. In retrospect.

Ralph Meier rose halfway to his feet, supporting himself on his undamaged knee. He still pretended to be laughing, but it was no longer real – if it ever had been. 'And you, you'd really better watch your step!' he said. As he said this, he rose further to his feet and pointed his index finger at my elder daughter. At Julia.

Julia shrieked. 'No!' she screamed. 'No!'

And she grabbed hold of her red bottoms with both hands. Her bikini bottoms.

I saw it quite clearly. The gesture could be explained in only one way. Ralph Meier was threatening my daughter with something. He was threatening to do something. Something he had done before. All as a joke. All with a knowing wink. But still.

It was, as I said, a mere detail. You've seen something, but you push it aside. Or rather, something in you pushes it aside. You don't want to think that way. You don't want to go looking for things that aren't there. You've been living next door to someone for years. A nice neighbour. A friendly neighbour. A *normal* neighbour, above all else. That's exactly what you tell the police detective when he comes for more information about your neighbour. 'Quite normal,' you say. 'Very nice. No, never noticed anything peculiar.' Meanwhile, inside the neighbour's house, physical remains have been found. Physical remains that perhaps come from fourteen missing women. In his freezer. In his garden. Then you suddenly remember something. The meaningless detail. You saw your neighbour go to his car a few times, carrying rubbish bags. Rubbish bags that he then placed in the boot. Not after dark or at some other 'suspicious' moment.

No, in broad daylight. He didn't even look around when he put the rubbish bags in the car. He did everything out in the open, where everyone could see. Then he would raise his hand and wave to you in greeting. Or come over and talk for a while. About the weather. About the new people across the street. A normal man. 'I have the feeling you've suddenly remembered something,' the detective says. Then you tell him about the rubbish bags.

Julia's reaction could only mean that Ralph Meier had tried to pull down her bottoms before. During a game, in the pool... I hadn't thought about it much at the time, but now, here at the beach with Caroline, I wondered whether I hadn't passed over it too lightly.

'I have the feeling you're thinking about something,' Caroline said.

I looked my wife straight in the eye. 'Yeah, I was thinking about what you just said. About Emmanuelle and Ralph. And about Julia.'

Now I was thinking about something else too. How would Emmanuelle have reacted if Ralph had pulled down her bikini bottoms? Or Stanley? I blinked my eyes again, but the black spots were still there.

'You should know,' Caroline said. 'You're a man. How do you look, Marc? Do you sometimes look at your own daughter as a woman? As the woman she's going to be?'

I looked at my wife. And I thought about it. She had asked me a question. I didn't think it was a weird question. In fact, not at all. It seemed to me like the only real question you could ask.

'Yes,' I said. 'Not just at Julia. Also at Lisa.'

A man has two daughters. From the time they are little, they sit on his lap. They throw their arms around him and kiss him goodnight. On Sunday morning they crawl into bed with him, snuggle up against him, under the blankets. They're girls. Your girls. You're there to protect them. You can see that, later on, they will be women. That they already are women. But you never look at them the way a man looks at a woman. Never. I'm a doctor. I know what should happen to those who commit incest. There's only one solution. A solution that's not open to discussion under a government constrained by law. But it's the only solution.

'I actually meant something different,' Caroline said. 'Are you able to imagine how men other than you, other than their own father, look at our daughters? No, wait, let's stick to Julia. How does a grown man look at Julia?'

'Come on, you know that. You just said so yourself. There are cultures where she might already be married. And look at Alex. Those two are completely in love. What do we know about what they'll do together later on? Or what they may be doing already? I mean, shouldn't we talk about that? Alex is fifteen. I hope they're aware of what could happen.'

'Honey, I'm not talking about fifteen-year-old boys. I think it's lovely to see the way those two revolve around each other. Yesterday they were holding hands. Under the table, at dinner. I mean, I think Alex is a bit slow, but he's a handsome boy. I understand completely. I know what I'd do if I was Julia.'

'So what do we call that? Women of a certain age who leer at pretty fifteen-year-old boys? Pederasty? Or is there a nicer name for it?'

I laughed as I said it, but Caroline didn't laugh back.

'It's only pederasty when you actually *do* something,' she said. 'I'm not blind. I see pretty fifteen-year-old boys. I enjoy looking at them. But that's where it stops. I don't take the next step. And that's the way men look at girls, of course. Most men. Maybe they fantasise a little more. But they don't *do* anything. Right? I mean, *normal* men don't do anything. That's what I'm really trying to ask you. As a man. To what extent do you, as a man, see this Ralph as being normal?'

'I think he's just as normal as all the men who go off to countries where the entire tourist trade is based on sex with underage girls. And then I'm talking about... what? Tens of thousands, maybe hundreds of thousands of men?'

'And do you think Ralph is one of those tens or hundreds of thousands? If you think so, then I want to leave here today. I'm not going to expose my daughter – or *daughters*, who knows how sick he is – to the randy eyes of a sex tourist any longer. Blegh! Just the thought of it!'

I thought again about Julia's hands clutching at her bikini bottoms. *No!* she'd shouted, *No!* And after that I thought about the raptor look with which Ralph had undressed my wife that time in the foyer of the old municipal theatre. How he had worked his jaws. How he had ground his teeth, as though he could already taste her on his tongue. Men look at women.

Women look at men. But Ralph looked at women as though he were flipping through a copy of *Playboy*. He squeezed his dick as he looked. In his thoughts, or for real. He pulled down the pants of thirteen-year-old girls. Or did he? After all, I hadn't seen him do that with my own eyes. It was always possible, of course, that my daughter only *thought* he was going to do that. Maybe the four of them – Julia, along with Lisa and the boys – had been yanking on each other's swimsuits in the pool earlier. As part of a game. An *innocent* game. Innocent among children between the ages of nine and fifteen; culpable for men in their late forties.

Perhaps, I thought now, I had accused Ralph prematurely in my mind. Plus there was something else: Caroline had just said that if Ralph posed a threat to our daughters, she wanted 'to leave here today'. Maybe that was rushing things a bit.

'And what do you make of this Stanley, actually?' I asked.

'What?'

'Stanley and Emmanuelle. What are we supposed to make of that? How old do you think she is? Nineteen? Eighteen? Seventeen? I mean, technically speaking she may be of legal age, but is it normal? Is it healthy?'

'But isn't that the ultimate, childish fantasy of every man over forty? A teenybopper? Then again… not every man. I don't think, for example, that that's a problem for you.'

'It's not about being a problem. Stanley can just do it. He's a celebrity. The teenyboppers are waiting in line for him. All he has to do is point. Maybe they get something in return. A minor role in one of his films. But maybe not. He doesn't even have to do that. To walk the red carpet with a celebrity, maybe that's enough for a teenybopper.'

'But is that all it is, Marc? That an ordinary family doctor can't get the teenage girls? I've never had the impression that you were even interested.'

'No, you're right. It would make me unhappy pretty quickly. I'd be up for taking a girl like that to a playground, but not to the disco, not any more.'

Caroline started laughing. Then she took my hand. 'You prefer women your own age, right, sweetheart?' she said.

'Yeah,' I said. But I didn't look at her when I said it; I turned my gaze towards the beach and the sea. 'That seems fairer to me.'

21

After a half-hour wait at the letting agency, we were told that the repairman would try to come by that afternoon to fix the water. The girl behind the counter consulted a calendar.

'Today's Friday,' she said. 'We'll do our best. But we're closed over the weekend. That would make it Monday.'

She was an extremely unattractive girl. About twenty-seven kilos overweight, and with scores of pimples and other irregularities on her puffy face. More than irregularities, they were stretches of no-man's land where nothing happened, that didn't move when she spoke, that remained blank when the rest of her face assumed an expression. Maybe she'd been in an accident, it occurred to me. Maybe, as a child, she had slammed her face against the inside of a windscreen.

I leaned a little further over the counter. Before I opened my mouth, I threw a glance, clearly visible to the girl, towards Caroline, who was standing by the door, looking at the photos of other holiday rentals.

'Are you doing anything this weekend?' I asked. 'Tonight? Tomorrow?'

The girl blinked her eyes. They were pretty eyes, it's true. Sweet eyes. She blushed. At least, the living parts of her face turned red, the blood beneath the dead sections probably met with too much resistance to reach the skin's surface.

'I have a boyfriend, sir,' she said quietly.

I winked at her. 'Your boyfriend is a lucky man. I hope he realises just how lucky he is.'

She lowered her eyes. 'He... he's very busy. But I'll ask him to come by this afternoon anyway to check the water at your rental.'

I stared at her. The repairman! The little repairman who had clambered up onto the roof with nude Ralph. Apparently he was a jack-of-all-trades, I reflected, apparently he knew how to unblock more than clogged water reservoirs. I tried to bring the two images together, but got no further than the repairman and the girl watching TV together on the sofa: they were holding hands, with his free hand he raised the thirty-two ounce bottle of Coke to his lips; her free arm was up to the elbow in a family-sized bag of crisps.

'Marc, take a look at this.'

'Look,' Caroline said. 'Isn't this our house?'

I looked where she was pointing. Pasted to a cardboard square were three photos: one of the house, one of part of the garden, and one of the swimming pool.

FOR SALE
summer house with swimming pool

Beneath the photos was a summary of the number of bedrooms and the square footage of both house and garden. At the bottom was the price, a phone number, and an e-mail address.

'That seems quite reasonable to me,' Caroline said.

'Well, it's right in the middle of a residential neighbourhood and a couple of miles from the beach. If I was going to buy something here, I would want it to be right on the beach.'

Caroline ran her index finger down over the other ads. 'Here you go. This one's on the beach.'

This house too was being offered as a 'summer house with swimming pool'. The difference was that it was perched high on a hillside above one of the bays; from the pool one had a view of the sea far below. The asking price was five times that of the house where we had spent the last few days.

'That's what I'm talking about,' I said.

Caroline took my hand, her expression was grave. 'What are we going to do?' she asked.

'Buy that house. After that, we'll see what happens.'

'No, I mean now. When are we going to leave? I really want to get out of that house, Marc.'

I thought about it. Or rather, I pretended to be thinking about it. In fact, I'd already thought about what I'd say when Caroline asked me this.

'Today's Friday,' I said. 'The traffic will be hellish tomorrow, Sunday too. And it will probably be harder to find a place to stay. At a campsite or whatever. So I'd say, let's go on Monday.'

'But then, really go, right?'

'Monday we are gone,' I said.

22

It was the following Saturday morning when Lisa found the little bird. It was lying beside our tent and had probably fallen from the olive tree that grew there.

'Daddy!' Lisa tugged on my sleeping bag. 'Daddy, come and look. A little bird's fallen on the ground.'

The fledgling lay on its side, it shivered and made a fruitless attempt to get back to its feet.

'I think it fell out of its nest,' I said, rubbing the sleep from my eyes. I peered up at the branches, but couldn't see a nest.

'I feel sorry for it,' Lisa said. 'But you're a doctor, Daddy. You'll make him better.'

I picked up the fledgling carefully. It pecked at my hand, but there was almost no force behind its beak. It had no broken legs or other injuries, not from the looks of it. Deep in my heart, I regretted that. A little bird with a broken leg could have been 'a project'. I'd done that kind of thing before while on holiday. The cat with the pinched-off tail on that Greek island two years ago. While I was disinfecting the bloody stump, the cat had bitten me so hard on the forearm that I had to get a tetanus injection myself and a whole series of painful rabies jabs. But it had been worth it. The cat's gratitude was limitless. Within three days it was eating raw lamb from our hands. When the bandages came off, there was a period of adjustment. The wound had healed neatly, but the cat now had trouble keeping its balance with only about an inch of tail left. It climbed into an almond tree and couldn't get back down. When I tried to help by climbing into the tree myself, the cat swiped at my face with its paw and tore open my left eyelid. Then it fell anyway, with a smack, fifteen feet onto the concrete terrace. But it never went away again. It followed us everywhere. In the house, in the garden, to the village, where it waited patiently outside the baker's or the butcher's until we had done our shopping – and it always walked with us the mile to the beach as well.

It was a difficult farewell. Julia and Lisa were in tears. No, we couldn't take the cat with us. It wouldn't be allowed in the plane, a cat without the required vaccinations, it would end up spending months in quarantine. And apart from that, Caroline and I tried to convince the girls, wouldn't the cat be much happier here on its own island? With its family and friends? Where it could hunt mice and lizards? Where the weather was always fine?

'But where is that family of his?' Julia wept. 'Why haven't they ever come by to see how he's doing?'

Whenever I think back on that last day, my eyes go misty. The cat thought it was supposed to come along, it was getting ready to jump onto the back seat. It trotted along behind the car as we bounced down the bumpy dirt drive to the road. In the end, the only thing I could do was climb out and throw stones at it. Our daughters refused to look, and lay crying on the back seat.

Caroline dabbed at her eyes with a tissue. And I cried too. I cried like a child as I picked up the first stone from the roadway. For a moment the cat thought it was all a game, but I aimed well, the stone hit it on the head. Hissing and with the fur standing up on the stump of its tail, it raced off towards the house.

'Sorry, Bert' – on the second day, Lisa had named the cat 'Bert', after a stuck-up teacher at her school – 'we'll come back someday to see how you're doing.'

Now I looked at the fledgling in my hand – and regretted that it was uninjured. It was only little. Too little and too vulnerable to take care of itself.

'Go into the house and be quiet, don't wake anyone,' I said to Lisa. 'A cardboard box, a shoebox or something. And some cotton wool and a face flannel from the bathroom.'

'They have a sort of zoo here,' Judith said. 'Before you get to the beach, if you turn left, the road that goes up the hill. We drove past it once. There's a wall and a fence and a few flags. There's a sign saying "zoo" above the gate and pictures of animals painted on the wall.'

It was breakfast time already, and we were on the patio. The fledgling was in a cardboard box that had once contained bottles of wine. The sides of the box were actually too high; when you looked over the edge and saw the little bird down there, snuggled up against the flannel, you couldn't help being reminded of a prison yard.

'What do you think?' I asked Lisa. 'He's not sick or injured. He's just really little. Too little to take care of himself. Shall we take him to the zoo?'

Lisa looked grave. The box with the bird in it sat on the chair beside her. Every twenty seconds she peeked into it. 'He's drinking,' she would say. Or, 'He's shivering again.'

I expected, no, I *hoped* that Lisa would refuse to take it to the zoo, that she would say she wanted to care for the little bird herself. Until it was big enough to stand on its own legs. Then we would let it go. This was not like with a dog or cat that becomes attached to you. With a bird, all you expect is that it will want to fly, that someday it will want to go away.

It would be a nice moment. A moment I'd be pleased to share with my youngest daughter. You hold the little bird carefully in the palm of your hand. You hold up your hand. The bird flutters its wings and takes off, hesitantly at first, clumsily. But then it regains its balance on a low-hanging branch. It sits there for a bit. It fluffs up its feathers and looks around. At us, its rescuers. It's grateful, we tell ourselves. Then it tilts its head to one side, fixes an eye on the sky and flies away.

The plan was that we would leave on Monday. I doubted whether the little bird would be strong enough in two days' time. But we could always take it along, I reasoned, in the box, on the back seat.

That was the ideal scenario. *My* ideal scenario. But Lisa asked: 'Will they think he's special enough, there at the zoo?'

'What do you mean, special enough?'

Lisa nibbled on her lower lip, then sighed deeply. 'In a zoo they mostly have tigers and elephants and stuff, right? And this is a really ordinary little bird. Maybe they won't think he's special enough.'

At that, everyone burst out laughing. Judith, Ralph, everyone – even Emmanuelle laughed along from behind her sunglasses, but without bothering to ask anyone what we were laughing about.

The zookeeper wore khaki shorts and a white T-shirt. When he peered into the box, a tender smile appeared on his face.

'It's really kind of you to bring him here,' he told Lisa. 'A little bird like this often won't survive a single day without its mother.'

'What's he saying?' Lisa asked.

I translated what the zookeeper had said. Lisa nodded seriously. 'So what are they going to do with him?'

'We'll keep him here for a few days,' the keeper said. 'For a week, if necessary. Until he gets his strength back. But you sometimes see, with birds like this, that they don't want to return to nature. That they've already become too attached to people. If that's the case, then he can stay here for the rest of his life.'

The zookeeper led us to the aviary, so Lisa could see where the little bird would be staying. I didn't see much in the way of spectacular animals along the way. A few deer, sheep with big horns, an immensely fat black pig, and a couple of peacocks and storks. A wolf stood rubbing its fur against the bars of a cage that was too small for it.

'Do you also have llamas?' I asked the zookeeper.

He shook his head. 'All the animals here are fairly common, as you can see. We have a chamois and a couple of springboks, but that's about all.'

'Imagine there's someone around here with a llama,' I said, 'and suddenly that person can no longer care for it. Or for his other animals. Would you take them in?'

'We would be very pleased to welcome a llama. But we draw no distinctions. We'll give shelter to any homeless animal. Temporarily or permanently. Sometimes we find a new owner for them. But we're very careful about that. We always look first to see whether someone is truly an animal lover.'

'That's nice to hear,' I said. 'If you give me your phone number, I'll think of you if I hear anything.'

At the summer house we found Alex, Julia and Thomas in the pool.

'Your wife went into town with my father and Stanley and Emmanuelle,' Alex said when I asked where the others were. 'My mother and grandmother are the only ones here.'

I looked up at the second floor of the house. I saw Judith's mother sitting in front of the kitchen window. She had her back to me. Lisa had already run to our tent to get her swimming things.

'Did they say when they'd be back?' I asked Alex.

'No. But they only just left. Maybe ten minutes ago.'

*

Judith and her mother were sitting at the little kitchen table. Judith was painting her mother's nails. Nothing flashy, something pinkish, almost transparent – a suitable colour for an old woman.

'Well?' Judith asked. 'Did you find the zoo?'

There was a pot of coffee on the stove and a saucepan with a little steamed milk. I looked at the clock above the kitchen door. Eleven-thirty. Why not? I didn't feel much like coffee anyway.

'They were very nice,' I said as I opened the fridge and took out a can of beer. 'That made it easier for Lisa to say farewell to her little bird.'

There was an empty chair at the kitchen table, but somehow I felt it would be unseemly to sit down beside the two women with a beer in my hand. So I remained standing. I leaned against the counter and opened the can. After only two mouthfuls it already felt light in my hand.

'Are you my daughter's new doctor too?' the old woman asked without looking at me.

'No, Mum,' Judith said. 'I already told you. He's Ralph's new doctor, that's all.'

Now Judith's mother turned her head to look at me. 'But when you called that time you said something else. You said—'

'May I?' I stepped forward quickly and picked up a pack of cigarettes and the lighter from the table.

'Mum, would you please sit still? Otherwise I'll get polish all over you,' Judith said.

'He said he was your doctor,' Judith's mother said.

I lit a cigarette and tossed the empty beer can into the pedal bin. Then I opened the fridge and took another one. Judith looked at me questioningly. I shrugged.

'I'm sure you're right,' I said, looking at Judith the whole time. 'I'm sure I must have made a mistake. I must have said I was your daughter's doctor.'

That always worked, I knew from a doctor's experience: complimenting old people on their ironclad memory.

'You see?' Judith's mother said, sure enough. Judith winked at me. And I winked back. 'You see, I don't have Alzheimer's after all.'

'You're much too young for that anyway, Vera,' I said.

Perhaps it was the beer that made me overconfident. I had never called Judith's mother by her first name before. But that always worked too, I knew, not only from the practice, but also outside the professional context: calling women by their first name. As often as possible. Preferably in every sentence.

Judith's mother – Vera – giggled.

'He's sweet,' she told her daughter. Her nails were finished. She stood up and flapped her hands. 'No, he really is sweet. I've seen the way he is around his daughters.'

Only then did she look at me. I saw two red blushes on her cheeks. Cheeks that were almost without a wrinkle. A cautious life. Without excesses. A life of whole-wheat bread and buttermilk. Of long bicycle rides through nature reserves.

'Oh yes,' she went on, looking me straight in the eye now. 'I have eyes in my head. I've seen how sweet you are with your daughters. Not all fathers are like that. And I've seen how your daughters show how much they love you. They're not pretending. It's for real.'

Now it was my turn to blush slightly. First of all, I couldn't recall ever having heard Judith's mother speak so many sentences one after the other – and especially not addressed to me. Secondly, I thought I detected a critical tone, a slightly sarcastic intonation when she said 'Not all fathers are like that'. I may have been imagining things, but I thought she glanced over at her daughter as she said that.

I looked her straight in the eye too. I tried to warn her against myself. Perhaps she was disappointed in the choice her daughter had made. *Not all fathers are like that.* She thought I was 'sweet'. Sweeter than Ralph Meier, from the sound of it. But then I wasn't all *that* sweet – at least not in the way she thought.

The sound of laughter came from the garden. Someone clapped his hands. Someone else whistled through his fingers. Judith's mother turned to the window, and Judith looked outside too.

'Oh, look at that!' she said.

Two steps and I was at the window. I had a choice between the left side of the kitchen table, beside Judith's mother, or the right side, where Judith was still sitting.

I chose to stand beside her mother.

Below us, at the pool, Julia and Lisa were standing by the diving board. Alex and Thomas were sitting on the edge of the pool, their feet in the water. First Julia walked forward, to the end of the board. She paused there for a moment, rose up on the balls of her feet and raised her arms in the air like a ballerina. Then she lowered her arms to her sides, spun around twice and walked back. Alex applauded, Thomas whistled loudly three times through his fingers.

Then it was Lisa's turn. She walked much more quickly than her older sister, in a flash she was at the end of the diving board, where she spun around so quickly that she lost her balance and fell backwards into the water. Now both boys clapped their hands. Alex picked up the garden hose that was coiled beside the pool and turned the spray on Julia. I expected my daughter to run away, but she stayed put. She even rose up on tiptoe as the water splashed across her bikini and bare stomach. She placed her hands behind her head, lifted her wet hair as though she were going to put it up, then shook it loose again.

'Are you kids being careful?' Judith shouted from the window. It was a needless warning: it was perfectly clear that the spraying was a matter of mutual consent. Fascinated, I looked at my eldest daughter. No, I wasn't mistaken: behind the jet of water, or rather, behind the space where the water created a fine haze of droplets, there danced the colours of a miniature rainbow.

'We're playing Miss Wet T-shirt, Mum!' Thomas shouted through cupped hands. 'Julia's winning!'

'No she's not!' shouted Lisa, who was just clambering up the ladder onto the side. 'Now you have to spray me, Alex! Now you have to spray me!'

Judith turned her head and looked at me. I could tell from her expression that she was trying hard not to laugh. I shrugged and smiled back.

'They're such sweet girls,' Judith's mother said. 'You're a lucky man, Marc, to have such lovely daughters. I'd take very good care of them if I were you.' She stepped away from the window. 'But now I'm tired. I think I'll go to my room for a bit.'

23

Then we were sitting across from each other at the little kitchen table. Judith had poured herself a glass of white wine and added two ice cubes. I had taken my third beer from the fridge. On the table between us was a bowl of olives. We had both lit another cigarette.

For a while we said nothing at all. We looked out of the window, at the garden, and the pool where the Miss Wet T-shirt contest had come to an end. Alex and Julia were lying together in a deckchair. Julia was leaning her head against Alex's upper arm, her open hand lay on his stomach, just below his navel. Thomas and Lisa were nowhere in sight, but from behind the house we could hear the sounds of a bouncing ping-pong ball.

For the first time since we'd arrived, Judith and I were alone together. I looked at her. I slid my hand across the tabletop, took her middle and ring finger between my thumb and index finger and gently pulled her hand towards me.

'Marc...' She laid her cigarette in the ashtray. She breathed a deep sigh, glanced outside and then looked at me. 'I don't know, Marc... I don't know whether—'

'We could take a walk,' I said. 'Or we could go to the beach. In my car.'

I was still tugging at her fingers. I caressed the back of her hand. I could drive us somewhere, I thought. Not to the beach, but into the hills, along one of those windy sand roads along the coast. I remembered a clearing in the woods and an almost deserted parking area we'd driven to once. From there it had been more than an hour's walk to one of Ralph's beaches. But we didn't have to go to the beach at all. The parking area would be good enough.

'I don't know whether my mother…' Judith said. 'I don't know what she'll think if she wakes up and we're not here.'

'We'll leave a note,' I said. 'That we've gone out to get something.' I held up my can and grinned. 'Maybe we'll run out of beer all of a sudden.'

Judith tossed a quick glance at the kitchen door, which was slightly ajar. 'Marc, this feels… weird.' She was speaking very quietly now, almost in a whisper. 'I think it's weird. I feel uneasy. My mother. The kids. Your wife… I mean, they could come back at any moment.'

I put down my can of beer and lay my cigarette in the ashtray too. 'Judith…' I leaned across the table, my face closer to hers. She looked out of the window, at the pool. 'Wait a minute,' she said. She pulled her fingers from my grasp, got up and walked on tiptoe to the kitchen door. There she turned and raised a finger to her lips. 'Just going to take a look,' she said.

She left the door open. I watched as she went, soundlessly still, into the living room and then turned left, into the hallway where the bathroom and bedrooms were. I raised my cigarette from the ashtray and took a drag. The first cigarette, the one I'd had a little less than a week ago at the campsite, had still tasted like the first cigarette ever. I had felt the same dizziness as back then, as an eleven-year-old boy on the playground. But in time the cigarettes had started to taste the way they had fifteen years ago, in the days before I quit. Normal. Like cigarettes. A few days ago I had bought a pack of my own.

I heard muffled voices from the bedrooms. I sighed and stood up. There was still one can of beer in the fridge. It was indeed high time for someone to do a little shopping.

I popped open the tab and raised the can to my mouth. I was still standing by the fridge when Judith came back. It went very fast. I put my arms around her waist and pulled her against me. First I kissed her neck. I put the can down on the counter. With my free hand I pulled her up tight and kissed her again, closer to her ear this time. She giggled; she placed both hands on my chest and acted as though she was trying to push me away. But she barely applied any force. I let my hands slide down to her rear, she was wearing only a thin, unbuttoned blouse over her bikini, I worked my fingers up from below, under the elastic of her bottoms.

'Marc,' she whispered. 'My mother… my mother is awake. She—'

'Judith,' I said into her ear. 'My sweet, lovely Judith.'

Then I felt her hand. Her fingers. They were doing something to the front of my body, around my stomach. I was wearing a buttoned sports shirt that hung loosely over my shorts. She pulled the shirt up and at the same time loosened two of the buttons. With her nails she tickled the area under my navel, then her fingers slid down. It was only a short distance from her ear to her lips. A short distance over which I tried to take an eternity. Meanwhile, I had my whole hand in her bikini bottoms. I spread my fingers over her buttocks and pressed, first gently, then harder. She tilted her head and stuck the tip of her tongue between my lips. She licked a little at the tip of my own tongue, then pulled hers back. I saw that she had her eyes closed. Like all women. I kept mine open. Like all men. And because I had my eyes open, I also saw the kitchen door. Behind Judith's hair. Behind my own forearm and the hand (my other hand, the hand that wasn't pressing against her buttocks) that still had its fingers in that hair.

You have it sometimes with a book you've left on the table. You go out of the room for a minute, and when you come back there's something different. In that same way, I knew for sure that Judith had left the kitchen door slightly ajar when she came back. Not closed, no, slightly ajar.

I remembered in any case that the door had been open a crack at the moment when I'd first pulled her up against me, and that now it was open just a fraction more. Still a crack, but a *bigger* crack.

At that same moment I saw something move on the other side of the crack. A shadow on the floor, nothing more than that. There was no sound. Sometimes seconds stretch out into a new unit of time. A unit that corresponds exactly with your heartbeat.

I stared at the door. Maybe I was imagining things. But then the shadow moved again. There could be no mistake about it. Someone was behind the door.

I pulled my hand out of Judith's bottoms and placed it against her stomach. I pushed her away gently, removing my hand from her hair at the same time.

Apparently Judith thought it was all part of a teasing sort of foreplay: that I was simply trying out a new variation. Attracting. Repelling. Delaying. She made a little sound, somewhere between a moan and a sigh, she smiled and wrapped her own hand around mine, which was pressing against her stomach.

But she did open her eyes. She looked at my mouth. At my lips, which soundlessly formed the words.

The door. There's someone behind the door.

Judith was still standing on tiptoe, now she slowly sank back down until she was three inches shorter again. She looked up at me and I saw her pupils, dilating and then contracting. She let go of my hand and pushed me away.

'Would you like another beer, Marc?' she asked. 'I'll take a look. I hope we still have some.'

Her voice sounded normal. *Too* normal. The way a voice sounds when it's doing its utmost to sound normal. She used both hands to arrange her hair. I pulled my shirt back down over my trousers and buttoned it.

And so we stood there, like two teenagers caught in the act. I saw the blush on Judith's cheeks. My face had undoubtedly changed colour too. Our hair might be neatly arranged, our clothing straightened as much as possible, but it was the blushing that would give us away.

Judith took a few steps back towards the door. At the same time she gestured to me: *open the fridge*.

But that isn't what I did. I did something else. Later, I would often ask myself why. A premonition, people say, but it was stronger than that. A shiver. A pounding heart. Or more like a heart that skips a beat. A moment in a horror film: the bloodied sheet is pulled back and, indeed, there is someone underneath. A corpse. A corpse with a crushed skull, the arms and legs have been expertly sawn off and divided among various rubbish bags.

I stepped to the window and looked out. There was no one by the pool any more. The deckchair where Alex and Julia had just been lying was empty.

'Mum?'

I turned around and saw Judith push open the kitchen door. 'Mum?'

I leaned out of the window, but it was one of those with a low frame; I leaned out so far that I almost lost my balance. The pounding of my heart was growing louder all the time. Panic. Adrenaline. The heart is preparing for flight, I knew that as a doctor. For flight or a fight. It pumps at full speed to get oxygen out to all parts of the body as quickly as possible. The parts where the oxygen is needed most badly: the feet for running, the hands to enable fists to be planted as hard as possible in an opponent's face.

I saw no one. I listened. *I pricked up my ears*, as they say, but only animals can prick up their ears. I didn't hear anything.

There wasn't a breath of wind. The leaves hung still and limp on the trees. You often heard crickets on hot days like this, but apparently it was too hot even for the crickets.

There was something missing, although at first I didn't know exactly what. A sound in the silence. A sound that had been there just a moment before.

Ping-pong balls! The sound of bouncing ping-pong balls.

I held my breath. But I wasn't mistaken. Behind the house, where the ping-pong table stood, everything was silent too.

'Mum?' Judith had now gone through the doorway and was standing in the living room. 'Mum?'

Now it was my turn to walk to the kitchen door. As calmly as possible. As normally as possible. Nothing had happened, I told myself. Not yet. I tried to smile. A light-hearted smile. But my lips were so dry they hurt.

I slipped past Judith and made a beeline for the front door.

'Marc...'

She was standing at the bathroom door, trying to open it, but it was locked. 'Mum? Are you in there?'

'I'll take a look outside first,' I said, and I was gone, out of the front door, down the stairs and the tiled path to the pool.

A little too quickly, I realised just in time. Nothing was wrong. Nothing unseemly had happened. If my daughters were still in the garden, it was crucial that I did not seem alarmed. A panting, red-faced father would give the wrong signal. *What's wrong, Daddy? Your face is all red! You're panting! You look like you've seen a ghost.*

I slowed down. Beside the deserted swimming pool, I stopped. For the space of one indivisible second I stared into the water. The glistening water that reflected the treetops and the bright blue sky. Squinting, I examined the bottom of the pool. But there was nothing there. No motionless body with hair fanning out from its head. Only the blue tiles.

I walked on, around the back of the house. There was no one at the ping-pong table either. The paddles lay on either side of the net. One of them was resting on the ball.

The tent. The zipper was closed. I didn't want to surprise or startle my daughters. So I coughed.

'Julia…? Lisa…?'

I squatted down and opened the zipper, but the tent was empty. I walked further, all the way around the house, till I finally got back to the front steps. Again, I had to force myself not to take the steps two at a time.

'My mother's taking a shower,' said Judith, who was still standing at the bathroom door.

'And the kids? Have you seen the kids?'

Without waiting for her reply I walked into the hall where the bedrooms were. I knocked on the door of the room Alex and Thomas shared. There was no answer, but I did hear something: a vague murmur, as though a radio were playing very softly.

I opened the door. Alex, Thomas, Lisa and Julia were lying together on the two single beds, which had been pushed together. Thomas, in the middle, had a notebook computer on his lap.

'Hi, hello!' I said cheerfully – much too cheerfully I realised right away, but by then it was too late. 'Is this where you guys are?' I said. What I felt like most was slamming my fist against my face. The way you slam your hand against the TV when the picture goes on the blink. I wanted to knock the false cheerfulness out of my voice.

Lisa glanced at me; Julia acted as though no one had come into the room. Only Alex shifted a little against the pillows, so that his arm hung a bit more loosely around the shoulders of my elder daughter.

Thomas laughed at something on the screen. Alex, Julia and Lisa didn't laugh with him.

'What are you watching?' I asked.

I had to repeat my question before anyone answered. It was Alex. '*South Park*, Mr Schlosser.'

Had he ever called me Mr Schlosser before? Not that I knew of. Not that I could remember. He always called Caroline 'Mrs Schlosser', even though we'd told him any number of times that that wasn't necessary.

I took a deep breath. No more cheeriness! 'Do you kids feel like playing ping-pong later? A tournament? All of us?'

Once again, at first, there was no answer.

'Maybe,' Alex said at last.

I looked at Lisa and Julia. I might have been imagining it, but it seemed as though Julia in particular wasn't really interested in the computer screen. As though she was doing her best to ignore me as completely as possible.

'Julia?' My heart started pounding again. I moistened my

lips with the tip of my tongue. The *guilty* tip of my tongue, it occurred to me at that same moment. I tried to obliterate the thought, but only half-succeeded. At all costs, I had to make sure nothing went shaky. My voice. My lower lip. My arms and legs. My whole body.

'Julia!'

Now, finally, she looked up at me. Listlessly. A neutral look.

'Julia, I'm talking to you!'

She held my gaze. 'I can hear that,' she said. 'And what was it you wanted to say?'

Indeed, what was it I wanted to say? I had no idea. Something about a ping-pong tournament. No, I'd already done that. I looked my daughter right in the eye. I saw nothing. No accusation. No sadness. Maybe she simply found it annoying that I was still standing there in the doorway.

'Are you drinking enough, Julia?' I said. 'I mean, it's very hot out. You have to watch out that you don't become dehydrated. All of you. Do you want me to make you a big jug of lemonade?'

It was way too much, all this crap I was coming out with. Too obvious. Julia looked back at the computer screen.

'Whatever,' she said.

'Yes please, Mr Schlosser,' Alex said. 'Or else maybe you could just bring us some Coke.'

I remained standing there for a couple of seconds. I could say something. I could raise my voice. *That's no way to talk to your father!* But something inside me whispered that this was not the right moment. *That I didn't have the right…* This was the other voice that was whispering to me, the voice of the *guilty tongue*.

I walked back to the hallway, where Judith's mother was just coming out of the bathroom. She was wearing a white bathrobe and had a towel wrapped around her head.

'Hello, Marc,' she said. She looked at me for a moment and smiled. Then she walked past me to her room.

I looked at Judith. Judith shrugged and gestured with her hands. A gesture meant to say *I don't know either*. At the same moment, we heard a car door slam outside. And then another. Four car doors in total.

'Jesus!' Judith said. 'They didn't waste any time.'

I went to her. I put my hand on her arm.

'Take it easy,' I said. 'We just act normal. Nothing happened.'

I walked to the front door and opened it. At the bottom of the steps, Caroline, Stanley and Emmanuelle were standing beside Ralph's car. Ralph was leaning over the open boot.

'Hello there,' I said. Cheerful again, but at least this time it sounded natural. I welcomed them with a wave of my hand. Only Caroline looked up at me.

'Hello there,' she said.

'Marc!' Ralph said. 'Give us a hand. You and Stanley. This is way too heavy.'

He pulled something halfway out of the boot. I saw the tailfin of a fish. A gigantic fish.

'A swordfish, Marc!' Ralph shouted. 'There was no way we could pass this one up. It's going on the coals tonight. This is the real thing, buddy!'

24

That Saturday evening the village was celebrating midsummer's eve. With fireworks and bonfires on the beach. You could hear the explosions all day long. The fireworks weren't like the ones at home. No rockets that blew apart in dozens of colours – only dark, heavy detonations. It sounded less like fireworks than like an artillery barrage or bombardment. Thuds you felt deep down in your chest. Beneath your ribs. Behind your heart.

The plan was that we would all go to the beach together. But first, of course, we had to eat. Ralph chopped the swordfish into pieces. With a hatchet, right on the patio tiles. At first the children found it fascinating, but with every blow of the hatchet they moved a few steps back. Organs appeared: the liver, bits of hard roe, the swim bladder, and a glistening, dark-brown organ the size of a rugby ball that no one recognised. On occasion, Ralph chopped right through the fish and splinters of tile flew in all directions.

'Be a little careful, dear,' Judith said. 'We still have to reclaim the security deposit from the letting agency.'

But Ralph was taking such obvious pleasure in the chopping that he didn't seem to hear her. He was down on his haunches and had kicked off his flip-flops. I looked at his bare feet; from time to time the hatchet came down awfully close to his toes on the tiles. I looked on as a physician. Just to be safe, I tried to work out what I would have to do first. If kept cool, toes and fingers could be put back on at the hospital. If Ralph planted the hatchet in one or more of his toes, someone would have to keep a level head. There was a doctor in the house. It would be up to the doctor to staunch the flow of blood and wrap the toes in a wet towel with ice cubes. Women and children might faint; perhaps only the doctor would be able to keep cool. *Judith, ice from the freezer! And a wet towel! Caroline, help me apply a tourniquet to his calf, he's losing too much blood! Stanley, start the car and fold down the back seat! Julia, Lisa, Alex, Thomas, go inside, you're only getting in the way. Leave Emmanuelle where she is, just put a pillow under her head, she'll come around in a bit…* It would be my opportunity to shine in a leading role, the role for which I was perfectly suited, but the hatchet came down only once within a fraction of an inch of Ralph's big toe, after that he became more cautious.

'What are you looking at, Marc?' he said. 'Ah, starting to get hungry already, are you? Listen, do me a favour and get me another beer.'

Darkness fell. Every now and then the flames under the grill shot up high. We were sitting around the patio, working on the beer and white wine. Judith had laid out plates of olives, anchovies and spicy little sausages. Chunks of swordfish hissed on the barbecue. Whenever I looked at Judith, at her face cast in a yellow-golden light by the fire, she lowered her eyes. Caroline stared straight ahead and took little sips of her wine. She also seemed to be doing her best not to look at me. *I'm sitting here*, her body language said. *I'm sitting here, but I'd rather be somewhere else.*

Thomas and Lisa were playing ping-pong. Alex and Julia were back in the deckchair by the pool. They each had a white earbud from Julia's iPod in one ear. In the last few hours I had tried a few times to establish direct contact with my elder daughter, but to no avail. Whenever I asked her a question she would shrug and breathe a deep sigh. 'Are you looking forward to the beach later on?' I asked, just for the sake of asking something. 'To seeing the fireworks?' And she shrugged. And sighed. 'Listen, if you guys don't feel like it, we can stay here,' I said, feeling my face start to flush. 'We can play Risk or something… Monopoly…' Julia pulled her hair up onto the top of her head and let it fall again. 'We'll see,' she said, and then turned around and walked away. Without giving me so much as a look. It was as though all the women were making a game out of not looking at me. The only exceptions were Lisa and Judith's mother. While the meal was being prepared, Vera smiled at me a few times. And while Ralph was whacking away at the swordfish, she had even shaken her head as she smiled at me. And Lisa? Lisa still looked at me the way eleven-year-old daughters look at their fathers. As though looking at the ideal man. The one they want to marry later on.

I had to try to catch Julia's eye, I told myself. Her eyes couldn't lie. One glimpse would be enough. In my daughter's eyes I would be able to read the awful truth. Or not. It was still possible, of course, that I was imagining the whole thing. Maybe something had happened between her and Alex. Maybe she had gone through a rapid process of 'growing up', as they call it, and no longer felt any desire for the obnoxious presence of a whining father. That was biology. There was no getting around biology.

'I thought that was pretty interesting, what you told us this afternoon, Stanley,' Ralph said as he distributed the first chunks of grilled swordfish. 'In the car. I think Marc would be interested too.'

I looked at Stanley, more out of politeness than interest. If I noticed the slightest disinclination in his expression, I would pursue it no further. He stabbed his fork into the swordfish, producing a puddle of juice on his plate, then cut off a good-sized chunk and put it in his mouth.

'Well, yeah,' he said.

At that very moment, in a neighbouring garden, a rocket took off. We had seen rockets taking off before, but never from so close by. Everyone held their breath while the projectile drilled its way into the sky with a hiss and a luminous trail of sparks. Then came the explosion. The explosion and the flash. Or actually, the other way around. The light travelled faster than the sound. Directly above our heads the rocket blew apart, our faces lit up white in the explosion, while the blast took a little more time to reach us. It was a blast like the earlier ones. Heavy and hard. A lightning bolt. A direct hit from a mortar shell. A car bomb. But so close this time that it seemed to fill your whole body. From the inside out. It started in the pit of your stomach, surged like rolling thunder along the inside of your ribs, only to leave the body at last through the jaws and eardrums. Women and children shrieked. Men and boys cursed. A bottle fell over and shattered on the patio. Somewhere down the street a car alarm went off. 'Holy fuck!' said Ralph, who had dropped an entire hunk of swordfish on the tiles. The blast echoed back and forth between the hills a few times. Then faded.

'Wow!' That was Alex. He and Julia had pulled the white buds out of their ears and climbed out of the deckchair. Julia was looking around in fright. She looked at her mother. At Ralph. At Judith. Even at Stanley and Emmanuelle. At pretty much everyone except me.

'Dad, Dad! Can we get some of those rockets too?' Thomas came running up from the ping-pong table. 'Dad! Are we gonna blast 'em like that too?'

'This is absolutely outrageous,' Judith said. 'What kind of pleasure can anyone get from that?'

I looked at Judith's face. It radiated sincere indignation. Caroline placed a hand on her chest and breathed in and out deeply a few times. At that moment I thought about the differences between men and women. The *irreconcilable* differences. The differences you can never explain.

Men go for the loudest bang. The louder the better. In women's eyes, that makes them more boyish. More childish. So boyish and childish that it makes women smile pityingly. *They never grow up*, they tell each other. And they're right. I remember how, as a boy of sixteen, I flouted all the rules when setting off fireworks. I never used a safety lighter. Always an open flame. A real flame. The flame from a match or a cigarette lighter. Fire was what I wanted to see, not some pussy glowing safety lighter. I didn't put the rockets in an empty bottle at a safe distance. I lit them in my hand. I wanted to feel the power of the rocket between my fingers. That way, something of that power became your own. The first time I held the rocket so tightly that splinters from the wooden stick bored into my fingers when the rocket yanked free of my grasp and raced for the sky. Later I learned the right way to do it. To hold it loosely. You had to give the rocket as little resistance as possible. The rocket had a will of its own. It wanted to go up. At moments like that I never thought about the evening's festive nature. Let alone about the new year that was on its way. I thought about war. About missiles and anti-aircraft guns. About rebel movements shooting the helicopters and transport planes of a technologically superior foe out of the air with portable, shoulder-held, surface-to-air missiles. Often I couldn't resist the temptation and aimed the rocket at an angle more oblique than might be considered strictly prudent. Then it would explode against the windows of the neighbours across the street. 'Sorry!' I would shout when a window opened and a startled neighbour leaned out. 'Sorry, it went completely in the wrong direction.' I would adopt my most hypocritical expression. The expression of the football player who slides into his opponent with his leg stretched out in front of him and cripples him for life. *Sorry, I guess I kind of slipped...* I aimed the next rocket at a group of partygoers further down the street. It was war. You're better off winning a war than losing it. History teaches us that. And biology. You're better off beating someone to death than being beaten to death. From time immemorial, the man has guarded the entrance to the cave. Intruders are sent packing. People. Animals. A persistent intruder can't say later that he hasn't been warned. 'A man avoids a fight only when the odds are too heavy,' Professor Herzl taught us in medical biology. 'When the opponent is his equal or weaker, he weighs his chances. He clenches his fists. He weighs the heft of the sword in his hand. Of the pistol. He turns the turret of his tank just a fraction of a second faster than the enemy. He aims and fires. He survives.'

Ralph bent down, stuck the barbecue fork into the piece of swordfish that had fallen to the ground and put it back on the grill. A broad grin appeared on his face. 'Go take a look in the shed, buddy,' he said. 'That door just past the ping-pong table. You too, Alex.'

As the two boys ran to the back of the house, I felt a sudden emptiness. An emptiness somewhere at the back of my heart. Ralph had bought fireworks. And I hadn't. Yesterday I had gone past one of the little stalls where they sold them. It was made of corrugated iron and stood at the edge of the village. I'd hesitated. I had slowed down. *Just take a look at what they've got.* But there had been no place to park, so I had driven on.

If I'd had two sons, like Ralph, then I would have parked the car even if I'd had to walk five miles back to the stall, I realised now. But I had two daughters. I remembered a particular New Year's Eve a few years back. Against my own better judgement I had gone out and bought a packet of rockets and firecrackers. At midnight I set up the first rocket in a wine bottle in front of our door. I tied together the fuses of three firecrackers, lit them and tossed them in the air. But Julia and Lisa only remained standing in the doorway. At the first explosion they ducked back into the house. Then Caroline appeared in the doorway. The three of them stood there and looked at me. I lit more rockets. I put an empty can on top of a firecracker to make a bigger bang. In the meantime Caroline had given each of the girls a sparkler, but they didn't really come outside after that. Standing in the doorway, they stretched their arms out as far as possible, so the sparks wouldn't fall on the welcome mat. From there they looked at their father. A father who was, to put it mildly, acting peculiar. *Like a twelve-year-old boy*. During wartime, the women sew the uniforms. They fill the grenades at the munitions factory. They contribute to the war effort, as they say. But the actual *throwing* of the grenades they leave to the men.

'Dad, Dad! Can we set one off now?'

Alex and Thomas had come back from the shed carrying two bundles of rockets, some of which were longer than they were tall. There were almost too many for them to carry. Two or three rockets fell onto the patio.

'Don't you think we should wait a bit?' Ralph said. 'We're all going to the beach in about an hour.'

'But the people next door lit one already,' Alex said.

'Oh, come on, Dad,' Thomas said. 'Please?'

Ralph shook his head. Laughing, he took an empty bottle from the table. 'OK, but just one,' he said.

I looked at the pile of rockets lying between the boys on the patio. Even the smallest ones were a yard long. Stacked up neatly on the tiles now, they reminded me of a captured arms cache. The secret munitions dump of a guerrilla movement or terrorist cell. The technologically superior foe had tanks and planes. The occupying forces had helicopters that could fire laser-guided missiles, but the primitive Qassam rockets, fired at random civilian targets, caused more psychological damage.

'No, not here,' Ralph said. 'Not so close to the other ones. One spark and we'd all be blown to kingdom come, along with the house. Let's do it down by the pool.'

'Are you sure this is a good idea?' Judith asked.

'Better wait till we get to the beach,' said Caroline.

'I'm going inside,' Judith's mother said.

But Ralph just laughed. 'Come on, boys will be boys, right? These guys can't wait.'

I looked away from the rocket, which Alex and Thomas were now positioning in the bottle at the pool's edge, towards my daughters. When the fuse flared they put their fingers in their ears. Julia shrieked when the rocket took off out of the bottle with a loud hiss, and the bottle fell over and broke. A few shards ended up in the pool.

The bang came much sooner than expected. Loud and deep, louder and deeper than the one the neighbours had launched just a few minutes earlier. It started beneath the soles of your feet and thundered its way up, used the space inside your chest to achieve its full wingspan, then ended up in your head. There was a brief instant when breathing came to a halt. This time a few car alarms started howling. Dogs began barking hysterically. Julia and Lisa screamed. '*Merde!*' said a woman's voice; when we turned around we saw Emmanuelle, holding only the base and the broken stem of her wineglass. The rest lay in shards at her feet. There were big red stains on her white blouse.

'Well, are you satisfied now?' Judith cried.

'Another one! Another one!' Thomas screamed.

'Fucking A!' Alex said, whistling low through his teeth. 'Heavy shit!'

'OK, one more,' Ralph said.

'Don't even think about it!' Judith said. 'Do me a favour, take that stuff down with you to the beach and have fun! Ralph, I suppose you heard me?'

Ralph raised both hands in a gesture of mollification. 'OK, OK, we're going to the beach.'

I was overtaken again by a deep sense of regret. Regret that I hadn't bought any rockets of my own. I wouldn't have given in as quickly as Ralph did. I tried to catch Caroline's eye. My own wife was perhaps no fan of loud explosions, but I didn't think – in all the years we'd been together – that I'd ever heard her say *Marc, I suppose you heard me?*

And at the same moment we actually did catch each other's eye. Caroline was standing beside Emmanuelle, she had one hand on Emmanuelle's shoulder, with the fingers of her other hand she was brushing at the wine stains on Emmanuelle's blouse. Then she turned her head and looked at me.

There was no mistaking it: my wife winked at me. I wasn't

completely sure whether the wink was only to do with the wine-stained T-shirt or with the whole situation and Judith's annoyance, but that didn't matter much. Above all, Caroline saw the *funny* side of it. She absolutely wanted to leave on Monday, so she'd said, but in her mind she had apparently already bade farewell to the Meiers and their summer house. No, not so much bade farewell: she had *taken a step back*. As I winked back at her, I thought about what had happened in the kitchen earlier that day. About the tip of my tongue against Judith's teeth, my hand on her butt. I thought about her fingers tugging at my shorts.

The rockets were scooped up, some of the group went inside to get sweaters or jackets, in case it got chilly on the beach later, and then we met at the cars. Emmanuelle announced that she didn't want to come, and Stanley didn't try very hard to change her mind. Judith's mother stayed at home too.

Julia and Lisa wanted to go with Alex and Thomas in the back of Ralph's car. There was a moment, just before Judith settled into the passenger seat beside Ralph, when she leaned against the open car door and looked at me. I looked back, I maintained eye contact with her the way you maintain eye contact with a woman when you have other motives. Ulterior motives. I saw the light from the lamp above the garage door reflected in her eyes. I thought about the possibilities of the beach. There would be a lot of people around. We could get separated. *Some people* could get separated. Others could definitely find each other.

'I was just thinking: maybe I'll stay too.' Caroline had showed up beside me and laid her hand on my arm.

'Really?' I said, turning my head a little to one side, so the light above the garage door no longer lit my face. 'Well, there's no reason for you to go if you don't feel like it. I don't mind. If you're tired, I'll go on my own.'

25

Sometimes you run your life back to see at what point it could have taken a different turn. But sometimes there's nothing at all to run back – you yourself don't know it yet, but the only button that's still working is forward. You wish you could freeze the picture… *Here*, you tell yourself. *If I'd said something else… done something else.*

I went to the beach that evening. And when I came back I was a different person. Not for a while, or for a couple of days, no: for ever.

You get a stain on your trousers. Your favourite pair of trousers. You wash them ten times in a row at 160 degrees. You scrub and scour and rub. You bring in the heavy artillery. Bleaches. Abrasive cleaners. But the spot doesn't go away. If you scrub and scour too long, it will only be replaced by something else. By a stretch of fabric that is thinner and paler. The paler cloth is the memory. The memory of the spot. Now there are two things you can do. You can throw the trousers away, or you can walk around for the rest of your life with the memory of the stain. But the paler cloth reminds you of more than just the stain. It also reminds you of when the trousers were still clean.

If you run things back far enough, the clean trousers finally show up. By then, you know that they're not going to stay clean. I know that I will keep running things back for the rest of my life. *Was this where it was?* I'll ask myself again and again. *Or was it further back? There?* I hit pause.

Here it's still clean.

And here, not any more.

We had barely lurched our way down the dirt drive to the street when Stanley Forbes fished a pack of Marlboros out of his shirt pocket and held it up in front of my face. Gratefully, I took one.

'Watch out,' he said.

'For what?'

'You're driving too far to the right, you almost knocked the mirror off that van.'

I belong to that category of men who can barely tolerate criticism when it comes to their driving. *Who can't tolerate it at all*, I should say. But being reasonable, I knew that Stanley was probably right. I knew that in any case I'd drunk too much to be driving a car. There had been a moment of hesitation. Stanley had been about to drive his own rented car to the beach, he was standing there with the keys in his hand, but finally he'd shrugged and gone along as my sole passenger.

'Thanks,' I said. 'You keep an eye on the right, I'll watch the left.'

I shifted down and slowed. About thirty yards in front of us I saw the red taillights of Ralph's Volvo disappear around a corner.

I was careful when I pulled the car over to the side. Even so, I heard the hubcaps scrape against the kerb with a sound like the gnashing of teeth.

'What are you doing?' Stanley asked.

'Listen, I was thinking: today's a public holiday. There might be police checks on the main road to the beach. I've really had a few too many, they'd confiscate my licence right away.'

'OK.'

'But there's another way to get to the beach. A sand road. We stayed at a campsite the first couple of days, remember? If I can find that campsite from here, that'd work too.'

It wasn't simple, we drove into a couple of dead-ends first, but finally we found a sandy road I was almost sure led to the campsite. There were trees along both sides of the road. I opened my window and turned the headlights on full beam.

'Those are trees on the right side, Marc,' Stanley said. 'On the left too, actually.'

We both burst out laughing and, to show how much I had the situation under control, I stepped on the accelerator just a little. The wheels spun in the sand and the car swerved and shot forward.

'Yeah!' Stanley said. 'Zebra One, we're on our way!'

That was probably a line from some film I should have recognised, but I had no idea. And I didn't feel like asking Stanley about it. In a pinch, however, I did have other things to ask the director. *How old is Emmanuelle, really? Does she fuck as lazily as she looks, or is it, as so often, a case of appearances deceiving; does she actually burn an old geezer like you down to the ground? Does she wear her sunglasses in bed, too?* But those were questions I didn't ask.

'What was that all about?' I asked instead. 'Ralph said something. Just before dinner. That you'd told him something that would probably interest me.'

'Oh, that,' Stanley said.

'You don't have to tell me now, not if you don't feel like it. Some other time.'

Meanwhile, the sandy road had taken a steep downhill turn; occasionally you could see little lights down below, between the trees, probably from the bars and restaurants along the beach. We were on the right road.

Stanley rolled down his window too. He tossed his cigarette out and lit another one. 'A few months after September 11, the Bush administration invited a few film directors to the White House,' he said. 'Mostly science fiction directors. Steven Spielberg, George Lucas, James Cameron. And me. I've directed a couple of sci-fi films. One of them was only released in Europe on DVD, but the other one was a real success over here. *Tremor*. Have you seen it?'

The title sounded familiar, but the last film of that kind I'd seen was, I think, *The Day After Tomorrow*. 'No, I'm afraid I haven't.'

'Doesn't matter. The point is the idea behind the invitation. We sat there in the Oval Office with the whole clique. George Bush himself, of course, and Dick Cheney and Donald Rumsfeld. George Tenet from the CIA was there, and a few other guys: the National Security Advisor, and a couple of generals. And the directors. They served peanuts and little snacks. And coffee and tea. But also beer and whisky and gin. After all, this was supposed to be about the imagination. About *our* imaginations.'

The sandy road grew narrower. There were more bends now. Switchbacks that you couldn't see around. I changed gears, braked with the engine, and through the open window I could hear pebbles bouncing off the bottom of the car. I smelled warm pine needles. And the sea. I thought about Caroline, who had stayed behind at the summer house. About the moment when we said goodbye and she had pecked me on the cheek. *Are you sure you haven't had too much to drink? Can you still drive?*

'The reason why we were invited was that we were supposed to let our imaginations run wild,' Stanley went on. 'Our sense of fantasy. I don't know who came up with the idea, whether it was Bush himself or one of his advisors. Anyway. We started off with coffee and tea, but then switched pretty quickly to beer and whisky. The president did too. He knocked back two double whiskies. Dick Cheney and Donald Rumsfeld were working on the gin. Somebody put on some music. First Bob Dylan, then Jimi Hendrix and the Dixie Chicks. Looking back on it now, it was fucking unbelievable. But we did what we were there to do: we fantasised. It had never occurred to anyone before 9/11 that terrorists might use a passenger plane as a weapon. Everything had focused on security in the plane itself. To prevent a bombing or a hijacking. Planes that flew into towers were simply *unimaginable*. So that's what they asked us to do: to imagine the unimaginable. Using our fantasy, the same fantasy we used to make aliens land on earth and avengers from the future appear in the present to settle accounts, they wanted us to imagine what the terrorists of the future might come up with. But then there's something else I forgot to tell you. *Tremor* was based on a book. A book by an American writer, Samuel Demmer. Ever heard of him?'

'I don't think so, no.'

'OK, doesn't matter. The point is, I'd read this book. *Tremor* by Samuel Demmer. And I saw a film in it right away. I started reading at midnight and I'd finished it by six the next morning. I called Demmer at eight. Myself. I usually have my agent call people for things like that, but I was so enthusiastic that I thought, I want to express that enthusiasm personally. Demmer had a reputation for being difficult. Never appeared on TV, never gave interviews. That's the most sympathetic kind of writer, if you ask me. Anyway, at first he was kind of cautious on the phone, he didn't seem to give a shit that someone wanted to make a film out of his book. But I also heard something else at the other end of the line. Something you hear more often when you talk to reclusive people. That in their heart, way down deep, they're glad to have someone call. To be able to talk to someone for a little while, even if it's someone they don't know. Or maybe *especially* if it's someone they don't know. I mean, characters like that often have to struggle with their own image. They have to live down their reputation, as they say in the States. He didn't mind at all, for example, that I'd called him so early in the morning. To make a long story short, we clicked. We jabbered a little about his book and the possibilities of filming it, and then at one point he asked me something that took me completely by surprise. Something that stopped me in my tracks, and that I've never forgotten. In fact, it became my own personal mantra. "Why don't you come up with something yourself?" he asked. I have to admit, that brought me up short. I didn't know what to say. "What do you mean?" I asked him. And I heard this deep sigh on the other end of the line. "I mean exactly what I said," Samuel Demmer said. "You sound to me like someone with ideas. Enough ideas of your own, I mean. So why would you want to make a film based on someone else's idea? Why don't you make up your own film?" We talked for about half an hour after that. About all kinds of things. About books we both liked. About films. Later on we met. It was an extremely enjoyable and inspiring collaboration. And Demmer's question changed my life for good. I made *Tremor*. But based only loosely on his novel, he thought that was OK. "Based on the novel by Samuel Demmer", that's what the credits finally said. And after *Tremor* I never adapted another book. Never. I took what Demmer said seriously and started coming up with things myself.'

In the headlights, I saw a sign at the side of the road. A little sign with a drawing of a tent and the name of the campsite where we had stayed for the first two nights. Another eight hundred yards. After that, as I remembered from the first evening, the road became even steeper going down – but after three or four tight curves you got to the beach. This was the final straight stretch of road. I gunned it a little.

'And what did all of you dream up, there at the White House?' I asked. 'Where is the next blow going to fall?'

'Well, that's exactly it,' Stanley said. 'Maybe it won't be a blow at all. I mean, there could be a blow too, but things went a lot further than that that afternoon. Trouble is, everything is classified top secret. We all had to swear that nothing of what we discussed would leave that room. Spielberg is the only one who revealed something later on. I don't even remember what it was, I think it was something pretty innocuous anyway, because that was our main conclusion at the end of that boozy afternoon: that it would all be a lot worse than anyone dared to dream. Or maybe not dared, but feared to dream. Anyway, it was horrible. A fucking nightmare. We're on the eve of a new age. Before long, nothing will be safe any more. Absolutely literally. *Nothing.* The Renaissance started with a new type of cannon. A cannon that could shoot right through the walls of a castle. That cannon put an end to the world as people knew it till then. Power shifted dramatically. Within a few decades, an end came to a thousand-year status quo. That's what's happening now too. We, the modern world, Western Europe, America, parts of Asia, we are that castle. We've been ruling the roost for a long time. But within the foreseeable future, something will come along that can shoot right through that.'

'And what's that going to be?'

'Like I said, I can't talk about it. But it's different from that cannon. It's not a single thing. It's a number of things, all at the same time.'

I couldn't help it; Stanley's story had interested me only mildly at first, but now I'd become curious in spite of myself.

'But you can tell me *one* thing, can't you?' I said. 'Honest, I swear I'll never tell anyone.'

As though to underline my words, I took one hand off the wheel, stuck two fingers in my mouth and then held them up as if I were taking a pledge, looking at him as I did. 'Cross my heart,' I said.

'Watch out!'

A car suddenly appeared from the right and shot onto the sandy road. Out of the blue. I hit the brakes and swung the wheel to the left. Maybe too slowly, who can say? We tell ourselves that we're still able to drive. But braking distance is a function of perception–reaction time. There was a scraping sound when the two cars made contact. To call it a crash would be an exaggeration. But there was contact. Metal to metal. Then we came to a halt, diagonally across the road. Or at least, *we* came to a halt. The other car just drove on. In the wink of an eye his red taillights had disappeared around the next bend.

'The fucker!' Stanley yelled. 'Did you see that? Jesus Christ! Fuck him! Fuck this motherfucker!'

I took one hand off the wheel and wiped my forehead. Hand and forehead were wet with sweat. 'Damn it,' I said. 'Damn it.'

'That shit didn't even have his lights on! Did you see that? He just came tearing onto the road with no lights.'

'But I saw his taillights. Just now, when he braked.'

'Yeah, exactly! He touched the brakes. But he didn't have his lights on. Really, he didn't.'

I noticed only then that my engine had stalled. Everything

had suddenly gone quiet. Two dry ticks sounded from under the bonnet. Now, far below, you could clearly hear the waves rolling over the beach. Along with the whiff of pine needles and salt, I now smelled burnt rubber.

'Come on, Marc. We're going to teach this motherfucker a lesson! Yes!' Stanley clenched his fist and slammed it against the glove compartment. I exhaled deeply. I squeezed the wheel with both hands. The wheel was wet too. 'What are you waiting for?' he said. 'Come on, start your engines!'

'Stanley. This is not a good idea. I've had too much to drink. We should be glad that bastard didn't stop. I would have got the blame anyway, with this much alcohol in my bloodstream.'

Stanley didn't say a word. He opened the door and got out. 'What are you doing?' I asked, but before I knew it he had come around the car and was opening the door on my side.

'Slide over,' he said.

'Stanley, this just isn't a good idea. I mean, you've been drinking too. Maybe even more than I have. In any case, no less.'

'Three glasses. It might look like I'm drinking as much as everyone else, but I take a long time over each glass.'

'Stanley…'

'Come on, Marc. Slide over, would you? We have to hurry. If that prick gets to the beach before we do, we won't be able to do anything.'

As I was struggling to crawl past the gearstick and sink into the passenger seat, I became aware for the first time of the heaviness in my head. The weight that pulls you down when the booze starts to wear off. I knew how it worked. The body demands moisture. Water. But in fact, by the time you feel that it's already too late. All you do then is go on. Straight on. I thought about a glass of beer. A big one. With beer you attack the heaviness from the rear, where it least expects it.

Stanley started the engine and hit the accelerator. Sand flew up from beneath the tyres. 'Yes!' he said when we shot forward at last. 'Hold on, Marc.'

At the first bend I heard the bottom of the car scrape across the rocks that lay in the road here and there. At the second bend he just missed a tree. 'Stanley,' I said. 'Stanley!'

'There he is!'

Barely thirty yards in front of us I saw the red taillights braking at the next bend. Stanley clicked back and forth between the headlights and the big beam. 'We're going to blind him,' he said. 'We've got him, Marc, we've got him.'

He downshifted and punched it. The engine wailed. 'Ever see *Speed Demons*?' he asked, without waiting for an answer. 'That was my first more-or-less hit in America. A shit story, frankly, but it was the only script I could get back then. About NASCAR races. A driver with cancer who wants to shine one last time. But they run him off the track and he dies in flames.'

'Stanley, please...'

'There's a bit part in it for his brother, the brother of the sick driver. I played the part myself. And that was the only fun thing about the whole shoot, that I was able to tear around in one of those stock cars the whole time. A hundred and eighty, two hundred miles an hour. And then giving the car in front of you a little tap so that it goes into a spin.'

We were now close behind the other car, an old Renault 4, I saw. Stanley hit the horn and kept hitting it. 'He has to keep going, otherwise it won't work. Come on, you fucker! Step on it!'

He yanked on the wheel and aimed for the right side of the rear bumper. Again there was the sound of metal on metal, louder than the first time. And I heard glass shatter. 'Got him!' The Renault slipped in the sand and spun on its axis. For a moment it looked as though it was going to roll, the wheels on one side were easily three feet off the ground, for a second it hung suspended in the air, but then it fell back anyway onto all fours. I thought Stanley would keep going, but he threw the car into reverse and manoeuvred back beside the Renault.

'Hairy cunt!' he shouted at the driver, who had his window open too and was looking at us, his eyes wide with fear. 'I hope the tumour in your brain explodes today, you fuck!'

Then Stanley raced off. Roaring with laughter, he steered the car through the last few bends before the beach. 'Jesus, Marc! Did you see his face? Oh, beautiful, these are the moments worth living for. And he got a free English lesson into the bargain.'

I didn't say a word. When the driver had turned and stared at us, I had pulled my head back so it would be behind Stanley's as much as possible. The other driver's hair was pretty mussed up. A bit mussier, in fact, than the first time I had seen him. But I recognised him immediately as the owner of the 'green' campsite who took such bad care of his farm animals.

Stanley was still dying with laughter. He turned to me and raised his arm. It took a moment before I realised that he wanted me to give him a high five.

'Two bottles,' he said.

'What?'

'I had two bottles of wine. And I'm not counting the couple of beers before dinner or the three brandies with the coffee. You have to admit, when you take all that into account, I'm not such a bad driver!'

26

The beach was crowded. So crowded that we couldn't find the others at first. We started off by looking in the open-air bars festooned with lanterns, then went further, past the bonfires, towards the sea. Rockets shot into the air to the left and right of us. In the pauses between the bangs you could hear a leaden disco beat rolling across the sand.

'Over there,' Stanley said.

Ralph and Judith were down close to the waterline, and almost right away I saw Lisa being chased by Thomas. Lisa screamed and fell onto the sand, and Thomas jumped on top of her.

'You guys are just in time,' Ralph said.

Ralph had buried a cardboard tube filled with explosives in the sand; it was about the size of a stick of dynamite, and now he was putting a pan over it. It was a heavy copper pan with a round bottom, apparently he had brought it along from the summer house – an antique soup pan, I guessed, the kind you see hanging on a chain above a fire.

'Get back,' Ralph said.

For a moment there was nothing. A split second later, thunder rang out and the pan was gone. We didn't see it fly into the air, no, it was simply gone. Where it had just been there was now a gaping crater about a foot across, with smoke curling up from it.

'Look!' Ralph yelled. 'There!'

He pointed. Against the night sky, lit by the glare of exploding rockets, we saw the pan. It was hard to tell how high up it was. A hundred yards? Two hundred? It tumbled as it rose, a tumbling dot, still rising. Just before we almost lost sight of it again, it began its descent. The pan's trajectory was fairly flat, and now it came hurtling down over the sea. For a moment we lost sight of it altogether, then it showed up for the last time about thirty feet above the waves.

'There goes our deposit,' Judith said as the pan disappeared for the last time.

'Jesus Christ!' Ralph said. 'Did you see that? Did you guys see that? What a boom. Here, look at this, this crater. Shit, man. I felt the pieces of seashell in my eyes.'

'And how are we going to explain this to the letting agency?' Judith asked.

'Oh, stop bellyaching, would you? I found that pan out in the shed, they won't even know it's gone.'

I glanced over at Judith. A little wrinkle had appeared on her forehead, just above her nose. On her cheeks and in her eyes flickered the golden glow from the bonfires.

I could do it, I thought. *I could just do it. This woman. Right this very evening.*

The next moment I thought about what had happened in the kitchen earlier that day. I felt a pang in my chest. And the heaviness in my head – which had gone away after Stanley had run the campsite owner off the road – came back. I thought about my daughter, about Julia, who must have seen us. Who else could it have been, if not Julia? Judith's mother? Maybe. It was possible. Thomas or Alex? Lisa? I dropped Lisa from the list right away. After all, Lisa was acting normally towards me. In fact, she was almost the only one. I now tried to picture *what* the person behind the kitchen door could have seen, exactly. Or heard. Maybe almost nothing, I told myself for one brief second. Maybe almost everything, I realised the next.

I thought about what I had to do. Julia. The best thing would be to be honest. Well, not quite honest: direct. *I don't know exactly what you saw, but Alex's mother was very, very sad about something. And I was trying to comfort her. She was sad because she… because of something grown-up women are sometimes sad about, I'll explain it some other time.*

'Judith?' Ralph called out. 'Judith, where are you going?'

Judith had turned on her heel and was taking big, angry steps through the sand towards the beachside restaurants. She didn't look back. Ralph grinned and shrugged.

'Don't mind her, Marc,' he said. 'When she's in one of those moods, it's better to just keep out of her way.'

For a moment I thought about following Judith up to the restaurants, but decided against it. That would be too much. An overly obvious signal. Later. A suitable opportunity would present itself. I could try to make Judith think that I was more sensitive than Ralph. What was I saying? I *was* more sensitive than Ralph. That's why I answered his grin with a gesture that was supposed to mean something like *women, one of life's great mysteries*.

'What is this, all this bitching about some old pan?' Ralph said. 'I mean, go figure.'

'Well, yeah,' I said. 'Caroline has those moods too. And then *we're* supposed to feel guilty and try to figure out what we've done wrong.'

Ralph stepped up to me and put an arm around my shoulders. 'Sounds like you know what's what, Marc. When it comes to women. But then you have them coming into your office every day.'

From up close, I could smell something on Ralph's breath. Swordfish… Halfway through dinner I had covered my own portion with a napkin, and after that took only a few pieces of French bread. Now I could feel the emptiness in my stomach. I needed to eat something first. Eat something, and then have a beer to get rid of that leaden feeling.

'Everyone get back!' It was Stanley. He had taken off his shoes and was standing up to his knees in the surf. In each hand he held a rocket, which he now pointed at us laughingly. I could see the sparks glittering at the fuses.

'Get away!' Ralph yelled. 'Away with that, you idiot!'

Only at the very last moment did Stanley turn a hundred and eighty degrees and point the rockets out to sea. Not at an angle, no, horizontally. At almost the same moment, the rockets flew out of his hands. One of them disappeared into a roller only about five yards from the beach. The other one skimmed just above the water's surface. There were people swimming out there, I saw now. Not a lot of them, maybe five, but still… The rocket drilled its way between the heads bobbing on the waves. For a few seconds nothing happened, nothing at all. Then there was a dull explosion and a fountain of water sprayed into the air. The swimmers started shouting and waving their arms, but Stanley only waved back and laughed.

'*Apocalypse Now*! *Apocalypse Now*!' he shouted, holding his hands up to his mouth like a megaphone. 'Ralph, Ralph,' he said. 'Give me another one of those. We'll blow them out of the water!'

It wasn't as if we'd forgotten about the first rocket. We'd just stopped thinking about it. There was an explosion. A deep thud. A sound as though an anchor had been dropped. An anchor slamming against a big rock under water. Seawater and sand and little stones came flying up. Something landed in my left eye. Stanley, who was standing closest to the explosion, lost his balance and fell face down into a wave. For a moment he went all the way under, then came back up, coughing and gagging. 'Fuck!' he shouted, picking an imaginary strand of seaweed from his tongue. 'Friendly fire! Friendly fire!' He laughed – the only thing you can do in a situation like that – just as Ralph had laughed at himself earlier when he'd landed on his knee beside the ping-pong table. Ralph and I laughed loudly too as Stanley clambered up onto the beach in his dripping shorts and T-shirt.

Someone grabbed me by the wrist. 'Daddy?' Lisa said. 'Daddy, can Thomas and I get ice cream?'

'Yeah, sure,' I said. I used the fingers of the other hand to rub my left eye, and blinked. The tears started flowing right away and

I felt a sharp pain. There was something in my eye. A piece of seashell or a grain of sand. 'Where's Julia?' I asked Lisa.

At that point Thomas came running up from behind and crashed into her, throwing her forward onto the sand. 'Thomas! Damn you!'

'Lisa!' I said. 'I don't want you to… you shouldn't talk…' Thomas pounded his chest with both fists and gave a kind of Tarzan yell. 'Where's Julia?' I asked again.

'How should I know?' Lisa said. She scrambled to her feet and smacked Thomas across the face with the flat of her hand – way too hard; harder, in any case, than she could have meant to.

'Fuck!' Thomas shouted. 'Slimy bitch!' He tried to grab her, but Lisa was already sprinting away across the sand.

'What do you think, shall we grab a beer?' Stanley said. He was soaked from head to toe, his wet grey hair was plastered down on his head, and you could see the white scalp shining through here and there.

Ralph was still hiccuping with laughter. 'That was a take, Stanley! You should have filmed that one!'

'Where's Julia?' I asked Ralph.

Stanley felt around in his pockets. 'Fuck! I think all my money… Oh no, there we go…' He pulled a few banknotes from his pocket. Soaked banknotes, stuck together. 'A hairdryer!' he shouted. 'My kingdom for a hairdryer!'

'Where are Julia and Alex?' I asked.

'They went to the club at that other beach,' Ralph said. 'There…' He pointed. 'You can see the lights, up past the bend.'

'Alone?' I asked. 'Just the two of them?'

I saw the lights Ralph meant. It was hard to tell how far away they were. Half a mile at least, I thought. Maybe a mile. Between this section of beach with its lit restaurant and bonfires and that club across the bay, there was nothing. Just a long and empty and darkened stretch of beach.

'Marc, you can't keep the kids on a lead. The last thing those two want is to hang around here with their parents.'

'No, I was just wondering… Julia could at least have waited till I got here.'

I tried to hide my annoyance at how Ralph had given my daughter permission to go to the other beach. Without bothering to ask himself whether I would mind. Was I being childish? I asked myself. Or would it have made more sense if he'd said, 'It's OK with me, but first we have to wait for your father to see what he says'?

'What's with your eye?' Ralph asked.

'Nothing. Well, there's something in it. Sand or something.'

'Beer all round?' Stanley said, holding the wet banknotes aloft.

27

Because all the tables were taken, we drank leaning on a bar that had been set up right out on the beach, probably just for this occasion. Judith was gone. Ralph didn't seem to worry much about losing track of his wife. At least he made no attempt to find her.

'Goddamn! Is a man supposed to take that lying down?' he said, slapping his beer mug down onto the bar. I followed his gaze and saw three girls in bikinis among the café tables, about five yards away. They had their backs to us and were trying to find an empty table. Ralph shook his head. 'Well, Marc, out of sight, out of mind. Oh, I'd be willing to commit a crime to get a little of that. Just a little.' He ran his tongue across his upper lip. He moaned and fiddled with the button on his shorts, his fingers slid down over his zipper. Suddenly I saw the raptor look again: the same look with which he had once undressed Caroline in the foyer. And this time too, a film slid down over his eyes as he examined the girls from head to toe, his gaze finally coming to rest on their buttocks.

'Hey!' Stanley shouted.

We turned and saw Stanley waving the girls over. 'Hey! Come on! Come here!'

Ralph shook his head, stared into his beer, and then grinned at me. 'We think about it, but he does it,' he said.

The girls seemed to be talking about what they were going to do. They had their heads together. They were giggling. I tried to picture what they saw: three middle-aged men in shorts, holding mugs of beer – the oldest of the three had taken the lead. If I were them I would have turned and walked away.

But, to my great amazement, after a moment's hesitation, I saw them coming towards us. Sometimes you misjudge women when you see them from behind. You see long hair falling over bare shoulders, but when they turn to face you they're suddenly fifteen years older. Here, however, that wasn't the case: all three of them could have stepped right off the cover of *Vogue* or *Glamour*. I tried to guess how old they were. Nineteen? Twenty? No more than twenty-five in any case, and in fact more girls than young women. I glanced over at Ralph, who took a quick sip from his mug, smacked his lips, and ran his hand over his belly. As though he were hungry. That's how he looked at the three girls too: as though he were at a party where the waiters come by with trays of croquettes, satay and liverwurst. A tasty morsel was heading his way, and he had already started licking his chops.

'No flies on them,' he said. 'Holy shit, they're real beauties.'

'Good evening, ladies. Drinks? What will you have? White wine? Margaritas? Cocktails?' Stanley looked at us mischievously. He was a fast worker. Even as he was still checking off the list of possible beverages, he had laid his hand lightly on the bare shoulder of the girl closest to him. They giggled again, but didn't walk away. One by one they held out a hand and introduced themselves. They told us their names, and Stanley asked where they were from. Two of them were from Norway, we understood, and the third was Latvian. Then Stanley asked whether they were here on business or on holiday. No, he didn't use the word 'holiday'. *Pleasure*, that was the word he used. *Business or pleasure?* He asked it in a suggestive tone of voice, as though the difference between business and pleasure was of piddling importance. It seemed to me like a last opportunity for the girls to walk away from us. But they just stood there giggling. By now, the two Norwegian ones were sucking on the straws in their margaritas. The Latvian girl knocked back her double vodka with ice in one go.

'So Marc,' Ralph said. 'You're the lucky one, with your better half safe at home. And so's he.' He pointed at Stanley. 'But I have to be very careful. Judith would have a fit.' He looked around, and I looked with him. 'The short one is completely wrecked,' he said. 'Yours for the taking, Marc.'

He nodded towards the Latvian vodka girl. Then he turned his own gaze back to the legs of the Norwegian girls and smacked his lips again. Meanwhile, Stanley had his arm all the way around the shoulders of the girl closest to him. He acted as though he were trying to wrap his lips around the straw of her margarita, then pretended to stumble and buried his nose in her neck. The girl pushed him away laughingly and said something in Norwegian to her girlfriend, who then took Ralph by the wrist and pulled him towards her.

'Whoa, whoa,' Ralph said. 'Wait a minute! Jesus, they're hot to trot, Marc. What did we do to deserve this?'

I saw him glance around quickly once again, then he threw his arm around the girl's waist and pulled her towards him. Or no, not around her waist: lower, just above the top elastic of her bikini bottoms. Within seconds his fingers were under the elastic. I looked at his hand. At his wrist. It was all completely out of proportion. Ralph's wrist looked thicker than the girl's waistline. I saw how he slid his thick fingers down between her buttocks, and I thought about other body parts. Body parts that were also out of proportion. But I didn't have time to develop this fantasy any further. The girl tried to push Ralph away, not half-jokingly, the way her girlfriend had just done with Stanley, no, in dead earnest. Ralph couldn't see her face. I could. Her mouth was twisted, as though she had tasted something filthy or felt a sudden pain, but because Ralph couldn't see this he only pulled her in even tighter, trying at the same time to plant his lips on her neck.

I heard a cry, a curse or term of abuse most probably. A term of abuse in Norwegian that sounded like *Varkensfetter*! Then she said something else, this time in English with a heavy accent. 'Fok of!' she said, and almost simultaneously brought her knee up hard into the crotch of Ralph's shorts.

Ralph's mouth fell open. He gasped for air and clutched at the front of his shorts (with the same hand that had just been under the elastic of the bikini bottoms), the better to cradle his genitals.

'Aw, fug!' was all he could say.

Now the girl threw the rest of her margarita, ice and all, in his face. It wasn't clear whether she really meant to do it or whether she'd just had too much to drink and wasn't completely steady. In any case the edge of her glass hit Ralph in the upper lip. Against his teeth. There was the sound of something breaking. A piece of tooth or a piece of glass, it wasn't clear which. Ralph raised his hand to his mouth. He ran his tongue over his front teeth, then looked at his bloodied fingers.

'You fucking shit whore!' he howled.

Before Stanley or I could stop him, he swung. He tried to punch the girl right in the face. But the knee in his crotch had thrown him, and the punch narrowly missed its mark.

'Ralph!' Stanley yelled. 'Calm down, man!'

'Dirty whores!' Ralph screamed. 'First you're the big cock-teasers, and then suddenly it's Mother Teresa. Bah! I shit on sluts like you!'

Now he had the girl by the wrist. He pulled her arm down hard, so that she lost her balance and fell onto the sand. She screamed. I saw Ralph swing his leg back. As though he was about to take a penalty. Just in time, I realised that he was going to kick the girl in the stomach.

'Ralph!' I shouted – I leaned into him, shoulder to shoulder. At the same time, I kicked him in the knee. As hard as I could. He was at a disadvantage. He was standing on one leg. If he'd been standing on both I could never have thrown him, but now he stood wobbling in place for a full second. Then he collapsed slowly, like a building demolished by charges in the basement.

The back of his head hit the bar with a loud crack. I couldn't tell whether the crack came from his skull or from the wooden bar top.

People were coming at us now from all directions. Men, mostly. Men who grabbed Stanley and me. Men who bent to help the Norwegian girl, who was halfway back to her feet. 'Hey, take it easy!' I heard Stanley shout, but I couldn't see him any more, he was no longer standing at the bar where he had been just a moment before.

'Stanley!' I shouted. Meanwhile, two men had forced me down onto the sand. A third one was sitting on my chest, letting his full weight rest on my ribs. I could feel the air being pressed out of my lungs. 'Calm down!' I peeped now. 'Calm down, please…' But I couldn't get enough air to say it very loudly.

Out of one corner of my eye I saw the Norwegian girl sitting on top of Ralph. She punched him a few times full in the face, until two strong men came and pulled her off him.

28

I was in the men's room of the restaurant where we had eaten that first evening, looking into the little mirror above the basin. I tried to keep my left eye open and look into it at the same time. I couldn't get a very clear picture, but what I could see, I saw well enough: more than a third of my eyeball was red with blood. A haemorrhage. Something – a grain of sand, a piece of seashell, a tiny stone – had flown into my eye. And hit the cornea. Or who knows, I thought as my breathing quickened and my heart began pounding more laboriously, who knows, maybe the grain of sand or tiny stone had actually *punctured* the cornea and was now stuck in the fluid inside the eyeball itself.

I've got this thing about eyes. I can look at anything – open wounds and fractures, a circular saw applied to a worn-out hip, complete with blood flying against the operating room ceiling, a trapdoor sawn in a skull, exposed brains, a heart pounding on a chrome tray, bloody rolls of gauze propped into a chest cut open from collarbone to navel – I can handle anything, except for things that have to do with eyes. Particularly things that don't belong in eyes: glass splinters, sand, dust, contact lenses that have slipped halfway behind an eyeball… Because of my oath as a physician I refer as few patients as possible to a specialist, but patients who sit in my waiting room spastically blinking their eyes don't even make it into my office. See that man holding the bloodied napkin to his eye? I say to my assistant. Get him out of here. Right away. Send him to emergency. Or write a referral to the ophthalmologist. I haven't had breakfast yet, I can't handle that right now.

I don't know why, it must have to do with something that happened a long time ago. Some event that I've repressed. Most phobias originate in the first four years of life: the fear of spiders, of water, of women, of men, of wide open spaces, or of towering mountain ranges that block out the sun, of toads and grasshoppers, fish heads on your plate with the eyes still in them, giant waterslides, furniture malls, pedestrian tunnels – there's always something to blame. A traumatic experience, people say, and they make an appointment for an exploratory meeting with a psychiatrist. After years of digging and delving, something finally bobs to the surface: a mother lost in the supermarket, a dripping candle, a snail in your tennis shoe, a 'funny' uncle who could blow smoke rings through a rolled-up newspaper but wanted to play with your willy at night, an aunt with warts and a bristly moustache who kissed you goodnight… a teacher taking a shower at a school summer camp; there is no clear demarcation between lower back and buttocks, after the tailbone the skin disappears into a dark, clenched crack; he stands there scrubbing at his pale, skinny dick with a pink washcloth – and after camp is over you have to do your best not to gag every time he draws an equilateral triangle on the blackboard.

A wide-open, watery eye reminds me of a fried egg. A fried egg that isn't nearly done yet, yolk and white are still largely liquid and lie there jiggling in the pan like a jellyfish on the beach.

Someone was rattling the handle of the toilet door.

'Go away,' I said in Dutch. 'Can't you see there's someone in here?

I was able to keep my damaged eye open only for a couple of seconds each time. Not only because it looked so hideous, but also because of the sharp pain. As though someone were stubbing out a cigarette in the white of my eye – *in the fried egg*, I couldn't help thinking.

There was a rattling at the door again. And no longer just a rattling: someone pounded on it three times. I heard a voice. A man's voice muttering in a language I couldn't quite make out.

'Jesus Christ,' I said.

I blinked my runny eye a few times. But it was no use. I couldn't keep it open any longer without feeling an unbearable, stabbing pain. I cursed. I took a length of toilet paper from the roll, wadded it up, and moistened it a bit under the tap. There was a brief moment of coolness and relief when I pressed the wet wad against my eye.

'Your turn at last,' I said to the man waiting in the half-darkened hallway beyond the toilet door. He was wearing shorts and a sleeveless T-shirt. His cheeks, chin and upper lip were sweaty and unshaven. I started to walk on, but then I took another look. His face seemed vaguely familiar, but I couldn't quite place it. And at the same moment I saw something else. The man looked at me too, as though he recognised me from somewhere: a slight gleam in his eyes, as if he were trying to connect my face to some memory.

'I sorry,' he said with a heavy accent. 'I hurry.'

He smiled. My gaze descended to his bare shoulders and upper arms. On one arm he had a tattoo: a bird, an eagle by the looks of it, clutching a dripping red heart in its talons. On his other arm were a few red stripes. As though he'd scratched at an injury. A cut or a mosquito bite.

He followed my gaze and brushed the wound with his fingertips. He rubbed it, his arm was wet with sweat, and when he took his fingers away all you could see were a couple of thin red lines. We nodded at each other again, the way distant acquaintances do, then he disappeared into the toilet.

At the front door of the restaurant I took a good look around before stepping out onto the patio. I looked particularly carefully at the beachside bar, where no more than fifteen minutes ago I had been forced down onto the sand by a group of men. But there was no one there any more. No trace of Ralph or Stanley or the three girls. Still holding the wad of wet toilet paper to my eye, I wormed my way past the tables. I may have been imagining things, but it seemed as though the eye had started to throb – not so much the eye itself, more like the space *behind* the eye. The place where the muscles and tendons were holding the eye in its socket, I recalled from medical school. From the ophthalmology lectures where I had only *pretended* to be listening. With each successive slide the professor flashed up on the screen, I sank further down into my seat. One of the slides showed an eye hanging out of its socket, connected to the skull only by bloodied veins. I had groaned so loudly that the professor had stopped the lecture to ask whether someone was in need of medical assistance.

Now I could feel the pounding behind my eye, a pounding that meshed seamlessly with the bass rhythm from the loudspeakers set up here and there around the patio – so seamlessly that there was no way to separate them.

Maybe I wasn't paying attention, or maybe walking around with one eye closed had affected my depth perception; whatever the case, the girl, when she stood up from her chair at the patio's edge, did so awfully fast and clumsily. Her left shoulder hit me just under my nose, I took a few shaky steps back and almost regained my balance before falling into the lap of a virtually naked man.

'Sorry,' I said to the man. I dabbed at my nose and looked at my fingers: no blood.

'Sorry,' the girl said now as well. She looked worriedly at the hand holding the wad of toilet paper against my eye, but before she could jump to any conclusions I said: 'OK, it's OK. No problem.'

The girl wasn't big, but she was fat. I took a better look at her now and, for the second time in the space of five minutes I saw a vaguely familiar face. This time it took only a few moments for me to place her: the girl from the letting agency… The girl who had promised us that the repairman would come by as quickly as possible to solve the water problem.

Suddenly I also knew who the man was, the one rattling at the toilet door. The repairman! The repairman who had climbed onto the roof to unblock the blocked water reservoir. Those two were a couple, weren't they? I looked at her eyes and noticed only then that they were filled with tears. Teary and red. She blinked a few times and spluttered another apology.

I held up my hand, as if to say *no problem*. Maybe the repairman had just broken up with her. There were red blotches on her cheeks. She had cried when they broke up. She had wept and rubbed her fingers hard over her eyes and cheeks. Was it unfair that girls who looked like this were frequently dumped? That was the question that flashed through my mind. Or was it something you took into account each time? Was it all you expected, and were you pleased enough when some sweaty repairman pressed his lips to your neck for a few weeks (or a few hours) and whispered sweet nothings in your ear?

'I... I have to get going,' I said. 'Are you OK?'

She nodded. It was hard to tell with all the red blotches on her cheeks, but it looked as if she was blushing again. The next moment she slid past me and headed towards the busier part of the restaurant.

When I walked past the beachside bar, no one seemed to notice me. The men who had thrown Ralph and me to the ground had apparently gone looking for fun elsewhere. A few hundred yards further I found Lisa and Thomas still chasing a football, along with a whole group of children their age. Fortunately, they hadn't noticed the fracas at the bar. Just before locking myself in the toilet to look at my eye, I had gone over to talk to Lisa.

'Stay close by, all right?' I'd said. 'I'll be in the bathroom over there if you need me.' I pointed at the restaurant, but Lisa didn't really seem to have heard me. 'All right,' she said without looking at me, then ran off across the sand in pursuit of Thomas and three other boys who were kicking the ball out in front of them.

In the end, Ralph had succeeded in freeing himself from the men who were pinning him down. Ranting and cursing, he grabbed the plastic bag of fireworks and strode off towards the sea. By that time they had already let go of me. 'Come on, Marc!' Ralph shouted over his shoulder. 'Let these shitheads play pimp to a bunch of whores, if that makes them feel good!' But he didn't look back to see if I was actually following.

Meanwhile, Stanley's whereabouts remained unclear. I stood up, brushed the sand off my shorts and shirt and looked around (with my one good eye).

Right then, the Latvian vodka girl passed out. One minute she was standing there beside us, empty glass in hand, the next, she collapsed. Without a sound. A leaf falling from a tree, no more than that. The men leaned over her. Hands slapped her cheeks. Someone held a pepper mill under her nose. Someone else fetched a wet cloth from the bar and dabbed at her forehead. One eyelid was lifted, but all you could see was the white of her eye. I turned away quickly and dabbed automatically at my own eye.

'A doctor,' someone said. 'We need a doctor.'

It was within the realm of possibility. I could have walked away. No one was paying attention to me any more. I took a deep breath and looked at the sea. The fireworks had almost died down by now, the sea lay black and darkened beneath the black sky studded with stars. In the pauses between the bass notes you could hear the hissing of the surf.

'I'm a doctor,' I said.

29

I often wondered later on whether things would have turned out differently if the Latvian girl had remained on her feet. Whether I would have been in time. I added and subtracted the minutes, but never really found a clear answer. It was like after you've made some remark to someone. A terrible remark. At least, that's what you think: that it was terrible. You lie awake all night, running back through the conversation. But as the hours pass, the words become increasingly vague. The next day you summon up all your courage. Did I say something terrible to you last night? you ask. What on earth are you talking about? is the reply.

The fact is that it took me fifteen minutes to bring the vodka girl back to her senses. I took her pulse, put my ear to her breast to hear whether she perhaps had fluid (vodka!) in her lungs. *Between* her breasts, I should say. It was a matter of life and death, I knew that from bitter experience. Girls her size – she couldn't have weighed more than eighty-five pounds, I noted later when I lifted her from the sand – can die almost immediately from an alcohol overdose. The body doesn't know where to put all that liquor. There's no room for it. The heart works overtime and pumps the overdose around and around, but the blood only goes on racing desperately through the veins. There's nowhere for it to go. After a while, the heart gives up. It pumps with less and less force. Finally, it stops. I had no time to wonder what the men leaning over us might think when I placed my ear between her breasts. They were little breasts that barely muffled the sound of the pounding heart. It was pounding slowly and laboriously. The final phase. Within the next five minutes it could stop. I placed my left arm under her head and raised it a little. At the same time I placed my right hand flat on her stomach. When I pressed my mouth against hers I could taste the vodka.

Mouth-to-mouth resuscitation. I hadn't used it often. One time with a drowned man, the father of three, at a campsite. He had come down the giant slide, slammed the back of his head hard against the edge of the pool, then sunk to the bottom right away. Another time was with an elderly writer in my office. While I was removing impacted wax from his ears, he lost consciousness. I remember it clearly: one moment I was staring at the metal bowl in my hand, at the black wad of earwax floating in the water. And then I looked at the writer. He had fallen on his side on the examining table.

As I often did, I thought at that moment about the choices I make as a doctor. About who you help first. Sooner or later, every doctor is confronted with such choices. Even though we would all deny it. In fact, they involve very simple considerations. Considerations you never talk about. The father of three has more right to mouth-to-mouth resuscitation than a writer whose work is more or less finished. Who is 'over the hill', as they say, without much chance that he'll come up with anything new. When a ship is sinking, it's the women and children who go to the boats first. In an ideal world, the old man would offer his place in the lifeboat to the young mother and her child. The old man is at the end of his biological rope. For a pretty young girl, it would be a waste to come all the way from Latvia to die of alcohol poisoning on some distant beach. I knew how it must have looked to the bystanders. They weren't seeing a doctor performing life-saving manoeuvres, they saw a grown man bending over a girl and pressing his lips to hers. His free hand hovers somewhere around her navel…

I pinched her nose shut and blew air into her lungs. At the same time I pressed hard on her stomach. I only had to do it once, and everything came out. I didn't even have time to take my lips off hers. A wave of vodka rushed into my mouth. And not just vodka. A noxious mixture of vodka, half-digested food and gastric juices. I yanked her upright, to keep her from choking on her own vomit. I licked my lips and spat a few times in the sand. The rest gushed down over her stomach and legs. But she opened her eyes. She made noises. An indefinable noise at first, a gargling coming from deep down, like a blocked drain that has suddenly come unblocked. Then came sounds and words. Words in her own language, from the sound of it. Latvian. I stood up, took her wrists and held her arms above her head. Air. Oxygen. What she needed most now was to breathe in oxygen. A few of the men who had pinned Ralph, Stanley and me to the ground a bit earlier now began applauding. Normally speaking, that's always the finest moment. The doctor. The doctor has just saved someone's life. For a few minutes he stands in the bright spotlight. The father of three came by the next day to give me a bottle of wine. It could have turned out much worse, they realise in a flash. After that they forget you again.

The crowd parted when I made for the restaurant, my left eye still closed tightly. A few people along the way patted me on the shoulder. Someone gave me the thumbs-up and winked. Words of praise were murmured in various languages. But what I felt most was a gnawing sense of discomfort. Maybe I had taken it all far too lightly, I realised now: the fact that my thirteen-year-old daughter had gone off to a beach club a mile away with a fifteen-year-old boy. I hadn't wanted to be petty. True enough, I was irritated that Ralph hadn't waited for me, but had simply given Alex and Julia permission. Then I forgot about it again, right away. I'd had – and it was only with difficulty that I admitted this to myself – *other things* on my mind. Those other things had pushed into the background the fact that a thirteen-year-old girl had walked across a darkened stretch of beach to a club further along. I tried not to let my imagination get the better of me. I did my utmost to make my imagination stop right there. *Take care of this eye first*, I told myself. With a painful, pounding and swollen-shut eye, I was nothing but a semi-invalid. But once I had gone into that bathroom and made a first attempt to look in the mirror, there was no stopping it. I thought the things every father thinks sooner or later. Every father with a daughter, that is. The dark stretch of beach. The dark stretch of park between school and home after the school party. There were a lot of drunken men walking around tonight. I thought about Alex. My daughter probably didn't have much to worry about on that score. Alex was a sweet, rather sluggish boy who liked to hold her hand – and who knows, maybe more than that. Also much too sweet and sluggish to be of much use when the drunken, nasty men tried to force themselves on my daughter. Somewhere along that dark stretch of beach or at the club. I didn't think about anything else. It didn't seem likely to me that Julia would let herself go like the Latvian vodka girl. When we were on holiday, and when we went to a restaurant, she was allowed to take a sip of our wine or beer. But it didn't really interest her much. She would raise the glass to her lips and make a face, almost as though she was doing it more to please us than to please herself. No, I was thinking mostly of drunken, nasty men who would see a thirteen-year-old girl as easy prey. Dirty men. Like Ralph, it flashed through my mind.

And I also thought about something else. I thought about Caroline. I've already talked about how I often play the role of the push-over father, the father with whom everything is permitted – well, maybe not everything, but in any case more than from the always-much-too-worried mother. That role suits me very well, as long as Caroline and I are both there. As soon as I'm on my own, though, panic descends. At an outdoor restaurant or in a department store, *at a beach!* – wherever there are lots of people, or perhaps even too few, or places that are too dimly lit, I keep looking around to make sure I haven't lost them. A bit less often these days than when the girls were little, but still… That panic had two faces. The first face was the straightforward fear that something might happen any moment: a ball rolling out onto a busy street, a child molester, a big wave that drags them out to sea. The second was Caroline's face. Or rather, her voice. *Why didn't you take better care of them?* the voice said. *How could you leave them alone there with all that traffic?* On occasion I've wondered whether I would be so panicky if I'd had to do it all alone. Really alone, I mean. A single father. A *widower*. But whenever that word popped up, the whole newsreel ground to a halt. My imagination would simply balk. Mustn't think about that, I'd tell myself – and the fantasy fizzled and died.

This time too I heard Caroline's voice. *How could you have let her go off alone with that boy to that beach club?* I looked in the bathroom mirror. Into my eye filled with blood. *I couldn't do anything about it*, that was how I formulated my answer in my thoughts. *They were gone when I got there. Ralph and Judith said they could…*

It was way too spineless an answer, I knew that. A flimsy excuse for an answer.

And even before Caroline's voice had a chance to pronounce the next sentence - *If I'd been there, none of this would have happened* – I had made up my mind.

30

The first thing I did, of course, was try her mobile phone. When she'd started high school a year ago, we had given Julia a phone. For safety's sake, we told ourselves. So she can always call us. And we can call her – we thought. But from the very start Julia showed great skill in turning her phone on only when it suited her. It was in my bag, I guess that's why I didn't hear it, she would say. Or, the battery was run down.

So it didn't surprise me at all when her mobile phone, after ringing three times, switched directly to the voicemail. Leaving a message was useless, I knew. She never, ever listened to her voicemail. It didn't surprise me at all, but on the other hand it didn't really worry me either. It was entirely possible that she hadn't brought her phone with her, that she'd left it behind at the summer house. And if she did happen to have it with her, well then, this was the evening of all evenings not to turn it on: out with a cute boy on the beach beneath the stars, what thirteen-year-old girl would want to be called by chronically nagging parents on a night like that?

'Have you seen Judith?' I asked Lisa, after I'd finally caught her attention and she came walking over to me with a sigh.

'Who?' She wasn't really listening, she never took her eyes off the boys playing football.

'Judith. Thomas's mother.'

There was no reply. Her face was sweaty, she brushed a few strands of hair from in front of her eyes.

'Lisa...'

'What?'

'I asked you something.'

'Sorry, what was it?' Now she looked at me for the first time. 'What's happened to your eye, Dad?'

I pinched my eye shut, then tried to open it. But it was no use. It started watering right away.

'Nothing,' I said. 'I have a... a thingumabob flew into it, an insect or something...'

'Thomas's mother is over there,' Lisa said, pointing across the stretch of beach they were using as a football pitch. There, where the beach sloped up right off the surf, Judith was sitting in the sand with her knees pulled up to her chest. She didn't see me at first when I waved, but then she waved back.

Go back to your game, I was about to say to Lisa, but she had already run off. I walked through the swarm of players to the other side.

'Well, well,' she said. 'Did you get to shoot off a lot of rockets?'

She was smoking a cigarette. I put my hand in my pocket and fished out my own pack. I leaned down so she could give me a light.

'I'm going over to the club at the other end of the beach for a look,' I said. 'See where Alex and Julia are.'

I tried to adopt the most lighthearted tone possible, but maybe there was still a little concern in my voice.

'Do you want me to come too?' Judith asked.

I took a drag of my cigarette. Less than five yards away from us the waves were pounding against the sand. Fine drops of seawater were atomised in my face. 'I don't know...' I nodded back over my shoulder, to where our youngest two were playing football.

'Oh, they're not really paying any attention to us. There are so many people around. As long as they stay put...' She stood up. 'I'll go tell Thomas, we'll be right back. What's with your eye?'

The dark stretch of beach was less dark than I had imagined. Here and there, behind and on top of the dunes, were summer houses, their patios lit. After about ten minutes the drumbeats behind us faded and the sound of the beach club ahead grew louder. Different music: salsa, or in any case something South American. Judith had taken off her flip-flops and was carrying them in one hand.

My fretfulness of a few minutes earlier had vanished just like that. I'd been worrying again for no reason, I told myself. What could happen here, for God's sake? Little groups of people came past us every now and then, walking in the other direction; young people mostly, teenagers in knee-length swimming shorts and bikinis, the occasional closely intertwined couple who stopped to kiss every five yards or so.

'Sorry I just walked away like that,' Judith said. 'But I can't stand it when Ralph acts that way. He's just like a big boy.

Sometimes he forgets that he has children of his own. It makes me so angry when he behaves like that around them.'

I said nothing. I walked a little closer to her, so that our forearms brushed. I smelled something vague: sea air mixed with a hint of perfume or deodorant. It was only a matter of time, I knew. Or rather, a matter of timing. To grab her around the waist now would be taking things too fast. I estimated the distance to the lights of the beach club. Ten minutes. Within ten minutes she would be all mine. But then I would have to be subtle about it. Not really subtle, of course, only subtle in her eyes.

'I can't help laughing sometimes, actually,' I said. 'The way Ralph can completely lose himself in things. Whether he's snorkelling or chopping a swordfish into pieces, he does it with the same kind of enthusiasm. The same kind of energy. Sometimes it almost makes me jealous. I don't have that kind of energy.'

Women complain about their men. All women. Sometimes they just need to air their grievances. But you should never join them in that. Never. You mustn't make them feel that they made the wrong choice. On the contrary. You have to defend the man who's being criticised. By defending the man who is being criticised, you indirectly compliment the woman on her good taste.

'Do you really feel that way?' Judith said. 'Sometimes I find it so tiring. All that energy.'

On the beach a little while back, after blasting the copper cooking pot into the air, Ralph had called his wife a bellyacher.

If you asked me, he was absolutely right. Judith *was* a bellyacher. Even back when they shot off the rockets in the garden at the summer house she had nagged and bitched *about nothing*. But she was pretty, and she smelled nice. It wasn't a good idea to marry a woman like Judith. If you did, you'd have to take your feet off the table every time she came in. You'd have to mow the lawn on time and not drink beer in bed. When you burped or farted she would adopt the same serious expression she'd worn when the cooking pot was launched. But I wasn't married to her. Fortunately. I had her only for this evening. Or at most for a few times after this, when we were all back from holiday.

It was hard to admit it, even to myself, it may even have been half-unconscious, but something about her bellyaching excited me. A woman who can't laugh when men fart. Who, if she had the chance, would send those men *out of the classroom*. We would have to wait in the hall until we were called back in again. I could feel my cock in my shorts searching for space at this fantasy. I fought back the urge to grab her right then and there and toss her onto the sand without further ado. To take the initiative. A half-rape, women always like that. All women.

'I can imagine you might get tired of it,' I said. 'On the other hand, you probably don't get bored often with a husband like Ralph. I mean, he's always coming up with something new.'

I myself would become bored to death with that, I knew. After a single day. But I wasn't a woman. I wasn't a woman like Judith. I wasn't a bellyacher. A prim bitch. A prim and horny bitch, true enough, but it was rather like all male fantasies about women in positions of authority (stewardesses, schoolmarms, whores), it was above all so terribly *transparent*. It was this transparency, I knew, which excited me most. Women who complain about everything. About rockets, about making too much noise for the neighbours and making soup pans fly hundreds of yards through the air, about their own husbands acting like little boys, but meanwhile… Meanwhile they whip it right out of your trousers and want you to stuff it in all the way – right up to the hilt.

'It's just that he treats me with no respect, a lot of the time,' Judith said. 'When other people are around, that's when it annoys me most. He always succeeds in making me look like someone who gripes about everything. And because it makes me so mad, in front of other people, I just go away.'

'OK,' I said.

OK, that was the new in-word. At first I'd objected weakly when I heard my daughters using it so often, but as is often the case with in-words, above all it was contagious. Its double meaning was precisely what made it so very useful: you were both saying *yes* and indicating that you understood exactly what the other person meant.

'I started paying attention,' Judith went on. 'He doesn't just do it with me. He does it with all women. I mean, on the one hand he's extremely charming, but he also just sees women as naturally more stupid than men. I don't know, something in his tone, the way he looks at them…'

'OK,' I said once again.

'Don't get me wrong: Ralph is a real ladies' man. That's why I fell for him. The way he looks at you, the way he looked at *me*, as a woman, it just makes you feel attractive. Desirable. That's wonderful for a woman, to see a man look at you like that. But it takes a while before you realise that a ladies' man doesn't just look at *you* that way, but at all women.'

This time I decided to say nothing at all. I thought about Ralph, the ladies' man. About how he had slobbered over Caroline.

'Hasn't Caroline ever said anything to you about that?' Judith asked. 'I mean, you have a very pretty wife, Marc. It wouldn't surprise me in the least.'

'No, not really. I don't think so. At least I've never heard her mention it.'

I stared straight ahead, at the approaching lights of the beach club. I was going to have to be quick about it, a few more minutes and it would be too late – but it was the wrong moment. The wrong conversation, that above all.

'And there's something else,' Judith said; she had stopped walking. That was good. As long as we weren't moving, time stopped too. 'But you have to promise not to tell anyone else. No one. Not even your wife.'

I looked at her. I couldn't see her face clearly, just her hair in silhouette against the background of the dark, murmuring sea. Only that, and something that was reflected in her eyes: a little light, a glimmer, no more than a candle's flame.

'I promise,' I said. The beach was deserted at this point. All I would have to do was take one step forward. One step, and I could run my fingers through that hair, press my lips against hers, and then further down – first we would drop to our knees in the sand, the rest would follow.

'Sometimes, not often but sometimes, he scares me,' Judith said quietly. 'We have a fight, for example, and then suddenly I see it in his eyes: now he's going to hit me, I think. Listen, he's never actually laid a finger on me. He's thrown whole dinner services against the wall, but he's never hit me. I just see it in his eyes. In his thoughts, he's hitting me right now, I think. In his thoughts, he's bouncing me off the walls.'

'OK,' I said, but suddenly that seemed too meagre. 'But as long as he only does it in his thoughts, it's not so terrible, is it?' I added.

Judith sighed deeply. She took me by the wrist. I fought the urge to pull her up against me with one move.

'No, but it makes you uncertain,' she said. 'I've never been able to shake the feeling that one day it might really happen. That he'll lose control and suddenly punch me in the face. Sometimes I think he knows that too. That I think that, I mean. And that's why it's never happened yet.'

'Have the two of you ever talked about this? I mean, mightn't it be better to talk about it? Before it actually happens, I mean.'

I was bullshitting. And I was very much aware of that. As a matter of fact, I didn't give a fuck about the whole subject. But I could never let her notice that, of course. I had to go on playing the interested, sympathetic man. To go on feigning sincere interest. Only the sympathetic man would get that to which he had a right.

'What do you think?' Judith asked. 'Do you think Ralph could suddenly turn violent, just like that?'

I thought about the Norwegian girl whose wrist he had twisted, a little less than an hour ago, until she fell to the sand, and how he had then tried to kick her in the stomach. In my mind I could hear him shouting *You fucking shit whore!*

'No, that seems very unlikely to me,' I said, taking Judith's wrist now. 'I mean, Ralph has a lot of surplus energy. People like that can sometimes get very angry. They have to expend their energy. But if you ask me, he makes sure that he expends it in time. With all the things he does, I mean. The way he dives into everything. Violence against women, against his own wife, isn't part of that, I think.' I caressed her wrist with my thumb. 'He's much too kind-hearted for that,' I added, just to sweeten the pot.

'Mum.'

We hadn't seen or heard Alex coming. Now, suddenly, he was standing a few yards away.

Judith and I let go of each other's wrists at the same time. Too quickly, I realised right away: caught in the act.

'Hey, Alex,' Judith said.

'Mum…'

He took two steps towards us. A few blond curls were hanging in front of his eyes. It was hard to see in the semi-darkness, but there was something glistening on his face. Sweat? Or tears?

'Where's Julia?' Judith asked.

'Mum...' he said again; I could hear it in his voice now: he was crying.

He took a final step towards his mother and threw his arms around her. He was almost as tall as she was. Judith laid her hand on the back of his head and pressed him against her. 'Alex, what's wrong? Where's Julia?'

31

Where's Julia? When I run my life back and hit 'Play', it usually starts with those words. Running it back any further is no use. You see a beach and a summer house, a swimming pool and rockets, chunks of swordfish hissing on a grill. Normal holiday snapshots. Snapshots with no hidden meaning. With no emotional charge. Starting with *Where's Julia?* my life only ran forward. It wasn't even that the holiday snapshots suddenly took on meaning or an emotional charge after the fact. No, it wasn't like that: I just didn't want to see them any more.

'What's wrong, Alex?' Judith asked, still pressing her son against her. He didn't reply, there was only the soft sobbing against his mother's breast.

I'm not trying to explain anything away. I did what I did. Next time I would do exactly the same thing, people say, in order to justify their own hasty actions. I don't say that. I would do everything differently. Everything.

'Where's my daughter, goddamn it!' I shouted, grabbing Alex by his upper arm and yanking him roughly from his mother's embrace. 'What have you done with her, you little prick!?'

'Marc!'

Judith took her son by the wrist and tried to pull him to her again.

'You,' I said calmly. 'You just shut up.'

She stared at me for a moment, then let go of Alex.

'Sorry,' I said, then I turned to the boy. 'Julia. Where is Julia?'

'I... I don't know,' he stammered.

Then he started telling his story, in snippets and in no fixed sequence. I had to do my best not to keep interrupting him. Concentrate, I told myself. Concentrate and try not to miss anything. My attentive ear. My attentive, doctor's ear. I could do it if I wanted. Deliver a diagnosis in a minute. Draw a conclusion. In one minute, in order to have the remaining nineteen minutes to myself.

They – Alex and Julia – had walked to the club at the far end of the beach. There they'd had a drink at the bar. 'Coke, Mum, I swear,' he told his mother. 'And Julia had a Fanta.' They watched people dance for a while. Julia wanted to dance too, but Alex didn't. She had tugged on his arm a little, he shouldn't be such a baby, come on, come with me, let's dance. He hadn't budged. There were other teenagers there too, but mostly grown-ups. And even the teenagers were older than them. They were really the youngest. He'd been too embarrassed to dance. Come on, let's go back, he said. They'll be wondering what's keeping us. She called him a wimp, said he was too afraid – and then she'd gone out onto the dance floor alone. He had stayed and watched her for a while, alone at the bar, how she pushed her way through the dancing crowd and then started dancing herself. She hadn't looked over at him any more. She danced. First with a group of girls who were all older than her, but there were also boys who came and danced around her. He'd felt torn. He could have done it; he could have gone to her, he could have danced, and then everything would have been like it was before – but he was afraid she would laugh at him, that she would really think he was a wimp then.

The story sounded familiar to me. The story of every man, credible if only for that reason. He had been angry too, he said. She shouldn't have left him alone there like that. At a certain point he had walked out of the bar, out onto the beach. He was going to repay her in kind, he figured. In a little while she'd go looking for him and not be able to find him. He had walked all the way down to the waterline. He had stood there for a bit, he didn't know how long, no more than a couple of minutes. His anger subsided. He walked slowly back to the club, out onto the dance floor. He was going to surprise her. He was going to dance with her. But she wasn't there. She was gone. He had looked all over the dance floor, front to back and left to right. A few times he was relieved when he thought he saw her, but it turned out to be someone else. A girl who looked like her. Then he had walked all the way around the club. After that, he tried looking in the ladies'. He'd tried to figure out what could have happened. She'd grown tired of dancing and gone looking for him. And when she couldn't find him, she had decided to go back. Back to the beach where his parents were. His parents and her father.

Didn't you have your phone with you? Judith interrupted him at this point. So what if? I thought. Was he supposed to call her? After all, Julia didn't have hers with her… But the next moment I realised that it wasn't such a dumb question after all. He could have called *us*. His mother. To ask whether we had seen Julia. No, Alex said. I left it at home, the battery was dead. He had walked around the building one more time. At the back, the beach stopped and a stretch of rocky coastline began.He had called her name a few times. Finally he decided that the best thing would be for him to go back too. He had walked down the beach in this direction for a while, but he soon started having misgivings. Would she have crossed this dark stretch of beach all alone? No, he realised. She never would have done that. Not even if she'd been meaning to make him worried by taking off without saying anything.

He went back to the beach club. He went up and asked the barmen. A thirteen-year-old girl? Long blonde hair? Wouldn't they have noticed that? He'd had to shout at the top of his lungs to be heard above the music. The barmen spoke only broken English. But indeed – one of them seemed to remember Julia. At least, his description fitted perfectly. But then he shook his head. He'd seen her, he said. On the dance floor. But that was a while back. Had she left with someone else, maybe? Alex asked. The barman shrugged. Sorry, he said. I didn't see her leave. At one point I just noticed that she wasn't there any more. Alex had started wondering again. Should he ask other people whether they had seen her? Should he go looking for her again? Or would it be better to walk back to the other beach? To us?

My mind was racing. Alex's story had already been going on too long, I felt. I felt no panic, more like a kind of icy calm. My heart wasn't racing, but actually pounding more slowly. Action. I was good at acting. At active intervention.

'But didn't the two of you see her then?' Alex asked.

I noticed something about him, something I couldn't quite put my finger on. Maybe it was the tone in which he asked that question: not so much as though it truly interested him, more like a question he logically *had* to ask.

He didn't look at me when he asked it either. He looked only at his mother. He's *afraid* to look at me, I thought. He feels guilty because he's lost something of mine. *My daughter*. He should have paid more attention. I never should have let my daughter go with him. But I hadn't! I realised the very next moment.

I had to restrain myself in order not to grab him again and shake him till his teeth rattled. We hadn't run into Julia. It was possible, theoretically it wasn't a hundred per cent impossible, that she had walked back alone to the beachside restaurants and that we had missed her. But only theoretically. Judith had been sitting in clear view on the higher part of the beach, watching Lisa and Thomas play football. I myself had spent no more than ten minutes in the bathroom at the restaurant. She would have had to see us. We would have had to see her.

Julia was still here, I decided. *Here* being in or around the beach club, which was only a few hundred yards away. My heart was beating more slowly, but also more heavily. Act now. There's no time to lose, every second counts, that's what popped into my mind – and I almost laughed out loud at that line, which seemed more like something from a TV cop show than from life itself – life (*my life!*) as it was unfolding right now.

Without looking back at Judith or Alex, I started running towards the club.

'Marc!' I heard Judith shouting behind me. 'Wait!'

I didn't turn around, I kept on running. Another ten yards or so. Then I realised that what I was doing wasn't wise: three of us could work more efficiently. We had to look for Julia, all three of us.

I stopped for a moment. 'Come on!' I gestured. 'Hurry up!'

While Judith went to look in the ladies' room, I had Alex show me the barman he'd asked about Julia. I flagged the man down and shouted in his ear. He screamed something back that I didn't understand. Then he pointed at the people who were crowding up to the bar to order. I'm her father, I screamed. He looked at me again. Maybe he was doing his best to share my concern, but he only half pulled it off. *Little girls grow up*, I read in his eyes. *They start doing things that Daddy doesn't have to know about*. I elbowed my way through the dancing crowd. Just asking random strangers whether they'd seen a thirteen-year-old girl didn't seem like a good idea. Beside the dance floor, a couple of aluminium barstools and tall tables had been set up in the sand. Judith was standing beside one of the tables.

'Where's Alex?' I asked.

'I sent him back,' she said.

I stared at her.

'I told him to go back as fast as he could,' she went on. 'That he should find Ralph, in any case. But who knows, maybe Julia's there too.'

I looked at her face, which was lit by the flashing red and yellow disco lights. It was still the same face that I had wanted to take in my hands before pressing my lips to hers, just a few minutes ago, but now what I saw in that face was above all the concerned mother. Concerned not about my daughter, but about her own son. I don't know whether it occurred to me then or only much later, but there was something about Alex's story that didn't make sense. The timing in particular. How long had he actually hung around there before deciding to sound the alarm? He had cried when he met us on the beach. But was he already crying, or did he start only when he caught sight of his mother?

'He could have helped us,' I said. 'He could have pointed out someone here. Someone he saw Julia dancing with, for example. Something might have occurred to him all of a sudden.'

'I think he should be with his father right now. He's completely confused, Marc. You saw how guilty he feels. Towards you.'

To be with his father, I thought, and almost burst out laughing. Indeed, maybe he was better off being with his father. His father could probably show him how to force girls down onto the sand if they put up a fight.

'Does he have good reason to feel guilty, Judith?' I asked – and right away I regretted having posed the question so directly. Even more, I regretted the accusatory tone. I had failed to camouflage my doubts about Alex's version of events. And that wasn't good. Now his mother was forewarned. That would make it much harder to catch him telling a lie later on.

'Marc, please…' Judith said; she blinked her eyes. 'Alex is still a child. He lost Julia. But you heard the way it went. Maybe it wouldn't have happened to us that way. But Julia is the one who walked away first, not Alex.'

I looked at her. In my mind I counted to ten. I looked at the light from the disco lamps playing across her forehead, cheeks and mouth. Was this woman simply stupid? Or was she in fact much more intelligent than I'd supposed? I had to watch what I said, but I could hardly contain myself. You're a woman too, you stupid cunt! I felt like shouting. You should know what can happen to women. A man has to protect a woman. *Even if he's only a child!*

I took a deep breath. 'You're right,' I said. 'We shouldn't jump to conclusions.'

Fortunately, one always has the clichés. The clichés that toss us the lifebelt when we're about to drown in troubled waters. I saw Judith's face relax. She pulled out her mobile phone and slid it open. 'Shall I try Ralph?' she said. 'Ask if Alex is already there? So Ralph knows he's on his way, in any case.'

Yes, do that, I thought. Call Ralph. He can tell you from experience that all women are whores. Then no one will need to feel guilty any more. I looked past Judith's head at the white, foamy waves curling and breaking against the beach. What I really felt like doing was leaving her here. Walking away without a word. But that would not be wise, I realised. For all sorts of reasons, that wouldn't be wise.

'Call him,' I said. 'Meanwhile, I'll go and look down there.' I pointed towards the sea, to the place where the sand stopped and the rocks began. The rocks in the water itself were fairly low, running out dozens of yards into the sea, but close to the beach they rose quickly. Behind one of those tall rocks, the moon had just appeared.

And it was in the pale light of that moon that I now saw the little group of people. They were standing together a few hundred yards from us, half hidden by one of the rocky outcrops close to the waterline. Five or six of them. They were looking at something. At something on the ground. They were standing around something.

'Ralph?' Judith said. 'Where are you?'

Someone left the little group and started running towards the beach club.

'What did you say? Where?' Judith stuck a finger in her ear and turned away from me. 'What do you mean? Why aren't you...?'

I didn't hear the rest. I took a few giant steps at first, then I started running too – towards the spot where the group had gathered, at the same time trying to cut off the man who was running towards the club: he was so close by then that I could see that it was indeed a man, a man in white cut-off trousers and a white T-shirt, wearing tennis shoes. White too. Those are the kinds of details you remember later. By that time you already know that both the little group and the man in white have something to do with you – have *everything* to do with you.

What is it? I shouted in English. What's happened?

An ambulance! the man shouted back breathlessly. We have to call an ambulance.

I'm a doctor, I said. For the second time that night.

Julia was lying in the wet sand between the rocks. The group parted when I knelt down beside her and felt her pulse. I laid my ear to her chest and spoke her name quietly. She was deathly still, her face felt cold, but I could detect a weak pulse. Weak but regular.

I put my forearm behind her neck and raised her head slightly. It was only then that my gaze travelled down the rest of her body. I was her father, but I looked with a doctor's eye. As a doctor I saw within those few seconds what had happened. The visible marks left no room for doubt. As a father, I won't go into detail about the precise nature of those marks. Not even so much because I swore an oath of confidentiality, but simply because of the right to privacy. My daughter's privacy, that is.

So I'll stick to presenting the thoughts that flashed through my mind at that moment.

The person who's responsible for this is alive only in the biological sense, I thought. He's walking around here somewhere right now, because that is what human organisms happen to do. Walk around. The heart pumps. The heart is a mindless force. As long as the heart keeps pumping blood, we keep moving. But one day it would stop. Better sooner than later. I, as a doctor, would see to that.

'Daddy…'

Julia blinked her eyes briefly, then closed them again.

'Julia.'

I shook her head gently; I lay my other hand against the back of it, against her hair. I dug my fingers into that hair and pressed her against my chest.

'Julia,' I said.

32

Caroline didn't say anything. At least, she didn't say the things I'd been afraid she'd say. For God's sake, how could you have let her go to that beach club all alone? Why didn't you go looking for her right away? If you'd gone looking for her right away, this never would have happened!

No, she didn't say anything as I lifted Julia from the back seat of the car and carried her up to the summer house. All she did was bury her face in her hands – only for a moment, two seconds at most. Then she pulled herself together and went back to being her daughter's mother. She caressed Julia's hair and whispered sweet things to her.

But even later on, she never said those other things. You sometimes hear that the first minutes and hours are crucial when there's a tragedy in the family. Those first minutes and hours determine whether the bonds are strong enough to survive the tragedy. A person who starts making accusations can cause irreparable damage. I was familiar with the statistics. Divorce was more the rule than the exception. You'd think that a tragedy would bring people closer together. That the bond would be strengthened by shared grief. But that's not the case. A lot of people actually want to forget the grief. And it's that other person who keeps reminding them of it.

I can't blame the people who choose to forget. And I don't mean to claim higher moral ground for us simply because we did draw closer together. I wouldn't even dare to claim that we *chose* to do that. It's just the way it went.

We were standing at the foot of the steps to the summer house. I still had Julia in my arms. There was a moment of hesitation. Did I really want to carry my daughter up there? To put her down on the sofa in the living room? Where everyone could see her? But Ralph and Judith's bedroom, or her mother's, or the boys', didn't seem like good options either. Better then to go to our tent. I knew what I wanted more than anything else. I wanted to hide my daughter from the eyes of others. I wanted to be alone with her. With us. I wanted her to be alone with us.

At that same moment Emmanuelle came out of the house. She appeared in the doorway of the ground-floor apartment and waved us over.

'Come,' she said. 'Come here.'

First I had carried Julia to the beach club. There I had a brief moment of doubt about what was best. Judith suggested we call an ambulance, but I cut her short. No ambulance, I said decidedly. I thought about the flashing lights, about the people crowding around the stretcher as it was slid into the back. About the siren. About the inevitable destination: a hospital. At the hospital, other people would see to my daughter. Helpful nurses. Doctors. I was a doctor myself. I had been the first to assess the situation. I had made the only correct diagnosis. There was no need for others to make that same diagnosis all over again.

Then Judith suggested that she get the car and that I stay with Julia. I have to admit, she reacted efficiently. She kept it together, as they say. To be honest, I was almost expecting her to lose control. But she remained dead calm. She didn't try to argue with me. OK, she said, if that's what you want, that's how we'll do it. She tried to lay a hand on Julia's forehead, but when I turned away from her she didn't try again. I wanted to get out of there as quickly as possible. People had already come over and were standing around us. I was enraged by the way they looked at my daughter. Too many people had looked at her already. I'm a doctor, I said. So please keep moving. Everything is under control.

No, I told Judith. We're getting out of here. I'll carry her.

And that's how it went. As I walked, Julia lost consciousness again. I shook her awake. She had to stay awake. At the first beach we found Alex, Thomas and Lisa. No trace of Ralph or Stanley. Given the circumstances, I remained fairly level-headed. I kept an eye out for Alex's reaction. He looked at Julia only quickly, then looked away. He didn't come any closer. Looking back on it, I suppose my body language was clear as a bell. I was like an animal that growls when an intruder tries to approach its young. No, I corrected myself: not *like* an animal. An animal.

The crucial thing now was Lisa. I saw her face as she came running up to us. 'Julia doesn't feel at all well,' I said quickly, before she could ask. 'Come on, we're going back to the house.'

Thomas danced around us a few times, yelling 'Football! Football!', until Judith grabbed him roughly by the arm and yanked on it so hard that he fell onto the sand. I saw the tears in his eyes, but Judith pulled him up just as roughly by both wrists. 'Just stop messing about, Thomas,' she said. 'Get moving!'

And that is how we walked to the car. Me, carrying Julia in my arms, and right behind us Judith, who was holding Lisa's hand, followed by Alex and a moping Thomas. On the way back from the beach club, Judith had told me that Ralph was already at the summer house, he had taken their car. Stanley was nowhere to be found.

'My God, what happened to your car?' Judith asked. She pointed at the front bumper, which was hanging loose on one side. The chrome ring around the left headlight was dented and broken in one place, the glass was shattered. *Go to the garage tomorrow morning and have them fix it*, Stanley had said to me just a few hours ago, here at this same spot. *I'll pay for the whole thing, it was worth every penny*.

'We took that dark road up there,' I said. 'I think we must have swiped a tree.'

Judith asked no further questions. She held open the back door so I could lie Julia on the seat. Then she crawled in beside my daughter and took Julia's head gently into her lap. Sliding up a little towards the middle, she waved to Alex to get in. She told Thomas and Lisa to sit together up front.

'But that's not allowed!' Thomas said. 'That's against the law!'

'Thomas...' Judith said – and that was enough; his arms crossed angrily over his chest, he moved in beside Lisa on the passenger seat.

Before I started the car, I called Caroline.

'Don't get upset,' I said quietly. 'It's not really all that bad.' It really was all that bad, but I didn't want anyone to panic before we got there. At the same time, I did my best to speak so quietly that Julia couldn't hear me. 'No one has been hurt,' I said. That, too, was a lie.

'I'm on my way now,' I said, and hung up.

Emmanuelle straightened the quilt on the twin bed and fluffed up the pillows. As I lowered Julia onto it, Emmanuelle went into the bathroom and came back a minute later with a towel and water in a porcelain bowl. She sat down on the other side of the bed, close to the head end, moistened one corner of the towel and held it gently to Julia's forehead.

'*Voilà*,' she said. Then she looked at me. 'Do you know what happened? Do you know who...?' I shook my head. Only then, when I looked straight at her, did I realise that she wasn't wearing her sunglasses. For the first time since we'd arrived. For the first time I was looking into her eyes.

'Mum...'

I took Julia's wrist. 'Mum will be here in a minute,' I said.

Judith and Caroline had gone upstairs with Lisa and Thomas. Judith had offered to stay with them and put them to bed, but after a brief exchange of glances with me, Caroline took Lisa by the hand and climbed the stairs with her. I could see in her eyes how torn she was; she wanted to be with Julia, first of all, but on the other hand she didn't want to leave her younger daughter with a stranger, not under these circumstances. Parents often forget one child when they're worried about the other. Caroline followed her intuition from the start. I tried to too, but I have to admit that it was harder for me.

Just then I heard a sound behind me. I turned and saw Ralph standing in the doorway. He looked as if he had just come out of the shower. His hair was still wet and plastered against his skull. And he had changed his clothes after coming back from the beach: he had on a clean pair of white shorts and a red T-shirt.

'I heard...' he began; he leaned with one hand against the doorpost above his head and made no move to come in. 'Judith just told me...'

My memory of what I did then is still utterly clear. I had absolutely no desire to see Ralph here in my daughter's presence. What I felt like most was telling him to buzz off and leave us alone. But I also thought about the future. About the various suspects. I had seen Ralph in action on the beach. I had witnessed the way Julia had grabbed at her bikini bottoms that time by the ping-pong table. Still, somehow, I found it too great a leap. The leap from the Ralph who slobbered over young girls, violent Ralph – to *this*. Logistically speaking, it also wasn't very likely. After what had happened on the beach, would Ralph really have walked all that way to the club, then back to the car, and then finally driven all the way home? I tried to squeeze it into a credible timeframe, but all things considered it seemed pretty improbable. We had still been at the beach club when Judith called home and got Ralph on the line. No, I corrected myself quickly: she got Ralph on the line, who *said* he was at home. I had to pay close attention, the way I had earlier with Alex. Not rule out anything or anyone in advance.

Now I was paying attention. I shifted my gaze from Ralph's face to my daughter's face. Julia had her eyes open. I saw what she was looking at. She was looking at Ralph. She blinked her eyes.

'Hi,' she said quietly.

'Hi, girlie...' I heard Ralph say.

Now I turned to look at him. I studied his face. I looked at that face the way I look at the faces of my patients. Through the eyes of a doctor. At a glance I could see whether someone drank too much, whether they suffered from latent depression, or whether they were weighed down by the burden of bad sex. I rarely get it wrong. I know when people are lying. 'Half a bottle of wine at dinner, doctor, no more than that...' I never let them fob me off with answers like that. *And what about after work?* I ask on. *Don't you stop at a bar for a drink then?* 'One or two beers, max. But that was only yesterday, I don't do that every day.' *Does your husband perhaps ejaculate prematurely?* I ask the woman with the deep, blue bags under her eyes. *Are there perhaps things you wish he would do with you but that you're uncomfortable talking about?* I hear someone whistling in the waiting room: when he comes into my office, he's still whistling. *Suicide is a realistic option*, I hear myself saying a minute later. *Some people take comfort in the realisation that they have control over the way their life ends. What they dread most of all is the implementation. The way in which. A train is so violent. Cutting your wrists in the bathtub is so bloody. Hanging is painful, it takes a long time before death comes. Sleeping pills may be vomited up. But there are substances that bring about a painless, easy death. I can help you to get them…*

Ralph Meier pinched the bridge of his nose between thumb and forefinger. He pressed his fingertips against the corners of his eyes. 'Aw, damn,' he murmured. Not for a single moment did I lose sight of the fact that he was an actor. One of the rare good actors. 'Do you want something to drink, Marc? Shall I get you a drink? A beer? Or maybe a whisky?'

I shook my head. I looked at my daughter again. When I saw her face, something fell from me. Something. Not everything. A tiny little part of the weight that had been pressing down on me for the last hour or so. That would continue to press down on me for the rest of my life, I realised that even then.

Still looking at Ralph, a faint smile had appeared on Julia's face.

'I'd like something to drink,' she said. 'I'm so thirsty. A glass of milk would be great.'

'A glass of milk,' Ralph said. 'Coming right up.'

33

That evening, the rest of our lives began. Let me say right away that I'm not a big fan of melodrama. I also have a natural aversion to dramatic statements. *The rest of our lives*… I'd heard people say that often enough. People who had lost someone or something. Who'd had something happen to them that you wouldn't wish on anyone – something you would never get over. Still, it had always sounded fake to me. It's only when it happens to you that you know it's not fake. There is simply no better description for it than 'the rest of your life'. Everything gets heavier. Especially time. Something happens to time. It doesn't really stand still, but there's no denying that it slows down. Like in a waiting room with a huge clock on the wall. You sit in the waiting room and, when you look at the clock five minutes later, only three minutes have gone by. The mind keeps a time of its own. A day during which we have all kinds of things to do 'flies by', as they say. A day you spend waiting slows down. All the more when you don't know what you're waiting for. You sit in the waiting room. You try not to watch the clock. You don't know what you're waiting for. The doctor's office or government institution to which the waiting room belongs probably closed a long time ago. But there's no one to wake you from your spell.

No one who comes by to say you might as well go home.

One moment you're a family with two lovely daughters, the next moment you're in a waiting room. You're waiting for nothing. In fact, you're waiting only for time to pass. All your hope is focused on the passing of that time. No, not all your hope. Your only hope. And the more time that passes, the further away you move from the point where the rest of your life started. But you don't know where it ends. The rest of our lives goes on and on to this day.

Later, I would keep reconstructing that first evening, down to the slightest detail. Ralph bringing the glass of milk and leaving again. Then Caroline coming downstairs. She took Emmanuelle's place at the head of the bed. She held Julia's hand. Every once in a while she ran her hand over Julia's head.

There was one moment I don't want to talk about much. For reasons of privacy. I asked Julia cautiously whether it was all right with her if I looked to be sure there wasn't… I was a doctor. But I was also her father. 'If you don't want that, just tell me,' I said. 'We can also go to a doctor here in town. Or to a hospital.' When I mentioned the word 'hospital', Julia bit her lower lip. 'No, it's nothing that bad,' I said quickly. 'We don't have to go to a hospital. But I do have to look at what we have to do. *Someone* has to look…'

She nodded and closed her eyes. I drew back the blanket carefully and looked. Years ago, Lisa had once slipped in the shower and fallen hard on a metal edge. She had bled a bit. Also… there. It wasn't too serious, she was more shocked than anything else. I calmed her down. As her father. And at the same time I did what I had to do. As a doctor.

I tried to do the same thing now. But this was different. Julia cried with her eyes closed. Caroline used the corner of the towel to wipe away her tears and whispered sweet words. I tried to ask as few questions as possible. I did what had to be done, then I pulled up the blanket again.

It was soon after this that Caroline and I looked at each other. We looked at each other: wordlessly, we both asked ourselves whether this was the right moment, or whether Julia should rest first. Sleep. We didn't want to remind her of the worst, but on the other hand, acting quickly was the only right option.

On the way from the beach club to the car park, I had already asked her once. I had whispered it in her ear, so Judith wouldn't hear. *Who?* I whispered. *Who was it? Someone you know?*

And at first, Julia hadn't answered. I started thinking that maybe she hadn't heard me, then she said: 'I don't know, Daddy…'

I didn't go on asking. Shock, that was my diagnosis. Shock blocks out what we don't want to see. What we don't want to be reminded of.

Now I nodded to Caroline. She was the one who had to do it, we agreed on that without speaking. This was a question a mother should ask.

'Julia?' Caroline said quietly, leaning over close to her daughter's face and at the same time laying the palm of her hand on Julia's cheek. 'Can you tell us what happened? Can you tell us who… who left the club with you? Or who you left with?'

Julia shook her head. 'I don't know,' she said.

Caroline caressed her cheek.

'First you were with Alex,' she said. 'And then? After that? What happened then?'

Julia blinked. Tears welled up in the corners of her eyes again. 'Was I with Alex? Where was I with Alex?'

Caroline and I looked at each other.

Julia had started crying again. 'I don't know...' she sobbed. 'I really don't know...'

Later that night, Stanley came home as well. He had walked the whole way, he told us. When he got to the parking lot there were no longer any cars he recognised, and he'd assumed that we'd forgotten him.

He came in for just a moment to say hello. Emmanuelle had already explained everything to him. He and Emmanuelle had decided that we should spend the night in their apartment and that the two of them would sleep in our tent. Normally speaking, when someone makes an offer like that, you tell them a couple of times that 'that's really not necessary' – but this wasn't normal. Nothing was normal. We didn't discuss it, we just accepted.

Later on, I went to our tent with Stanley to take out some of our things, so they would have more room. Stanley put his arm around my shoulders. He said again how terrible he felt about all this. For us. For Julia. He swore. In his American English. Also in

American English, he went on to say what should happen to men who did things like this. I could only agree with him.

Then he clasped my hand. He pulled out his packet of cigarettes and offered me one.

'There's something else…' he said.

We stood and smoked in front of the tent while Stanley told me how he had walked back to the summer house. Along the same high, sandy road that we had taken on the way down. And so he had also come past the spot where we had run the man from the green campsite off the road.

'His car was still there,' Stanley said. 'At exactly the same spot. It was really weird. I mean, it looked as though, after us, no one else had come past there. But it gets even weirder…' He glanced over towards the house. 'I tried the door,' he went on, almost in a whisper. 'And it was open. And the window was rolled down the whole way too. That's strange, isn't it? I mean, who would leave a car behind like that? I took a good look, but it didn't look like it was stuck in the sand or anything. I think he could have just driven away…'

'Maybe he couldn't get it started?'

Stanley shook his head. 'No, it's not that. Listen, I did something that maybe wasn't such a good idea. I leaned in through the window and I saw that the key was still in the ignition.'

Now, for the first time, I felt a shiver run down the back of my neck. The kind of shiver you feel at the cinema when the film takes an unexpected turn.

'Jesus,' I said.

'So I climbed in the car and turned the key. And it started right away...'

I said nothing. I took such a deep drag on my cigarette that I started coughing.

'I got out again. I even did what they do in the movies. Because I didn't have a handkerchief or anything like that, I took off my T-shirt and wiped down everything with it: the key, the steering wheel, the door. Then I walked around the car. There's a pretty steep slope on the other side there. I climbed down a little, but then I started to slide. I had to grab hold of a bush. Besides, it was pitch dark up there. I shouted. Once. Then I came back here on foot.'

'But do you think he...'

'I don't know, Marc. I just think it's weird that he didn't keep on driving. And if he couldn't, for whatever reason, then it's also weird that he would leave his door unlocked and the window open and the key in the ignition. Something doesn't add up.'

I felt that shiver down the back of my neck again. I thought about the campsite owner who for some reason had walked around his car and then fallen down the hill.

'Maybe his nerves were shot,' Stanley said, as though he could read my mind. 'Maybe we scared him more than we thought. Who knows what somebody does when they've been run off the road.... I just wanted you to know as soon as possible. Even in this situation. Especially in this situation.'

Now I was the one who got to read Stanley's mind. But I didn't say anything. I let him say it.

'Sooner or later they're going to find that car, Marc. Who knows, maybe not tonight, but for sure tomorrow morning, once it gets light. The first thing they'll do is go looking for the driver. Maybe he just walked home, who knows. But maybe he didn't… They're going to notice the damage to the back of his car. Your car has some damage too, Marc. There's no connection, not yet. Besides, that guy has no idea who we are. But in any case, I wouldn't take your car to a garage here. I'd head out. Maybe not tonight. But tomorrow morning for sure.'

34

Julia was asleep. Caroline and I had carried two chairs out and were sitting outside the apartment with the door ajar. We were smoking. Caroline looked at her watch.

'We have to go to the police, Marc,' she whispered. 'We have to report this as soon as possible. Maybe now, right away. Or do you think we should wait till morning?'

'No,' I said.

My wife looked at me. 'No, what?'

'I don't want that. I don't want to take Julia to a police station. All the questions they would ask... I mean, something happened. We *know* what happened. You and I know. And she knows too, even though she can't remember anything right now. Maybe that's better too, that she doesn't know right now.'

'But Marc, we can't do that! Who knows, that man may still be walking around somewhere. They always say that when there's been a crime. That you have to act fast. The first twenty-four hours. They're the most important. The sooner we report it, the less chance that bastard has of getting away. The greater the chance that they can find him.'

'Of course. You're right, Caroline. Completely right. But we can't take Julia to a police station right now. You don't want to do that to her. And I don't either.'

'But the two of us could go, right? Or at least one of us. One of us goes to the police and the other stays with Julia.'

'OK,' I said. 'I'll stay with Julia.'

'No, I will.'

We looked at each other. Caroline had wiped the tears from her face. Her expression was grim, that above all.

'Marc, I don't want to whine about who she needs most right now, her father or her mother. I think it's her mother. You can go to the police.'

I could have told my wife that at this point what our daughter needed most was *a doctor*. Maybe not so much her father as the general physician I was too. A doctor who sat beside her when she came out of her initial shock and started remembering things. But in my heart I knew that Caroline was right. Julia had to be able to hold her *mother's* hand. Her mother, who was a woman as well. A woman. Not a man, not at this point. Even if that man was her father.

'I don't know, Caroline,' I said. 'I mean, imagine I go now, then they're going to ask if they can question Julia later on. Tomorrow. We don't want that, do we?'

'But there's no use in questioning her, is there? She doesn't remember anything anyway?'

'Do you think they'll be satisfied with that, with our word that our daughter can't remember anything? Caroline, please! They'll come in here with the whole CSI team. With psychologists and specialists. With understanding female officers who've seen it all before. Who supposedly know how to get rape victims with amnesia remembering and talking again.'

'But still, that's what we want.'

'What?'

'For her to remember something. That she remembers what happened. What that bastard looks like.'

I tried to remember what I knew about amnesia. What I had learned about it at medical school once, long ago. Memory loss was often selective, I remembered that. The brain blocks out a traumatic experience. Sometimes that experience never comes back at all. On the beach Julia had recognised me right away, as well as Judith later on, her little sister, Thomas, Alex, her mother, Emmanuelle and Ralph. With total amnesia, people often don't even know who they are: they no longer recognise their own faces in the mirror, let alone the faces of other people.

Under the circumstances, I hadn't wanted to ask Julia, but it seemed as though the memory loss went before all that. *Was I with Alex?* She still knew who Alex was, but she couldn't remember that they had walked the length of the beach to the club together.

And there was something else too. That afternoon and evening, my daughter had tried to ignore me as much as possible. When I asked her a question, she barely answered. She probably hadn't looked me straight in the eye even once.

After she'd seen me in the kitchen. With Judith.

But from the moment I'd found her on the beach, and as I was carrying her to the car, and after that, here, in Stanley and

Emmanuelle's apartment, while I had been examining her, she had only looked at me sweetly. Sadly, but sweetly.

Was it possible? I asked myself now. Was it possible that Julia's amnesia went all the way back to the early afternoon, or maybe even before that, and that she no longer knew that she had seen me with Judith in the kitchen?

I couldn't ask her straight out, it had to be something casual. A remark about something else, about that same Saturday. I reconstructed the day from start to finish. The fledgling. Lisa finds the little bird that fell out of the olive tree. Breakfast. After that, Lisa and I go to the zoo. And when I came back... When we came back, Caroline was gone. And Ralph and Stanley and Emmanuelle too. I had gone upstairs. To the kitchen. Judith and her mother and I had looked out of the kitchen window... That was it! Miss Wet T-shirt... Julia and Lisa had taken turns walking the diving board as though it were a catwalk. They had let Alex hose them down... I thought about my daughter, about the coquettish pose she'd assumed, how she'd pulled her hair up at the back of her head and then let it fall...

That was what I needed to ask Julia about when she woke up. In my mind I tried to formulate a casual question (*Remember this afternoon / yesterday, when Alex sprayed you with the hose down at the pool? You guys really had fun, didn't you?*) but it didn't seem quite right. The word 'fun' in particular seemed out of place.

'I've been thinking,' Caroline said. 'Maybe you're right. Maybe we should keep Julia away from too many prying eyes at this point. I hadn't thought about it that way: that they would want to ask her all kinds of things. It would probably only make her more confused. The police and everything. But then what are we going to do? We have to do something, don't we? I mean, we can't just let that bastard walk away, can we?'

'We could call. We could place an anonymous call and say that there's a rapist on the loose.'

Caroline sighed, and at that same moment I saw how senseless it would be to make a call like that. I thought about Alex again. About the way he'd acted on the beach. I couldn't see him as a potential rapist. But I still had a nasty feeling that he hadn't told us everything.

'Marc,' Caroline said, placing her hand on my forearm. 'You're a doctor. You can tell. How bad is she? Should we take her to a hospital? Or is it better to let her calm down as much as possible? Let her rest for a few days, and then go straight home?'

'She doesn't have to go to a hospital. She doesn't know what happened. I mean, she knows *something* happened. And she probably also knows what. She's thirteen. I gave her something to stop the pain. But she's... she feels...'

I felt my voice falter, there was high wheezing in my throat, and I started coughing. Caroline squeezed my arm.

'OK,' she said. 'Then that's what we'll do. We'll let her take it easy for a day. Tomorrow. And then we go on Monday, if you think she can handle the drive. On the back seat. We can make a bed for her on the back seat.'

'It would be better...' I looked at my watch. It was two-thirty in the morning. 'It would be better if we left today. Later on, as soon as it gets light.'

'Isn't that kind of rushing things? We haven't even slept yet. And for Julia—'

'It's just better,' I interrupted her. 'For her sake. We have to get away from here as soon as possible. We need to go home.'

35

It was a couple of hours later – I was still sitting in my chair in front of the apartment, smoking; Caroline had crawled into bed with Julia – when Ralph came down the steps.

'I figured, maybe he could use some of this,' he said. He had a bottle of whisky under his arm and two glasses filled with ice in his hands.

We sat beside each other for a while, not saying a word. Somewhere in the dry brush on the far side of the pool, a stubborn cricket persisted in rubbing its hind legs together. That and the ice tinkling in our glasses were the only sounds in an otherwise silent garden. The first daylight had appeared in the eastern sky. I stared at the motionless water of the pool, lit from below. Then I looked at the diving board. It was the same diving board as yesterday, but it was a different board nonetheless. The garden and the summer house were a different garden and summer house too. And not only that. For the time being, I didn't want to see another garden, summer house or pool. Maybe never again. I wanted to go home.

Ralph rubbed his right knee. 'That was a good kick, Marc. Where did you learn that? In the army? At school?'

I looked at his knee. You couldn't see anything on the outside, it looked like a normal, hairy, male knee, but on the inside all the muscles and tendons were stretched to the limit, I knew that. I hadn't paid attention when he came down the steps and sat beside me, but he would almost certainly be limping for the next few days.

'What did you do after that?' I asked. 'Did you go home right away?'

'I walked along the beach for a bit. Along the sea. Well, walked... it was more like hobbling. At first I didn't feel much, but after that it started pounding and throbbing inside there.' He tapped his knee. 'I figured, what am I doing here anyway? I'm going home.'

I have to admit that I hadn't taken Ralph's knee into account in my earlier calculations. I had thought about whether he could have walked to the beach club and back. And whether he could have been home by the time Judith called him. But I had forgotten all about the knee.

Why would Ralph Meier have walked more than half a mile to that club with a painful, pounding knee? And then back again? It seemed not only highly improbable, but also nearly physically impossible.

'You have to keep moving it, that's important,' I said. 'If you sit still the whole time, it will get stiff.'

Ralph stuck his right leg out in front of him. He wiggled his fat toes in their plastic flip-flop. He groaned. He was biting his lower lip, I saw when I glanced over. If it was all playacting, it was good acting. I wasn't ruling out anything. I still took into account the possibility that the whole business with his knee was *a performance*. That he was using his knee as an alibi.

'I talked to Stanley and Emmanuelle,' he said. 'You can stay in the apartment as long as you like. We'll come up with a solution.'

I was about to reply that that wouldn't be necessary, that we would be leaving in a couple of hours, but stopped myself in the nick of time. Who knows, maybe he would be relieved to hear that we were leaving. I didn't want him to be relieved. Not yet.

'Where's Alex?' I asked.

As I stared straight ahead, at the glowing blue water of the pool, I stayed alert to any physical reaction on Ralph's part. And indeed, he shifted in his chair. He leaned forward a bit, ran a hand over his face, then sank back.

'Upstairs,' he said; now he crossed his right leg over his left knee, this time without groaning. 'He's asleep. Want some more?' He had picked up the whisky bottle from the tiles and held it above my glass.

'OK. Did he say anything to you?'

Ralph topped up his own drink before answering. 'He's incredibly upset. He feels guilty. I told him there's no reason for that.'

I took a deep breath. I raised the glass to my lips. The ice had already melted, I tasted lukewarm, watered-down whisky.

Why shouldn't he feel guilty? Maybe he has every reason to feel guilty.

That was what I could have said. But I didn't. I felt my face growing warm, but that wasn't good. I had to keep a cool head. Literally.

'No, he doesn't have to feel guilty,' I said for that very reason. 'It's just that I think he saw something. Something he's afraid to tell us. Precisely *because* he feels guilty.'

'And what do you think he might have seen?' Ralph shifted in his chair again and took a few quick gulps of whisky. Body language. If his body language told me anything, it was that he wasn't telling me everything he knew either. Or else he was simply trying to protect his son.

Then I realised something else. Something that hadn't occurred to me before, strangely enough. Julia couldn't remember anything. But I had not told Ralph that. I hadn't told Alex either, or anyone for that matter. No one but Caroline and I, in fact, knew about Julia's memory loss. Or did they? I tried to run back through the last few hours, down to the smallest detail. Who had been here in the apartment at which moment, and who hadn't.

They had all given us as much room and asked as few questions as possible. Judith... After she'd put Thomas and Lisa to bed, Judith had come down and asked something. Whether Julia knew anything. She's still in shock, we answered. She doesn't know. Her memory is probably blocked, I'd said, it happens more often with things like this. We were whispering. And when Julia opened her eyes partway, we stopped. Emmanuelle hadn't asked any questions; Stanley hadn't either, later on. It was quite possible that Judith had told Ralph what she'd heard. But even then... Was it likely that Ralph would have sat down beside me with a bottle of whisky if he knew that it was only a matter of time before Julia identified the man who had attacked her?

Unless... my temples started pounding. Unless Julia was already unconscious at the time... You read about things like that. That they put something in your drink when you're not looking. A pill that makes girls get drunk faster. That makes them giggly. *More accommodating*. Or that knocks them out altogether. That makes them throw caution to the winds and go along with a man they shouldn't go along with. Sometimes the combination of alcohol and pills is too much, and they lose consciousness.

I tried not to think about it, but I did anyway. A man – a grown man probably – who takes advantage of an unconscious, thirteen-year-old girl. Sick, people say. A person like that is sick. But that's not it. It's not a sickness. Sicknesses can be cured, or at least treated. This was something different. A defect. A design glitch. A bottle of fizzy drink explodes and is taken off the shelves. That's what should happen to men like that. No treatment. More like a factory recall. The whole batch is destroyed. No burial. No cremation. We wouldn't want the ash, the residue to mix with the air we breathe.

I blinked my eyes. Only my *right* eye, I realised right away: I hadn't stopped to think about it, but after coming back from the beach I hadn't been able to open my left eye any more. It didn't hurt, no, it was just closed tightly. First I tried to raise my eyelid in the normal fashion, but when that didn't work I pulled carefully on the lashes. I rubbed the closed eyelid, pressed against it with my knuckles, but the eye remained shut. That was not a good sign, I knew. Before we climbed into the car in a couple of hours, I was going to have an unpleasant task on my hands.

What's with your eye? almost everyone had asked me by now. *Do you want me to take a look at your eye?* Caroline had asked as the one and only. *No*, I'd snapped.

I looked over at the big body of the actor beside me. He was leaning over now, resting his elbows on his thighs, his head in his hands. *The first twenty-four hours are crucial*, Caroline had said. I had to do something. Something I couldn't do later. Later he would have had enough time to think. To choose his answers carefully. Now it was five in the morning and he had downed half a bottle of whisky.

'What was going through your mind, actually, when you twisted that girl's arm and put her in the sand?' I asked calmly.

There was silence for a few seconds.

'Excuse me?' he said. 'What did you say?'

'I asked what you were thinking. When you tried to kick that Norwegian girl.'

He snorted loudly. He looked at me out of the corner of his eye. I looked back. I held his gaze, as they say. With only one eye, of course, but with my good eye I did my best to hold his gaze. I tried not to blink.

'Are you dicking with me, or what?' He grinned, but I didn't grin back.

'Is that your standard reaction when a woman, or in this case a girl, rejects you? To beat her brains out? Or kick her into A&E?'

'Marc! Come on! Who did the kicking around here? I mean, listen to who's talking! Kick her into A&E...' He rubbed his knee again, with a face supposedly contorted with pain. I saw what he was doing, he was trying to turn things around and at the same time laugh it off, but he didn't entirely succeed. I saw it in his look, in his watery eyes – like a frozen pond with a thin layer of water on top: beneath the skim of water the ice is hard as rock. I suddenly knew where I'd seen that look before: during ping-pong games, when he tried to smash the ball. And also that time when he had slipped and fallen, during the first few seconds, when no one dared to laugh: all he felt was pain and he hadn't yet decided how to react.

'Julia told me,' I said. 'About what you did.'

I looked him right in the eye as I said it. Through the water, I was looking at the ice. I was testing to see how thick it was.

'What are you talking about?'

'You know very well what I'm talking about, Ralph. I've seen how you look at women. At all women, regardless of their age. And tonight I also saw how you react when those women don't do exactly what you want.'

There was no body language this time. Unless you can call the absence of body language body language too.

He stared at me, unruffled. 'What did Julia tell you?' he asked.

'That you pulled down her bikini bottoms. And that she didn't like that at all.'

'What? Did she say that? Damn it...' He brought his fist down on his knee. 'That was a game, Marc! A game! We were all pulling down each other's swimsuits. Alex, Thomas, Lisa, Julia too. She pulled down *my* trunks. We almost died laughing. The one who got tagged had to dive in the pool and fetch a coin. Jesus

Christ! A game. And now she's saying... Is she saying that I...? Oh, please no, where the hell does that come from?'

Deep inside my chest, my heart had started pounding. Fast and heavy. But I couldn't let it show. I had to go on.

'Do you think that's normal, Ralph? Do you think it's normal when a grown man pulls down little girls' pants? I mean, maybe a couple of days ago I would thought it was normal, but after tonight on the beach, not any more.'

Now something shifted in Ralph's look. The moisture in his eyes seemed to have dried up just like that. In the whites I saw only the red branches of burst blood vessels.

'What are you trying to say, Marc? Are you trying to make something dirty out of something normal? Just because your daughter's hormones are starting to act up and she suddenly feels bad about a game that she never, not for a single second, let on that she didn't like? I swear, I would have stopped immediately as soon as I noticed that it bothered her. I swear.'

I gulped something down. But there was nothing to gulp. My mouth was dry.

'What did you say?' I asked. 'What was that about hormones?'

'Anybody can see that! Jesus, Marc! Alex was the first victim. First she teases him for days, and finally she drops him anyway. And then she goes running to Daddy to complain about some innocent game. Come on, you're her father. You've got eyes in your head.'

All I did was store up this new information: had Julia dumped Alex? Since when? Yesterday evening they were still in love.

Apparently something had happened at that beach club that I didn't know about. But first I had to concentrate on Ralph.

'You keep talking about innocent games,' I said. 'But how innocent is it when Julia is actually already a woman? Or at least a girl whose hormones are acting up, as you put it. I mean, let me put it this way: Emmanuelle. Did Emmanuelle take part in your little game too? Did you pull down her pants too? Did she have to dive and fetch a coin after you yanked down her bikini bottoms?'

Ralph sprang to his feet. His chair crashed over backwards. He took one faltering step and turned. Now he was standing right in front of me, less than two feet away. He pointed a thick finger at me. The fingertip almost touched my nose.

On the one hand, I was afraid. Afraid he was going to do something to me. On the other, I couldn't have cared less. Ralph was drunk. If he hit me he would knock me out right away, and I wouldn't notice much after that.

'You know what it is,' he said, and I felt a few drops of saliva hit my face. 'You ought to ask yourself who the real degenerate is around here. You're the one who starts thinking about dirty stuff when we're talking about a game. Not me. I can see how your daughter plays the innocent little girl when it suits her. When she goes crying to Daddy. But she already knows exactly how to handle men, Marc. I've seen it with my own eyes. How she flirts and gets everyone going with her cute little dance steps on the diving board. With her little smiles. The way she walks around! I mean, who knows exactly what happened at that club. Who knows who she was enticing with her little fashion model tricks.

Maybe Daddy's blind to it, but every man turns his head when your sweet little daughter walks past. Maybe you don't *want* to see that. Maybe you want her to stay your little girl for ever and ever. But your little girl has already grown up, Marc! And she's just as crafty as the rest of them!'

Now it was my turn to get up from my chair. Placid on the outside. Calmly, without knocking the chair over. But inside I was ready for anything. Ralph was bigger and stronger than me. I would lose. But I could damage him first. For life. I was no fighter, but I knew the weak spots like no other. I knew how to destroy a human body with a few simple interventions.

'What did you say?' I tried to make my voice sound calm too, but there was a quiver to it. 'What was that about how Julia walks around? Are you trying to say that it's her own fault, what happened to her? The way it's ultimately every woman's own fault? Because of the *way they walk around*?'

A window slid open above our heads. The kitchen window, we saw when we looked up.

'Could you two keep it down a little?' Judith said. 'They can hear you a mile away.'

36

We drove north. First along the little coastal roads till we reached the highway. Lisa had fallen asleep in the passenger seat, her body hanging limply in the safety belt, her head leaning at an uncomfortable-looking angle against the car window. Caroline and Julia were asleep as well, I saw in the mirror. We had laid Julia on the back seat, under a sleeping bag, with her head in Caroline's lap. When we lifted her into the car she had woken up for a while, but for the last two hours she'd been sleeping like a log.

It was Sunday morning, traffic was light. But driving with one eye still took a fair bit of effort. I could see the other cars, but it was hard to tell how far away they were. I knew all about it, I'd read about it, at medical school they'd talked about it: you lost your ability to perceive depth. I had never known exactly what I was supposed to imagine by that, but by now I did. It's not like when you just close one eye for a bit. Then the other eye *remembers* depth for a while, it takes about half a day for the world to go flat. As flat as a photograph – there's perspective, but no movement. Experience is all you have to help you get by. You know the dimensions of a car. Experience tells you that a car that's small at first but quickly becomes bigger is probably coming in your direction.

It was already light out. The sun flared on the road's white concrete slabs. I longed for my sunglasses, but was afraid my vision would only get worse if I put them on. The next exit was a petrol station, and I took it: there was enough in the tank, but I needed to get something into my stomach. A cup of coffee. And a sandwich or a chocolate bar.

Caroline nodded groggily when I stopped the car, then opened her eyes. I gestured to her to climb out. She carefully pulled the sleeping bag off Julia, rolled it up into a pillow and stuffed it under her head.

'I have to pee,' I said. 'And then I'm going to get something to eat and drink. Do you want anything?'

Caroline rubbed the sleep from her eyes. She shook her head.

'I've been thinking,' I whispered. 'We could drive home in one shot, but maybe that's not a good idea. I mean, we have to stop somewhere along the way anyway, I can't keep this up all day. So I was thinking: aren't we just making it a whole lot worse by going home right away? We could stop at a hotel somewhere. Along the coast. Or in the mountains. Do something *nice* first. For later. So she has some good memories, too, not just the nasty ones.'

I had spent the last two hours thinking. In particular about something that had happened to me when I was young. I was wondering whether I could keep driving. Whether that was wise, seeing the quantity of alcohol still in my blood and the way my head was buzzing from lack of sleep. I had to take care of my family. I couldn't drive us off the road. But I might fall asleep at the wheel at any moment. I knew the symptoms. You start blinking your eyes, and the next moment something has disappeared: a billboard on a hill, a mansion surrounded by cypresses, a skinny donkey behind a stretch of barbed wire. You've been asleep. For no more than three seconds, maybe, but you've been asleep. From one moment to the next, the billboard and the donkey have vanished. It would get only a short mention in the newspaper. On page two. *Dutch family (...) through the guardrail and into oncoming traffic...*

When I was about thirteen, my father gave me my first driving lessons. We started off in a car park, but before long we took the car out onto the road. Some people don't like driving. Under normal circumstances I enjoy it a lot, and I always will. And the foundation for that love of driving, I'm absolutely sure, was established when I was thirteen.

One afternoon we were going down a narrow, winding road through the woods of eastern Holland. I was behind the wheel, my father was sitting next to me, and my mother was in the back. We came up to a sharp left-hand bend in the road. By that time I had already reached the point where driving had become completely automatic. The dangerous phase, when concentration flags. A car came from the other direction, but I saw it too late. I yanked on the wheel and we swerved to the right. We went off the road, the verge was fairly steep, I was able to avoid the trees, but we finally came to a halt with a bang against a wooden picnic table. My father climbed out and inspected the damage. Then he took over from me at the wheel and drove the car back up onto the road.

I thought that was it, that he would keep driving, but he stopped and climbed out again.

'It's all yours,' he said.

'I don't know…' I squealed; my forehead and the palms of my hands were covered in sweat. There was only one thing I knew for sure, and that was that I never wanted to drive a car again.

'You have to go on now, it's important,' my father said. 'Otherwise you'll be afraid to, later on.'

That was what I had thought about during the first hours after we left the summer house. I thought about Julia and the risks of a holiday cut short halfway through. We had driven more than eighty miles by then, we were far enough away – but it was still a long drive home. At home there were people. Friends and family who would ask questions. Both answering and avoiding those questions would cause a certain degree of damage. Here, there were just the four of us. Maybe it was better to stay with just the four of us for a little while.

'I don't know,' Caroline said. We were standing beside the car, we looked through the rear door, which was still half-open, at our daughter asleep on the back seat. I laid a hand on my wife's shoulder. I brushed her hair back with my fingers.

'I don't know either,' I said. 'It was just an idea. A feeling. But to be honest, I really don't know. That's why I'm asking you. It's your call.'

Two hours ago I had woken Caroline gently. 'We have to get going,' I'd said. 'I'll explain later.' Caroline went upstairs and got Lisa out of bed. We let Stanley and Emmanuelle sleep on. 'The tent will get back to us at some point,' I'd said. 'We're not going to use it now anyway.' We didn't see anyone around the house. They were all asleep. Ralph was probably still awake, but he didn't come out either when I started the car and rolled it down the little dirt drive to the road.

I was just about to turn onto the asphalt when I saw something moving in my rear-view mirror. I braked and took a good look. Judith's mother was standing at the top of the outside steps. She was waving. Or rather, she was gesturing with her arm for us to stop. The next moment I saw her, still in my mirror, coming down the steps. I thought I heard her shout something. Then I touched the accelerator and drove away.

37

The little hotel was beside a mountain stream with a watermill. Further down in the valley, brown cows grazed among the trees. The bells around their necks clanked softly, fat bumblebees zoomed from flower to flower, the stream gurgled across the rocks. Here and there along the mountaintops in the distance you could see white patches of snow.

That first day Julia stayed in her room. Occasionally she woke up, and all she wanted was something to drink: she wasn't hungry. Caroline and I took turns sitting with her. The first evening, Lisa and I stayed in the dining room together. She asked me what was wrong with her big sister; I told her I would explain it all later, some other time, that it had to do with what girls have sometimes when they grow up.

'Is she going to have her period?' Lisa asked.

When I woke up the next morning, my eye was throbbing. I went into the bathroom and looked in the mirror. Beneath the lid was a bump the size of an egg. The skin on my eyelid was stretched to the limit, and had taken on the colour of a mosquito bite, with a few dark spots here and there. My eyelashes were clogged shut with dried yellow pus. The whole thing pulsed and pounded – like an abscessed finger. That's what it was too,

I knew: an abscess. An untreated sore, even on a fingertip, could lead to blood poisoning and amputation. If the pressure on the retina became too great, it would tear. Under great pressure, pus and blood inside the eyeball would search for a way out. By that time, the eye itself would be more or less a write-off.

'I need you to take Julia downstairs in a little while,' I whispered to Caroline. 'I don't want her to stay here.'

I was holding a face flannel to my eye, so my wife couldn't see anything.

'Do you want me to help?'

I shook my head. 'You'd be helping me more if you stayed with Julia.'

Only much later – days later – did I feel disturbed in retrospect by the way Julia didn't protest at all when Caroline gently pressured her into getting up and getting dressed. 'Come on, we're going downstairs to have a nice breakfast,' she said cheerfully to both her daughters as she pulled the curtains aside. 'It's a beautiful day.'

I lay on the bed with the flannel still over my eye. I watched as Julia went into the bathroom with the little pile of clothes her mother had handed her. After a while I heard the hissing of the shower. Fifteen minutes later it was still hissing.

'Julia?' Caroline knocked on the door. 'Is everything OK? Do you need us to help you with something?'

We looked at each other. The look of panic in Caroline's eyes was undoubtedly an exact copy of the panic she was seeing in mine right then. Meanwhile, Lisa had climbed out of her own bed and snuggled up to me. I pressed her against me even closer, I lay my hand over her head while my lips soundlessly formed the words 'the door… try the door'.

'Julia?' Caroline knocked again, then tried the door handle. She looked at me and shook her head. At the same time her lower lip began to quiver, her eyes suddenly filled with tears. 'Don't do that! Don't…' my lips were still saying without making a sound.

'Daddy?' Lisa said.

'Yeah?'

'Daddy, is it all right if I call Thomas later on?'

At that moment the hissing of the shower stopped.

'Julia?' Caroline quickly wiped the tears from her eyes and knocked on the door again.

'Mum?' The door opened a crack; from where I was lying I couldn't see my elder daughter's face. 'I'll be finished in a minute, Mum,' Julia said.

In Caroline's travel kit I found a needle that I held over the flame of my lighter. I had everything laid out on the edge of the basin: cotton swabs, gauze and iodine, as well as a hypodermic with a painkiller – which was only for emergencies. I didn't want to numb the eye, in as far as that was even possible. Pain here was the only good counsel. The pain would tell me how far I could go. An abscess is sort of like a fort bristling with weaponry. A hostile bridgehead in an otherwise healthy body. Or maybe more like a terrorist cell. A relatively small number of armed militants is holding a large group hostage. Including women and children. The terrorists have equipped themselves with hand grenades and sticks of dynamite that they will set off if attacked. Using the middle finger of my left hand I pulled the eyelid up a little. I poked carefully with the hot needle. If it went in too far it could cause permanent damage. Not just the abscess, but also the eye itself would drain. A rescue attempt that results in dozens of dead hostages can only be considered a failure. For the moment, the needle met with little resistance. There was no pain. With my good eye, I was just trying to estimate in the mirror how far in I was, when I suddenly heard sounds. Voices. I looked to one side. The voices were coming from the transom above the toilet. The transom had a frosted glass pane, and it was open. I recognised Lisa's voice, even though I couldn't make out what she was saying. They were probably sitting on the outdoor terrace, just under the window. Carefully, without removing the needle from my eye, I took two steps and quietly closed the window. At that same moment I felt something sticky on my fingers. When I stepped back to the basin, I saw the blood. It was streaming down my face and falling in thick drops on the white porcelain. I pulled the needle back and pressed against the eyelid. More blood. It spattered on my T-shirt. And on my feet on the tiled floor, and between them. But I also saw something else. A substance the colour of mustard. Mustard that was way past its best-before date. Now I smelled it as well. A stench somewhere between old water from a vase and spoiled meat. I gagged, and the next moment a wave of bile came up that I spat into the basin, amid the blood and pus. But meanwhile I was cheering inside.

Soundlessly. I increased the pressure on my eyelid. And there at last was the pain. You have two kinds of pain. Pain that warns you not to go any further, and pain that comes as a relief. This pain came as a relief. I opened the tap. I pressed against my eye. I pressed until it was completely drained. I pulled off a yard of toilet paper. Only after I had cleaned the entire area around my eye did I dare to look. It was nothing short of a miracle. From beneath the residue of pus and strands of blood, my eye appeared. Undamaged and clear, gleaming like a pearl in an oyster. It looked at me. It looked grateful, I imagined. It was visibly pleased to see me.

Ten minutes later I joined my family on the outdoor terrace. On the breakfast table sat a pot of coffee and a jug of warm milk. There was a basket of croissants and French bread. There were little packets of butter and marmalade. The cowbells clanked. A bumblebee disappeared into a flower that sagged beneath the insect's weight. The sun warmed my face. I smiled. I smiled at the mountains in the distance.

'Shall we start the day with a walk?' I said. 'Shall we try to find out where that stream goes to?'

And walk we did. Julia did her best. Higher up along the slope the stream vanished into a forest of huge spruce trees. We crossed at a ford, hopping from stone to stone. Later we came to a waterfall. Lisa wanted to go swimming. Caroline and I both looked at Julia.

'It's OK,' she smiled. 'I'm fine here.'

She sat on a big, flat rock with her arms around her knees.

There was something wrong with her smile. Something wrong too about the way she was doing her best – *for us*, it seemed. She was doing her best not to ruin the holiday any further.

'Or would you rather go back to the hotel?' Caroline asked. She asked the question at the same moment I was planning to. Or no, I was actually planning to ask if maybe she would rather go home.

'No, it's fine,' she replied.

Caroline sighed deeply and looked at me. 'Maybe you're tired. Maybe you'd like to take a rest.'

'I'm perfect here,' Julia said. 'Look, that's so pretty, that light through the trees.'

She pointed up, to the tops of the spruces. She squinted against the broad bands of sunlight falling through the branches. Meanwhile, Lisa had undressed and plunged into the water. 'Whaaa, that's cold!' she shrieked. 'Are you coming in too, Dad? You coming?'

'Julia?' I said.

She looked at me. She smiled again. I felt something: a sudden weakness that began in my knees and moved up, to my chest and head. I took a step back and sank down onto a stone.

'Do you want to go home, sweetheart?' I asked. 'If you do, just say so. Then we'll leave tomorrow.'

My voice had sounded normal, I thought. At most a little too quiet, perhaps, but I didn't think anyone had noticed that.

Julia fluttered her eyelids. The smile was gone. She bit her lower lip.

'Yeah,' she said. 'Could we do that?'

38

And that is what we did. We left early in the morning and were home by midnight. Lisa went to her room and played there for a bit. Julia took a shower – again, for more than fifteen minutes – then fell asleep almost right away.

Caroline opened a bottle of wine. With two glasses and the wedges of cheese we'd bought at a convenience shop beside the main road, she came and lay down beside me; it was the first time we'd been alone together since we left the summer house.

'So what do we do now?' she asked.

In the car we had barely spoken. Julia had slept almost the whole way. Lisa had listened to music on Julia's iPod. I'd had time enough to think.

'For the time being, nothing,' I said. 'That seems best to me.'

'But shouldn't we take her to a hospital, now that we're here? Or at least to a specialist?'

Caroline pronounced the last word without emphasis and as casually as possible. She knew how I felt about 'specialists'. She also knew how sensitive I could be when aspersions were cast on my own, limited medical knowledge, especially by my own wife.

'You know what it is?' I said. 'I don't think that a more thorough examination is going to help her at this point. I've looked, and you'll have to trust me on this: there's damage, but no lasting damage. As far as the psychological damage goes, it's too early to say. She doesn't remember anything. If she goes to a hospital, they'll start asking questions. A specialist will want to know everything. Here, she's with us. With you and me. With her little sister. I really think complete rest is the best thing right now. Just let time do its work.'

'But is it normal that she can't remember anything? I mean, maybe it would be painful if she remembered it all, but ultimately, wouldn't it be better? How damaging can it be when something stays buried in your unconscious mind for ever?'

'We don't know. No one knows. There have been cases of people who have gone through something horrible, but repressed it so thoroughly that they were able to lead a normal life. On the other hand, there have been cases of people under hypnosis who dredged up all kinds of misery they couldn't deal with afterwards.'

'But we want to know, don't we? Maybe not right away, but in the end we want to know, right?'

'Know what?' I held up my empty glass and she filled it.

'Who it was. Oh, I don't want to think about it, but I get so furious when I do! About the kind of bastard who would do something like that! They ought to arrest him. They ought to take him off the street for the rest of his life. He should be… he should be…'

'Of course we want to know. I do, just as much as you. All I'm saying is that we have to be careful not to do more damage. If we try to force everything to the surface, our daughter might experience more damage from that than from leaving things for a while. For the moment.'

During our hike along the stream I had walked beside Julia for a while. I had brought up the afternoon by the pool as casually as possible. The fashion show on the diving board and getting sprayed by Alex and Thomas: the Miss Wet T-shirt contest. 'I was standing at the kitchen window,' I'd said. 'I saw you guys. I laughed so hard.' And Julia had frowned, deep in thought. As though she was hearing about this for the first time. 'When was that?' she asked.

'Marc...' Caroline put her glass on the bedside table and grabbed my wrist.

'Yeah?'

'Do you think...? Do you think that...? I mean, we talked about it when we went to the beach. Do you think that Ralph could do something like that?'

I didn't answer right away. I acted as though I was thinking about it. I breathed a deep sigh and rubbed my knuckles against my left eye. The eye that didn't hurt any more, only itched.

'I've thought about that too,' I said. 'But it doesn't add up. I was with him most of the time. And when I finally lost sight of him, he went home almost straight away. So at one point I sat down and did the arithmetic. Ralph could never have walked to that other beach and back in such a short time. And he was limping too.'

'Yeah, I noticed that,' Caroline said. 'How did that happen?'

'We were messing around with those rockets. One of them

went off in the waves. Close by. It startled the hell out of him and he fell. Landed badly.'

I closed both eyes. I heard the edge of the wine glass tick against Caroline's teeth.

'But what I asked was whether he could do something like that,' she said. 'Whether he's capable of it.'

I said nothing.

'Marc?'

'Yeah?'

'I asked you something.'

'Sorry. What was it?'

'Whether he's capable of it. Ralph. Of doing something like that.'

This time I answered right away. 'Oh, absolutely,' I said.

A few days later, Judith called. On my mobile. She asked how we were doing. And how Julia was doing in particular. I was sitting on the sofa in the living room. Julia was lying on the floor, reading a magazine. Lisa was at a girlfriend's house. Caroline was shopping. I stood up and walked into the kitchen. I said it was going reasonably well, under the circumstances.

'I keep thinking about the four of you,' Judith said. 'Oh, Marc, it's so horrible for all of you. For Julia. And that it had to happen here. Ralph is completely devastated too. He sends you all his best. Stanley and Emmanuelle too. They're going back to the States tomorrow.'

In the silence that followed I heard something: a familiar sound.

'Where are you?' I asked.

'I'm sitting by the pool. With my feet in the water.'

I closed my eyes for a moment. Then I walked over to the kitchen door and looked around the corner. Julia was still lying on her stomach on the floor, immersed in her magazine. I closed the door almost all the way and went back into the kitchen.

'Thomas keeps asking about Lisa,' Judith said. 'He misses her a lot.'

'Yeah.'

'I have the same thing. That missing feeling.'

I said nothing. I turned on the tap, took a glass from the counter and filled it.

'I miss you too, Marc.'

39

A week before the end of the school holiday I opened the office again. But the inspiration was gone. Maybe the inspiration was never really there anyway, but now, in any case, it was gone. Despite my distaste for the human body, I had always done my work well. I almost never had complaints. The serious cases, I referred on in plenty of time. The less serious ones received the right prescription. This was in contrast to the vast majority of cases: the people who had nothing wrong with them whatsoever. Before the summer holiday, I had listened patiently. For twenty minutes I would wear my most understanding expression. Now I couldn't even make it through the twenty minutes any more. After about five, cracks must have started appearing in that understanding expression: patients would suddenly stop talking after those five minutes – sometimes even in mid-sentence. 'What's wrong, doctor?' 'Nothing, what could be wrong?' 'I don't know, you look as though you don't believe me.'

I used to let the patients talk for the full twenty minutes. After that they would go home feeling relieved. The doctor had given them a prescription and urged them to take things a little easier. 'See my assistant for a new appointment on the way out,' I said. 'In three weeks we'll see whether there's been any improvement.'

I couldn't bring myself to do that any more. I lost my patience. 'There's nothing wrong with you,' I told a patient who had come in for the third time to whine about dizzy spells. 'Absolutely nothing. Be glad you're so healthy.'

'But doctor, when I suddenly get up out of a chair—'

'Did you hear what I said? Apparently not. Otherwise you would have heard me say that there is nothing wrong with you. Nothing! So do me a favour and just go home.'

A number of patients changed doctors. We would get a letter or an e-mail saying that they had found another general physician 'closer to home'. I knew where they lived. I knew they were lying. But I let it go. The appointments stopped arriving back-to-back. A twenty- or forty-minute gap between patients became much more common. I could have gone out during those breaks. Taken a walk around the neighbourhood. Picked up an espresso or a cheese sandwich at the café around the corner. But I always stayed in, in my office with the door closed. I would lean back in my chair and close my eyes. I tried to work out how many months it would take before I had no more patients at all. It should have been an alarming thought, but it wasn't. I thought about the natural course of things. People were born. People died. They moved from the countryside to the big city. The villages emptied out. First the butcher would throw in the towel, then the baker would close up shop. Wild dogs would take over the deserted, darkened streets. Then the last inhabitants died. The wind had free play. Sagging barn doors creaked on their hinges. The sun rose and set, but its rays no longer illuminated and warmed anything.

Occasionally, during a moment of clarity, I thought about the financial consequences. Not for too long, because the solution was obvious. A successful medical practice in a good area was worth a lot of money. Young family doctors just out of medical school would give their eyeteeth for a practice like mine. Astronomical sums were paid for them, usually by private contract, as they put it. Key money. Officially it wasn't allowed, but everyone knew that's how it went. I could place an ad. Purely for show, the young whippersnapper fresh out of medical school would adopt a doubtful expression when I mentioned the astronomical sum I was asking. But his eyes would be unable to lie. His slobbering look would speak volumes. 'You'll have to decide quickly,' I would say. 'You'd never believe how keen everybody is to get started here.'

I myself shouldn't wait too long either, I realised during the moments of clarity. A practice with a number of patients was a goldmine. A practice with no patients at all was not. I added it up. The four of us should be able to live three or four years on the proceeds. After that, we'd see what came up. Maybe some cushy job. As a company medical officer. Or even something completely different. A radical change. Hotel doctor on one of the Canary Islands. Tourists who had stepped on sea urchins. Been burned by the sun. Had their intestines thrown for a loop by olive oil heated up once too often. Maybe the radical change would be good for Julia too. Taking her away from her familiar surroundings. A new start. That was what I thought about during my moments of clarity. Sometimes one of those clear moments wasn't quite over when the next patient came into my office.

'Why do you think that?' I asked the homosexual TV comedian who thought he'd contracted AIDS. Then came the stories, descriptions of parties I didn't want to hear about. I tried to think about a beach instead. A golden-yellow beach with a clear blue sea. After my office hours at the hotel I would walk across that beach to the sea. 'Did he come in your mouth?' I asked the comedian in the meantime. 'And have you been to a dental hygienist recently?' When the gums are inflamed, the infection can go by way of the semen into the bloodstream. By then I was up to my waist in the blue sea. The moment right before the plunge. The lower part of the body is already cold, the torso is still warm. I looked at the comedian's mouth and tried to imagine his lips wrapped around a dick. For some reason it was a pale dick, a dick like a winter leek, and it was all the way in: in that mouth. The comedian sucked on the leek, nibbled on it teasingly. 'Oh Jesus, I'm coming!' the dick's owner moaned. The floodgates were opened. The first wave of semen hit the roof of the comedian's mouth. The waves that followed landed on his inflamed gums. It was more effective than a lethal injection. For a brief moment there is the cold when your head disappears beneath a wave. The rush of water in your face. But then you resurface. Your hair hanging in wet strands around your head. Salt stings your eyes. You lick at the snot on your upper lip: the taste of algae and of oysters. You look back at the beach where you just were. Cleansing, that's the first word that pops into your mind. The comedian was rather tubby, but in another month or so no one would recognise him. Emaciated.

There is no better word for it. AIDS destroys the body from the inside out. It presses a jackhammer against a boundary wall. The kind of jackhammer road workers use to pry tram rails out of the tarmac. The structure begins to creak. Three storeys up, fractures appear in the supporting walls. Bits of paint and plaster come raining down from the ceiling. It's like an earthquake. Huge buildings sometimes fall before clay huts do. The comedian didn't stand a ghost of a chance. He should have brushed more thoroughly. He should have gone to the dental hygienist on time. Now the wave of semen against his gums had sounded his death knell.

I still pretended to be listening, I pretended to take notes on my prescription pad, but meanwhile I was looking at the clock on the wall behind the comedian's head. How long was this going to take? Barely four minutes had passed. Even so, I didn't want to hear any more. No more details. I wanted the comedian to leave my office. To die quickly. Preferably without darkening my door again. Animals go looking for a quiet spot to die. A cat hides behind the bottles of cleaning fluid under the sink. In eight months or so I would read the obituaries in the paper. A *whole page* full of obituaries, most likely. A funeral with more than a thousand attendees, at the cemetery on the bend in the river. Speeches. Music. A posthumous tribute on TV. A special re-run of his best show. Another couple of half-baked anecdotes on a chat show – then, after that, the inevitable silence would settle.

I smiled. A reassuring smile. 'Oh, it's not that bad,' I said. 'The chance of infection is relatively minor. And even then, AIDS inhibitors are getting more sophisticated and more effective all the time. Tell me, was there also anal penetration?'

I posed the question as casually as possible. As an unprejudiced general physician. A physician has to be above all prejudices. I am above all prejudices. There's no two ways about it. But standing above them is not the same as being able to eliminate them altogether. During anal penetration the tissue is stretched to the utmost. Bleeding occurs more often than not. No one has ever become pregnant from anal penetration. That is not a prejudice. Those are the facts. In biology, everything has a goal and a function. If we were meant to stick our dicks in someone else's arsehole, the opening would have been made bigger. Or, to put it differently, the entrance is as tight as it is in order to warn us *not* to stick things in there. The way the heat of a flame warns us not to hold our hand above it too long. I looked at the doomed comedian. I could examine him. I could come up with something about swollen glands. The glands in your groin *are* a little swollen, but that doesn't necessarily mean anything. On the one hand, I felt like getting rid of him with something that sounded reassuring but sent him home reeling in panic; on the other, today I wanted to see as little of him as possible. No bare skin, no hairy buttocks or – who knows – shaved pubes. As I said, I harbour no prejudices, but there are some things that stretch one's empathy to the breaking point. I took a blood test form out of a drawer and checked it off at random. Cholesterol. Blood glucose. Liver function. I looked at my watch. I could have told the time from the clock above my patient's head, but the glance at my watch sent a signal. 'If you go by the lab on your way home, we'll know more in a few days' time,' I said. I stood up. I held out my hand. I handed him the form. Three minutes later the patient was out on the street. I dropped down into my chair and closed my eyes. I tried to get the beach back. The blue, cleansing sea. But then there was a knock. My assistant stuck her head through the door. 'What did you say to him?' she asked.

'What do you mean?' I asked.

'The patient who was just in here,' she said. 'He left in tears. He said he was never coming back. He said you could... well, sorry... I'm only repeating what he said.'

I looked my assistant straight in the eye, I held her gaze. 'And what was it he said exactly, Liesbeth?'

My assistant blushed. 'He said... he said that you could stuff it up your... well... there, he said you could stuff it up there. I thought that was so rude! I was speechless!'

I took a deep breath. 'Liesbeth. The man most probably has AIDS. He got it because he let someone spray semen all over his bleeding gums. When a man drives his motorcycle into a tree without a helmet on, we say it was his own fault. But a person who lets someone else stick their dick in his mouth without any precautions gets no more pity from me than that motorcyclist without a helmet. As far as I'm concerned, he can stuff it up his *own* arse. What am I saying? That's exactly what he does!'

40

I didn't return Judith's call. She called me.

'We still have your tent here,' she said.

I felt like saying she could burn it in the backyard, because we would never go camping again.

'I'll come and pick it up when I have the time,' I said.

It was quiet for a moment at the other end. Then she asked how Julia was doing. I don't know exactly what it was, but I thought there was something indifferent about the way she asked – something routine, as though there were no way she *couldn't* ask. I replied in kind, as briefly as I could. And indeed, she didn't ask any more questions. Another silence fell. I expected her to say that she missed me. That she wanted to see me. But she didn't.

'Ralph was sort of listless, those last few weeks of the holiday,' she said. 'And he still is. I ask him what's wrong, but he just shrugs it off. I'm sort of worried, Marc. I thought maybe you could look at him sometime. He doesn't actually admit it to himself. It's impossible to get him to see a doctor.'

It seemed an eternity since we had left the summer house. Julia was still unusually subdued. She took a shower two or three times a day – rarely for less than fifteen minutes. Physically, she had made a good recovery, as I'd been able to determine first-hand, after emphatically asking her again whether she didn't mind. Whether she wouldn't prefer to be examined by another, 'neutral' doctor, and not her own father. But she said that she wouldn't want any other doctor to do that.

Caroline and I had agreed to wait a few months and see how things went. And only after that, if there was no visible improvement, to get outside help. We decided not to inform Julia's school either.

'Have him come by sometime,' I said, even though I wasn't too keen on that. I tried to imagine a listless Ralph. For a split second I considered asking about Alex, whether perhaps he was listless too, but I immediately decided against it.

'I thought, maybe you could come by and pick up the tent and then, sort of in passing, ask whether everything's OK with him,' Judith said.

'Sure, I could do that.'

I heard Judith take a deep breath. 'It would be nice to see you again,' she said. '*I* would like to see you again.'

The obvious thing would have been for me to say 'me too'. But it would have cost me an enormous effort to make it sound sincere.

I closed my eyes. I tried to imagine Judith on the beach, and when that didn't work, under the outdoor shower beside the pool: how she pulled her wet hair back and closed her eyes against the sun.

'Me too,' I said.

*

A few weeks later, her mother suddenly called me. I hadn't seen or spoken to Judith's mother since I saw her come down the steps of the summer house that morning. I hadn't even thought about her since then, I was almost sure.

She asked how things were. Especially with Julia. I told her. I didn't tell her everything. I left out, for example, the fact that Julia still remembered nothing about that particular evening. But she didn't ask about that. I tried to keep the conversation as short as possible, by giving only summary replies to her questions.

'So that's all there is, more or less,' I said in an attempt to bring things to a close. 'We try to live with it, as far as is possible. Julia has to try to live with it.'

I heard myself talking. Sentences were coming out of my mouth, but they weren't mine. Freestanding sentences are what they were. I was only saying them together. I thought she was about to say goodbye, when she said instead: 'There's something else, Marc.'

She had called during one of my moments in-between; the last patient had already left, the next one still had to arrive. I don't know whether it was her tone of voice or the fact that for the first time during our conversation she called me by my first name, but now I stood up from my desk and walked to the office door, which was open a crack. I peeked through the crack and saw my assistant sitting at her desk. She was busy writing something on an index card. Quietly, I closed the door.

'Yes?' I said.

'It's... well, I don't know how, or even if I should be saying it,' said Judith's mother. 'But it's been bothering me for a long time. Ever since that night, actually.'

All I did was make a little sound. The sort of little sound you make when you want the person at the other end to know that you're still listening.

'I've hesitated until now, because I didn't want anyone to jump to any conclusions,' she went on. 'And I hope you won't do that. On the other hand, I thought it was irresponsible to simply keep it to myself.'

I nodded – and because I realised at the same moment that she couldn't see me, I made that little sound again.

'On the night of the fireworks, when all of you went to the beach, I went to bed early. I read for a while first, then turned off the light. I didn't wake up until much later. I can't remember exactly what time it was, but I had to get out of bed. That happens to me more often in the middle of the night.' She paused for a moment, then said: 'All the lights were out, so I assumed your wife had gone to your tent and that Emmanuelle was in the apartment downstairs. I went to the toilet in the upstairs bathroom. I'd only been sitting there for a minute when I heard a car down below. A car that came up the drive and stopped. I heard the door slam and someone walk up to the house. I don't remember exactly why, but I flushed quickly, turned off the light, and went back to my room. Someone came into the house. Someone who walked straight through to the bathroom. My room was right next to the door, so I heard the washing machine being opened and closed again. Then the machine started up. And a few minutes later I heard the shower.'

Ralph. Ralph was the first to go home. Alone. In his car. Leaving his family behind. So far, the story Judith's mother was telling me fitted the facts.

'After a little while I heard sounds coming from the kitchen. I waited a bit, then got up. Ralph was in the kitchen. He was leaning against the counter, drinking a beer. His hair was still wet. When he saw me, it was obvious that he was startled. I told him I had to go to the toilet, even though I'd just been. But he didn't know that.'

On the beach, Ralph had been hit in the mouth with a margarita glass. Blood had flowed. After that, the Norwegian girl had punched him a few times in the face. Maybe there was blood on his clothes.

'The washing machine was running in the bathroom,' Judith's mother went on. 'I looked through the glass to see exactly what was in it, but there was too much foam. I couldn't see very well. I remember that even at that moment I thought it was rather peculiar. I mean, you come home and maybe you want to put on some clean clothes, but then you just throw your dirty stuff in the clothes basket, don't you? You don't do a wash right away? In the middle of the night?'

41

One morning, it must have been in mid-October, Ralph Meier suddenly walked into my office. Unannounced, as always. He didn't ask whether he had come at a bad moment. He didn't ask whether he could sit down. He dropped down into the chair across from my desk and ran his fingers through his hair.

'I… I needed to talk to you,' he said.

I held my breath. I heard my heart begin to pound. Could this really be happening? After two months of uncertainty, could he really be about to come up with a confession? I didn't know how I would react. Whether I'd grab him by the shirtfront and pull him across my desk. Or start screaming – spit in his face. My assistant would come rushing in. Or would she call the police right away? I could also remain calm. Icy calm, as it's called. I could pull the wool over his eyes. I could act as though I found his confession touching. Then I could give him a lethal injection.

'How are all of you getting along?' he asked.

That was not exactly the question you'd expect from someone who was about to confess to having raped a thirteen-year-old girl. Maybe *he* was the one pulling the wool over *my* eyes.

'We're getting along,' I said.

'Good.' He ran his fingers through his hair again. For a brief moment I wondered whether he had even heard me. Then he said: 'I really admire the way you people are dealing with it. Judith told me about it. Judith told me how strong you've been.'

I gaped at him. At the same time I tried not to gape too much. I didn't want him to see my bewilderment.

'I'm faced with something very disturbing that needs to be dealt with in fullest confidence,' he said. 'That's why I came to you.'

I forced myself to stop staring. I tried to adopt an interested expression, in as far as I was able.

'Everything we discuss here remains between these four walls,' I said, waving my hand at my office. I smiled. My heart was still pounding: smiling, I knew, helps lower your pulse rate.

'Most important of all is that Judith doesn't find out about it,' he said. 'I mean, she insisted that I come and see you, but if it's something serious, I don't want her to know.'

I nodded.

'There something wrong with me,' he said. 'I'm afraid there's something wrong. Maybe it's all bullshit, but Judith always gets into a state about terrible diseases. I don't want her fretting. Over nothing.'

Listless, Judith had said. *Ralph was sort of listless, those last few weeks of the holiday.*

'It's good you came in,' I said. 'Usually these things turn out to be a storm in a teacup, but it's better to be safe than sorry. What are the symptoms exactly? What do you feel?'

'For starters, I'm tired all the time. Ever since the summer actually. And I don't feel like doing anything. I've never had that before. But OK, I figured maybe I've taken on too much work lately. But about two weeks ago I got this....' He stood up and without further warning unclasped his belt and dropped his trousers down around his knees. 'This...' He pointed, but even if he hadn't it would have been impossible to miss. 'Three days ago it was half the size. It's hard as a rock, and when I press against it, it hurts.'

I looked. I know my business. At a single glance, in fact, I knew there was only one possibility.

Ralph Meier needed to go to the hospital that week. Preferably that same afternoon. Maybe it was too late already, but the earlier you dealt with it the better your chances were.

I got up out of my chair. 'Let's go into the other room...' I said.

'What is it, Marc? Is it what I think it is?'

'Come with me. I want to take a better look.'

He pulled up his trousers halfway, to just below his buttocks, and shuffled into the examination room beside my office. I asked him to lie down on the table.

Laying a fingertip carefully against the bump, I pressed gently. It didn't give, it was indeed just as he'd said: hard as a rock.

'Does this hurt?' I asked.

'Not when you press that way, but if you squeeze it I see stars.'

'Then we won't do that. And there's no reason to. In ninety-nine per cent of all cases, these are just nodes. A sort of growth under the skin. Unpleasant, to be sure, but nothing to get worried about.'

'So it's not... Not what I thought?'

'Listen, Ralph. We can never be a hundred per cent sure. But we want to rule out that one per cent too.'

'What are you going to do?'

He was no longer looking at me. He was looking at my hands, which were pulling on the rubber gloves. At the scalpel I had placed in readiness on a clump of cotton wool, beside his bare thigh on the examining table.

'I'm going to remove a tiny piece of it,' I said. 'And we'll send that to the lab. In a couple of weeks we should know more.'

I disinfected the area a couple of inches around the bump. Then I stuck the scalpel into it. I cut. First superficially, then deeper. Ralph made a noise, he gasped for air.

'This might hurt a little,' I said. 'But it will be over in a second.'

There was almost no blood. That confirmed my initial diagnosis. I pushed the scalpel in until I reached healthy tissue. By cutting into the healthy tissue I established the connection. The cells from the bump would get into the bloodstream and be disseminated all over the body. *Disseminate*... I've always found that a nice word. A word that covers all the bases, as they say. At this moment, I was sowing something. Planting something. Within the foreseeable future, the seeds would germinate. In other parts of the body. Parts where they couldn't be seen with the naked eye.

For the sake of appearances I scraped off a little tissue onto the edge of a glass jar and used the tip of the scalpel to push it in. For the sake of appearances I wrote something on the label, which I then stuck to the jar. I applied a gauze square to the wound and fixed it with two bandages.

'You can put your trousers back on,' I said. 'I'll write you a prescription. For more of those pills you had before. We all have trouble sometimes getting back into the swing after a long holiday.'

At the door of my office, I held out my hand.

'Oh yeah,' Ralph said. 'I almost forgot. Your tent. Judith gave me your tent to give to you. It's in the car. Can you come out and get it?'

We stood beside the open boot. I was holding our tent in my arms.

'I have to go out on a shoot soon,' Ralph said. 'You know, that series Stanley was talking about? *Augustus?* They're about to start filming.'

'How is Stanley?'

He didn't seem to hear my question. Right above his nose, between his eyebrows, a wrinkle had formed. He gave his head a little shake. 'Do you think it's safe for me to go?' he asked. 'It's a two-month shoot. If I have to stop halfway through, it would be a disaster for everyone.'

'Of course,' I said. 'Don't worry about a thing. It's usually nothing at all. We'll just wait for the tests to come back. There will be enough time after that.'

I waited until his car disappeared around the corner. Halfway down the street there was a skip. I dropped our tent into it and walked back to my office.

The waiting room was empty. In the examination room I held the little jar up to the light. I squinted, studied the contents for a few seconds, then tossed it into the pedal bin beside the examination table.

42

I'd thought it would all go quickly, but it didn't. Ralph left for Italy to shoot *Augustus*, and two months later he came back. Only then did he call me to ask about the test results.

'I never heard anything back from the hospital,' I said. 'So I assume they didn't find anything.'

'But then they usually say something anyway, don't they?'

'Usually. I'll call tomorrow, just to be sure. How are you feeling otherwise?'

'Good. I still get tired easily, but then I take one of your miracle pills. That works fine.'

'I'll call you tomorrow, Ralph.'

I was relieved to hear that he was still tired. I had prescribed Benzedrine to repress the symptoms of fatigue and give the disease time to spread through his body. But it was taking longer than normal. I started doubting myself. My skills as a doctor. Maybe I had seen it all wrong.

The next day I called him back, but got Judith on the line.

'Is it about the test results?' she asked right away.

For a minute there, I didn't know what to say. 'I thought...' I started.

'Yeah, Ralph told you not to tell me anything if it was serious.

But you left him feeling so reassured that he told me about it right away. That you said that it wasn't anything. That's right, isn't it, Marc?'

'I told him it *probably* wasn't anything. But to be completely sure, I also sent a sample to the hospital.'

'And?'

I closed my eyes. 'I called today to ask about the results. There's nothing to worry about.'

'Really? I mean, if there really *is* something, I want to know, Marc.'

'No, there's nothing wrong. Is there something that makes you suspect there's more to it than that?'

'He's still tired all the time. And he's lost weight, even though he still eats just as much. And drinks just as much.'

'I took a bit out of his leg. Can you still see that? That spot?'

'No, the bump's still there, but it's not getting any bigger. I don't *look* at it every day, of course. But sometimes I feel it. Sort of surreptitiously, if you know what I mean. So that he doesn't notice. Or at least I hope he doesn't notice.'

The bit about Ralph losing weight was good news. And also the fact that the bump wasn't getting any bigger made sense in terms of the clinical picture. The hostile army had established a beachhead. The attacks were being coordinated from there. Only limited commando forays to start with. Clandestine operations behind the lines. Hit-and-run actions. The terrain was being reconnoitred. Brought into readiness. Later, the main forces would meet with no resistance worth mentioning.

'It's probably just a fat node,' I said. 'It can't really do any harm in that spot, as long as it doesn't bother him. But if he wants, I can remove it for him.'

'Isn't that something they usually do at the hospital?'

'At the hospital you end up on a waiting list. This kind of thing can be done really quickly. He can come by any time. As far as I'm concerned, he doesn't even have to make an appointment.'

Lisa asked about Thomas sometimes. Julia never asked about Alex.

'Of course you can call him,' we told Lisa. 'You can ask him to come over and play.'

But as the school year progressed, she asked less often. Her school friends crowded her summer romance into the background.

Things were different with Julia. We had the feeling that, for the time being, she wanted nothing whatsoever to do with boys. And especially not with the boy who would remind her of this last summer holiday. In that context, the word 'remind' was not entirely appropriate. Julia remembered things about the summer, but not everything. So she probably remembered Alex too. But up to what point? To what moment? We didn't ask her about it. It seemed best to leave things as they were.

Ralph didn't drop by again. Apparently he was sufficiently reassured and had indefinitely put off having the 'fat node' removed. That, in fact, was a favourable sign. Maybe the disease simply needed more time.

Early in the new year we received another invitation to a first night. This time it was Chekhov's *The Seagull*. We didn't go. We had adopted a policy of passive deterrence. We were trying to establish as much distance as possible between ourselves and the Meiers. I emphatically say 'we' here – Caroline felt exactly the same way.

It was while we were having dinner out. A few days after the invitation to *The Seagull* arrived. Just the two of us out for dinner, for the first time in a long time. When the second bottle of wine arrived, I made my move.

'Do you know why I didn't want to go to that opening night?' I asked Caroline.

'Because plays make you hyperventilate,' my wife laughed, clinking her glass against mine.

'No, this is different. I didn't want to tell you at first. I thought it would stop by itself. But it didn't. It's still going on.'

It was the truth. Judith had tried to call me again a couple of times, but every time I saw her name on my phone's display I hung up. When she left a message on my voicemail, I didn't call back. I had instructed my assistant not to put her through to me if she tried to call me at the office. Which indeed she did a few times. My assistant told her I was seeing a patient. That I would call back later. Which I then did not do.

A couple of times she tried our private number. Both times she got Caroline on the line. I could tell from my wife's replies that it was Judith. No, we're getting by… a little better lately… *I'm not here!* I signalled to Caroline and kept as quiet as possible till the conversation was over.

'Besides that, I didn't want to go to the premiere because I didn't feel like running into Judith there,' I said. 'I don't know whether you've noticed, but that woman wants something from me. Even then, at the summer house. She tried something… It was obvious, she thought I was nice. Nicer than normal nice, I mean.'

I looked at my wife. She didn't seem shocked by this revelation. On the contrary. She seemed more amused than anything else. A smile played on her lips.

'What are you grinning at?' I said. 'Did you notice, or not? That Judith was chasing me, I swear.'

'Marc… I just had to laugh. About you. Don't be angry, I didn't mean to laugh at you, but I think you have the tendency to make assumptions pretty quickly: that a woman is after you when she acts a bit flirty or does her best for you. I noticed it at the summer house too, but, if you ask me, that Judith is the kind who does that with all the men. A little uncertain of herself, the type who tries to appeal to every male.'

I had to admit that, on the whole, I was disappointed with Caroline's reaction. She'd viewed it all as an innocent flirtation. She really hadn't caught on. That's how easy it was, I thought.

'She calls me on my mobile all the time, Caroline. She says she misses me. That she wants to see me again.'

Caroline shook her head laughingly and took a big slug of her wine.

'Oh, Marc, she's just one of those women who wants a bit of attention. I'd probably be the same way if I had to live with a big boor like Ralph. That's what it's about. Attention. The doctor's attention. Maybe that's what she wants. Maybe she wants you to *examine* her.'

'Caroline...'

'I hate to have to disillusion you, but you brought it up. Judith acts like that with all men. I saw how she acted towards Stanley. A little giggly, a little running her hands through her hair, sitting on the diving board, supposedly lost in thought, dangling her feet in the water, all those tedious old female tricks. In fact, I'm surprised that you would fall for it so easily. And by the way, she had more success with him than she did with you.'

I stared at her.

'What are you staring at? Oh, Marc, are you really so naïve? You think the women are swooning over you, but a woman like Judith knows exactly what she's doing. I was going to tell you about it, but I forgot. Until you started up about her just now. Whatever, it was one afternoon by the pool. You'd all gone to the village. Ralph, you, the kids. Emmanuelle wasn't feeling well, she was lying indoors with the curtains closed. There had been something in the air for a long time, a sort of charged tension between those two. At a certain point I went upstairs to get something to drink. And when I looked out of the kitchen window I saw them. Judith was lying in her deckchair and Stanley was leaning over her. He started with her face and then he licked her all over, Marc. And I mean completely. I made sure the glasses rattled loudly enough when I came down the steps. And when I got there they were both lying neatly in their own deckchairs. But I saw what I saw. I could tell from Stanley's swimming trunks. I probably don't have to explain what I saw. And the next moment, there he went, right, splash, into the water.'

About a month after the premiere of *The Seagull*, I came across a little item in the arts' pages of the newspaper:

Performances of *The Seagull* cancelled due to leading man's illness

The article was no more than ten lines long. '(…) Ralph Meier (…) cancelled until further notice.' It didn't say anything about what kind of illness it was. I was already standing there, phone in hand, then I decided it was better to wait a bit.

Judith called the next day.

'He was admitted to the hospital last week,' she said. She mentioned the name of the hospital. It was the same one to which I'd sent the sample – or rather, to which I *hadn't* sent the sample.

I pressed my phone against my ear. I was sitting at the desk in my office. The next patient – in fact, the last patient of the day – wouldn't be coming in for another hour. This time I had been sure to answer as soon as I saw her name come up on the display.

I asked a few general questions. About the symptoms. The probable therapy. Her answers confirmed my earlier diagnosis. Ralph's body had put up a fight for a long time – longer than normal – but now there was no stemming the tide. The disease had already skipped a few stages. The stages at which treatment might have some chance of success. I was reminded of trenches. Entire networks of interconnected trenches being overrun one by one. Because Judith didn't ask about the tissue sample, I brought it up myself.

'It's strange,' I said. 'They really didn't find anything at the time.'

'Marc?'

'Yeah?'

'How are you doing?'

I glanced at the clock across from my desk. Another fifty-nine minutes separated me from my next patient. 'I'm getting by,' I said.

I heard her sigh at the other end. 'You didn't call me again. You don't call me back when I leave messages for you.'

I was silent for a moment. During that silence I thought about the tissue sample, about the glass jar with the bloody piece of flesh from Ralph's thigh, which I had tossed into the pedal bin.

'I've been pretty damn busy,' I said. 'And then what with Julia, of course. We're trying to get our lives back on track, but it's not that easy.'

Was it really me who was threading all those words together into sentences? It was all made easier by the fact that I was alone in my office and that Judith couldn't see my face – in order to concentrate, I even kept my eyes shut tightly.

'It would be nice to see you again,' I said.

*

That was how our renewed contact began. I simply told Caroline the truth. I'm going to have coffee with Judith Meier, I said. She's pretty upset about Ralph's illness. At first we met in cafés, later more and more often at her place. I didn't have many patients left; it was no problem for me to pop out for an hour or longer. And otherwise I just waited until my appointments for the day were over. Alex and Thomas were still at school around that time, I'm not trying to justify anything, things often happened quickly, usually we didn't even make it to the bedroom. Sometimes, afterwards, we would go and visit Ralph in the hospital. The first operation didn't have the desired results, and a second one 'offered little prospect of improvement', according to the specialist in attendance. Alternative treatments were suggested. More radical treatments. He could decide for himself whether he wanted to stay in the hospital for those, or commute back and forth from home each day.

'Maybe you'd rather be at home,' Judith said. 'I could drive you here every day.'

She didn't look at me when she said this, she was sitting in a chair beside the bed, her hand on the blanket, close to her husband's.

'It can be more pleasant to be at home,' I said. 'But it can also be very taxing. Especially at night. Here in the hospital they have everything you need within reach.'

A decision was made to try for the best of both worlds, a compromise whereby Ralph would come home at the weekends, and sleep at the hospital during the week. I continued to go to Judith's for coffee once or twice a week.

I don't know whether it was Ralph's generally dazed state, or the operation, the medication, and the often highly unpleasant treatments, but he never mentioned the first time I had examined him that last October. During one of our visits, when Judith left the room to buy some magazines for him at the newsagent on the ground floor, I seized the opportunity.

'It's strange how things can go with an illness like this,' I said. 'One moment you have a node examined and there's nothing wrong, and a few months later it goes wrong anyway.'

I had slid my chair up closer to Ralph's bed, but I still didn't have the impression that he understood me.

'I had a patient once who thought he'd had a heart attack,' I said. 'He came in to see me, he was in a panic. With all the symptoms. Chest pain, dry mouth, sweaty palms. I took his pulse, it was over two hundred. I listened to his heart. "Did you eat cheese fondue yesterday, by any chance?" I asked him. The patient looked at me with big, round eyes. "How did you know that, doctor?" he asked. "And I suppose you knocked back quite a bit of white wine along with it," I said. Then I explained it to him. The molten cheese, the ice-cold white wine. At the bottom of the stomach it all clumps together to form a huge clot that can't go anywhere. When that happens, people usually show up in casualty in the middle of the night, but this case was waiting for me when I came in at nine.'

Ralph had closed his eyes, but now he opened them again.

'But here's the zinger,' I said. 'I send the patient home. Completely reassured, of course. And two weeks later he actually dies of a heart attack. A complete fluke. If you used that story in a book or a film, no one would believe it. But this was real. The fondue and the heart attack were totally unrelated.'

'That's what you call tough luck,' Ralph said, and he smiled feebly.

I looked at the shape his body made under the blankets. It was still the same body, but it looked as though it had collapsed a bit here and there – in fact, he looked like a party balloon the day after a birthday party: a balloon that has lost half its air.

'Exactly,' I said. 'Tough luck.'

With Julia, meanwhile, things were going a bit better. That was our impression at least. She began bringing her girlfriends home more often, at the table she sometimes told us about things that had happened at school, without our having to ask first, and she had started laughing again. A hesitant little laugh, to be sure, but still a laugh. On other days, however, she spent most of her time alone in her room.

'It's probably the age she's at,' I said.

'That's the worst thing, as far as I'm concerned,' Caroline said. 'That we'll never really know any more. Whether it's just part of the age she's at or whether it's because of… because of that other thing.'

Sometimes I studied Julia's face, when I thought she wasn't

looking. Her eyes. Her look. That was *different* from the way it had been less than a year ago. Not so much sadder, but more serious. More inward-looking, as they say. Caroline was right. I had no idea either whether it should be attributed to her growing up or to the – unremembered – events on the beach.

43

That next summer holiday we went to the States. *A change of scenery*, that was the idea. A change of scenery from the usual holiday at the beach (or poolside). More of a trip than a holiday. A trip with lots of distractions, new impressions and little time to ponder – to fret, to lie awake at night.

A trip might not 'heal' Julia, but it could have a healing effect, we reasoned. Cathartic. Purging. Maybe, after a trip like that, we could start with a clean slate.

We flew to Chicago. We took the lift to the top of the Sears Tower and looked out over the city and Lake Michigan. We took a downtown tour in an open double-decker. We had breakfast at a Starbucks. At night we ate at restaurants where they served Julia's favourite food. Italian. Pasta. But even at the table she kept the white pods of her iPod in. It wasn't that she shut herself off completely: she smiled gratefully when the plate of ravioli was put down in front of her and the waiter sprinkled grated cheese over it. She laid her head on Caroline's shoulder and stroked her mother's arm. The only thing was, she barely spoke. Sometimes she hummed along with a song on her iPod. Usually we would have said something. 'We're at the table now, Julia. You can listen to music later.' But we didn't. She should do whatever she feels like, we thought. Apparently it's still too early for that clean slate.

We drove west in our rented car, a white Chevrolet Malibu. We saw the countryside grow barer and emptier. In the back seat, Lisa shrieked in excitement when we saw our first cowboy and our first bison. But Julia kept her earpods in. To make contact, we had to shout. 'Look, Julia,' we shouted. 'Up on that rock. A vulture.' Then she would pull one bud out of her ear. 'What did you say?' 'A vulture. Over there. Oh, no, he flew away.' At Badlands National Park we saw signs warning for rattlesnakes. At Mount Rushmore we took pictures of the sculpted heads of the four American presidents. That is to say: Lisa took the pictures. She was the one with the camera. I've never had the patience to take pictures, Caroline took photos when the kids were little, but stopped after that. Lisa enjoyed it; she started taking photographs when she was about nine. At first mostly holiday snapshots of butterflies and flowers, but later our family began appearing more often in her pictures.

Julia did her best. She summoned up a smile for each photo. But it was as though she were doing it for us. As though she felt guilty about her own gloominess. At Custer State Park, where we rented a log cabin for a few days, she actually apologised. 'Sorry,' she said. 'I'm probably not the best company.'

We were sitting outside the log cabin, at a picnic table beside the barbecue where the steaks and hamburgers were hissing and steaming. 'Don't be silly, Julia,' Caroline said. 'You're the sweetest, nicest daughter we have. All you have to do is what you really feel like doing. Come on, we're on holiday.'

Lisa was standing at the barbecue, flipping the meat. 'And what about me?' she shouted. 'Am I the sweetest and the nicest too?'

'Of course,' Caroline said. 'You too. Both of you. Together you're the loveliest thing I've got.'

I looked at my wife. She bit her lower lip and rubbed her eyes. After a few moments she stood up. 'I'll go and see whether there's any more wine,' she said.

'There's wine here, Mum!' Lisa shouted. 'It's right here on the table!'

In Deadwood we ate at Jakes, Kevin Costner's restaurant. All through the meal a pianist played loudly on the grand piano, making a normal conversation almost impossible. Julia kept her earbuds in, took two bites, then pushed her plate away. In Cody we went to a rodeo. At Yellowstone National Park we saw even more bison, as well as moose, and different types of deer. We climbed out at a spot where a lot of cars had parked along the side of the narrow road. People with binoculars were pointing at the hill on the far side of a stream. 'A bear,' a man said. 'But he just disappeared behind those trees.' We parked at Old Faithful, the geyser that blows its white, foamy plume into the air every fifty minutes. 'Ooooh!' Lisa cried when the geyser blew. Julia smiled and swayed her head to the music from her iPod.

We headed south. We saw our first Indians. We drove through Monument Valley and stopped at an almost deserted car park where there was an American flag and a silvery trailer where they sold Indian bric-a-brac. 'Don't you want to come out and take a look?' Caroline asked Julia, who had remained in the back seat. But Julia just shook her head and rubbed her eyes. 'Shall I come and sit with you?' Caroline asked.

At Kayenta we were told that the entire Navajo Indian reservation was dry; you couldn't get a drop of alcohol anywhere. Not with dinner, but also not at the supermarket. 'It's like Iran,' Caroline said, taking a sip of her Coke. 'But right in the middle of America.'

At the first lookout point along the Grand Canyon, Julia began crying. I was alone with her just then, Caroline and Lisa had disappeared into a brick toilet block. We were standing at the edge, on a little, unfenced promontory, further away from the larger groups of tourists.

'Look at that,' I said, pointing to a bird of prey, an eagle probably, that had come soaring by within five yards of us, silently, on motionless wings. 'Do you want to go back to the car?' I asked. I looked over, and only then did I see that Julia had taken out her earbuds. She wasn't making a sound, the tears were simply running down her cheeks.

'I can't even see how beautiful it is any more,' she said.

I felt a cold shiver down my spine. I stepped towards her and held out my hand. I did it very carefully, I tried to get hold of only her wrist. Ever since the last time I'd examined her, about eight months before, she had done her best to avoid all physical contact with me. I thought it would go away by itself after a while, but it didn't. Whenever I held out my hand to her, she turned away immediately – during this trip, we hadn't touched each other even once. 'That's OK, you don't have to,' I said. 'You don't have to think it's beautiful now.'

I took her hand. We stood there like that for a moment, then she looked down, at her father's hand holding hers, and shook it off. She turned around and walked back up the path, towards the toilet block, where Caroline and Lisa were just coming out. When she saw her mother, Julia quickened her pace. The last bit she ran. Then she threw herself into Caroline's arms.

That evening we stopped for the night in Williams, a town along the old Route 66. We ate outside, on the patio of a Mexican restaurant. Caroline and I drank margaritas. While we were eating our starters, a cowboy came out onto the patio with a guitar. A few yards from our table he put down a soapbox and climbed onto it. I looked at Julia as the cowboy started in on his first song. Her enchilada was still lying untouched on her plate. She had taken out her earbuds and was looking at the cowboy. In her eyes I saw the same look as the one with which she had viewed the Grand Canyon that afternoon.

The hotel was close to the railway line. I lay awake in the dark and listened to the freight trains that passed every half-hour. You could hear them coming from a distance, first the whistle: a wailing sound like the call of an owl, or of an animal lost in the night. The trains were endlessly long. I tried to count the cars, but with every train that passed I forgot to keep counting halfway through. I thought about the Grand Canyon and the singing cowboy. About Julia's fit of weeping and the look in her eyes, back at the Mexican restaurant.

'Marc?' I felt Caroline's hand on the back of my neck. 'What is it?'

'Are you still awake? You should try to get some sleep.'

Caroline's hand had reached my face by then, her fingers touched my cheeks. 'Marc, what's wrong?'

I had to clear my throat to make my voice sound normal. 'Oh, nothing. I was just lying here listening to the trains. Hear that? Here comes another one...'

Caroline moved up against my back. She placed one arm under my head and put the other around my chest. 'You don't have to be sad. I mean, of course you can be sad. I'm sad too. But have you noticed that she doesn't have her iPod in all the time any more? She's starting to look around again. Just this evening, in the restaurant. There really is something changing, Marc.'

I don't believe it for a minute, I felt like saying. But I didn't. I lay there for a while, completely quiet, and counted the boxcars. 'I think I can probably go back to sleep now,' I said.

In Las Vegas we spent most of the time in the deckchairs beside one of the many pools at the Hotel Tropicana. Caroline and I drank even more margaritas. During happy hour we sometimes ordered as many as four in a row. We threw a few dollar coins into the one-armed bandits. In the evening we strolled the neon-lit streets, past the casinos. We looked at the fountains in front of the Bellagio Hotel, as they performed a water ballet to music. By that time the margaritas had worn off; I listened to the pounding in my head and didn't dare to look over at my elder daughter. Caroline held Julia's hand. Lisa cried 'Oooh' and 'Aaah' at every new flourish of water and took photos. I bought us all ice cream and Coke from a street vendor, but even the Coke couldn't make my tongue any less dry.

'Maybe we should do something different,' Caroline said later, in bed. The girls had a room of their own next to ours. I was staring at a poker tournament on TV.

'Oh yeah?' I said. I raised the little can of Budweiser I'd taken from the mini-bar and emptied it in one swig.

'Something restful,' Caroline said. 'Maybe it was a bad idea, taking this trip. Maybe there are just too many new impressions for her, all at the same time.'

I suddenly felt my eyes sting. 'Oh, damn it,' I said.

'Marc! Is that the only way you can deal with it, to sit around knocking them back all day? This is about our daughter. About *her* sorrow. Not about ours.'

'What?' I said, much louder than I'd planned. I wiped the tears from my face. 'Listen, who's knocking them back around here? You haven't quite been avoiding those margaritas yourself. Even though you can't hold your liquor at all. Not at all! You should see yourself. And hear yourself! That fake, cheerful tone of yours. Lisa winked at me this afternoon, when you were sitting there in your deckchair giggling again, when you knocked over that whole fucking bowl of popcorn. I mean, Julia doesn't say anything, but do you think it's fun for her to have to see her mother sloshed all day long?'

'Me? Me sloshed? Marc, you don't know what you're talking about. Julia is old enough by now, she knows damn well that her mother sometimes acts a little giddy when she's had a few. Why else would she always walk beside me and hold my hand? With you it's different. You undergo a personality change when you've been drinking. She's really scared of you then.'

I felt the air disappear from my lungs, as though my chest had suddenly imploded. 'If she's scared of me, then it's because of you!' I climbed off the bed and hurled the empty beer can at the wall. 'Because you can't come up with anything except to play the nice mother. The nice mother who's oh-so understanding of her little girl who's been raped. You know as well as I do that before last summer she could hardly stand you, you with your constant harping about what time she had to be home. That she always thought I was a lot nicer than you. Jesus Christ, that kind of behaviour makes me puke. Sometimes, deep down inside, I think you're happy to finally be able to play mother hen to your poor, miserable raped daughter. But she's not a little girl any more, Caroline, you're not doing her a favour by mothering her. All you're doing is pushing her down deeper into her own mire!'

Someone pounded on the wall. We both covered our mouths with our hands and looked at each other in horror.

'Quiet over there!' we heard Lisa shout. 'We can't sleep!'

During the last week we rented an apartment in Goleta, a seaside suburb of Santa Barbara. We ate crab at the pier, Lisa photographed the huge seagulls that swooped down brazenly onto the wooden tables and made off with the leftovers. We sauntered down the shopping streets. Julia bought herself a blouse. Then she bought a pair of Nikes. Sometimes I would wait outside after she had grabbed her mother's hand and pulled her into yet another boutique.

But every once in a while she laughed too. More and more often. Real laughter now. At the apartment she spent a long time in front of the mirror, then came to show us her new acquisitions. 'Yeah, does it really look good on me?' she asked. 'Isn't it a little too tight around the shoulders?'

Lisa took pictures of Julia posing on the balcony in one of her new outfits. She raised her leg and rested her heel against one of the low iron railings. She put on her new sunglasses, then slid them up onto her hair like a hairband. Lisa squatted down, the camera glued to her left eye. 'Now look into the sun,' she said. 'And now look back at me... Right, like that... that look... Just keep looking like that.'

On one of our last days there we went out for a Mexican one last time, at a restaurant with a patio dotted with palms and cacti, not far from the beach.

'A margarita?' I asked Caroline.

'I guess one couldn't hurt,' my wife replied, winking at me.

Later there was a parade down the main street of the town. Our daughters elbowed their way through the crowd to get a better look, while we stayed back a bit, on the pavement – without losing sight of them for a moment.

'You're right, it was a bad idea,' I said.

My wife tilted her head to one side and laid it against my shoulder. I felt the warmth of her hair against my cheek.

'It sure was,' she said.

44

One Sunday, a few weeks after we got home, I looked at the photos Lisa had taken in America. I had transferred the entire contents of the camera to the hard drive of my laptop. Then I clicked through them, from back to front. The most recent photos first, and then further and further back to the start of our trip.

Let me say right now that it was no accident, my going through them in that order. There was something I feared, I didn't quite dare to admit it to myself, but what I feared were the photos from the beginning of the holiday. Or rather, the photos made around the time Julia had wept at the Grand Canyon.

I clicked a little more quickly past the pictures of the illuminated casinos on the Strip in Las Vegas. There was one of the singing cowboy on the patio of the Mexican restaurant in Williams. There were pictures of Caroline and me drinking our margaritas through straws and waving cheerfully at the photographer. In the next picture, Julia stared straight into the lens. On the plate in front of her lay her enchilada, untouched. I forced myself to look my elder daughter straight in the eye. I saw what I was afraid to see. But I also saw something else. Before what happened at the summer house, Julia had had a different look in her eye.

Uninhibited. *Undamaged*, I corrected myself immediately. That was how I viewed the damaged look in my daughter's eyes, while I tried to think about nothing. I knew I would be lost as soon as I thought about anything.

I closed my eyes and pressed my fingertips hard against my eyelids. For thirty seconds, maybe longer. Then I opened my eyes again. I looked again. And now I saw something different. It was impossible *not* to see it.

Julia had always been a pretty girl. An uninhibited, pretty girl, that's right, a girl some grown men turned their heads to watch when she walked by. But on the patio of that Mexican restaurant she looked anything but uninhibited. It wasn't even a sad look that I saw in my daughter's eyes. It was a grave look. Julia was fourteen now. She no longer looked into the camera as a girl, but as a young woman. A young woman with eyes that had seen things. That *knew* things. It made her even prettier. She had changed from a normal, pretty girl into a dazzling beauty.

I clicked further back in time. I saw dry, empty landscapes with cacti. Petrol stations and Burger Kings. Endless freight trains. There was a photograph of Caroline, Julia and me sitting at a wooden picnic table at the viewpoint on the Grand Canyon. It must have been taken just before Julia's crying jag. *I can't see how beautiful it is any more*, that's what she'd said. But in her face I already saw the first signs of the change that had become definitive by the time of the photo on the patio in Williams. Even further back, posing in front of the presidential profiles at Mount Rushmore, she had looked at the camera almost searchingly.

Really searchingly, as though she were looking for something. Maybe she was looking for herself, it occurred to me now.

The photo series ended with the skyscrapers of Chicago, the view of Lake Michigan from Sears Tower. At least I thought it did. But there was more. After a photo of a departures screen at Schiphol, zoomed in on our destination (Kl0611 – Chicago – 11.35 – C14), there was suddenly a picture of a flower. Some kind of flower, not one I knew the name of myself, taken from very close up. At the bottom of the screen I saw that this was photograph number sixty-nine. Sixty-eight more to go before the first… I clicked again: a picture of a butterfly on a white wall, and then a portrait of a cow. It was a brown cow, with a thick copper ring through its nose.

I knew it even before I clicked further back. I could tell by the way I was breathing. It was a camera with a memory large enough for more than a thousand pictures. Lisa had taken at least three hundred in America. Plus another sixty-nine during our holiday before that. At the summer house. And apparently not a single photograph in the entire year between the two summer holidays.

A few photos back in time I saw my own face at a breakfast table. The breakfast table at the little hotel in the mountains. My half-open, bloodshot eye on the morning that I had operated on myself in front of the mirror. I hesitated for a moment about clicking further back. These were the pictures I had never wanted to see. Or, to put it more accurately, the pictures whose *existence I had denied.* I had never wanted to look at them: at normal holiday pictures that would never be normal again because you knew what had happened afterwards. *Carefree* holiday pictures in which everything, as they say, is just peachy. Your own thirteen-year-old daughter on a green inflatable crocodile in a pool. Your *laughing* daughter – back then, still.

But now everything was different, because of what I'd seen in the pictures taken in America. Now I wanted to see with my own eyes whether it was true: whether one year ago Julia had still been a girl, but now wasn't any more. So I kept clicking back. I saw Julia sharing a deckchair with Alex, each of them with one white earbud. I saw Ralph chopping the fish into pieces. Ralph and Alex and Thomas at the ping-pong table. Julia and Alex up to their waists in the sea at one of the remote beaches; Julia was waving at the camera, Alex had his arm around her. Caroline lying on her stomach, asleep on a beach blanket, Judith posing with a tray full of glasses and a pitcher of pink lemonade. I saw myself as well, down on my knees, digging a trench in the sand; I wasn't even looking at the photographer, that's how absorbed I was in my work. Then came the pictures of the hosing-down at the pool: the afternoon of the Miss Wet T-shirt contest. I spent a bit more time looking at a picture of Julia on the diving board. She had adopted the pose of the consummate fashion model, looking into the lens with eyes closed to slits while the water from the garden hose spattered against her stomach. 'Consummate' was indeed the right word for it. Professional. But it was a make-believe professionalism; one year ago she only did a very good imitation of the models in magazines. Now, one year later, she 'did' nothing at all. Nothing extra.

At the next photo, my heart suddenly began to race. There I was at the kitchen window, beside Judith. We weren't looking at the photographer, we were looking at each other. In the background you could vaguely see a third person. Her mother. During what must have been about five seconds, my finger hovered above the delete key. Then I decided that that would not be a good idea. Who knows who might have seen these pictures already. Lisa in any case, perhaps she had already copied them to the computer she shared with Julia. A deleted photo would probably be more conspicuous than one in which you couldn't actually see that much. I took a good look now. The picture was taken from too far away, you couldn't see *how* Judith and I were looking at each other.

There was one photo of the little bird that had fallen from the tree, in its cardboard box. It was huddled up in a corner, against the water dish and the face flannel. It was a picture, a still image, but I could almost *see* it shiver. Next came a few photos that seemed to have been taken at night, in the tent, when Caroline and I were already asleep. In the beam of light, probably from a torch, Julia was making shadow figures on the canvas with her fingers. A rabbit. A snake. I'd been able to hold it back till now, but suddenly I felt my eyes growing wet. I clicked on quickly.

More pictures from beside the pool. Julia, her knees pulled up, on a deckchair. Julia sitting on the edge of the pool. In one picture she was wearing her bikini; in the next she had a towel slung over one shoulder in a way that made it look more like an article of clothing (a vest, a shawl) than a towel. There were a number of photos like that. It took a few seconds before I realised what I was looking at.

Julia was *posing*. She was posing with different articles of clothing, or at least she was pretending to be posing with different articles of clothing. But in none of the pictures was she looking into the lens. Not at the photographer. Not at Lisa.

Julia was looking at something else. At someone outside the frame of the photo.

I quickly clicked further back. At last, in the final three photos, you could see who she was posing for. He was squatting in front of her while she stood under the shower beside the pool. She had one leg raised in an unmistakable pose, her sunglasses pushed up onto her wet hair, and she was looking provocatively at the photographer squatting in front of her. He held his camera pressed against his eye, just like in the next two photos.

Stanley Forbes was grinning broadly as he photographed my daughter in the shower. In the next two photos he just looked as though he was concentrating deeply. In one of them Julia had dropped the top of her bikini and was holding her hands in front of her breasts in mock shame. In the other she was smoking a cigarette, she blew the smoke into the photographer's face in close-up.

'Lisa, could you come here?'

My youngest daughter was lying on the bed in our room, watching a *South Park* DVD. She gestured to me to be quiet, until she saw my face. She picked up the remote, hit pause and got up off the bed.

'What were you two doing here?' I asked, letting the poolside photos pass one-by-one. I was doing my best not to sound alarmed, but I could almost hear my own heart pounding.

'That's Stanley,' Lisa said.

'Yes, I can see that. But what were you doing. What was *he* doing?'

'He took pictures of Julia. He told her she could work as a fashion model, no problem. He was going to make a whole series of her and then send them around in America. To *Vogue*, I think that's what he said. He took pictures of me too.'

I took a deep breath. 'What are you telling me, Lisa?'

'Daddy, what's wrong? Why do you look like that? He made a whole series of me too. He said that fashion magazines are always looking for pretty young girls. He said that was how Emmanuelle got started. That he'd made a whole bunch of photos of her first, and that then she got famous.'

'Lisa, I want you to look at me. And I don't want you to lie to me. What kind of pictures did he take?'

'Don't be weird, Dad. Julia and I are both friends with Stanley on Facebook. We sent those last pictures to him too. He asked us to.'

'Wait a minute. Last pictures? Which last pictures?'

'The ones from America, Dad. He asks us all the time whether we have new pictures of ourselves, so we sent him the holiday pictures. The ones with us in them, of course. Well, it's mostly

Julia, because I took most of them. Stanley's really famous. He says we just have to be patient, but that later maybe both of us can be models. In America, Daddy. In *America*!'

45

I waited. But I didn't wait too long. The time difference with California was nine hours. Stanley had given me his number back at the summer house. If I was ever in the neighbourhood of Santa Barbara, I should give him a ring, he'd said. A few months ago I had indeed been in the neighbourhood of Santa Barbara. But by then things had already happened. It had seemed to me better for Julia, for all of us, not to get in touch with the film director.

At five p.m. Dutch time I dialled his number. It was eight a.m. in Santa Barbara. For the element of surprise, the best thing was to wake Stanley Forbes with my call.

'Stanley…' He'd answered almost immediately, and he sounded far from sleepy, I noted to my regret.

'This is Marc,' I said. 'Marc Schlosser.'

'Marc! Where are you? Long time no see. Are you in town? Are you coming by?'

'I know about the pictures, Stanley. The pictures you took of my daughters.'

There was a few seconds' silence. A fraction longer than the normal silences that always punctuate an international call.

'Aw, that's too bad,' he said. 'They wanted it to be a surprise for the two of you. Especially Julia.'

Now it was my turn to be silent for a second longer.

'Marc? You still there? Listen, now that you know anyway, take a look at my website. I put a selection on there. A selection from the series I made beside the pool.'

'Actually, I'm calling about something else, Stanley. I'm calling because I'd really like to know where you were that night, at the midsummer party. After Ralph tried to beat up that girl. I lost track of you after that. Until you came back to the summer house, really late. Did you go wandering around the beach that evening, Stanley? Did you perhaps go looking for one of your models?'

I was taking it too fast, I realised too late. I shouldn't have accused him right away. I should have given him more rope. Stanley Forbes was a grown man – a dirty, old, grown man, I heard myself think – who took pictures of young girls and made vague promises about modelling careers. For that alone he could be arrested these days and put behind bars for a long time.

'Marc, come on!' he said. 'I really can't believe you'd think that about me!'

I said nothing. I waited for him to say too much. Maybe I should have been taping this conversation, I realised now.

'Listen, Marc. I realise you're all confused because of what happened to Julia. But everything's taking a turn for the better now. Julia and Lisa sent me those last pictures just a few days ago. The ones from America. I'd already signed them up with a modelling agency here. They were definitely interested, but now, with these new pictures, especially the ones of Julia, they're going completely nuts. There are a couple of them... I guess you've seen them. Julia on the patio at some restaurant. It's the look in her eyes… Those pictures at the pool were missing something. But the way she looks at you in that one… And then that other one, beside the Grand Canyon. She looks… how should I put it… she looks the way she looks, Marc. I sent her an e-mail a couple of days ago. She should really come over here for a new shoot. I could do it in Holland too, but it's about the light. The light here's different, I could never fake that in a studio. If you ask me, she's afraid to talk to you about it. She's afraid you won't let her come. But she's in good hands with me, Marc. And otherwise, just come along with her for a few days. You and Caroline. Or all four of you. My house is big enough. It's not right on the Pacific, but you can hear it from here. And I've got a pool. And by the way, why didn't you come by this summer? You guys were right here, I saw that in the pictures the girls sent. That parade through Santa Barbara? Emmanuelle and I were there too.'

I wanted to ask Stanley again exactly where he'd been between midnight and two on that particular night – but suddenly I didn't believe in it any more. Stanley had talked about the pictures at the Grand Canyon and on the patio of the Mexican restaurant in Williams. He'd seen the same thing I had.

'And what about Lisa?' I heard myself ask.

'Oh yeah, sure. Lisa. You guys should bring Lisa along too. But just between the two of us: she's going to have to wait for another year or so. It's different. She's still so young. A different thing, if you know what I mean.'

46

One by one, I looked at the pictures on Stanley's website. The pictures of my elder daughter. There were ten of them in total. Lovely pictures. Especially the one of Julia under the shower with her sunglasses slid up onto her head: in the spray of droplets above her wet hair you could see a miniature rainbow.

There were other photographs as well. Not only of Julia, also of other girls. *Teen Models* was the title Stanley had given the series. There was a picture of a girl in a Jacuzzi, somewhere outside in a garden with palm trees and cacti in the background. On the edge of the Jacuzzi was a bottle of champagne and two glasses. There were fluffs of foam on the water, only partly covering the girl's torso. She was looking straight into the lens. The picture could only have been taken from that angle if the photographer himself was in the Jacuzzi as well.

Only when I looked again did I recognise Emmanuelle. A younger Emmanuelle. Younger than she was now, in any case. No older than fifteen, I guessed.

There were even more photo series on the site. Series with titles like *Deserts*, *Sunsets*, *Water* and *Travel*. I clicked past some photos of camels and pyramids, and then a whole row of sunsets. The *Travel* series was categorised according to place and year.

There was also a photo series under the name of the coast where we had spent our holiday at the summer house a year ago. I clicked past a few pictures I'd seen before: monasteries and castles, things Stanley had shown me back then on his camera's display. Emmanuelle posing on a wall or beside a statue. Some of the photographs were new to me: lobsters, rays and shrimp on display at a street market; shells and jellyfish in the sand; a white tablecloth with breadcrumbs – and then I suddenly saw myself. And not just me: we were all in this one, sitting at a richly covered table in the garden of the summer house – Ralph, Judith, Caroline, Emmanuelle, Alex, Thomas, Judith's mother, Julia, Lisa, and me – we were looking at the photographer and raising our glasses in a toast.

Then came more photos from the summer house. Ralph chopping the swordfish into pieces on the patio; Lisa leaning over the cardboard box containing the little bird; Judith in a deckchair beside the pool; and one in the garden, of a man I didn't recognise, a man in shorts and a sleeveless T-shirt; his arms folded across his chest, he was looking into the camera with a grin. In the next photo the unknown man was holding the garden hose in his hand, a jet of water was spouting straight into the air; after that came a photo of the same man standing between my two daughters: he had his arms around their shoulders and was beaming at the camera. In this picture you could clearly see how small he was, he was a good inch shorter than Julia.

I clicked back to the first photo. For the second time that day, I called for Lisa.

*

'That's the guy who came to fix the water,' Lisa said.

We looked at the photos together. In all three of them you could clearly see the tattoo on his upper arm: an eagle clutching a bleeding heart in its talons.

'He was really nice,' Lisa said. 'He joked with us. About him being so little. He kept going up and standing beside Julia and shaking his head and laughing. We couldn't understand everything he was saying, but he said something about Dutch girls, about them being so much taller than the men there.'

I counted back. On Friday morning Caroline and I had gone to the letting agency. The girl behind the counter had said that the repairman would try to come by that afternoon. The unattractive girl, who was also his girlfriend. Then Caroline and I went shopping. We'd stayed away much longer than usual, because neither of us felt like going back to the house right away. We had wandered around the market, and before that we went to have lunch somewhere. I couldn't remember whether the water was already fixed when we got back, but the Saturday after that the boys had been spraying the girls on the diving board, so it was fixed by then, in any case.

Then I thought about the Saturday evening. About the night on the beach. In front of the men's room in the restaurant I had run into the repairman. I remembered the tattoo on his sweaty arm. On his other arm he had a cut. Three red stripes… His homely girlfriend was crying out on the patio. Maybe they'd just had a fight. Perhaps he'd been feeding her some line about why he'd been away for so long. Who knows, maybe she'd smelled it on him. Maybe she'd seen the cuts on his arm. And maybe, because after all she was a woman too, she had immediately recognised them as scratches that could only be inflicted by a woman's nails.

A girl's nails, I corrected myself.

47

The Monday morning after I'd looked at the site, I suddenly saw the TV comedian sitting in my waiting room again. The same comedian who had shouted a year ago that I could stuff it up my arse and that he would never come back here again. I hadn't taken a good look at the list of patients my assistant had drawn up for that morning – or rather, I had stopped looking over the list in advance months ago; I 'took things as they came', as they say.

'I went to another doctor for a while,' he said, once he was sitting across from me in my office. 'But I found him, how shall I put it, just a bit too chummy. More chummy than you are, in any case.'

I looked at his round, not unhandsome face; he looked healthy, the AIDS infection had apparently been a false alarm.

'Well, I'm pleased that you—'

'And there was something else,' he interrupted. 'Something about the way he acted made alarm bells ring. I don't know whether you've ever experienced it, I'm sure you have, but there are people who go to great lengths to show how terribly tolerant they are of homosexuals. That they think it's all completely *normal*. Even though it's not normal at all. I mean, if it's so normal, why did it take me five years to work up the nerve to tell my parents? That was what irritated me about that new doctor. Once he started, for no good reason, talking about Gay Pride, how fantastic it was that all that was allowed in this town. Even though, as a homosexual, the one thing that disgusts me most are all those pumped-up male bodies dancing on a boat with only a shoestring between their buttocks. But that never occurs to some people, some *tolerant* people, that you, as a homosexual, might not think that's so great.'

I said nothing, just nodded and worked my face into a smile. The clock across from my desk said that five minutes had already gone by, but it made no difference: I had plenty of time.

'Listen,' the comedian went on. 'It's great that we all have equal rights these days, sure. On paper. But that doesn't mean you have to think it's *charming*. People make that mistake. They're afraid to be discriminating. That's why they laugh even more loudly when an invalid in a wheelchair tells a joke. The joke isn't funny, and besides, you can barely understand it. The invalid has an untreatable progressive illness. When he laughs at his own joke, the drool runs down his chin. But we laugh along with him. What was it again, Marc? You have a son and a daughter, don't you?'

'Two daughters.'

'So would you think it was charming if one of your two daughters, or both of them, turned out to be lesbian?'

'As long as they're happy.'

'Marc, come on! Don't try clichés like that on me. That's exactly the reason why I came back to you. Because you've never tried to hide it. Your aversion. Well, maybe "aversion" is putting it too strongly. But you know what I mean. Am I right or not?'

I smiled again: a real smile this time.

'See!?' the comedian said. 'I knew it. But why is it then that I feel so much more comfortable with you than with people who try so hard to find homosexuals *charming*?'

'Maybe because you don't find them charming yourself,' I said.

The comedian began laughing loudly, then grew serious again. 'I guess "charming" is the key word here,' he said. 'It wasn't particularly easy for my parents to accept that from me. To accept my boyfriend. To, as you said before, only care about my happiness. But they really don't think it's *charming*. No parent thinks it's charming. Have you ever heard a father or mother say that about their son or daughter, that they found it so *charming* when they heard about it? That they were so pleased and relieved to find out that their son or daughter, thank God, at least wasn't *heterosexual*? I mean, I'm a comedian, in my shows I've always tried to deal with that side of it too. If I didn't, I wouldn't be able to take myself seriously. Well, seriously… you know what I mean.'

'That's right,' I said. 'I know exactly what you mean. So what else can I do for you?'

He sighed deeply. 'My prostate,' he said. 'It only drips lately, no powerful jet any more. I thought… well, you know what I thought.'

I looked at the comedian's hairy bottom on my examining table. I couldn't help it. I couldn't help but think of the words of my professor of medical biology. 'I'm only going to say it once,' Aaron Herzl had told us. 'If God had meant for a man to introduce his sex organ into the anal opening, he would have made that opening larger. I intentionally use the word "God" here, but I could also have said "biology". There's an idea behind everything. A plan. Things we shouldn't eat stink or taste bad. And then there's pain. Pain tells us that it's not a good idea to stick a fountain pen in our eye. The body gets tired and tells us we should take a rest. The heart can only pump out so much oxygen to all the body's extremities.' Here Professor Herzl took off his glasses, for a full minute he had let his gaze wander over the seats in the auditorium. 'I'm not out to pass moral judgement here,' he went on. 'Everyone should be able to do what they want in all freedom, but a swollen dick penetrating the anus hurts. *Don't do that*, the pain says. *Pull it out now, before it's too late*. The body has a tendency to listen to pain. That's biology. We don't jump out of a window on the seventh floor, not *unless* we want to destroy that body.'

It happened quite suddenly. I guess I must have been repressing it, or maybe I'd simply forgotten, but now, suddenly, I remembered what Herzl had said after that. First I felt my eyes grow misty, then – there was no stopping it – my lower lip began quivering.

'Everything about a small child is smaller. Everything. That too is biology. Little girls can't get pregnant. As far as that goes, they're conversely identical to women over forty. Keep off, biology says. There is no biological sense in having sex with a girl who is not yet sexually mature. Once again, the opening is too small. And then there is the hymen. One of the most wonderful inventions biology has bestowed on us. Almost enough to make you believe in the existence of a God.'

There was some chuckling in the auditorium; most of the students were grinning, a small minority was not.

'I'd like to once again summon up the image of a big, swollen dick. The male sex organ in erect state. When a dick like that tries to enter the too-narrow opening of a sexually unripe girl, there is, first of all, pain. *Don't do that*, the girl herself probably says as well. In our society, the arrangement is that men who try to penetrate little girls, or boys, are locked up. Our moral code in this regard is so pronounced that, even within prison walls, child molesters' lives are worth nothing. Thieves and murderers consider themselves *superior* to child molesters. And for good reason. They react elementally. In fact, they react the way all of us should react. The way we reacted once, long, long ago, in the days when biology was still more powerful than the rule of law. *Get rid of it! Get rid of that trash! Destroy those freaks!*'

Now the auditorium was deathly silent. The proverbial pin. The breath that was held longer than was good for you.

'It's not my intention to advance solutions to this moral dilemma,' Herzl said. 'I simply want to get you to think first before you blindly accept the moral codes of your own day as being the only proper moral codes. Therefore, by way of conclusion, here is a simple hypothetical case that I'd like you all to think about for next week.'

By now I had been standing at the examining table too long. More time had passed than the comedian could be expected to consider normal. I had washed my hands. I had pulled on the rubber gloves. Something had to happen. The examination. The internal examination of the prostate by way of the anus. But I could no longer interrupt my own train of thought, I had to keep going first. All the way to the end. I took a deep breath. To gain time, I placed one hand on a hairy buttock and took a deep breath.

'We consider an adult who tries to impose himself sexually on a child to be abnormal,' Professor Aaron Herzl had said. 'Someone with a deviation. A patient in need of treatment. There begins the dilemma, and the question for next week. Because *what* treatment is required here? Before going into detail, I first want you to ask yourselves the following: of those present here today, ninety-one per cent feels attracted to members of the opposite sex, nine per cent to those of their own sex. Less than one per cent feels sexually attracted to children, so fortunately I can assume that there is no one like that present here today.' Laughter from the auditorium: slightly uneasy laughter that tried to sound relieved. 'But let's turn the whole thing around. Let us, the better to understand this example, imagine that our own sexual proclivity were to be banned. That we would be arrested if caught having sexual intercourse with an adult of the opposite sex. That we would then be locked up for years in a prison or clinic. And that during that period of detention we would be talked to by a psychologist or psychiatrist. We have to convince that psychologist or psychiatrist that we are willing to work on our own cure. In the end, we have to make that other person believe that we *have been* cured. So that the psychologist can write a report that says we no longer pose a risk to society. That we, as men, have kicked the habit of feeling attracted to women, or as women to men. Meanwhile, however, we know better. We know that that's impossible. That we cannot be "cured". All we want is to get out as quickly as possible and once again interfere with women or men.'

I moved my hand one inch further over the comedian's buttock. As though I were going to *do* something. What came after this was a part of the lecture that I could no longer remember clearly, but that undoubtedly had to do with the 'curing' of child molesters. All I could remember was the pan of mussels at the end.

'Take, for example, a pan of mussels,' Herzl had said. 'Before you on the table is a lovely pan of cooked mussels. Healthy mussels. Tasty mussels. But if everything is as it should be, we have learned not to eat those few mussels that don't open of their own accord. Because they can make us ill. I want you to think about those mussels as you think about next week's assignment. Those mussels themselves are ill. Some of them are even already dead. Are we going to apply force to break open that mussel and eat it anyway? Are we going to make it converse with a prison psychologist for two years, and then put it in our mouth anyway because the prison psychologist has assured us that the mussel is by now edible? Or do we throw it away? See you next week.'

The comedian shifted on the examining table. He lifted his head and glanced over his shoulder. At me. I saw the startled look in his eye.

'Marc,' he said. 'What's wrong?'

I tried to grin, but it hurt somewhere. There was a dry click somewhere at the back of my jaw. 'What could be wrong?' I asked.

But I couldn't kid myself any longer. I had looked at his hairy backside. I knew that a hairy male bum was not my kind of thing. That a bum like that did indeed induce in me a healthy aversion: a plate of nasty or rotten food that you push away gagging. *Don't eat it!* I was 'normal'. I thought about women. Not just Caroline or Judith, about women in general. That was biology, Professor Herzl had taught us. A man who doesn't look at women in general is like a car with the accelerator and the brake held down at the same time. A car like that first starts to smell of burnt rubber, in the end it breaks down or catches fire. Biology dictates that we should impregnate as many women as possible. I made the same mental leap I'd made thirty years earlier during Herzl's lecture. Could I ever cure myself? Would I be able, if society were to label my own healthy urges as sick, to convince a prison psychologist that I had meanwhile been 'cured'? I thought I could. But as soon as I was out on the street, I would fall back into my old ways within twenty-four hours.

I don't mean to place myself on a higher moral level than those men who feel drawn to young girls. All men feel drawn to young girls. That, too, is biology. We look at those girls with an eye to future generations: whether they, within the foreseeable future, will be able to guarantee the continuation of the human species.

But it was taking things a step too far to actually act on that attraction. Biology had its own warning systems: with little girls, all systems were no-go. *Don't! Keep off! If you go on you will break something.*

'I think it would be better if you returned to a sitting position,' I told the comedian.

He righted himself, sat with his legs hanging over the edge of the examining table, pulled a white handkerchief out of his pocket and handed it to me.

'Here,' he said. 'Don't worry, I washed it,' he added with a wink.

'Sorry,' I said. I tried to blow my nose, but my nose was already empty. 'If you could come back... otherwise I'll give you a referral to emergency.'

'You don't have to tell me anything, OK,' he said. 'But if you feel like it: I've got all the time in the world.'

He spread his arms. I looked at his round, open face. I told him. I told him everything. I left out only a couple of things. With an eye to the future. My plans for the future, that above all.

'And you still have no idea at all who could have done it?' he asked when I was finished.

'No.'

'Shit. Someone who does something like that, you could just...'

He didn't finish his sentence, but it wasn't necessary. I thought about the pan of mussels: about the mussels that didn't open.

48

The shot glass with the lethal cocktail was on the table beside Ralph's bed. Also on the table was a half-finished container of fruit yoghurt with the spoon still in it, that morning's paper and a biography of Shakespeare that he'd been reading for the last few weeks. There was a bookmark between the pages, not even halfway through. He had asked Judith and his two sons to leave the room for a moment.

When they were gone, he gestured to me to come over.

'Marc,' he said; he took my hand, held it against the blanket, and put his other hand on top of it. 'I want to tell you that I'm sorry,' he said. 'I wouldn't have... I never would have...' He fell silent for a moment. 'I'm sorry, I guess that's what I'm trying to say.'

I looked at his face, emaciated and swollen at the same time: at his eyes that were still seeing me at this point, but which, as from a moment between now and an hour from now, at most, would never see anything again.

'How is it … with her?' he asked. I shrugged.

'Marc,' he said. I felt the pressure of his hand on mine. He tried to tighten his grip, but I could feel how little strength he had left. 'Could you tell her… from me… could you tell her what I just said to you?'

I averted my eyes; effortlessly, I pulled my hand from his grasp. 'No,' I said.

He sighed deeply, closed his eyes for a moment and then opened them again. 'Marc, I've hesitated for a long time about whether to tell you this or not. I thought, maybe I'm the last person he wants to hear something like this from.'

I looked at him. 'What are you talking about?'

'About your daughter, Marc. About Julia.'

Involuntarily, I glanced at the door, then at the shot glass beside his bed. Ralph saw what I was looking at.

'In the end, I decided that you need to know. It may be a little late, but I haven't known about it so long myself. Just a couple of weeks, actually.'

For a split second I thought he was going to say something about Judith: that he knew about the two of us, for example, that she had confessed everything, but that he wanted to wish us all the happiness in the world. The next moment I realised that, no, he had clearly said *about your daughter. About Julia*.

'Alex made me swear to keep quiet about it. He knew I wasn't going to be around for long, that's why he told me. He had to get it off his chest, he said he would go crazy if he kept it to himself any longer. His mother doesn't know. He's the only one. Him and Julia.'

I thought about that night on the beach. About the way Alex had acted when he came across Judith and me near the club. He's hiding something, I'd thought even then. He isn't telling us everything.

'Do you remember that repairman who came by a couple of times to fix the tank on the roof? When we didn't have any running water?'

I probably blinked, or else I was wearing a blank expression, because Ralph said: 'The repairman. From the letting agency. A little guy. Late twenties, early thirties...'

'Yeah, I remember... a repairman... for the water. What about him?'

With difficulty, Ralph drew air into his lungs, it sounded like an air mattress deflating. 'Julia had arranged to meet him that evening,' he said. 'The repairman. I don't know when they actually agreed to meet up, I guess one of those times when he came by. Or who knows, maybe in the village or on the beach. Whatever it was, they agreed to meet at that beach club on the night of the midsummer party. Alex tried to talk her out of it, he had an uneasy feeling about it. I mean, it was already bad enough for Alex that she wasn't content with just him. She told Alex that she thought he was still too much of a baby, that she went more for real men. Well, anyway, that evening... that night... Alex finally went along with her. Because he had a bad feeling about it, like I said. And then what happened happened. The guy threatened Alex, Marc. He threatened to do something to Alex if he ever said anything to his parents. Oh, if I'd only known that back then... The bastard wouldn't have lived to talk about it!'

'But... but how did Julia...?'

'Wait a minute, I'm not finished yet. Julia and Alex agreed

not to say anything. Actually, she made him swear not to say anything. Back on the beach. After it happened.'

'But I found her... When I found her...'

'She was so ashamed, she thought it was all her own fault. She thought you and Caroline would think it was stupid of her and you would never trust her again. That you would never let her go anywhere alone again after that. That's why she came up with the idea of pretending to be unconscious. So she could tell the two of you that she didn't remember anything.'

Half an hour later Judith and I were in the corridor. Alex and Thomas had gone to the hospital cafeteria. Judith had just said that she was so glad I had been there. And I had said that Ralph had 'gone with dignity'.

Then Dr Maasland came along with his griping about the tissue sample that had never arrived. He'd asked Judith for permission to perform an autopsy.

'That's really strange, isn't it?' Judith said after Dr Maasland left. 'You really can't remember what happened back then? I remember you telling me that the hospital had said it was nothing serious.'

'It *is* strange, that's right,' I said. 'And that arrogant bastard acting as though it was *me* who lost it, even though they were probably the ones who should have been more careful.'

'But just now, the first thing you said was that you couldn't remember. Why did you say that, Marc? I don't get it, not at all. I thought there was something else going on. Something between you and Ralph. What did Ralph want to talk to you about, anyway, just before? Did that have anything to do with it?'

'Listen, Judith,' I said. 'I think it would be better for both of us if we didn't see each other for a while. And maybe not just for a while. What I really mean is, for an extended period. I've been there for you up till now, but now I have to kind of get my own life into shape. Too much has happened. Things you don't have a clue about. At this point, I just can't have you around.'

49

Two days later I received a call from Dr Maasland. I was right in the middle of my daily appointments. I was with a female writer whose excessive consumption of red wine made her look twenty years older than she really was – or at least eighteen years, judging from the photoshopped portrait on the back of her latest book.

'Can I call you back in a little bit?' I said. 'I'm with a patient right now.'

'I'm afraid not, Dr Schlosser. This is too serious for that.'

In the last few years the author's face had aged with increasing speed. Red wine drains the skin from underneath. It's like with a receding water table. The moisture draws back beneath the skin's surface. The skin itself becomes a wasteland. All life dies off. Animals go looking for a place where there's more water. Plants wither and die. The sun and the wind have free rein. Cracks appear in the soil. Erosion. Drifting sand wears away at the surface.

'Have you people been able to track down that tissue yet?' I asked Dr Maasland. 'The tissue I sent you back then. I mean, it's awfully strange that something like that could just go missing.'

There was a loud sigh at the other end. The sort of sigh that specialists breathe when they have to explain something complex to a general physician. Something that's beyond the ken of a simple family doctor.

'We haven't got to that yet, but that's really not the issue here. We performed an autopsy on Mr Meier's body yesterday. It showed, beyond a shadow of a doubt, that someone, and we can also assume that someone was you, Dr Schlosser, removed tissue from Mr Meier's thigh—'

'That's exactly what I've been trying to tell you the whole time.'

'Please let me finish, Dr Schlosser. What it's all about, in fact, is that *too much* tissue was removed. From much too large a surface. While every doctor ought to know that when there is even the slightest suspicion of such a serious illness, one is better off not removing anything at all. That you first need to look at the white blood cell count, and only then, perhaps, take a sample. That's first-year medical school stuff, Dr Schlosser.'

'I thought I was dealing with a fat node. In view of Mr Meier's eating habits, that was not particularly unlikely.'

'Due to your rigorous incision, the cells most probably entered the bloodstream. From that moment on Mr Meier didn't stand a ghost of a chance. I therefore reported this immediately to the proper authorities. These things usually take weeks or months, but because of the dire nature of this case and the fact that our hospital's reputation is also involved, they found a chance to fit this in as a matter of extreme urgency.'

'Fit this in?'

'At the Board of Medical Examiners. You are expected there next Tuesday at nine a.m.'

I flashed a grin at the lady writer, who was beginning to show signs of impatience, shifting back and forth in her chair.

'Next Tuesday...' I said. 'But the funeral is this Friday. I thought—'

'Dr Schlosser, I hope we understand each other clearly. I believe the family would hardly appreciate your presence at the funeral. At least, not after we've informed them of the results of our investigation.'

'And when will that be? Is there such a big rush? No verdict has been passed, has it? That can't happen before Tuesday, right? Or maybe not even then? Maybe the Board will want to take its time examining things.'

I realised I was asking too many questions at once. *Nervous* people ask too many questions at once. But I wasn't nervous, I tried to tell myself. It was just that I had never before been forced to use the term 'Board of Medical Examiners' in front of a patient.

Again, that same deep sigh at the other end.

'We always send our conclusions by letter. That, in fact, is the only thing I can do for you. We're obliged to inform the family, but by doing that in the form of a letter we comply with the regulations, while the doctor in question gets a day's reprieve. See it as a helping hand, from one colleague to the other, Marc.'

50

'Herzl here.'

The human voice doesn't age. Even if he hadn't stated his name, I could have picked out my former professor of medical biology's voice in a crowd.

'Professor Herzl,' I said. 'How are you?'

'I should probably be asking *you* that, Marc. Are you alone? Can you speak freely?'

I was indeed alone, at my desk in the office. The waiting room was unusually crowded: there were no fewer than four patients waiting to be called in one by one, but I didn't feel like dealing with patients, so I just let them sit there.

'I'm alone,' I said.

'Right. Please excuse me if I skip the preliminaries and get right to the point, Marc. I propose that you listen to me first and only then, once I'm finished, do you ask a question. Just like the old days, during lectures, in fact. Is that a problem for you?'

'No.'

'Right. Listen. Since my expulsion from the university I've worked in all kinds of capacities, but I'm not going to bore you with the details. Holland is a totalitarian state. Anyone who falls from grace can go to work cleaning toilets. In my case things didn't get that far, but for years I worked in places where I shouldn't have. In any event, the ideas I expressed back then are now widely accepted, but don't think anyone ever came to me to apologise. For the last five or ten years, though, I have been getting work that is better suited to me, if you can put it that way. For the last couple of years, for example, I've been a freelance consultant to the Board of Medical Examiners.'

Here Aaron Herzl let a brief silence fall, but I kept hold of myself and didn't ask. I did, however, hold the receiver a little more tightly against my ear.

'Right,' Herzl said. 'All I do is offer advice, I have no power of decision. Sometimes I see things other people don't. A few days ago, your case landed on my desk, Marc. I recognised your name right away. General practitioner. I always felt it was too bad that you didn't go on, you were certainly capable enough. Tomorrow morning, nine o'clock. The hour of truth. I've examined your case in great detail, it's not every day that one of my former students is summoned to appear before the Board. I say "great detail", but that wasn't even necessary. In fact, I saw it right away. Listen carefully, Marc. I'm going to ask you a few questions. The best thing would be if you could answer only with "yes" or "no". It's all off the record. But I can only help you if you're frank with me. At the same time, it's in my own interests not to know everything. I hope you understand that.'

'Yes,' I said. At that moment, my assistant stuck her head around the door. She raised her eyebrows inquiringly and gestured over her shoulder, towards the waiting room. I didn't make a sound; I formed the words with my lips. *Go away!* She got the message right away and slipped out again.

I thought Herzl was going to say 'right' again, but he didn't. Or maybe I had missed it.

'Removing tissue for a biopsy is not something the family doctor does, Marc, I don't have to tell you that. And especially not when one suspects that it might involve a life-threatening illness. Technically, one can't even speak of a medical error here. More like temporary insanity. A family doctor is allowed to burn away a mole. He's allowed to remove a lipoma. As soon as he has even the slightest suspicion that it could be something serious, he doesn't touch the mole or lipoma. That's not what happened here. To make things even worse, the tissue was removed in so rigorous a fashion that, in the case of a life-threatening illness, it could only serve to accelerate the spread of that illness. Am I right so far, Marc?'

'Yes.'

'Then, the tissue never arrived at the hospital. It's possible, of course, that it got lost somewhere. But it's also possible that you *forgot* to send it. Pay attention, Marc. Only yes or no. Did you forget?

'Yes.'

I heard Professor Herzl breathe a deep sigh. It sounded like a sigh of relief. Then I heard him shuffling through some papers.

'I'm glad you're being so honest with me, Marc. Now let's get to your patient. The deceased patient... Ralph Meier. An actor. I had never heard of him, but that doesn't mean much. I tend to stay at home. I read, or I listen to music. But down to business. Was there something that made you want to get rid of this particular patient? And I don't mean that you hoped he would start seeing another doctor. No, I mean literally get rid of him. In the sense of *wiped off the face of the earth*. As is, strictly speaking, the case now: the patient is in his grave. Was something like that running through your mind, Marc?'

'Yes.'

'Something happened that meant, in your eyes, that Ralph Meier no longer deserved to live. That's possible. We all think things like that about other people at times. We are, after all, only human. I assume you had your reasons. What I'm going to ask you now, in fact, has nothing to do with this case or with the way the Board will deal with it tomorrow. This is purely my own, personal interest. You have every right not to answer, of course. I haven't gone rooting around in your private life. I came no further than the fact that you have a wife and two young daughters. My question is very simple. Does the death of Ralph Meier have something to do with your family, Marc?'

I hesitated. 'Yes,' I said then, but Aaron Herzl must have heard my hesitation.

'Once again, if you don't want to answer, just don't,' he said. 'I won't hold it against you. So it has something to do with your family. With your wife?'

I hesitated again. One side of me wanted to end the conversation right there; the other no longer wanted to give only 'yes' and 'no' answers. That side of me wanted to tell my former professor of medical biology the whole story.

'No,' I said. 'That is to say, at first... No, not really.'

'I don't want to sound overly acute, Marc, but that didn't seem very likely to me either. My guess was more that it had something to do with your daughters. How old are they now? Fourteen and twelve, if I remember correctly. Is that right?'

'Yes.' I had felt like telling Aaron Herzl everything, but that wasn't even necessary. He already knew.

'Marc,' he said. 'I realise that you may be tempted now to say more than might be good for you. Good for either of us. But we really need to limit ourselves to the facts right now. That's why I'm going to ask you again, emphatically, to answer only with "yes" or "no". On one occasion I was handed a file that, strictly speaking, had only marginally to do with the Board of Medical Examiners. The case of a grown man who had interfered with a twelve-year-old girl. And who actually claimed that she had "liked" it. That's what they all say. We medical people know better. It's a defect. A defective batch is removed from circulation. At least, that's what we *should* do. But I'm digressing. Was it something like that, Marc? Only yes or no.'

'Yes.'

'Then you did what you should have done,' he said. 'You did what any father ought to do.'

'Yes,' I said again, even though Herzl hadn't actually asked a question.

'The point is that you can't present this to the Board in that way,' he went on. 'They don't give a damn about fathers with healthy instincts. I could always try to steer it in the direction of *negligence*. But it's all much too much out in the open. This is not going to be a few months' suspension, Marc. This is more like having your licence revoked. If it even ends there. I'm talking about prosecution. You don't want to do that to your family. You certainly don't want to do that to your daughter.'

'Then what?' I asked. 'What am I supposed to do then?'

Professor Aaron Herzl sighed deeply. 'First of all, don't show up tomorrow morning,' he said. 'That would only make things worse. Personally, I would advise you to disappear completely. Literally. Go abroad. I would decide about that today if I were you, Marc. Talk to your family about it. Go away. Start anew somewhere else. If you need references somewhere, contact me. I can help you. But at this point, that is really the only thing I can do for you.'

After hanging up I sat at my desk for a bit, trying to resolve things in my mind. I could always ask my assistant to send the patients home. I needed time to think. On the other hand, I could mull things over just as easily while listening to their interminable blather. Even more easily, sometimes.

I pushed the button on the intercom. 'Liesbeth, send the first patient in,' I said. 'I'm finished.'

Keep acting normal, I told myself. Everything needs to seem as normal as possible. I looked at the clock on the wall. Ten past ten. I had all the time in the world.

But then, while my first patient of the day was just getting settled, there was suddenly a huge ruckus at the front door. 'Doctor!' I heard my assistant call out. 'Doctor!' There was a sound like a chair being knocked over, and after that I heard a second voice.

'Where are you, you piece of shit?' Judith Meier shrieked. 'Are you scared to show your face?'

51

I leafed through the file. I acted as though I was looking for something. It wasn't Ralph Meier's file. It was some other patient's, one I had taken off the shelf at random: not too thick, not too thin. I didn't even have a file for Ralph Meier.

'Here we are,' I said. 'Ralph came to me in October of last year. He didn't want you to know anything at that point. He was afraid you would become upset for no good reason.'

I glanced up at her. Judith averted her eyes right away. She snorted and drummed her fingers on the armrest.

'At first I didn't think it was anything either,' I went on. 'In most cases it isn't. OK, he said he was tired. But there can be other reasons for that. He worked hard. He always worked hard.'

'Marc, spare me your little asides and excuses. We're way past that point now. Dr Maasland has briefed me in detail. You should never have performed that little biopsy. Under no circumstances. And what the Board of Medical Examiners doesn't know yet is that you prescribed that junk that suppressed his symptoms. At first I had no idea he was taking those pills. I found them by accident, in a compartment of his suitcase. He told me everything then. Including where he got them from.'

'Judith, he was *tired*. Over-tired. He had a two-month shoot. I told him he shouldn't place unreasonable demands on his body. That it was only for those two months.'

I felt extremely composed. Calm. By that point I 'had myself well in hand', as they say. The mere fact that I had come up with an expression like 'unreasonable demands on his body' – an expression I would never use otherwise – showed that I was back on top. I looked at the clock on the wall. We had been here for fifteen minutes already. I'd heard some vague sounds coming from the waiting room, then I'd heard the front door slam. Now it was quiet. Everyone had left.

'Why now, all of a sudden, Judith?' I said. 'Why do you come here, calling me a murderer in front of my patients and my assistant? Last Friday, at the funeral, I figured you were confused by all that horseshit Maasland has been trying to feed you. But it seems like you really bought it. And besides, you haven't actually seemed too mournful about Ralph for the last few months, to put it mildly. At least I never heard you complain, all those times I came by for a cup of coffee.'

Then Judith began crying. I sighed. I had no time for this. I wanted to go upstairs; I had to talk to Caroline about what we were going to do. The autumn holiday was starting in a couple of days, and all four of us were going to fly to Los Angeles. I needed to confer with Caroline, to see whether maybe we should leave a few days earlier – without mentioning my conversation with Aaron Herzl, of course.

'You said you couldn't have me around, Marc!' Judith wailed. 'That we shouldn't see each other any more. Those were your exact words. "Too much has happened. I just can't have you around." I couldn't believe my ears! How could you be so cold? Ralph had been dead for less than half an hour!'

I stared at her. Was I hearing things? I had always prided myself on being able to figure out what was wrong with someone within sixty seconds, but I wouldn't have believed this was possible, not in a million years. I looked at her face. Besides being covered in tears, it was above all marked by dissatisfaction. Deep-lying dissatisfaction, the kind a person is born with. Nothing helps to drive out that dissatisfaction. Expensive espresso machines, attention, a new wing on the house... for a fleeting moment the dissatisfaction disappears into the background, but it's like a leak coming through the wallpaper: you can cover it with new wallpaper, but after a while the brown spots soak through anyway.

There's not much you can do about it. You can muffle it for a bit with medication, with what they call 'mother's little helpers', but in the end it only comes back with renewed strength.

Only an injection, I knew, would help to wipe the dissatisfaction off Judith's face. Once and for all.

I thought about her reaction on the beach when Ralph had blown that soup pan into the air. Her whining about loud bangs in general. Her bellyaching about the security deposit she might not get back from the letting agency. And then I thought about what Caroline had told me. About Stanley and Judith beside the pool. *He licked her all over*, Caroline had said. *And I mean completely*.

I knew what I had to do. I got up out of my chair and came around from behind my desk. I laid my hands on Judith's shoulders. Then I leaned down, until my face touched hers.

I had expected heat. A wet but hot face – but her tears were cold.

'My sweet, lovely Judith,' I said.

52

We were sitting by the pool. Just Julia and me. Caroline and Lisa had gone into Santa Barbara to do some shopping. Stanley had a meeting somewhere in Hollywood about a new project. Emmanuelle was upstairs taking her afternoon nap.

Julia was lying on her stomach on a lilo, in the shadow of a palm tree. I was sitting in a deckchair, leafing through some magazines I'd brought out from the house. The latest *Vogue* and *Vanity Fair* and *Ocean Drive*. In the distance you could indeed hear the ocean, just as Stanley had said. And the occasional train whistle. Between Stanley's house and the beach was an unguarded, single-track crossing. The train whistles sounded different from a year ago, in the hotel in Williams – but it was also very possible that I was listening to them differently.

I looked at Julia. Maybe she was asleep. Maybe not. Her iPod lay beside the pillow section of the lilo, but she didn't have the earbuds in. In Holland this was autumn. Here you had to sit in the shade because it was too hot in the sun. I had expected a call from the Board of Medical Examiners, asking why I hadn't shown up that Tuesday. But no call came. During the next few days there was no news either. On Friday I called at last and spoke to a secretary, who told me that all current cases had been 'put off' until after the autumn break. She asked me to repeat my name. 'Dr Schlosser,' I said. 'Oh yes, here it is. Your name is marked with a red arrow on my computer. That means your case will be given priority treatment. But the ruling will only come during the week after the break. You'll be informed by the end of that week, at the latest.'

The autumn holiday started the next day, and the four of us flew to Los Angeles. Stanley had offered to pick us up at the airport, but I'd told him that wouldn't be necessary. The drive in our rented car along Highway 1 to Santa Barbara took less than two hours.

The first few days we did pretty much nothing at all. We hung around the pool and sauntered down shopping streets. We ate crab on the pier again.

'I have a theory,' Stanley said on the third day. 'I've thought about it for a long time. But then again… not really even that long.'

We were at a fish restaurant on the beach. The sun had just gone down. Caroline, Emmanuelle, Julia and Lisa had gone for a walk along the surf. Stanley took the bottle of white wine from the cooler and refilled our glasses.

'The midsummer night party,' he went on. 'Last year. We were on the beach with those girls. Ralph tried to kick that Norwegian girl. Then we lost sight of each other for a few hours. In the meantime, your daughter was… well, what happened happened. *You* do the addition, you figure one plus one is two. Not long after the summer holiday, Ralph becomes ill. Deathly ill. One year later he's dead. I'm no doctor. I don't know, technically speaking, how it works, but maybe you could explain that to me.'

I said nothing. I only smiled and took another sip of my wine.

'I'm going to tell you something else, Marc. Last year, as you probably remember, we shot *Augustus*. I gave Emmanuelle a minor role too. As one of the emperor's illegitimate daughters. But one day Emmanuelle comes to me and says she doesn't want to be in the series any more. She couldn't stand it any more, she said, the way Ralph behaved towards her. The way he looked at her. On the set and off. So I went and had a talk with Ralph. I warned him, in no uncertain terms, to stop what he was doing. He acted as though it was all a big joke, as though Emmanuelle was *exaggerating*, but he stopped. I had to promise Emmanuelle that she would never have to see him again, once the series was finished.'

It was tempting. It was tempting to tell Stanley, if not everything, then at least something. I'd had almost a whole bottle of white wine. A good story, I thought. I could make a good story out of it.

'That Ralph was completely mental,' Stanley said. 'The way he acted with women. But both of us were there, we saw it. I don't really mind that much that he's not around any more. I'm just curious. Purely from a technical point of view. Technically speaking, by the way, it seems to me pretty improbable that he got to Julia… He could barely walk after you kicked him in the knee like that, remember? But that's not the point. The point is that you *thought* he was a possible culprit. So you did something. Maybe that very same evening...'

Close, but no cigar, I felt like saying. But I said something else instead. 'Come up with something yourself,' I said.

For one whole second, Stanley stared at me. Then his eyes began to twinkle. The next moment he burst out laughing. 'Very good, Marc! No really, very good. Say no more. I think you've answered my question sufficiently. More than sufficiently.'

That afternoon we looked at the photos Stanley had made last year, during the holiday at the summer house. I had asked about them as casually as I could. Whether he had other photos besides the ones I'd already seen on his site.

We sat around Stanley's desk, he had closed the venetian blinds to keep out the bright sunlight as he clicked through the pictures on his monitor.

Caroline and Emmanuelle were out beside the pool. Lisa and Julia were standing to Stanley's right, leaning against his desk. I was sitting on a stool to his left.

There weren't all that many new ones, in fact. I looked at Julia out of the corner of my eye as the pictures of the repairman came by. There was one new photo: Julia and the repairman standing across from each other, with Julia holding out her arm, palm down, to indicate the difference in height between them. They were both laughing.

I was waiting for the moment when Julia would look over. At me. Weeks ago, I had already decided to wait for the right moment. But as time went by, I began having more and more doubts about that right moment.

If she had looked over right then, we would both have known what the other knew. As far as I was concerned, that would have been enough.

But she didn't look over. She only giggled and urged Stanley to click on through to the next photo.

'Look!' Lisa shouted suddenly. 'It's that donkey!'

All three of us looked at her.

'That donkey from the campsite!' Lisa said. 'That poor little donkey, Dad!'

I leaned over a little closer to the screen. Indeed, you could see a donkey, sticking its head over a wooden fence.

'Do you recognise that donkey, Lisa?' Stanley laughed. 'Maybe you saw it at the zoo. That's where I took the picture. They have a kind of zoo there, you know, just a normal-animal sort of zoo. By the time I went there, you guys had already been gone for a while… Wait, what am I saying? Of course you knew about it! That's where you took that little bird. You and your dad.'

'But that donkey wasn't there then,' Lisa said.

'How can you be so sure it's *that* donkey?' I said quickly.

'I can just tell,' Lisa said. 'There was a llama too. Did you take pictures of the llama too, Stanley?'

Stanley sank back in his chair and put one arm around my younger daughter.

'I didn't photograph a llama there, sweetheart,' he said. 'But I believe you one hundred per cent. I think there was a llama there too.'

'Hey, Dad, are you coming in?'

I'd had my eyes closed and now opened them again. There stood Julia, with one foot up on the diving board. The sun was so bright it made me squint, so I couldn't see her face clearly.

'OK,' I said.

Stanley had already taken a whole series of photos of her. Here in the garden. On the beach. Tomorrow there was going to be an official shoot. With a costume assistant and a make-up artist. Nothing was certain yet, Stanley had said, but there really was a lot of interest. He mentioned the name of a few big fashion and cinema magazines. He took a few photos of Lisa too.

'How old are you now?' he asked her. 'Twelve? That's great. Maybe you'll have to wait a little while, but you never know, there could always be some magazine. You might be exactly what they're looking for.'

I hadn't thought about the repairman again, not since our arrival in America. At most, I'd thought of him as an organism. An organism that breathes. A heart that beats. I looked at Julia, who was halfway along the diving board by now. I tried again not to think about him. And I succeeded. I smiled at my daughter.

'Dad, come on…'

I started to get up, but then sank back in my chair. I waited until she got to the end of the board.

She turned her face towards me. The right moment had passed for ever, I'd decided by then. The right moment belonged to the past. My daughter on the diving board was the future.

We looked at each other. First I looked at her as a girl. Then I looked at her as a woman. Then she took off.

Note on the Author

Herman Koch is a Dutch writer and a renowned actor. His novel *The Dinner* won the prestigious Publieksprijs Prize in 2009 and went on to be a huge international bestseller. *Summer House with Swimming Pool* is his seventh book. He currently lives in Amsterdam.